DARKSHIP
REVENGE

BAEN BOOKS by SARAH A. HOYT

Draw One in the Dark
Gentleman Takes a Chance
Noah's Boy
Night Shifters

Darkship Thieves
Darkship Renegades
A Few Good Men
Through Fire
Darkship Revenge

To purchase these and all other Baen Book titles
in e-book format, please go to www.baen.com.

DARKSHIP REVENGE

SARAH A. HOYT

Darkship Revenge

A Baen Books Original

Baen Publishing Enterprises
P.O. Box 1403
Riverdale, NY 10471
www.baen.com

ISBN: 978-1-4767-8192-1

Cover art by Steve Hickman

First Baen printing, May 2017

Distributed by Simon & Schuster
1230 Avenue of the Americas
New York, NY 10020

10 9 8 7 6 5 4 3 2 1

Pages by Joy Freeman (www.pagesbyjoy.com)
Printed in the United States of America

To Ray Carter, whom I met when he had
too little time left, and who—in a month—managed
to teach me more about writing action and fights than
I'd learned in the previous thirty years of writing.
Thank you and farewell.

BEGINNING AND END

Battle Born

I NEVER WANTED TO BE A MOTHER. I ALWAYS GET WHAT I DON'T WANT.

My name is Athena Hera Sinistra. I was meant to be the woman without a mother, the mother of a race of gods. Bioengineered madmen created me, assembled me protein by protein, to be the Eve of a new race, the start of a new humanity.

It didn't work out that way.

But I did become a mother. Suddenly. By surprise.

Alright, so it shouldn't have been a surprise, but the thing is I had no idea how easy making a human being was. My foster mother disappeared when I was six, and my so-called father, the old bastard in whose image I'd been made, was never interested in forming my mind, only in keeping my body healthy. Sure, I'd got the usual lectures. Which I'd ignored. And nothing had happened even when I ignored them.

There were reasons for that, of course. Most of my lovers were genetically incompatible. And for those who weren't, I'm sure my father had kept me on a contraceptive implant, perhaps installed at my annual exams. Preserved free of taint until he was ready to begin the breeding program.

I hadn't noticed. I thought it was lucky I never caught.

I'd found out I was pregnant while I, my husband, and our friends were under siege in Eden, suspected of treason or worse.

Even after we were freed and proven innocent, I didn't want my child to be born in a place where it seemed like every hand was against us, and everyone suspected us of something awful. And I didn't want to stay in Eden longer than absolutely necessary.

So, when Kit said he wanted to go on a powerpod-collecting trip, from our hidden colony of Eden to Earth orbit, three months away, I'd said yes. I hadn't told him I was pregnant either, because then he wouldn't go. I knew men had a near-superstitious fear of birth and babies. But I figured if primitive humans could give birth without assistance, surely I, who had been bioenhanced to be stronger, faster, smarter, would have no trouble.

I'd give birth in our darkship, the *Cathouse.*

It would be me, and Kit, and we'd have three months to get used to being parents before we came back to Eden. By which time, hopefully, things in Eden would be better too.

Did I mention that things never happen the way I expect them to?

My child was born during a battle. A strange battle started when an unknown ship, of an unknown, lithe design, attacked the *Cathouse,* the darkship my husband, Kit, and I flew to steal powerpods from Earth orbit to power Kit's native colony of Eden.

We were three days from the powertrees in Earth orbit. We didn't even see the other ship before it fired on us.

One moment we were under way, still too far away from possible near-Earth traffic for either of us to man our stations, the other moment our alarms were blaring that our ship was damaged.

I abandoned the reader where I'd been searching for instructions on how to give birth, and Kit came running out of the exercise room.

And we fought our attacker with all we had. It wasn't much.

The *Cathouse* was ill-equipped for battle. It only had weapons at all—energy cannons mounted on the surface—because Earth had recently started trying to capture ships from Eden colony when they came to collect powerpods. And some of us had finally decided it was better to fight than to just commit suicide in order to avoid interrogation.

But our weapons were small and relatively ineffective. Built to discourage rather than to destroy. Built to allow us to fire a warning shot and run away. Built to save on weight and therefore fuel and leave more space on the ship for the harvested powerpods. But also built not to create such outrage at us that Earth dropped everything to find and destroy us.

Before the alarms had stopped sounding, Kit and I were at our battle stations, also known as our powerpod-collecting stations and also our landing stations. They were all the same, just two rooms on opposite ends of the spherical ship, where all the navigation and piloting took place. One was for the navigator and one for the pilot. I was clicking the lock on my belt, when I felt Kit's baffled shock. I *felt* it because, to avoid detection, the pilots and Navs from Kit's world had a form of telepathic communication. It was engineered into them for the purpose, and it had been engineered into me for completely different reasons, which didn't matter, because it still worked.

To my wordless question, he returned the image he could see on his screens:. Kit's eyes had been enhanced to be able to pilot in near-perfect dark. He could see what I couldn't. His screen, which would look dark to me, showed him a silver ship: triangle-shaped, but with added flips to the wings.

I was already calculating coordinates in my head, to target our defensive shot, and rattled them off to Kit via mind-link. My normal work aboard was to calculate coordinates and maneuvers for Kit to pilot without lights in the tight confines of the powertrees, where any wrong move could bring you in contact with a ripe powerpod and to sudden, explosive death.

But the ability to calculate coordinates on the fly and to communicate them to my husband served us well in this too. He spun the *Cathouse* to aim our weapons at the attacker, and let fly with a blast of power.

Our opponent . . . flipped, like a falling leaf twirling in an impossible wind. I guessed the purpose of the maneuver and directed Kit to move us sharply down, which he did, avoiding the return blast, which flew by above us.

Before Kit was done plunging, I'd directed him to fire again.

We did, and targeting light from our weapons played across the other ship, which seemed to me to falter for a moment.

I remembered some genius of the twenty-first century had written a treatise on how space battles were impossible, because ships could always evade other ships in three dimensions. It hadn't occurred to said genius that in that case, as in air battles between airplanes, one ship could follow the other.

I just thought we should follow the ship and—

A sharp pain cut through my middle. It hurt almost as badly as when I'd got stabbed in the gut in a back-alley fight when I was twelve. Almost as bad as when I'd crashed my antigravity wand—broom in slang—against a wall when I was fourteen.

For a moment I lost breath and the ability to focus. *Thena?* Kit screamed in my mind.

We got hit. The ship shook. Our sensors started blaring.

I sat, frozen, not because I was afraid this ship would destroy us. I was afraid of that too, but mostly I was shocked I'd wet myself. I'd never wet myself in any of the fights I'd got into, in mental hospitals and military camps, not even when my father had sent my very young self to them in hopes of taming me.

And then pain rippled through me again, thought-stopping. I'd read something—

Kit, Kit, I think the baby is coming. And then, by an effort of will, I sent coordinates. Shoot at 45-26-10.

Over the mind-link with Kit, I received wordless irritation and panic. The ship shook again, and a blinding flash of light burst from my screens.

Alarms screamed. And Kit was there, unstrapping me, pulling me away from the seat, pulling me out of the navigator's room.

You have to fire on them. They're going to destroy us otherwise. Go. I can give birth alone. I'll give you coordinates. I tried to pull away from his hand, back to the chair.

He suggested I do something biologically impossible to the coordinates, and got a hand under my knees, pulled me off my feet, and ran carrying me.

You can't do this, I wailed at his mind. Another pain—contraction?—hit, and another explosion hit somewhere on the skin of the *Cathouse.* I tried to scream at Kit that the attackers' weapons clearly weren't any stronger than ours, otherwise we'd already be dead, but if they kept at it, they would eventually do real damage. But what came out was an ululating, incoherent scream.

He dumped me on my back, on our bed, and started frantically stripping me. He looked at my lower portion with an expression of utter horror, which, frankly, was a new reaction.

"Push, Thena, Push," he said, both mind and voice. I tried to tell him what to do with this instruction, but my mouth wouldn't work right except for screaming.

I panted through the pain, and groaned in frustration, because I could push, but it didn't seem to do anything except bring on more pain.

I'd read just enough in the last few months to know all the things that could go wrong with a birth. Too big a head, too-big shoulders, hemorrhage, death, and that was just for the mother, without counting on things like the baby being strangled by the umbilical cord.

Maybe the civilizations who didn't teach women to read had been right. "I'm scared," I managed to say between screams.

Kit's eyes widened. He grabbed our medkit from under the bed, and brought the examiner gadget, which looked like a giant magnifying glass, to bear on me.

"This thing doesn't work," he said, in a distracted tone. "It has no setting for giving birth. It says you're experiencing muscle-contraction pain, and that your heart rate is elevated. And the baby's heart rate is fine."

Pain struck again, stronger this time. As it receded, I found I'd grabbed hold of Kit's tunic, and pulled him really close. Really close. I must have used the super strength with which the mad genetic engineers had endowed me, too, because he was a shade of purple as the tunic collar tightened on his neck. And he was trying to pry my hands loose.

I forced myself to let go, and heard him take deep breaths. *I'm trying to help,* he mind-sent in a tone of great and offended dignity.

Which he was, for all the good it did us. And of course the medical gadgets wouldn't work. They had no setting for pregnancy. In Eden most people decanted their children from artificial wombs. Those who didn't would plan the time and manner of their children's arrival so it didn't happen aboard a darkship, months from civilization.

Kit had a smear of blood across his forehead; his feline eyes were wide open in terror. He looked like some sort of primitive god, who kept screaming for me to push, interspersed with "Damn you, damn you, damn you, damn you. What possessed you to come on a long trip alone with me when you knew this was coming? Damn you. Push, Athena, push."

"But it shouldn't be difficult," I wailed back, between screams, as the pain struck me. "Humans have been doing this forever. It should be natural."

He made a sound that might be a laugh. "Push, Athena."

It all seemed like a crazy dream, and I kept noticing things that I'd failed to register. Like how there was blood everywhere, but I didn't remember bleeding. I should have been clearheaded. I mean, I'd had no drugs.

We didn't have any of the drugs women commonly use to eliminate pain in childbirth, and of course Kit didn't want to give me any of our other painkillers because he wasn't sure how they'd affect the baby.

Our gravity cut out, and Kit slammed a hand in my middle, to keep me from floating, while he stayed in place by holding onto the bed.

"There should be better ways to do this," I yelled. "This is a bad design."

He laughed again. "Come on, Athena. The baby has crowned. I hope you like hair because this one has a lot of it."

I thought crowned meant he could see the head. Why didn't he pull it out, then? I yelled, "It's a bad design."

"Granted," he said. "That's why we have biowombs. Push it out, damn it. Push!"

A big explosion hit the outside of our ship. We were just getting pounded, and we weren't returning fire. Even if the baby and I survived, we were going to die. "We're all going to die."

"Not on my watch!"

Ship alarms blared. Blood was everywhere.

"Let me die in peace! The people who wrote about the beauty of birth lied," I said. It might have come out as an incoherent wail. "They lied!"

There were clots of blood floating in the air and Kit—with his feline-looking eyes, his calico hair—looked like a blood-smeared nightmare as he yelled, "Push, push. Push."

"You push!" I yelled.

Suddenly gravity cut in again. Pain sliced me in half. And then there was a sudden, astonishing relief. The type of relief that calls for angels singing and choirs of joy.

Kit did something. I tried to look down. There was a baby, but I couldn't muster the strength to reach down and pick it up. It made faint mewling sounds.

Kit took off running. I lay there, exhausted and bonelessly relieved. *Had he run away from the baby? Did the baby have three heads?* Before I could grow alarmed enough to sit up, Kit ran back in, babbling something about no vital systems being affected, and auxiliary artificial grav having kicked in.

He picked the baby up. "We...we have a daughter."

The creature he showed me was wrinkled and red, but I'd been told this was normal, by various stories. In this, they were apparently right. He picked her up, cleaned her, burnt the end of her umbilical cord—who thought up that system? It's as though humans were born unfinished—set her down on the bed again, examined me through one of the med sensors, muttered something about not needing stitches, then sat on the side of the bed, slowly bent to rest his crossed arms on his knees and his face on his crossed arms and looked like he'd like to pass out, as if he and not I had done all the work. He was saying "light, light, light," in a slow chant. Since "light" was close to a swear word for pilots of darkships, this sounded a little crazed. "Kit?"

He shook his head. "I thought you were going to die. I thought you were both going to die." His hand was shaking, as he rested it on my knee. "Are you all right?"

"I'm fine," I said. "I know I'm tired, but don't feel it. May I see her?"

He made a sound that was either a sigh or a chuckle. "She's not much not look at," he said, as he picked her up, and handed her to me.

She wasn't much to look at. She was small, wrinkled, with a head covered in tight black curls, and big blue eyes with puffy eyelids, as if she'd been crying for a long time. And she was glaring at me as though I'd offended her mortally.

I probably had, ejecting her from the only world she'd ever known and into...this. I counted her fingers and toes. Yes, I know it's stupid, but I'd read somewhere if they had all their fingers and toes, they'd be all right. And with Kit and I both being the product of labs and test tubes, you never knew. But she was perfect, not a tentacle in sight. "Shouldn't you go see if there are any affected systems, besides grav?" I asked Kit. "And see if you can make them stop attacking us."

"I told you the systems are fine for now. They've stopped attacking us. The shot that took grav out was the last. When I checked on systems, they'd left." He raised his head slowly. He was shaking and his eyes looked like he was somewhere far, far away. He took a deep breath and shook his head. "They... They seem to have disappeared, too. I can't find them on any view screens." He took a deep breath. "I'll need to go outside and repair connections and sensors," he said. "But we're not in danger anymore. And it's repairable. Everything on this ship is."

"That makes no sense," I said. I tried to figure out how to nurse, even though I'd only experienced it in sensies before. You'd think it would be self-explanatory, too, I mean, what else were my breasts for but to feed babies? Beyond Kit's amusement, of course. But it turned out to be pretty complicated. Maybe evolution coded for aesthetics more than for function? I pushed my nipple at the baby, but it just glanced off her lips. And then, when she got hold of it, it was to the side, and her sucking hurt like the devil. I said a string of bad words, as I put my finger in between her mouth and my breast to break suction.

"Athena! Don't swear in front of the baby!" Kit said. I swear he actually said that.

"Your daughter can't understand how to feed herself, much less bad language. She obviously gets this from you. Both problems."

"I doubt it," he said. "I always understood female breasts." I realized that I had no idea if Kit had been breastfed, or even how many people in Eden breastfed. I suspected most used some kind of biofeeder, like the wombs. I mean, navigators and pilots had babies while out on pod-collecting trips. Perhaps what I was trying to do looked as archaic to him as it did to me. But we had no baby formula aboard the *Cathouse*.

Just then she latched. Properly. Her eyes went really big at the sensation or the taste of milk, and I looked up at Kit. "The ship attacking us and leaving makes no sense. Why would they attack us and then leave?"

"I don't know," Kit said. "Maybe it was a case of mistaken identity. Earth is at war, after all." He frowned. "Several wars, I expect, by now."

"But that shouldn't extend to space," I protested. "There really is no space presence beyond Circum."

"Maybe," he said. "But your idea of how things were and how they *really* were aren't always the same. Maybe the Good Men had secret bases in space. They were secretive bastards."

I inclined my head in semi-agreement. The last few years had been a series of shocks about how the world really worked and what history really had been. "Maybe."

We were both covered in blood, I was naked, and the room, between lack of gravity and the dirty aspects of birth, looked like particularly messy barbarians had stormed through.

My child sucked, greedily, completely absorbed in her task. I held her and looked down at her, thinking how odd this was. How strange that I could become a mother so—Not easily, no, not quickly, but almost accidentally.

Kit looked at us, with that odd look of reverence that males reserve for things that scare them more than a little. "We have a daughter," he said. He sounded like he wasn't sure what to do with the situation.

I nodded. This small creature was utterly dependent on me and would surely die without me. I'd never had anyone utterly dependent on me. Yes, I'd rescued Kit from some horrible situations, but he'd rescued me too. It wasn't a one-sided relationship. And he could go on living without me, no matter how little he would like it. But with my daughter . . .

The word tasted wrong, as something that could not possibly apply to me. She looked small, unfinished, and red, with a face the size of a large orange, and the most determined expression I'd ever seen. She clenched her fists, as though she were engaged in a difficult battle, and she glared up at me as though she couldn't trust me.

Kit stood up, by the side of the bed, looking down. "She has your eyes," he said.

"Sure," I said. And since his eyes, feline-shaped and to a certain extent feline-efficient, were the result of a bioengineering virus introduced in the first trimester of gestation, I added, "We didn't pay extra for her to have yours. Still, she might make a decent navigator yet." Both navigators and pilots—colloquially called Cats in Eden—were bioengineered. Navigators' improvements were largely invisible: things like visual memory, very good sense of direction, and an ability for mechanical reasoning. I had those, engineered into me for other reasons than to become a navigator. Which is why I could fly pod-collecting missions with Kit. And our daughter, while obviously not inheriting his eyes, could have inherited my characteristics.

He did a laugh that sounded like a hiccup. "I hope—"

"Yes?"

"Nothing. Foolishness," he said. "I was going to say I hoped the world would be kind to her, but I don't think that's how it works."

"No, we each have to make the world as kind to us as we can."

"And we'll have to protect her until she can look out for herself," he said.

"Yes," I said. This *tasted* strange, but it also felt right. I didn't want it to be true, but if I didn't owe anything to someone I'd created, to whom would I owe anything? She couldn't look after herself. And I'd brought her here, on purpose or not.

He got up. "Right," he said. "I'm going to see about fixing those sensors. And then I'll come back and help get you cleaned up."

It was the last I saw of him aboard the *Cathouse*.

Between Space and a Hard Place

I WOKE UP ON THE RUMPLED, SWEATY, BLOODIED BED, WITH MY daughter tucked into the crook of my arm, asleep.

She was not beautiful. She was barely human: all wrinkly red skin, tightly clenched eyes, and an expression like as soon as she was awake she'd have words with whomever had sent her here right now. I knew she'd grow up to look more human. Or at least, I'd seen this in a million sensies. I had trouble believing it.

Yet she was mine, and I was responsible for everything pertaining to her. I panicked. On the verge of feeling resentment, I frowned at her. I didn't want this. I didn't ask for this. I was not fit to be anyone's mother. She sighed in her sleep. Something irrational rose up. My thoughts stopped. In their place there was a feeling, ancient and immense, like a bottomless sea.

I'm not good at love. Like everything I can't understand, it makes me uncomfortable. So I'm not going to say that's what I felt. I've come to accept that I love Kit, because no other explanation suffices for my not having killed him yet. In the same way, I suppose he loves me, because he actually wants to spend time with me, and hasn't taken to beating me every other day just to stay sane. So he loves me. I still don't understand how. It makes no sense at all.

13

I don't know if that's what I felt for my daughter. All I knew was that I'd put a gory end to anyone who tried to hurt her. I pulled her closer to me. She nestled closer, like a cat.

I wondered how long I'd been asleep, precisely. It could have been hours, or just a few seconds. I didn't remember falling asleep.

I started to open my mouth to call to Kit, but then decided not waking the baby was highly advisable, and mind-called, *Kit?*

Calling with your mind is not the same as voice-calling: in your mind, you know when you call out and the message is not received. You know if it just wasn't heard, or even if it was ignored. If you mind-call and there's no reply of any kind, not even the sense of someone at the other end, the only possible conclusion is that there is no one to answer. Even if the object of your call is asleep, impaired or in a vegetative state, there is a feeling that he is there. Non-responsive, but there.

Kit? I called, again, in my mind.

Have you ever entered an empty house? No matter how large it is, or how much it looks like it should be inhabited, you know the house is empty and that there is no one at all in any part of it? That the dark and cold extend forever, unbroken by human presence?

It felt like that. The *Cathouse* was empty, save for myself and the baby.

Kit, Kit, Kit, KIT! The call went out and was swallowed by nothingness, like a pebble falling into an endless hole.

I carefully extricated myself from my daughter, leaving her asleep on the bed, as I rose.

I didn't know if I should stand up. Some of the books and sensies said you should stay in bed for months. Others that it was highly advisable to get on your feet and go weed rice paddies. I was fresh out of rice paddies, but I had to get up. I had to go look for Kit. If he was in trouble, I was the only one who could help.

I closed my mind to the thought that the lack of return on my call meant not that he was in trouble, but that he didn't exist. Or that he was so far from me I couldn't sense him and he couldn't hear me.

But how could he be that far away from me in space, with no vehicle but the *Cathouse* nearby?

So I got up. Had to, even if it meant I could bleed to death, or pass out cold on the floor. Besides, I told myself, that only happened to women in sensies.

As it turned out, there was no dying, no passing out. There was a wave of dizziness, but only because I was still so tired. And things, to include most things below my waist, felt sore, but it was a soreness short of pain.

Through my childhood and teen years, between running away from home, mental hospitals, reform homes and boot camps, getting in burner fights and broom accidents, not to mention Daddy Dearest's version of loving correction, I'd often felt worse. Well, not in those specific places, but worse anyway.

Walking gingerly—all right, like a duck—getting used to soreness, I called, mentally, *Kit?* No one answered. I didn't expect an answer, but the idea that he had simply disappeared made no sense either. Perhaps I'd only slept a very short time, and he was still outside fixing whatever damage the unknown ship firing on us had done? Perhaps my being so tired meant that my mind-call had less range than normal?

I went to the pilot's room first. There are sensors built into the wall of the ship that will show you what's wrong with it, and what is in the process of being repaired.

I turned the lights of the screen up so I could see it, since I didn't have Kit's modified, feline-like eyes. And stared unbelievingly at the devastation.

The *Cathouse* is not the most up-to-date ship. Its circuits are more vulnerable than any sane designer would want. It was a retired training ship when Kit—who, back then, flew alone—persuaded them it was a low enough risk to rent it to him.

Somehow the unknown attacker had managed to destroy most of our air scrubbers' ability, which meant that between myself and a little one, we would exhaust the air in a couple of days. By that time we'd be without water. Also, the ability to drive the *Cathouse* had been destroyed. Our thrusters were either burned out or disconnected from the power pod. If I didn't repair them, we'd drift aimlessly through space, forever.

I bit my lip and stared at the list of damages and waited for Kit to do something out there, and for me to see the condition of something change.

Come on. Something change. Kit, do something.

He'd heard me mind-call across much greater distances. Not

all distances. There was a definite limit to those. But greater distances. I couldn't possibly be that tired? Perhaps birth changed telepathic ability? It wasn't like I could communicate with anyone but Kit, anyway.

My query, *Kit?* returned nothing. No sense of him. And the screen didn't change.

There were three answers for this. One was that my telepathy was broken. Possible, but not likely. Then again, the only other telepaths I knew were in Eden, and they didn't usually have children. Not gestated and delivered from their own bodies, so who knew?

Two was that Kit had died. Perhaps something had gone suddenly wrong with him, and he was dead somewhere in this ship, or even outside. The idea induced a sort of panicked denial. Kit couldn't be dead. He just couldn't. Of course, I knew he was mortal. But surely if he'd died, I'd have felt it?

The third one was that he was alive but simply not here. This last would be the most plausible, except for the part where it was impossible. It didn't require me to have ignored his death mind-call. It didn't require me to believe the effort of giving birth somehow destroyed telepathic ability. It just required me to believe that Kit could fly unassisted through space, and breathe vacuum. There was nothing in the *Cathouse* beyond the range of mind-call. And there was nothing outside. Just endless space. Sure we had suits and oxygen bottles. But not to get significantly far from the ship.

The *Cathouse* was a collector ship. It was all it was designed to be. Everything else about it had been stripped down to allow for more storage of powerpods. There were no hidden rooms, no vast labyrinths.

From the beginning, powerpod collections, from the powertrees in Earth orbit, had been done without consent from Earth, and in fear that Earth would realize it and find and destroy Eden. There were no lifeboats aboard. There was nothing you could take to get away from the ship.

If you suffered a problem near Eden, they could send someone to evacuate the ship. Anywhere else, you were as good as dead. In fact, if something went wrong near Earth, rather than asking to be rescued, you were encouraged to simply commit suicide so you didn't risk betraying the secret colony.

So, Kit couldn't have run away. Good to know. And I couldn't picture him committing suicide by jumping from the ship to outer space with only the limited oxygen in a spacesuit. And so, the second place I checked was the suit storage locker.

Spacesuits from Eden are made of material unavailable on Earth. They look and feel like a soft knit, but somehow lock when outside, to keep internal pressure. The same for the helmet, which looks like a hood with a transparent view window.

Our suits normally hung in a closet, side by side.

Kit's was gone.

So, he'd gone outside, wearing a suit and intending to repair the ship, as he'd said he would. It was always possible, of course, that an unexpected tear in the suit or something could have killed him without his realizing it was coming. It was a risk we lived with.

I stood in the bedroom, watching my daughter sleep in the middle of our very large bed. If Kit was gone, I must go outside and fix what was wrong with the ship, otherwise we were going to be dead. And while life without Kit seemed horrible, I was responsible for that little creature: responsible for making her, responsible for bringing her into the world, and responsible for choosing to take this trip while pregnant. Moisture formed in my eyes and rolled down my cheeks.

None of this felt fair, and the injustice of it all galled me. It made no difference. There was no one to see me cry, and even if there were, who would care? No one ever did anything for me because I cried, except maybe Kit. I was in charge of saving myself and my daughter. And, by damn, I was going to do it.

Tears continued to flow as I decided the first order of business was to clean myself and the baby and to diaper her and dress her in something. Then I'd leave her on the bed and go outside to fix the ship. I felt a twinge at this, but didn't know what else to do.

First of all, the bed had a horrible organic mess that I suspected, from reading, was the placenta. Have I mentioned this is a stupid design? I disposed of it down the incinerator.

I got in the fresher alone, first, cleaning the blood and sweat and other residues of the messy process of bringing a human to life right down the drain.

Then I came back to the room, still naked, picked my daughter up, and took her back with me to the fresher. The business of being born must be even more tiring than the business of giving birth. Though I'd set the fresher for water, she didn't awake when I washed her, merely grumbled in her sleep and half opened her eyes, before closing them again.

She woke as I was drying her and set up a scream that wouldn't stop. Since I assumed she didn't object to being dried, I diagnosed the problem as hunger.

Once she had been nursed, she dozed again, not waking as I diapered her, using for the purpose a quick reengineering of feminine hygiene products, provided in the normal stocking of the ship, but not used by me at all this whole trip until now.

One of my tunics, stylishly tied around her feet, served as further clothing.

She slept through all this, but opened her eyes when I put her back on the bed. And I stopped.

I stopped, staring at her blue eyes and thinking that Kit had gone outside and something had happened. What if I went outside and something happened to me?

Then I'd leave her behind here. And she couldn't even feed herself.

"Okay," I said, surprised and annoyed at the sound of tears in my voice. "That's so not happening."

The spacesuits stretched. Not far, granted, but they did stretch.

It was uncomfortable and the baby squirmed. It took some doing to squeeze into it with my daughter tied around my middle, with the excess of her tunic's sleeves. Her nose protruded just below my chin, safely within the helmet and able to breathe, her back supported against me. One thing I had managed to understand from the stories was that human newborns lacked spine strength. This again seemed like a design flaw to me. We're a lousily engineered race.

It was uncomfortable as hell, but not as scary as leaving her alone in the ship while I went outside to work on the shell of the *Cathouse*. And it made me feel less abandoned, less alone, safer. It made no sense, because a little baby had no way of keeping me safe, but that's how I felt.

She seemed to agree. She fell back to sleep as we proceeded through the airlocks and outside. She didn't even wake as the suit stiffened in response to outer vacuum.

I hate being outside the ship in space. I always have. I know the shoes that come with the spacesuit attach to the ship and that as long as I took care not to jump and have both feet off the ship, I'd be fine. As the resident repair mechanic, given that the *Cathouse* was designed almost as badly as the human body, I'd been outside many times.

It doesn't make it any more comfortable. I hate the idea of being in a place where you can fall, in any direction, without stopping, ever. It's not a fear of open spaces so much as a fear of lack of control.

This whole situation was tweaking that fear. I wanted Kit back, and I wanted to know where he was. I wanted my life back.

I got the little tool kit and walked in an unnatural duck-walk, so the entire sole of the suit made contact with the ship, to the air processing nodule first. It wasn't actually the air processing mechanism, merely the linkage of power to the air processor. It was a bubble-like protrusion in the skin of the ship, and opening it, I looked at charred internals and blinked.

It wasn't the charred internals that disturbed me. There were replacement wires—only they weren't exactly wires, being bioed, and technically I *think* living creatures—in the bottom of the tool box, and I had expected the ones in place to be charred.

No. What I was staring at was characters, written in the charred remains of the connectors. Two words. *Kidnapped* and *Earth*.

"At least it isn't 'Croatoan,'" I told no one in particular, thinking of a particularly scary story about a lost colony, which I'd read long ago in my father's library.

It made no sense, but then the ship attacking us made no sense either. Had they lurked around to kidnap Kit? How does one lurk in open space? And how easy was it to kidnap my husband? I couldn't imagine him going without a fight. Then I thought again. He might not have wanted them to notice he was not alone. He might have gone quietly if he saw no chance of fighting them off without endangering us. He might have sacrificed himself to save us. At least sacrificed himself to the extent of allowing himself to be kidnapped. Which meant it was my job to set things right and free him. Besides the fact that I'd gotten used to him and had no intention of living without him for any length of time.

I had to stay alive for my daughter, and life without Kit

would be unbearable. Therefore, my daughter and I would have to go and find him.

It was getting really tiring calling her *the baby* or *my daughter*. Kit and I had only spoken of names in jest. If I'd had a boy I'd probably have named him Bartolomeu. Or Jarl Bartolomeu, after the closest thing Kit had to a biological father and his mentor. But I didn't. And we'd never agreed on a name for a girl.

Men had strange ideas, and my husband might be the strangest of all. The only name he'd proposed for a girl was unsuitable. I was not going to call my daughter after Kit's first wife. There are limits to what love can cause me to do. Through a moment when I'd shared his memories accidentally, I'd formed my opinion of that lady. And it was not so complimentary that I wanted my daughter's name to pay her homage. On the contrary. And it didn't matter how much Kit's guilt and his illusions made him like the name.

I thought of Kit, kidnapped and taken to Earth, and of the circumstances of my child's birth. There was really only one name for her. "It's alright, Eris," I said, though she was probably asleep. "We're going to go to Earth and get Daddy back."

Into the Known

GOING TO EARTH INVOLVED GOING TO CIRCUM TERRA, IN EARTH orbit. If it were held by friendlies, I could get military-level help in finding Kit.

Circum Terra is an old space station. Rumor has it that it started, long ago, in the mists of the twentieth century, as the international space station, but no one knows if that is true.

Between us and that time on Earth lay several world wars, several new ways of living and storing information, new ways of governance, the rise of the seacities, the fall of the continents, the imperium of the biolords everyone else called Mules, the Turmoils, the rise of the Good Men, and three hundred years of so-called peace and stability.

Even the records of Eden, which were more reliable than those on Earth, couldn't say for sure how Circum had started. Some said it was what remained of the building of the only interstellar vehicle Earth had ever constructed, the *Je Reviens*, which about half the biolords had taken when they'd escaped Earth, after the Turmoils. It had certainly been used for that.

If it had been the international space station, no more than a little core of it remained, built around and around with new stuff. Whenever Circum had been built, it had been built on a grand scale. That would fit with its near-Earth orbit, its neat

21

doughnut-like structure, and its haphazard utilization. It had as many closed and forgotten docking bays as open and operational ones, for instance. And it was huge for something used only for research, scientific experimentation, and some communication relay.

We got to Circum on the third day after Kit disappeared. In a way it was reassuring to see its lighted doughnut shape in the sky, next to the haphazard, rambling, and also glowing thicket of the powertrees.

The powertrees had been seeded back in the twenty-first century, and they were biological constructs designed to collect solar energy and relay it to Earth—mostly in a beam—and were still used, both by Earth and by Eden, though the Eden usage was somewhat less than authorized.

I hadn't sped up the *Cathouse* to catch up with the ship that had taken Kit. For one, because I couldn't. The *Cathouse* didn't have a button or pedal for "make it go faster." But even if it had had such a thing, just based on how the triangular ship had disappeared, I doubted it could be caught by something like the *Cathouse*.

Instead, we'd used the three days to sleep a lot, feed Eris a lot, and—Heaven help me, did babies run up a lot of waste products. It seemed like my days were entirely bounded by Eris's physical needs. And I missed Kit. Not only because he was an extra hand to change diapers, either.

I had to find Kit. Which was going to be interesting, with a baby. Sure, in my younger days I'd terrorized reform schools, psychiatric hospitals, and the occasional broomer lair. But not with a tiny creature attached to me who couldn't even hold up her head.

The first thing to do, I realized, was scout the lay of the land. I told Eris this. Two hours or so out from Circum, I picked her up from a nap, dressed her in one of Kit's undertunics, and explained the plan. "You see, with Earth in a civil war, we really can't assume that Circum is on our side or their side. So we need to do some listening in on communications and see if we can determine it."

She crossed her eyes, pushed out her tongue. "Yeah, I understand," I said. "We shouldn't have a side, really. But we do, because most of my friends are on the Usaian side, the side of the revolution against the Good Men. And if they're in control of Circum, then we might be able to get in touch with someone, and make our going to Earth much easier."

She frowned.

"Of course I left my friends in charge of Circum, but you know what men are. Okay, I guess you don't, but you will. If you don't check on them every minute they lose stuff. So, it's possible that in the months we've been gone, the Good Men have taken over the station, in which case we'll have to kidnap someone, steal a ship and make it to Earth. Inconvenient. And more protracted."

From her intent, glaring frown, Eris would seem to agree.

Unfortunately, the scanning of communications frequencies was less than enlightening. I guess a research/scientific experimentation/powerpod harvesting station has the same kind of communications every day, regardless of who is holding it. Unless it is during an active takeover.

Most of what I got consisted of this:

"...must send someone to harvest quadrant five of the powertrees. Several powerpods will blow and seed or reseed there if not taken soon."

"...Hold full of powerpods. Permission to dock in fifth dock, port?"

"...Found a fascinating genetic mutation in mice raised under null-gravity conditions..."

"...Solar flares...intermittent."

Any and all of those could be taking place under control of the Good Men, the now-diminished but even a year ago all-powerful oligarchy that had held tight control over most of the Earth. Or it could be happening under the control of the Usaians, a semireligious sect based on the governing principles of the old North American territories, whose revolutionary forces had wrestled control of some portion of the Earth from the Good Men.

I'd been away five months, and left Circum in control of the Usaians, several of whom were my friends or old broomer-lair mates. They might by now have won their war and be in control of Earth as well as the station. Or they might have been exterminated. The effect on what I'd overheard emanating from Circum would be next to nothing. Stupid scientists and harvesters! They'd go on the same way, about their routine, no matter what the changes in government.

"Okay," I told Eris. "We do this the hard way."

Which involved going below the powertree rings, and under most of Circum, to the unused side of the station.

The used side faced the powertrees. They were called the powertree ring, and I understand once upon a time they'd been planted as such so that they could be accessed and harvested from outside or inside. But as biological, living plants, which harvested solar energy and concentrated it in their fruits, the powerpods, they were of necessity unstable. At some point, between the rule of the biolords who'd built them and the Turmoils, during which the old beanstalk was still used to send organic material to feed them but the harvesting was irregular and infrequent, they'd exploded and reseeded and exploded again. Now they looked like a spiney ball, a tangled patch of dark diamond-hard trunks, with glowing, unstable powerpods sprouting at random.

Harvesting them was dangerous work even for the official Earth collectors, with lights and locators. It was worse for the darkships of Eden, which collected blind. But we managed.

I considered briefly navigating through the forest of trunks and powerpods to get to the other side, perhaps harvesting on the way.

But it was not something you should do alone, even if my husband had done so for over a year, between becoming widowed and meeting me. It could also be argued that at that time he'd been suicidal.

I wasn't suicidal and I had no intention of risking Eris. So I dove under the powertrees, under most of Circum, in the shadow of it, which helped conceal the *Cathouse*. This was helped by the fact that the *Cathouse* was, being a darkship, painted in black, unreflective paint, which melded with the shadows.

I came up on the other side of Circum, totally unused the last time I'd been here.

It still looked unused. I couldn't see movement of ships around the periphery, and there were no lights save for beacon lights, and those were weak.

So far, so good. Finding an unused bay was relatively easy, too. Well, finding a bay. It was almost impossible to tell if it was unused or not, until you were entering it. There were membranes at the entrance to all the bays. Two sets of membranes, forming an airlock. And maybe the membranes had been transparent at one time, but they were all opaque now.

Given the size and lack of maneuverability of the *Cathouse*, that meant things could get dicey. It was kind of like going into a mountain tunnel in your flyer without knowing whether there was a flyer already in there, coming the other way. There were no traffic lights to help guide you on the way.

Eris didn't like it. She was strapped on, under my suit, to my chest, her head just beneath my chin. I wouldn't subject her or myself to the helmet until I had to, and I would only use the helmet because some portions of Circum didn't even get oxygen and I couldn't be sure where I'd end up.

She hated the pressure of the belts across her front, and the fact that I was concentrating on piloting and not on her. Being my daughter, and not liking something, meant she kept up a continuous, low-grade complaint. Only, of course, because she couldn't kick my ass.

I realized stealth might not be possible with her. Ah, well. All I could do was try. Most people would probably frown at taping the baby's mouth shut. Kit would if—when I found him. I held my breath and plunged through the first membrane that covered an opening large enough for the *Cathouse*.

Inside the tunnel was dark as the distant reaches of space. I took another deep breath. Backing out of here was going to be a right bitch, if I needed to do it.

There shouldn't be anyone inside, not in this part of the station. Why couldn't I just turn the lights on? *Because, idiot, there might be someone,* I told myself. *And that would be disastrous, if Circum is in enemy hands.*

In front of me, more guessed and "felt" than seen, was another membrane, this one, probably from being sheltered from the vacuum, still semitransparent. I held my breath as I plunged through the membrane, afraid I'd find it occupied at the last moment, and have to pull back, a maneuver easier described than done in a completely spherical, almost-too-large ship, piloted by someone who was no pilot and who had a squirming baby strapped to her midriff.

I pushed all the way in, and when no other ship materialized, turned on my lights.

Eris continued squirming and complaining, in a thin, creak-like cry, as I brought the *Cathouse* to rest on the floor of a cavernous and abandoned warehouse.

I made all secure, removed any materials—mostly data gems—that would give away where the *Cathouse* had come from, or that it had come from somewhere else, armed myself with all the burners onboard, strategically distributed about my person and Eris's, put the diapering material in a bag slung over my shoulder, put the helmet of the suit on, and locked down the *Cathouse*.

I didn't like leaving the *Cathouse* behind. It wasn't just that Kit and I had a substantial portion of our net worth, or rather our net debt, invested in the ship. It was also that, no matter how carefully scrubbed, if it fell in the wrong hands, it would give people who might want to destroy us or Eden substantial information that would make it easier. Eden might not be the refuge I'd once hoped it would be, but it was still Kit's beloved homeland. I couldn't risk seeing it destroyed. Or his family, who had welcomed me with open arms.

On the other hand, I couldn't "park" the *Cathouse* in space. Sure, I could set it in orbit somewhere, but without a lifeboat, there was no way to leave it. And it was more likely to be detected in orbit than in a Circum bay.

Which didn't make it any easier to walk away from it and towards the inhabited side of Circum. I needed to get to those areas if I wanted to steal a ship that could take me to Earth.

It took a long time. I walked towards the busier parts of Circum along a corridor that went from derelict and dust-covered to looking like warehouses filled with cases and warehouses filled with scientific equipment.

I knew I was approaching the inhabited parts of the station when I started hearing human steps and muffled voices a long distance away.

If I could have come across a bay with one of the Earth-bound ships that took packages to Earth and brought supplies back, or even one of the bigger harvesters that could withstand atmospheric reentry, I'd have stolen it and have left Circum with no more trouble. Contrary to what Kit and friends of mine have said at various times, I don't actually *try* to leave a trail of destruction in my wake. Not on purpose. It just tends to happen.

And this time, it just happened that, as I rounded a corner of a pile of crates, I ran headlong into a young man. We both stepped back, and he hesitated a moment. Long enough.

Part of the way I've been bioimproved is to be faster than

anyone else. Than anyone else who wasn't bioimproved, at least. So when he hesitated, I pounced, jumped behind him, and grabbed him around the chest, pinning his arms. I was completely out of shape, but still had naturally improved strength. He struggled, but not long, because I'd pulled a burner and had it to his head.

I had to speak louder than I intended, because Eris had started crying louder, but I was speaking almost in his ear, so he couldn't avoid hearing it. "Stop struggling right now. If you do what I tell you nothing will go wrong. I just need a ship."

He stopped struggling. He was a little taller than I, not much, and thin to the point of stringy. His sparse blond hair looked like it had been self-cut, in the dark, without the benefit of a mirror. One of the scientists in Circum, I imagined. Though there were exceptions, they tended not to be magnificent physical specimens.

He was trying to look at the burner, with his head somewhat turned, and his eyes trying to escape sideways off his face. "Is that really a burner?" he asked, his voice very low.

"No, it's a toy. What do you think?" I asked.

He swallowed. "I think it's a burner."

"Bright boy."

"Would you really shoot me?"

"Only if I have to," I said. "I don't want any trouble. I just want a ship back to Earth."

A long shudder went over him, as though he tried to recoil from my touch at the same time that he was trying not to upset me. "Are you . . . can I ask a question?"

"Sure. But then we have to go find me a ship."

"Okay. Okay, but . . ." His voice was very low and hard to hear over Eris's crying. "Look, do you really have two heads?"

"What?"

I think it was the surprise of this and also the racket that Eris was making that made it possible for me to be ambushed the way I was.

Just after I said "What?" I felt something heavy hit my skull, and then everything went dark.

In the darkness there were voices. Male voices, almost whispering, not so much as though they were trying to avoid waking me but as though they were trying to be respectful in the presence of the dead, which I was almost sure I wasn't.

"...materials are of unknown manufacture," one said.

"She looks familiar," the other said. "I've seen her somewhere before."

There were other voices, too low to be understood, and I didn't have time to waste on them. I was taking stock, instead.

It is something I tend to do early every morning, anyway, which amuses Kit because he says I'm the only person he knows paranoid enough to think through everything around her every morning, and make sure her body is still all there, and that no one has captured her during the night. Which just shows two things: first, that I sometimes talk as I'm coming awake; and second, that the foolish man doesn't go through that verification routine when he wakes up. Entirely his problem the day he wakes up body-swapped with a tentacle horror and captured by spider aliens. And I didn't know why he'd laughed when I'd told him so.

But in this, case, having been out, taking stock of myself and my surroundings was even more important. First, because they might have done something to me while I was out. Once, when I'd been unconscious for an extended period of time, someone had stripped me naked and strapped me to a hospital bed, under armed guard. You just never knew. And second, because I had to know how many of them there were, how well armed, and if they were prepared to fight. Which was essential if I was going to escape.

And I was going to escape. As I had from that hospital bed, under guard.

I was lying down on something soft. Nothing was broken. They must have removed my helmet because I could smell the air in Circum with its tinge of staleness and—Eris wasn't on my chest.

My taking stock of myself and the situation stopped. My heart sped up, and panic invaded my mind.

Eris wasn't on me. She wasn't attached to me. "Eris!" I said, sitting up. And as I sat up five males took simultaneous steps back. There was the blond guy I'd held hostage and four other men, all of them looking like scientists. I had the vague impression they all looked alike. It probably wasn't true, but they were all tall, skinny, and had that look of having spent the last thirty years awake and studying.

Three had their hands up, in a fending-off gesture. The fourth, darker-haired than the one I'd first captured, stood with his arms akimbo and looked openmouthed at me, as his lips worked silently, as if he were doing difficult calculations. He cleared his throat loudly, snapped his mouth shut and croaked "Discordia?"

By this time I was standing up. His word barely registered, and I found I was yelling "Where is my daughter? Eris? What have you done with my daughter?"

They crowded together, as a group, as if by standing back to back they could avoid my killing them. Ah. My father, were he still alive, could have told them better. It just gave me an easier time targeting.

The guy I'd first taken hostage was making obvious efforts to speak, but seemed to have lost his voice. He pointed behind me, and I looked at the bed, and there, sprawled next to where I'd been, was Eris. She looked unconscious, but as I picked her up, she opened her eyes and made a gurgling sound.

"We...we changed her and fed her," one of the other guys offered, as if he were trying to appease me. "She wouldn't stop screaming till we did."

I sniffed. She did smell clean and had that look she got after eating. I might have to let these idiots live. "What did you feed her?" I had nightmare visions of them expressing my milk while I'd been unconscious.

"We had some baby formula," one of them said, and to what must have been my stunned look, because save for occasional and rare visits, everyone on Circum Terra was male and fully grown, he swallowed, "Well, old formula powder, which I think was meant to be loaded in the *Je Reviens*."

Well, great. My daughter had just been fed some formula more than three hundred years old. And the greedy-gut had eaten it, too. On the other hand, I knew some of that food had been preserved for the long haul in deep-frozen stasis. Though what the all-male Mules wanted with baby formula was beyond me.

I looked at Eris. She looked fine. Which was good. If she so much as spit up, though, someone was going to die a painful death.

One of the scientists cleared his throat. "You seem to be lost and disoriented. We imagine you ditched from a ship in distress?"

I raised my eyebrow at him. They looked back at me with a mixture of fear and worry. I swear I can't generally hear thoughts other than Kit's, but I had the impression I could hear the guy I'd first taken hostage thinking *yeah, she distressed the ship, then left.*

"I mean, I mean," the man said. "We have contacted Olympus Seacity and as soon as possible, they will send someone up to take you back and . . . and restore you to . . ." My expression must be too easily read. His speech had slowed down as he talked, and he was looking at me as if realizing he'd said something wrong, or at least that his explanation wasn't going over the way he'd expected.

For my part, I was thinking, very quickly. First, they'd contacted Olympus Seacity. Last I'd heard, that island was the center of the Usaian rebellion, and that meant that, at least if the rebels hadn't been utterly eliminated—

I stopped, because that was possible, in which case it was quite possible that Olympus Seacity just meant another center of the power of the Mules, who had once been the biolords and who, after the Turmoils, had taken over again under the guise of "Good Men" and pretending not to be bioimproved. And if that was the case, then I was in de facto enemy territory.

I cast about for something to tie Eris to myself. Look, she was my daughter and I would look after her, but a baby in a fight is a liability, anyway. A baby you have to hold with one hand while fighting is a worse liability. I didn't want her getting dropped, tossed, or worse, captured. There'd been a little piece of cloth by her side, which probably had been over her to begin with. I grabbed it and tied it around me and over my shoulder as a sling, into which I settled Eris. She was looking at me with big, expectant eyes, and I smiled reassuringly at her. Then I looked up at the men, who were staring at me with a confused expression.

"You see, Madam," one of them said, apologetically, "as soon as we can, there will be help—"

I nodded. "I presume you talked to Good Man Keeva?" I asked.

Good Man Keeva, aka Lucius Keeva, was the most prominent of the Usaians, and incidentally a friend of a friend. Okay, technically the lover of a friend, though it was none of my business.

If he was still in power, I'd be safe. Not that I actually expected my captors to have talked to him. It was far more likely they'd talked to an underling ten levels down.

But what I got were raised eyebrows, a confused expression and "Who? No—He is not in charge—"

It was all I needed. They'd taken the burner I'd carried, of course, but thank heavens for small favors, scientists are not usually trained in searching women for weapons. Or, to be fair, searching women. If that were part of scientific training, research would attract an entirely different kind of man. While I asked the question I'd reached the most accessible of my hidden weapons, and no, I'm not going to tell you where I'd hidden it. I might need it again in the future. I pointed it at them.

They looked surprised. One of them opened his mouth.

"Shhh," I said. "Not a sound. Do not under any circumstances call for help. Who else knows I'm here? Who called Earth?"

"I—We—d-d-d-"

It was the blond man I'd first held hostage. "Easy now. Who else in Circum knows? Where are we? How do we get out of here? How can I get an atmosphere-capable vehicle?"

"We didn't think you really meant to kill anyone!" one of the other scientists managed to get out.

"I don't," I said seriously. "Unless I have to. Who else knows I'm here? What kind of guard would I have to defeat on the way to finding a vehicle?"

Two of them looked at each other. "We didn't tell anyone else," one said. "You looked harmless, just a little confused. I mean, you have a baby. We just thought if we got you help and if you calmed down, everything would be okay."

"Ah," I said. I'm many things, but I'm *not* guileless and trusting, and they were speaking a little too fast, a little too glibly. I smiled maniacally at them. "You see those wires there?" In the corner of the compartment, with the bed and the covers, there were a bunch of circuits and wiring. I'd bet money this was one of their rooms and that they used it as a place to tinker with computer equipment. I pointed the burner at the scientist I'd first captured. "Easy now, I want you to tie all your friends' wrists and ankles with those, and no funny business because my burner is going to be pointed at you. And I'm going to be verifying the tying job."

I once escaped twenty people, surrounding me, holding burners. Not something I'd want to do while holding a baby. But I had advantages over the scientists. The first was the ability to speed up to a speed that most normal people couldn't even see clearly, much less respond to. It wasn't as fast as the speed of movement engineered into Eden's Cats, but it was fast enough, for long enough. The other was that I'd gotten into so much trouble

growing up that it had become a training of sorts. I knew exactly
how far I could push a situation, how I could deceive my oppo-
nents into giving me the advantage, and how to escape a bind.

Because this scientist might have the same sort of propensi-
ties, I watched carefully, while staying out of range of a sudden
turn-and-punch, or even a sudden stretch-and-reach.

Weirdly, neither the guy I had the burner pointed at or his
friends tried to fight it. This was good, because if they had, I
would have had to shoot them. Once upon a time it wouldn't
have bothered me at all. To be honest, it still didn't much. A
little, I suppose. I'd come to realize other people, even those who
opposed my objectives, were people. Someone's son or daughter,
husband or wife, father or mother. Sure. I sort of got that. In the
sense that I knew it, and I'd figured out that shooting people I
didn't have to kill was bad. But I still did not get it at the level
other humans did. It came from not having been raised like a
real person, from never having had to think of other people as
being like me. From my earliest remembered thoughts, I'd been
different, separate, set apart. As the daughter of the Good Man,
and then, in Eden, as Earth-born.

My upbringing had been isolated, apart, and frankly unpleasant
enough that I'd never bonded with anyone outside my broomer
lair. For them, or now Kit or Eris, I would die or kill. Anyone
else didn't much matter.

But Kit cared. He'd be very upset if he found out I'd killed
random people who weren't even, properly speaking, friends or
foes. And having Kit think well of me had become one of my
primary objectives in life.

So I was very glad the scientists didn't fight back, and even
let my hostage gag them. Of course I tied him and gagged him
in the end. Just before I did, I asked him again where to find
the ships that could take me down through the atmosphere.

His nervous stammer came back, "That—th-tha-tha-tha—"
He pointed to the right.

From which I assumed that meant I should go to the left.

Which is what I did, after looking out of the door and making sure no one was watching the hallway.

It was the same hallway I'd been walking down when I'd been
hit on the head. I started trotting to the left, around a bend—And
almost into the arms of an armed guard, who shouted "Hey!"

Either the scientist was very, very cunning, or, more likely, so simple that he had outwitted me by telling me the truth.

The man didn't draw his weapon immediately. I think this was because I had a baby. In most circumstances, most men aren't ready to fire on a woman. I'd taken advantage of that any number of times. But a woman with a baby seemed to be a force multiplier. I needed to remember this.

He didn't even threaten to fire on me. As I turned and started legging it the other way as fast as I could go, he shouted to my back, "Hey, hey," and then started running after me, but the expected "stop or I'll shoot" never came. Of course, perhaps he was a mechanic and figured his pay didn't include grappling with crazy women.

I ran as fast as I could, until I caught sight, out of the corner of my eye, of a bay with a shiny ship parked on it. It wasn't as big as my father's space cruiser had been, and it looked much like the air-to-space my friend Good Man Simon St. Cyr of Liberte Seacity had once used to bring me to Circum.

A ship like that was much like a flyer, meaning it was probably only one room and there was slim to no chance anyone could hide in it. A larger ship would be hard for one person to control, but this—

I continued running till I clambered aboard. There were two young men in what appeared to be sky-blue uniforms there. Sky blue was Olympus, but they'd told me Luce was no longer the Good Man of the City, so there would be no point in trying to appeal to his authority. Instead, I motioned to them with my burner and said, "Out. Now."

They looked at me, looked at the baby and backed past me, without reaching for the weapons at their belts. I really must remember this baby as a magical shield thing. It almost compensated for the disadvantages of having a helpless and noisy human strapped to my front.

I closed the door of the air-to-space, just as I heard my pursuer arrive running. There were shouts from outside the ship as I dropped into the pilot seat and checked the fuel gages. Miracle, it was fine.

Eris started crying as we took off. I'd have to feed her as soon as we were out of range of Circum weapons.

Broom It!

EARTH, EVEN UNDER THE GOOD MEN REGIME, WHERE THEORETI-cally about fifty men split all the power of the Earth and its resources between them, had always been fairly chaotic.

A Good Man would control certain continental territories, islands, seacities, or a combination thereof. And because whatever they controlled was too large for them, under them would be a confusing, mostly hereditary bureaucracy of directorates, satrapies, principalities, secretariats, and whatever someone thought to call a group of people obeying a single person or family.

At this level territorial feuding and poaching were common. Not that they weren't at the Good Man level too. They were. But they were usually at least dressed up as something more sedate.

Which meant everyone on Earth was more or less paranoid about territory and invasions of territory, from the lowest shopkeeper to the Good Man with the largest domains. Or not paranoid, but whatever you call someone who is afraid of something that is actually trying to harm him. Alert, maybe?

The alarms didn't even startle me. I'd heard them before. I'd barely gotten to Earth atmosphere level when they started, blaring through the com on my air-to-space, telling me I was violating this territory, disturbing the peace of that other, and I should definitely provide credentials to that other.

Because air-to-space vehicles break atmosphere at a slant, to avoid going too fast and catching fire—I assume, I never studied aerospace engineering—I was flying at the highest level possible over a number of territories. It was a jurisdiction-a-second tour and it sounded something like this:

"...Garble, garble, identify self or..."

"...breaking the airspace of..."

"We shall send missiles to..."

"Restricted territory of..."

On and on and on. All of this with one person speaking over the other, and all mixed in with those people speaking languages I did not understand, which added a level of din to the already noisy warnings. There were also blaring music, screams, whistles, and sirens to add to the charm of the moment.

Eris, in her rigged strap-in in the copilot chair, slept through all of this. I had to put my hand on her twice to make sure she was still breathing.

She slept happily through all the screams and warnings, as I held on, trying to pilot us to what I hoped would be a safe landing place, in this case the waters off Liberte Seacity, the hold of my friend and sometime lover Simon St. Cyr.

For a moment there, I glided over my former home, what used to be my father's domain of Syracuse Seacity. I only knew we were over it because of my superhuman sense of location, not because I could see it. But I knew we were almost over it when I caught...

Not a mind-call from Kit. Nothing as defined as that. Just a sense of nearness and his being alive. Which could mean he would be anywhere within a day's flyer journey from that location.

This was both bad and good. Bad because it was an enormous area, more or less encompassing all of my teenage stomping grounds, i.e., the places I could reach easily enough on my broom, and where my friends, my associates and my broomer lair ranged.

Good because in this area I did have friends, at least if they hadn't all been killed, and some of these friends would have the means of listening to and looking out at the sky, which means one or more might have traced a triangular ship making it through the atmosphere. In fact, it was almost sure to have been tracked or at least filmed.

Unless the triangular ships had somehow become standard design for air-to-space vehicles since I'd been away, and I didn't believe that, as it had been only six months or so, I should be able to trace our suspected attackers and, presumably, Kit's kidnappers.

I looked at the displays on the dashboard that told me how far I was dropping and how fast.

I had, of course, not being completely stupid, removed the trackers from my stolen vehicle, right after I'd changed Eris and strapped her down in her own seat. The units were two small, card-sized transmitters that gave anyone with the right receptor the location, type and ID number of this vehicle. In a normal Earth situation, I'd have sent them flying out the window, but in space I'd had to be contented with grinding them under my heel.

The problem was that I couldn't, not while flying and needing to be strapped in for most of it, do a thorough dismount of the engine and make sure there were no other hidden trackers. Oh, sure, for flyers this was usually easy. There were two places they put trackers, and you could remove them and that was it.

But air-to-space were considerably more expensive, which meant they were considerably better protected. And by better protected I mean that while I might have got rid of everything that would blare a specific ID to the world—and even this was not a certainty—I couldn't get rid of everything that would blare a location. Not without a full engine inspection and clean-up, which by definition couldn't be done while the air-to-space was in the air. Or in space.

If I hadn't got rid of the ID, then there would be an alert out for me. After all, the scientists might be the worst fighters in the world, but they wouldn't cover up the theft of an expensive vehicle from Circum.

If I had got rid of the ID, then I was still in danger, as this was an unknown vehicle, coming in at speed, not blasting an ID, and violating all sorts of national and international boundaries.

Which meant by the time this baby splashed into the ocean, somewhere near Liberte Seacity, I wouldn't be on board. In fact, I should leave the vehicle as soon as we descended and slowed enough that I could without actually catching fire or freezing to death. Some of those territorial defense forces had always had itchy trigger fingers, and when you added that most of the Earth seemed to be engaged in war right now, that made the itchy trigger fingers all the more dangerous.

Every flyer, and every air-to-space designed to function within

Earth's gravity—even freighters—have one elementary safety precaution: brooms.

Named after the supposed mount of witches, in ancient times, these antigravity wands could be as small as two feet long, with no saddle, no obvious mount, and just a series of buttons to control speed and altitude.

Or they could be up to five feet long, and have any of the following: minimal, sculpted saddle, cushy saddle with stirrups and seat belts, oxygen masks and minimal tanks/oxygen extractors and concentrators, speed, altitude and steering controls.

The brooms were the only real way for someone who wasn't a professional parachutist to survive a bailout from a flying vehicle when something went wrong. And they allowed you to survive crashes at altitudes where parachutes failed.

That was why they were in every vehicle, in a closet with a door that read "Break only in case of emergency."

They were also highly illegal everywhere on Earth as autonomous transport. Brooms, at least brooms that had had their "brains beaten out," or were manufactured for the underground market, could not be tracked, and allowed people to go where they wanted and do what they wanted with no reference to their lords and masters, something that no government could tolerate and that the would-be total government of the Good Men despised and loathed.

Which meant there were illegal broomer gangs all over the Earth, most of them engaged in low-level petty criminality, like drug running or illegal gambling, or petty theft or smuggling. I'd been a member of a broomer lair, the Brooms of Doom, before I left the Earth.

This was very good as it meant that I was prepared for what I had to do. I knew how to ride a broom, I knew how to avoid arrest, and I could and would do both.

I broke the door seal before it was an emergency and grinned at the brooms in the closet, because—I guess I should have expected it—this being a top-of-the-line air-to-space, the brooms were high quality with a saddle and oxygen mask and all. There were two of them. One to ride and one to sell, if I should need the currency; that is, if I didn't make contact with friends or at least nonhostile acquaintances soon enough.

Of course these brooms being about four feet long, with a saddle, the only way I could—at five feet and some change—carry the spare, or my own, would be on my back, which, with Eris on my front, was about to get crowded and make me less mobile.

More importantly, though, both brooms had oxygen tanks and masks and also, hanging beside them in the closet were two brooming suits, of the kind used by people who'd never broomed and who were afraid of catching their death in the air; that is, a lot more beefed up and protective of one's tender extremities than what regular broomers wore.

Instead of just leather with decent padding, gloves, and a helmet of sorts, there were layers and layers of insulating fabric under leather that covered everything from toes to top of head.

I wondered briefly whether these people were stupid enough to think that if they insulated the suits enough they could ditch while cutting through the atmosphere. If so, I didn't think they understood physics. But then again air-to-space were either owned by the very rich or by governmental organizations, both of which could afford to be stupid and still survive.

My utility to my broomer lair had come mostly from my mechanical ability, which allowed me not only to keep our brooms in running order as to make them better or change them in specific ways we needed.

I had the experience I needed to steal an extra oxygen mask from the spare broom and split the oxygen line of my broom to cover both. Making something that would cover Eris without either putting her inside my suit or smothering her was a little more difficult, as the air-to-space lacked a vibro unit that could do alterations in clothing. Honestly, I don't know why the very rich or governmental organizations wouldn't want to alter clothes on the run, but there it is. I certainly had had one aboard Daddy Dearest's air-to-space.

There was, fortunately, a small repair kit, of the sort every provident housewife can use to fix some wardrobe malfunction on the way to a party.

I wasn't your average housewife, and if my clothes had malfunctioned while I was being raised on Earth, there would have been a seamstress, wardrobe mistress, or housekeeper not only to deal with it, but also to answer to why the malfunction had happened in the first place. And what I needed was considerably more than a mere repair.

But everyone knows how to use fix-it glue and tape, right? And I certainly knew how to cut.

The result would never have passed muster at one of those places for baby gear that I used to pass by and wonder why women spent so much time in there. But it would keep Eris warm and unfrostbitten. And attached to me. I'd changed the suit and its hood into a little sack with a hood, with face protections still in place, and with straps to attach the sack to me, so she would be warm and cushioned by my body.

I beat the brains out of both brooms, and in this case was quite sure that I had stopped all possible mechanisms for tracking the vehicles. Not hard, as there really isn't much space inside a broom, besides the antigrav unit, the fuel unit, and, in this case, the oxygen tank.

Then I put Eris in her sack, put my suit on, strapped the broom to my back. I put the oxygen mask on Eris and topped it off with my helmet from the Eden space suit, to make sure it didn't fall off, and to make sure her head didn't get frozen, since she only had little dark curls over it. For me, a hood pulled up around my head and the oxygen mask on my face were enough.

With things strapped front and back, my mobility was some-what diminished, but it wasn't an unusual situation. When the broomer lair had to transport extra brooms, usually acquired in a raid, I was often the one to carry them. My enhancements made me fight better than most of them, and I was the mechanic.

I reset the angle of flight and speed of the little air-to-space, felt its instant and accommodating response, and tamped down a pang that I couldn't save it from destruction. But there was nothing for it. If the air-to-space was being tracked, the only way I could survive this without my arrival making me the object of a manhunt—or womanhunt—was to get rid of it in a way that spelled out accident.

The route I'd calculated would drop this little vehicle in the middle of an ocean, with sufficient force to break it. I didn't want to crash it into populated land.

Having checked route and programming twice, I counted under my breath to estimate the time when the air-to-space would be lowest and slowest, before I punched the button to open the bottom emergency hatch. I was already straddling the broom.

"It's time to broom it up," I shouted, and jumped.

Eris's little face looked up at me through her visor, as blank and devoid of expression as an egg.

And the Rock Cried Out

ERIS CRIED ALL THE WAY ON THE WAY DOWN. I KICKED THE broom into as shallow a descent as I could, but I had the vague and possibly wrong idea that babies' eardrums were more sensitive than adults', and I assumed the pressure changes bothered her.

We glided over blue ocean, tinged gold here and there by the setting sun. Above us, the air-to-space sped up on its final journey.

Eris cried.

She was still crying—it is entirely possible that babies crying are the most underestimated force in the universe—when we approached the ocean. I changed my flight path, adjusting from memory to fly at that one peculiar height that was rarely tracked. Too high for the normal everyday flyers, but not so high that I impinged on the path of intercontinental or inter-island traffic. It was the level at which broomers lived. Other than the occasional peacekeeper broomer or flyer looking for broomers, and that only when broomers had been particularly troublesome.

There were neither broomers nor peacekeepers. In fact, there was no one around.

I let my memory play back what I'd seen while coming down through the atmosphere, and while getting ready for the broom, and oriented myself. If I was right, Liberte Seacity would be... north. About an hour.

Long before I'd flown the full hour, I was tired of listening to Eris cry, and felt like I'd been flying for years or perhaps centuries. My back ached and I couldn't move it, couldn't make myself comfortable with Eris and the broom both strapped to me.

It felt oddly more vulnerable and desolate to have Eris with me than to be alone. I was responsible for her, so it wasn't simply a matter of looking after myself. And part of me hated being responsible for her, and having the extra burden of making sure she was well, and the other part of me despised myself for thinking it.

When we got near Liberte, even from the air, I could tell something was wrong. In fact, it was as much of a shock as I'd sustained when first seeing my native city of Syracuse from the air last time I'd returned to Earth.

Liberte—unlike Syracuse—had always been a beautiful seacity. Part of it came from its being the ruling city of the empire ruled by Good Man St. Cyr who, for the last ten years or so had been my friend, Simon. His domains included Liberte, sure, but the real workhorse of his fortune was the seacity of Shangri-la, known mostly for its production of mind-altering—and in many jurisdictions illegal—drugs and the algae farms that surrounded it, which fed half a continent, if one were to believe the reports put out by St. Cyr. Of course, I didn't believe the reports. It's something one learns when growing up in an oligarchy. Never believe the official reports. But I still knew the St. Cyrs had commanded impressive wealth for a long time, and that very little of it was produced in Liberte.

This left the city where administrators and bureaucrats lived a beautiful place, resembling a dimatough wedding cake, climbing layer on manicured layer till it achieved the pinnacle, where Simon's palace stood, itself like a wedding cake, all glistening white dimatough, layer on layer, to the turret on the top, where the ballroom had been located.

It had been one of the most beautiful seacities to look at from the air.

Had been.

Half the palace looked ruined—blackened and burned—as did many of the other levels of the seacity. Even from the air I could see entire streets where once-airy mansions had been torched.

There were signs of rebuilding, as I got nearer the palace:

Scaffolds and heavy machinery, some of it obviously dimatough extruders, stood close enough to the palace that it was obvious that they were repairing some of the damage. But who was repairing the damage? Who was in control?

The same events that had propelled me out of Earth and into Kit's native Eden, and that had caused a quasi revolution in Eden, had made it so that there was a revolution or the start of one on Earth.

Now, Earth, unlike Eden, was a vast place, with more than three billion inhabitants—how many more was a matter of great debate, because, as I've said before, the Earth was divided not only into the domain of fifty Good Men, but into countless principalities, governorships and satrapies under them. And none of the absolute rulers or their absolute underlings trusted each other's numbers. So estimates of the numbers of humanity on Earth ranged from ten billion to three billion, and there was no consensus.

But even at three billion, there was no way a single revolution, even one propelled and masterminded by the Usaian cult, which seemed to be everywhere, could by itself span the globe. However, it was enough that it had started chaos in the areas I was most familiar with. My own native city, Syracuse Seacity, had been destroyed by a bomb, and the last time I'd been on Earth, war ranged across all of Syracuse's continental dependencies, and Olympus Seacity's also.

That it had extended to Liberte was not a surprise. Simon, though not a Usaian, had aligned himself with them. And the Good Men still in control of most of the seacities and territories on Earth would attack him as well as the rest.

But the question was—who had won? Who was in control of the island?

If it was the party of the Good Men, my landing there and making myself known might at best get me killed, or, more likely and worse, get me captured and made into that "Mother of the Race" thing they had planned for me.

I listened to Eris's now-hoarse cry and decided I wasn't absolutely sure I was ready to be the mother of one child, much less of a race. This was absolutely not happening.

So, instead of landing near the top, where the palace was; instead of trying to make contact with Simon and asking for his help in finding Kit, I circled the island and came in on the north side, the lowest level.

The way the seacities were built, level on level, the level above cut off most of the light and air to the lower one. Perhaps because of that, the lower levels tended to be far cheaper than the top levels, and the areas where the supports for the top level anchored often were dark and difficult to get to, which made them ideal for a criminal or at least shadowy element.

Now most levels of Liberte housed at worst minor bureaucrats and an educated middle class. But there still needed to be a place for the servants and gardeners, the cooks and cleaners catering to the rest of the island. Shangri-la was too far away for a daily commute for those who had neither a flyer nor a broom. And I've yet to see a place, on Earth or not, that doesn't have an area where a shadow economy can flourish. In Liberte, that was only the lowest level of the seacity.

I landed there, in a secluded place I knew from visits with my broomer lair. My appearance attracted a few looks, even after I pulled off the oxygen mask and stowed it and removed my Eden-made helmet from Eris's head and folded it into my pocket. Possibly because my suit was more expensive than normally seen in these parts, but also—likely—because it was unusual to see a broomer carrying two brooms on her back and an infant on her front.

The minute I removed the helmet from Eris, she had stopped screaming and fallen asleep. This told me she really didn't like her head confined, but there was something more. From the whiff emanating from her we'd need to find a place to change her too. Materials too. I wasn't used to this being a mother thing. I had completely forgotten to pack diapering material.

Everyone gave me a wide berth, and I walked more or less aimlessly, but taking stock of what was available, as well as think- ing through my next move. I needed to know if Simon was safe and still in control, but if he weren't that might be a perilous or even deadly move. The easiest thing would be to listen to people talk, but that wasn't going to happen on the streets. It might very well happen while shopping for diapers, or looking for food. But for that I needed money.

I knew where to go. Look, my lair did not engage in the normal criminal pursuits of broomer lairs, but it was impossible to exist—even as a semi-recreational broomer lair—without getting into battles with other lairs. And in those battles we often took spoil, which was mostly brooms. So we needed a place to dispose of stolen brooms. And I'd in the past had occasion to dispose of other spoil. Or at least of things I'd stolen from my father's house, in order to finance my lair or a new broom. Mostly things no one but me even remembered existed, like one of those musty old books in the library, printed on twenty-first-century paper with ink that was fast fading.

Most of the places we traded with were in Syracuse Seacity, but we had places of resort in other isles and continental settlements, at least within our broom range.

In Liberte the place was Lupin and Sons. Its door looked like a gash in the base of one of the dimatough columns that supported the next level. From the fact it was much taller than most normal doors, it probably had started out as a bubble in the dimatough, with an opening. Well, two openings, because next to the strangely shaped door was a strangely shaped shop window.

The shape of the shop window did not begin to be as odd as its contents. In higgledy-piggledy fashion, the display showed off—if you can call it that—anything from tarnished silver candlesticks to brand-new, shining burners that looked like police issue.

In the center of the shop, holding pride of place, was a stuffed squirrel outfitted in miniature broomer kit, with a burner in its hand. By pride of place I mean that it was upright and could easily be discerned from its surroundings. It was, however, covered in a thick layer of dust and a dusty cobweb linked its tufted ears to—presumably—the distant, darkened ceiling of the shop window.

Its dull glass eyes seemed to look me over banefully as I passed by to enter the shop.

The man behind the counter was old François and his helper was his son Louis. They were both thin and I presumed they had both once been dark-haired. The only way I'd ever known them, François's ponytail was all white, and there was a distinct bald circle on top of his head.

They looked like perfectly respectable merchants, except for a slight look of . . . expectancy. Behind their eyes lurked the sort of alertness that indicated they were looking for something or waiting for something. People said no one tried to rob Lupin's twice. People—and by people I mean broomers—also said that in the basement of the shop there was a powerful hidden incinerator that was used to dispose of more than damaged merchandise.

As a matter of curiosity, I'd often wondered if there was any truth or if these were rumors carefully set about to make sure that no one tried anything funny the first time. It didn't matter. I'd never been willing, or in fact interested in, trying anything new the first time around, and I surely wasn't about to do it now, with Eris dependent on my staying upright and breathing. If I died, heaven only knew what they'd do to Eris.

An unexpected, disturbing image, of a stuffed Eris in the shop window, in a miniature broomer suit, holding a burner, made me shudder, and I realized both men were looking at me expectantly and also with a scared expression. The expectant part made sense. They probably remembered me. The scared? Not at all.

I kept my eyes and ears open for any movement behind or to the sides of me, but there was nothing. The crowded little shop— with brooms hanging from the ceiling, used furniture and books cramming the corners, and for whatever reason, a batch of white rats in a cage—looked perfectly still, and sounded perfectly still, except for the rats and the men behind the counter. And trust me, if there had been anyone else there, even just breathing, I'd have heard them when I was listening that intently and that alert.

The last time I'd used the code that told Louis and François that I was a broomer with something illicit to sell, it had been "at the orders of Marat."

Now in the old days, the password had changed every few months, and I was never absolutely sure how it was changed or how it was passed down. We just knew it by word of mouth. Mention in any broomer bar that you were going to visit Lupin's and someone sooner or later told you the new code.

Only I'd been away from Earth for well over six months. I was sure it had changed, but not how. So I approached the counter and gave the old sign. "At the orders of Marat."

Pierre's watchful, laid-back look changed. He blinked. I had the impression he'd bit his tongue. He said, in something less than a whisper, "Louis, secure."

I tensed. For a moment I thought he was telling his son to secure me, which even with Eris strapped on and brooms on my back would not go well at all well for him.

But Louis slid quietly around me as I tracked him, and closed the door, then threw a switch somewhere in the shadowy edge of the walls. I wasn't sure what the switch was, or even if there was one, but I was aware a distant hum had quieted.

François gave me the once-over. "Well, 'demoiselle, now we should be safe. I should tell you never to say those words again, and not in public. We are good citizens, and good subjects of the Emperor Julien, alors."

If my eyebrows climbed any further, they would become part of my hairline. "Emperor Julien?" I asked. My voice cracked a little. I didn't know anyone named Julien, and really, Emperor? It didn't sound like someone who served under the sphere of the Good Men. The highest title I knew they allowed was king, and mostly because the British, an ancient, proud and quite possibly mad race, had refused to surrender their ancient pomp and dignity.

"Emperor Julien Beaulieu," he touched his forehead, in what seemed to be some kind of gesture. "The Protector of Liberte, grantor of our liberties and keeper of our people."

Uh-uh. There was one thing I knew for sure. When someone called himself the grantor of anyone's liberties, those liberties were long gone, if indeed they had ever existed.

I tried to look calm and uncaring. It didn't help that Eris chose this moment to wake up and give me a look like she was astounded at my incompetence. All right, so I was probably reading that into her wide-eyed look. But I felt incompetent, and was afraid of getting us both killed. "What happened...I've been away...ah. Out of the reach of news. What happened to Good Man St. Cyr?"

François didn't look shocked. He tightened his mouth so much that it looked as though he were trying to make his lips invisible. "I suspected you might have been away, 'demoiselle." His eyes narrowed too, and he made a gesture with his head, as though pointing his rather sharp chin at Eris. "Judging by your company."

I almost corrected him and said I was Madame, as befitted a married woman, but I didn't, because he was going on, "The Good Man, so called, got deposed and executed for his crimes against the people."

For a moment the room swayed and it seemed to me like darkness crept from near the walls to press in on me.

"Mademoiselle!" It was Louis, and he'd held my arm near

the elbow. I didn't think I'd almost passed out, but I must have swayed, from his gesture.

"I'm fine," I said, steadying myself, and standing on my own two feet. "I'm fine. I just didn't know." Poor Simon.

He'd been somewhat of a pest. If I understood what Kit had said—after he'd found these things out from the memories of the man he was cloned from—Simon's own original had been created as a spy, a chameleon who could fit in anywhere, unnoticed, who could penetrate all levels of society and the most closed of conspiracies.

And Simon's own history, with his father becoming incapacitated when Simon was very young, and Simon being required to step into the work of government, while at the same time keeping the insurgence against the *mode* of government alive, had caused him to develop a fake personality, a face he wore in public, which I had reason to believe concealed a much deeper and thoughtful young man.

But for all his flaws—and sometimes I wasn't sure where the flaws ended and Simon began—he had been one of my earliest friends and one of my first lovers. Even the last time we'd met we'd flirted, and to be fair to him, he'd given me and Kit and our companions all the help we needed in getting what we needed from Earth.

"Well, now, 'demoiselle, we all had our own private feelings for the Patrician. And that's how they should remain. Private."

François was watching me closely. I nodded. I shook Louis's grasp away from my elbow. "Indeed," I said. "Indeed, we must be loyal subjects of the ah—Emperor Julian."

François smiled approvingly. He made some kind of head gesture at Louis, who disappeared into the shadows, and, if my ears were tracking right, into a corridor somewhere near the back of the shop. "Now," he said. "Before we open the door, demoiselle, how may I help you?"

I took the extra broom from my back and laid it on the counter.

He looked at it, nodded, then ran his fingers over it, as though studying it by Braille. "It's not one of the standard commercial models," he said. "Nor one of the military models."

I kept my mouth shut. I really had no need to confess to the theft of an air-to-space, much less precisely to where I'd stolen it or why.

"On the other hand," he said, largely—I think—speaking to himself, "it is not one of those rescue brooms that fly only down, right? So. Let me see what I can give you for this?"

He bit the corner of his lip. It was said among the broomers that François Lupin had a computer between his ears. A highly specialized computer that could calculate to the last centime exactly how much he would get for an item, and then offer you half.

But when he spoke I was shocked. "How about two hundred beaulieus?" he asked.

I raised my eyebrows. "Beau—" The currency not just in Liberte but over most of the hemisphere was narcs, which was an abbreviation for "narcotics" which had been a form of currency in the Turmoils, before the Good Men had taken over and restored peace.

"It tracks more or less with the old narcs," the man said. "Because they were only replaced a week ago. It's a thousand beaulieus to the ounce of gold," he added, helpfully. "Give or take. Emperor Julien has placed us on a gold standard." I noticed once more he touched his forehead with his fingertips when talking about the emperor. It really gave me a creepy crawly feel up the spine, but I turned on the calculations instead.

One thousandth of an ounce per narc, give or take, and depending on fluctuations, had indeed been the price of gold in the old days. I knew because I often bought raw gold to have it fashioned into jewelry that was exactly what I wanted.

Given that, a hundred was unusually high for a broom with its brains beaten out, which made it clear it was stolen. I must have murmured something about high price, which just shows you I wasn't functioning. I'm not in the habit of arguing against myself.

I didn't realize I'd done it, till I saw François's smile widen, with his lips still closed. "Well, 'demoiselle," he said, his voice slightly hoarse. "It is what you can expect when war is so widespread that all flyers and brooms go up in price, as the military are buying them." He looked at the broom on my back. "If you sell me that one too, and your suit, I can raise it to four hundred nar—beaulieus."

I shook my head. The entire situation was making my skin crawl, and I did not want to leave myself without the means to escape this place as soon as possible. I did not know anything about the Emperor Julien, his rule, his domains, or even his policies. But I knew anyone who talked loudly about how much they defended liberties, let alone anyone who named a currency after himself, was not a benevolent or lax ruler.

"One broom," I said, my own voice hoarse. "And what is the price in gold?"

"One tenth of an ounce," he said. "Would Madame prefer it in coins?"

I was Madame now. And Madame was not outfitted to check the gold composition of coins, and wasn't completely stupid.

I ended up selling the broom for a tenth of an ounce, deposited in the Interplanetary Bank, an old and respectable institution at least three hundred years old and if anything a little stodgy. The deposit was in gold, but retrievable in any currency of my choice by means of a fingerprint, a voice code or a typed number code, both of which I memorized.

When I asked how much of that I'd have to pay for a packet of diapers—the smell was really near unendurable, and I suspected the screaming was about to resume—they told me it was no charge, and brought out from the back a dusty, ancient but sealed packet of newborn-sized diapers, and even threw in a shoulder sack to carry them in.

I changed Eris in a little room at the back of the shop—one that contained two cots and a tiny cooker—where I couldn't avoid the suspicion the father and son lived.

And I left wondering if I'd sold the broom so cheap that it warranted throwing in freebies, or if Gallic courtesy had taken over.

I thought of this to avoid thinking of what had happened to Simon. Or of what might happen to me and Eris, in a world where no one had any reason to be well disposed towards us.

Kit? I mind-called.

But there was no answer. Which only meant I had to find him, if I had to turn the Earth upside down and give it a good shaking.

Sanctuary

WHEN I GOT TO THE EDGE OF THE LEVEL IN WHICH LUPIN'S WAS located, and could get a good look at sky and sea without the encumbrance of a dimatough platform overhead, I saw that light was dwindling.

I might have stayed in Liberte, I supposed, but I was haunted by both the knowledge that they'd killed Simon and the vague, undefined suspicion that I was being followed. And it came to me, clear as day, that I didn't know what Louis had gone to tend to when he'd gone to the shop's corridor, or perhaps its backroom, while I was haggling with his father.

It wasn't as though I'd never been tracked or followed before.

My father had liked to at least make sure that my body was safe, which often meant having people follow me or having devices placed on me to track me. Which was part of the reason I'd taken payment in the form of an account elsewhere, instead of a credgem I could hold. Credgems are trivially easy to bug. All electronics are.

I had no reason to think that François Lupin as I'd known him would have me followed or tracked, but I also no longer knew what the society was like on the seacity or what his incentives were. Under some circumstances, in some societies, even your best friend, who wishes you well, will spy on you. And Lupin was not my best friend.

My experience allowed to check for pursuit without appearing to check. I listened attentively, but heard no single pattern of steps following me. Casual glances revealed no consistent shape or body type. And yet I was sure I was being followed.

Fed and changed, Eris slept peacefully and I thought to myself that the instinct for being followed or not being wished well had kept me safe more than my enhanced hearing or my enhanced vision. More even than my enhanced speed.

If I assumed I was being followed, what was the downside if I weren't? Well, I'd spend some uncomfortable hours and might put myself to a great deal of unneeded trouble.

But what if I were being followed and assumed I wasn't? I could get killed. Or worse.

At the edge of the platform I took the long, circuitous road around that level, walking briskly along the side of the road, on which flyers traveled fast at the low heights that were the only height allowed within the seacity.

From somewhere came the idea that one of those flyers could slow and someone could grab me.

I said, "Right," got the Eden helmet from my pocket and put it and the extra oxygen mask on Eris's face, then slipped my own oxygen mask on, mounted the broom and took off into the distant sunset.

I can't say I saw any flyer take off after me, or that I had any proof of ever being in trouble, but I know the further away I flew from Liberte, the safer I felt.

Of course, I hadn't thought of where to go until I was in the air, and then it was more or less obvious.

Some poet or other once said that you could never go home again. In my case, this was very true, of course. There was no way I could walk in through the front door of the house in which I was raised, or, as had been my custom, crawl in through the half-open library window. None of those were there anymore. Or at least the portions still standing weren't structurally safe. The palace had got bombed out, actually during the war over the possession of Syracuse, when my father had died. I'd seen the ruins from the air.

But Syracuse was still there, and I doubted the levels below the palace had been substantially ruined, and I needed a place to say. Just for the night, with Eris.

If that failed I had some vague idea of going to one of those places prostitutes rent by the hour. Father had been very strict about their being clean and vermin-free, and I was sure it would take them more than the two years or so since his death to fall into bad habits. And those establishments were known not to ask for ID or anything else but money.

But when I approached the seacity, the palace looked less ruined than I'd expected. Oh, still a burnt ruin, don't get me wrong, but not ruined all the way down, and I thought I'd land and go see what remained.

I don't know what I expected. The funny thing is that I expected it to either be completely ruined or inhabited. After all, in the lowest levels of the seacity people would take over any space, even those spaces that were left over by imperfections in building the seacity.

There were tents and huts in those levels far less luxurious than these ruins.

My first thought on landing was to note that the external walls hadn't been broached and the vast dimatough gates were still locked. This seemed strange to me, since I presumed when the palace had been bombed there had been a full complement of servants in residence, and even if most of them had been killed during the attack, there should have been corpses and the disposal of the dead.

But the glimmering black dimatough walls were unbroached and the gates locked. I circled, from the air, three times, to make sure, but I saw no movement whatsoever. True, it was getting dark, but even so, you can tell when someone is living somewhere. Well, you could if the very poor had moved in. There would be cooking smoke, and at least makeshift lights.

Nothing. The gardens had gone wild, and nothing moved inside the perimeter of the walls. So I did what any sane person would have done. Or perhaps not any sane person, since I was, after all, of the same line that had built this house, and the one thing we couldn't claim, just looking at the floor plan, was any sanity.

I landed in front of the gates, found the genlock in the dima-tough, and put my finger in the lock. The lock was a genlock and had been keyed to my supposed father's genes. I wasn't sure, though Kit could probably give you an exact description, of the manipulations that had gone into making me, but I knew that it was close enough for me to open all the locks.

This one was no exception, and the gates slid open with a protesting creak.

I took a step into the patio-driveway in front of the house, and then saw it coming towards me. It looked like a serving robot that someone had crossed with a kitchen mincer. What I mean is that it was a cylindrical column, with multiple arms coming out of its center, at all different angles. Each arm was equipped with a cleaver or knife or, yes, I was sure of it, serving fork.

One thing is to think that if you're caught here or there you're going to be lunch, and another and completely different is to be faced with what looked like a butler robot gone wild.

I screamed and fried it right through the chest with my burner, only to have the burner ray glance off the black dimatough carapace, as the thing lurched closer at an incredible speed, and I shot the burner again, this time at the light on top, amid the whirring arms.

The light exploded, the robot stopped. It started to emit a high-pitched whine and Eris woke up and started crying.

Through all this din, I heard a much-too-familiar voice say "Thena?"

There was only one person in the world who could sound like that, managing to make his voice waver, and hit several pitches at once.

I turned around and saw him loping towards me, at an uneven gallop, his hair—what remained of it—standing on end, his clothes looking like what someone would wear if he dressed in the dark, after severe brain damage. Which applied. I said, "Fuse," and put my burner away.

Fuse was—I suppose you must call him a member of my broomer lair, only some special conditions apply. Fuse had started out, like me, the child of a Good Man and raised in the lap of luxury. Until he'd discovered the secret underpinning the entire regime of the Good Men and he'd run from his father's vengeance. An accident while going through an old piece of port machinery had rendered him safe from retribution. And brain-damaged. Only one thing remained between the old Fuse and the one after the accident: an unnatural enthusiasm for making things explode.

One side of his body was close to paralyzed, he had missing tufts of hair, but it seemed to me as he got closer, that the expression in his eyes was less vague and wandering than it had once been. Half of his face remained slack and drooping, but it didn't look like he was drooling, his mouth wasn't loose, and it looked like his eyes were actually focused.

He stopped short of me and stared uncomprehendingly at Eris, tied to my front. She'd stopped screaming, but was making little snuffling sounds of displeasure.

I smiled at him. Fuse was, or had been, at about a six-year-old's level of understanding, and if you introduced something or someone new to an interaction, you were likely to confuse him. "This is Eris," I said. "My daughter."

"Your…" He blinked. "You have a daughter?" He came around with great curiosity to peer into the helmet at Eris's sleeping face. "Tiny," he said.

"She'll grow," I said. Then added, "Fuse, what are you doing here?" at the same time as Fuse looked at the robot I'd shot and said, "You've broken Nellie."

And then he said "My father," at the same time I replied "Nellie?" and then I said "Your father?" at the same time he said "Nellie, my robot. You broke her, and it took me so long to build her." And then reproachfully, "The Sinistra house doesn't have many things to build things. They're all for other things. I had to improvise."

The word improvise, despite the muddled nature of the rest of the talk, had been beyond Fuse when I'd last seen him, as had, also, the idea of building a robot. Before his accident, Fuse had been a master of explosives, building bombs for fun. After his accident he'd retained that knowledge. That, I understood, was not that hard, as passions and strong interests might leave something behind, even as a brain was damaged. But even if he'd had some mechanical knowledge before his accident—I hadn't been close enough to know it—I'd never seen him show it before or since.

I proceeded with caution.

"What does your father have to do with your hiding out in the ruins of *my* father's house?"

Fuse blinked at me. "My father is trying to catch me," he said. "For the surgery. Jan suggested I hide here."

"The…surgery?" It occurred to me that perhaps there was some treatment that might fix Fuse and perhaps it had already started. There were ways to rescue victims of brain injury, I knew that. The only thing that had made Fuse's injury so bad was that he'd not reported immediately to a med center for regen. But at the time he'd been running from his father.

"The surgery for him. He has a disease. My body will do for his brain."

It was my turn to blink, both because that was one of the most coherent explanations I'd ever heard out of Fuse and because his eyes looked full adult and intent, and sad.

The truth about the Good Man regime, which Fuse had learned just before his accident, was that while, throughout the rule of the Good Men, supposedly genetically pure and unenhanced "humans," instead of son following father, the Good Men, who were actually the Mules and the biolords of old, had had themselves cloned and their brains transplanted to the body of a supposed son.

After his accident Fuse had been deemed unusable by his father. Not because his brain had been damaged, since that wouldn't count once the surgery was accomplished, but because he was known to be brain-damaged, and so it would be very hard to believe that he was well enough to inherit. His father had had a new, younger "son" made, and Fuse was deemed not important enough to kill, but also not important enough to control. He'd spent most of his time at the broomer lair, more or less looked after by anyone who had the time and energy. Most of looking after Fuse consisted of keeping him from blowing something up.

He looked at me impatiently and said, in a snappish tone I was not at all used to hearing out of Fuse, "My brother was killed. Assassinated. My father made me come back and started using treatments," he raised a tremulous hand to the side of his face that was slack and not fully under his control. "To repair this. Some nano thing. The thing brought me back. Brought some of me back. I remembered. I understood my father wanted to bring me back, so he could say I was healed and have the surgery. He has a disease. He needs out of his body."

It was one of the longest speeches I'd ever heard Fuse make, and the most coherent. "I see," I said.

"Hid for a while. Old lair. There is no one old lair. Everyone is fighting the war. Nano thingies continued working," he said. "Called Simon. Simon said call Jan. Jan said go old Sinistra house. It's abandoned but defen— defen— defen—" His face scrunched in frustration. His mouth pursed. "Can keep intruders out. Even my father. If he thinks to look here, and he won't. So I moved in, and live in secret place. Place that closes. But I built Nellie to protect me." He looked at the robot. "You killed Nellie."

I wondered what he meant by secret place. If it was my father's secret office-and-fun-rooms, I wondered how he'd discovered it and more importantly how he'd gotten into it. I, myself, had only been able to find it because I'd seen my father go into it once. "I'm sorry, Fuse," I said, not sure which mental age I was talking to anymore. "Nellie would have carved me to pieces otherwise. You understand I don't want to be carved."

He nodded, forlornly, so forlornly that I added, "If we take her inside I might be able to fix her. You remember I'm good with machines?"

His eyes lit up. "You fix," he said. Then he looked up apprehensively. I realized that though he'd come close to me, he was still in the shadow of the house and wouldn't be fully visible should anyone or anything fly overhead. "You know we're not supposed to be out. Someone might see."

I agreed with him that far. I grabbed hold of one of Nellie's arms, beneath a cleaver end, and pulled it along. Fortunately it had wheels, and allowed itself to be pulled fairly easily.

We went in to the home of my childhood by what used to be the doorway to the secondary kitchen.

In its heyday, as in when I'd grown up here, the house had had a population of a few hundred people, between maids, guards, cooks, gardeners and rarer occupations like seamstress or shoemaker. To serve this population, it had two kitchens, each with a dedicated staff: One of them catered to the family, that is Daddy Dearest and I, and any guests we might have at any time. It specialized in whatever food was trendy or fashionable at the time.

The secondary kitchen catered to the staff, and while the food there wasn't bad—my father believed in giving people incentives to stay loyal and to remain working for him—it was cooked on a grand scale and for a small multitude. As such, it was plain, plentiful, and nutritious but not in any way fashionable.

The secondary kitchen was magnitudes bigger than the primary kitchen, and it had been a very full place. Now only the furnishings remained, the staff having either died in the explosion or dispersed. It contained two very large, industrial-scale cookers, and a huge table, right down the center. Bits and pieces of what I assumed had been kitchen equipment remained scattered around, but the pots and pans that used to hang from the ceiling and the plain white ceramite service for four hundred that used to be stacked on the shelves near the cookers were gone. I assumed they had been looted and that the only reason the cookers and table were still here was that they'd been assembled in the kitchen and were too large to simply carry out and too complex to be assembled by the uninitiated.

As we entered the kitchen, perhaps triggered by the change between light and dark, between warmth and relative coolness, Eris resumed screaming.

Fuse looked back, alarmed, and I said, "It's all right. She's just scared. She doesn't understand what's happening."

He nodded and resumed walking, out of the kitchen and into a hallway that I remembered having been furnished with oriental carpet and holograms on the walls, but which was now just bare, black ceramite. He spoke without turning back, in a sort of toneless, flat voice, "I remember not understanding," he said. "It's very scary."

And I realized that having been severely hampered and recovering might be worse than never having recovered. I stared at Fuse's broad back, as he limped rapidly ahead of me, and felt a sudden surge of pity.

At the end of the hallway, past doorways that led to what used to be other parts of the house, was a large bare room. It used to be the administrative room for all of my father's domains, and I wondered who had got the computers with their data, as well as all the other accoutrements necessary for running what had been the Sinistra empire.

The room was so bare and spare that even the places where wires ran into the wall had been excavated, to remove the last bit of wire-metal that people could possibly reach.

Fuse paused and said, "First night here, I looked at wires and where wires went," he pointed at a section of wall behind denuded built-in storage. The storage was in molded dimatough and looked like it had been poured at the same time as the wall, which probably explained why no one had tried to remove the shelves. They had removed the doors that had been wood, and which had once hidden the shelves. "I was bored," he explained. "And I realized that some of them had to be for a secret door. So I got wires from other places. Some of the bombed, unstable places still had everything. And I got components and I refixed the entry."

I remembered the door to my father's secret domain had once been operated by manipulating a faun's statue and some accouterments on the shelves. Those were gone, but Fuse now reached beneath a shelf, touched a point on the wall, which looked to me indistinguishable from any other point on the wall, kicked a distant shelf. Part of the wall slid away, revealing a hallway. He smiled back at me, an echo of his old lopsided smile, "Come," he said. "Once this is closed we'll be safe here. Even if they know there used to be a secret place, they won't know where to look."

I hesitated. I had known Fuse well before, and while I wouldn't say I'd have trusted him with my life, since his impairments made trusting him with anything but the ability to "make a big boom" perilous, I had known how his mind worked and his proclivities. I knew Fuse had been a good-natured child, at heart. Now—

Then I thought that once Fuse's personality had been stripped away by the accident, what had remained, at the heart of it, was his own basic inclinations, which seemed to be rather well-intentioned and perhaps even, at least when applied to the old Fuse with his impairments, sweet. I remembered he used to greet me with wholehearted hugs, for instance, and I didn't even remember a single instance of his throwing a tantrum.

And while brain injury could and did change people's personality, the vague memory I had of Fuse before his injury was of a quiet, somewhat shy, but helpful and rather gentle young man. Besides, if he tried anything funny, I could fight him off. I'd fought off bigger men before. And even if he had the same enhancements I had—or so close as made no difference—being also the clone of a Mule-biolord-Good Man, he hadn't full control of his body yet. That much was obvious from his dragging right foot, his trembling right arm.

I nodded and followed him, pulling Nellie the Robot. He noticed this and said, "It's okay. I'll take Nellie. You have a baby," and reached to pull the Ms. Cleaver Robot himself.

Inside the secret door, it looked far more as I remembered my father's house looking. There were deep rugs on the floor, and shelves and cabinets everywhere, many of them crammed with mementos of my father's long and disreputable career.

Most of these mementos were perfectly innocuous, consisting of things he'd been given by his subordinate rulers, usually a slightly higher version of the sort of souvenir people bought in souvenir shops. Things made of seashells, and seashells of monstrous proportions, and fossils, and holos and . . . And then there was his office, a far more utilitarian space, with a link and things that Father wouldn't want anyone else to see. And then there were the private rooms. For a moment I entertained the hope that Fuse hadn't penetrated the private rooms. Father had rather peculiar tastes, we'll say it that way, the result of which had been not only dark stains on the floors of those rooms but the sort of mementos that I understood all serial killers kept: bits of humans. Usually small and desiccated, but unmistakably human bits of people who were no longer alive by virtue of Father's agency. There had also, I think, been holos and sensi recordings. I wasn't absolutely sure, as I hadn't activated the holo apparatus or played the sensis. In fact, since, at a relatively young age, I had realized what Father did in those rooms, I had tried to stay out of them and keep my ignorance of what happened there as much as possible.

So I'd hoped that Fuse hadn't opened those rooms. I didn't know what his recovering mind would make of it, and I wasn't sure I wanted to know.

But when we got to the central hall of the place, the door to Father's most secret room, which had once been secured by genlock, stood open, blasted, the lock burned away. Fuse looked at it, then stopped dead.

He turned around to face me. "I have thrown away everything from those rooms," he said, with a slightly worried look, as though he thought I might object. And, to my enthusiastic, "Good," he hesitated.

"I burned them," he said. "Or threw it in the sea. I cleaned. I got a bed from upstairs and . . . and things . . . and I sleep there. But you don't want to sleep there. It was a bad place."

I had no idea how he'd intuited I didn't want to sleep in that place. Perhaps he'd noticed my expression when looking at the blasted-open door. Or perhaps he'd recovered enough memories and enough of his mind to realize what the place must have been and was gallantly trying to protect me. Impossible to say. I simply didn't know the new Fuse.

"No, I don't want to sleep there," I said.

He grinned, with an echo of the Fuse I'd known, and possibly an echo of someone he'd been in childhood, and went into that space, and dragged back several blankets. "We'll make you a bed in the office," he said. He hesitated. "I don't want to go upstairs and see if there are some mattresses. You don't mind, do you? Some places are very unstable."

I didn't mind at all. I'd flown enough above the mansion's ruins to think that Fuse shouldn't have risked it in the first place. Yes, the way the shell was split, and only selectively burned, there were probably entire rooms untouched, but the way the walls leaned at crazed angles, it was entirely possible for the entire thing to collapse at the smallest weight. In fact, Fuse had colonized just about the only safe area in the house, since Father's holy of holies plunged under the dimatough top of the island and was therefore probably safe even in case the structure above collapsed.

The assemblage of blankets Fuse arranged was more of a nest than a bed, but it was surprisingly comfortable. Or maybe I was that tired.

Fuse watched in solemn, owlish interest as I changed Eris, and, because I couldn't figure out how to get rid of him, while I nursed Eris, although I did cover the process with a draped corner of a blanket.

At the end of it, while Eris lay in my arms, falling asleep, he gave her his finger, which she grasped with a determination that I suspected meant a whole lot of stubbornness as part of her inborn character.

He looked down, fascinated at her tiny fingers squeezing his. "She's holding so she won't fall," he said, very gently. There was a long silence. "I felt like that. When I was ... when I was really not well. I kept trying to hold on to the little bits that were me," he said. "But I kept falling."

I didn't say anything. There didn't seem to be anything I could say. Eventually he shambled off to the rooms I'd rather never enter again, and I closed the door to the office and locked it.

Look, chances are he could get in if he tried really hard. And he probably had a burner about him, somewhere. And I'd once fought off an armed and armored man using only my boot. But I like to sleep more or less undisturbed. And what if he came in and took Eris off with him, while I slept? Let's suppose he even did it with the best intentions in the world: Did he know he was supposed to support her spine? Even if he had known that about babies long ago, while well, did he still know it?

I shoved one of the armchairs against the door in such a way that getting in would take time as well as effort. Time would mean time enough for me to wake up, time enough to prepare defense.

I bedded down on the untidy nest of blankets and eiderdowns on the floor, with Eris on my chest.

It smelled as though it had been exposed to the outside air for a long time, which was probably true, before Fuse had rescued the covers.

As I started sliding down into sleep, I had an idea. But even the idea was not enough to keep me awake.

Mapping the World

I WOKE NOT KNOWING WHAT TIME IT WAS, WITH ERIS COMPLAIN-ing. It was her "I am wet" complaint. It's amazing how in a very few days I'd come to know her range of sounds. The wet cry was not a full-throated cry, like the one when she was dirty or needed food. Rather it was a low, rambling complaint, as though she were muttering in her sleep.

I said "Light" and the light came on, as it had been pro-grammed in most of the house. For the first time it occurred to me to wonder where the energy for this part of the house was coming from, considering the stripped condition of the house above. Then I nodded to myself. Of course Father must have had a backup power source for this place. If he hadn't, someone who helped run the rest of the house—housekeeper, butler, or manager—would have noticed the power consumption and initi-ated a search for where it was going, thereby risking disclosing the secrets Father would like to keep secret, including but not limited to the fact that he'd lived for over three hundred years and was one of the dreaded Mules once created to administer entire countries.

Possibly, too, this part of the house had some sort of emer-gency power supply, since I had the vague idea that it had been meant as a safe place, where Father could ride out a full attack on him. Wars between the Good Men for various purposes, including trade advantages, hadn't been unusual in the three hundred years since the Turmoils.

I changed Eris, and put the used diaper down an incinerator chute, wondering if it would in fact get incinerated or if that system was now disabled and if it was just falling into some place below, from where no one would retrieve it. Not that I cared much either way, it was just an odd feeling not to know which systems I could count on.

Eris went back to sleep almost immediately. I had no idea what time it was. The only thing approaching a window in the room was the repaired place where I'd once smashed a chair through to create an impromptu exit.

I looked at it, amused that it had been inexpertly repaired. I suspected Father had had this place built long ago and the workers who'd built it assassinated. So to repair it without being discovered he'd likely have had to do it himself in the scant time between my causing the damage and his death.

Then I remembered my idea. I set Eris down in the nest of blankets and slid into the chair behind the desk with dad's link, the one that had kept all his secret projects, reports of his prisons, and who knew what else.

To begin with, the link gave me the most immediate information I needed. It was in fact seven in the morning. Outside, the sun would be shining still pale, and veiled, from behind the clouds. How pale and veiled depended on the season, which I tried in vain to calculate before looking at the calendar in the link's memory and finding out it was November. So the sun would be very pale and veiled indeed, I thought, as I started poking around the link, trying to find my way.

The last time I'd used this link or its predecessor, I was looking for something very specific, to be precise, where exactly my father had hidden my husband.

Now, while my husband was still hidden and I could not find him, and a forlorn attempt at calling him, just now, with *Kit?* brought no answer, I didn't think I could find the location in my father's files.

In fact, since my father had been dead for two years or so, I couldn't find the answer to any current problems in his records. It was not his records I wanted. It was recent news that I wanted to search for any mention of a triangular ship, and any reference to anyone arriving from space recently. In addition I'd like to know if any of my old friends were still in power and could lend me help. I presumed Jan Rainer, of Sea York Seacity was still alive, or had been at a recent time. But whether that meant he was still in control of anything, I couldn't know, and I didn't also know if Fuse could even understand the concept of a Good Man's power.

So I slid in front of the link full of determination.

I'm not a programmer or anyone who can bend computers to her will. Of the two of us, Kit was better with that. I'm simply good with machines, and because of that could, sometimes, with much effort, alter programming and make things work the way I wanted them to.

Daddy Dearest's system proved a pain in the behind. In truly paranoid fashion he'd hidden all his records behind multiple passwords. Fortunately I now knew enough of his past to crack those. Not that I did it at first. What I didn't expect and only a truly insane man would do is that he also had locked all the search functions of the link behind multiple passwords.

While floundering around, trying to get the link to do what I wished, I activated something, which projected a holo onto the desktop. I took in sharp breath at the sight of it. I'd seen it before, much faded and discolored and in small format, in the house of a man in Eden. Or rather in the house of one of two Mules who'd stayed behind in Eden, with the bioed but human Mule servants. The rest of the Mules had continued their voyage to the stars in the interstellar spaceship tragically named *Je Reviens*. That Mule, Dr. Bartolomeu Dias, had been the one who'd decanted Kit and was, truth be told, the one who had saved Kit's life before he was even born. He'd served as a sort of surrogate father to my husband.

The holo showed him as a young, tanned man of Mediterranean looks, short but muscular with dark, curling hair and dark, smiling eyes. He was leaning on a tall, red-headed man who, except for hair color and the fact his green eyes were perfectly normal human eyes, was a dead ringer for Kit, which made sense since this was Jarl Ingemar, the originator of the genetic code Kit carried. I wasn't so stupid as to think I knew Jarl. But his personality had been accidentally superimposed on my husband's for a brief time, when Kit had been given a cutting-edge treatment to restore brain function after an injury. I wondered sometimes if parts of him still remained in Kit. Then I wondered if the treatment they'd given Fuse was of the same kind, and wondered what personality they might have given him.

Leaning on Jarl from the other side was another young man, also much shorter than Jarl, and also vaguely Mediterranean. Dark hair, and blue eyes, a lithe build and a more-pretty-than-handsome face. The young man could have been my brother. Which he was in a way, since he was the originator of the genetic code to which I'd been built, even if they'd somehow managed to gender-shift me.

At the time this holo had been taken, they were very young. Even though Mules aged slower, and it was possible that they'd looked this young over the next thirty years or so, I knew they were young from the attempted insouciant poses, the white suits, which looked like they were the somewhat expensive but not tailored, the kind of clothes that young bureaucrats would wear.

I assumed this had been before the Fish War, the first war between the land nations and the seacities, which, in collapsing society and destroying much of the world, had first catapulted the bioengineered young men into power as biolords, the same young men who would, after the Turmoils, rule under pretense of natural humanity, as the Good Men.

Not for the first time, it occurred to me that these bioimproved men had been given everything, or at least everything that the bio science of the time could give them. They'd been made superhumanly intelligent, agile, strong, and healthy. Other talents had been heaped on them depending on who had built them and for what purpose: Simon seemed to have been a naturally good actor, like I was an instinctive mechanic, for instance.

But at the end, all of it hadn't done much for them. Oh, they'd acquired great power not once but twice, world power, the kind of power that controlled entire territories, peoples and lands.

None of which seemed to have made them happy. What I'd known of Dr. Bartolomeu and of Kit's brief struggle with Jarl's personality, and what I remembered of my father, had revealed unhappy personalities, forever seeking for something they couldn't find, and for which power and wealth, possessions and adulation could not compensate.

I'd come to believe it was that they'd not been raised as humans but as something both better and worse, both superhuman creatures capable of saving mankind, and as things: artifacts made and operated for a purpose.

The split between the two sets of expectations had cleaved their souls. So it hurt to see a picture of these three, young and seemingly happier in their friendship, their new freedom, and their newfound ability to travel than they'd ever be again, even at the pinnacle of power and strength.

I managed to turn the holo off, which was good since it had gone blurry as though my eyes were filled with tears, which was stupid, because what was there to cry about? They were all dead and beyond hurt.

The next attempt at breaking into the outside world with this link actually got out and I found myself setting a search on the news. There were about a million news items about ships: launched ships, stolen ships, war ships, bombed ships, ships in engagements in war at sea. There was nothing about triangular ships, and the search brought up no images that looked like the ship that had attacked me.

A momentary panic assailed me, the fear that I'd dreamed it all. In some of the books I'd read there was stuff about pregnant women hallucinating or going insane. But surely hallucinating an entire battle was beyond even my ability. And it would mean Kit had what? Fallen off the surface of the ship?

No.

I started searches on the names of my friends. Jan Rainer came up in reports of military actions. Sieges and assaults and the like. I judged he was likely to be a commander in the active war, and therefore not someone whom it would be safe to try to contact. I noted in some interest that he was still called the Good Man.

I then searched for Simon St. Cyr. What came up was a holo of someone holding up a decapitated head. I blinked. Then swore and turned it off. It felt like I'd been punched in the stomach and it took me a moment of shaking before I collected myself. There might have been tears. I'd never loved Simon. At any rate not like I loved Kit. It was more that we'd been friends since we were very young, and I'd liked him a great deal. We'd been lovers more out of boredom than out of love, but we'd belonged to the same broomer lair. We'd planned operations together, we'd fought together. And most of all, he'd listened to me, and I'd listened to him.

Kit thought he was many kinds of reprehensible, and truth be told, he was, but it wasn't bad reprehensible. What I'm trying to say is that in the end I'd be able to trust him with anything, just as he could trust me.

That severed head. Those staring eyes. The blood. I swallowed down hastily. I couldn't imagine Simon losing control of the situation to that point. What in holy hell had been happening on Earth while I was gone?

Half blinded by moisture in my eyes, I typed in Lucius Keeva's name. It came up almost immediately, in page after page after page. Apparently Luce had been doing broadcasts of some sort every week to rally the troops. They called him Lieutenant Colonel Keeva. I realized with a pang that when I'd asked for him on Circum as Good Man Keeva I'd been wrong. No wonder they'd been confused.

But even though I should feel upset that I'd run in such a precipitate way and ruined a good air-to-space for no reason, I was so relieved that someone I knew was alive and in power of some sort, after I thought he'd been killed, all I felt was relief.

I sat there for a moment, then started looking again at Keeva's location. Yeah, the military title might mean that he was away at war, in some dangerous location, but then the weekly broadcasts argued against that. I found a reference to Lucius being quartered in Olympus, and I thought I must get to him. If he had his finger on the levers of military bureaucracy, he would be able to tell me if those triangular flyers even existed.

I decided it was late enough—or early enough, depending on how you looked at it—to get going, and I got up, changed Eris again and fed her, then wrestled her into the improvised infant brooming suit. It seemed to me that human infants had been maximized for difficulty of dressing, moving every which way except the way that would help you dress them. As she became more awake, it was sort of like trying to wrestle a greased octopus into a party dress. Her arms flung everywhere except where they needed to go, and when I pulled them into the right place her legs started kicking. And then she smiled, as though it were the best game ever. I had a vague impression this one was going to be trouble.

She stopped smiling when, after I'd dressed, I strapped her to my middle. She made a face like she was going to cry, but then thought better of it, as I opened the door. Fuse was waiting. I had a moment of alarm, but he looked worried, not menacing.

"Thena?" he said, staring at me. "Where are you going?"

"I need to go to Olympus Seacity," I said. "I need to find Lucius Keeva."

"Who?" Fuse said. And I realized even though his brain might be getting fixed by whatever the nanocites were he'd been given, he wasn't going to remember or to remember very clearly the things that had happened while he was brain-damaged. I said, "Max's older bro—" Then remembered he knew as well as I did why we'd been made, that is, as body-replacements for near-immortal and unable-to-reproduce Mules. "The first clone Dante Keeva had made. He was rejected beca—He was rejected and sent to prison on trumped-up charges, because they thought he'd realized about the brain transplants, but his father didn't want to discard him in case he needed—"

"An extra body," Fuse said. "Like my father." He seemed already more coherent than yesterday. "I see." He frowned. "I have a vague memory he'd murdered someone..." He shrugged. "But those things can be faked. He's Good Man again? I remember him in the lair. Looking for Nat."

I frowned. "He's a Usaian, and he's serving in the army of Olympus Seacity."

"Oh. Was Max a Usaian? Did I forget?"

"No, I think Lucius converted."

"Why do you want to see him? You're safe here. Why would you go out of here?"

I told him. I told him as simply as I could. He didn't ask me to repeat but he did frown as though he were making an extraordinary effort to follow the thoughts. At the end he nodded. "I shall go with you," he said.

"No. You're hiding here for a reason. If Jan finds out that you—"

"Jan can boil his head," Fuse said. "He's not my boss. I'll be with you. You won't let my father take me. You're better than Nelly."

In the context, being considered better than a single-column robot with cutlery arms was high praise. After all he'd built Nelly himself.

"I'll fix Nelly," I said, feeling guilty. "As soon as I can."

He shook his head. "Don't worry. I'll just go with you. I remember how you fight. I'll be fine."

He disappeared towards his room and I considered getting dressed very quickly and escaping, but Fuse did seem to be much better and he didn't deserve for me to behave so churlishly to him.

So in addition to Eris, I'd have a half-child I'd be responsible for. I missed the days when I was only responsible for myself.

Lost and Found

OF COURSE ERIS STARTED CRYING HALFWAY THROUGH THE TRIP, above the ocean. She cried so loudly even Fuse could hear her. I realized he'd flown closer and was making the sign-language gestures for "What is wrong?" over and over frantically.

Strangely, broomer sign language did not contain terms for "her diaper needs changing, she wants to nurse, and she's probably upset at changing air pressure." So I flashed back, quickly, "nothing" and "uncomfortable."

He must not have believed the first part, because he flew close to us for a while.

Olympus Seacity is a sprawling seacity. They used a lot of white dimatough in making it, so it manages to give an impression of Mediterranean beauty. I wanted to fly the way I used to when Max was alive and a member of our broomer lair—to the side, and land on the terrace next to the sea. We used to gather there often before a raid or a party.

But even from the sea I could tell that Olympus was now a military center, and as such I could not possibly just land anywhere. Or I could, of course, but I wasn't interested in getting shot out of the air. People fighting a war didn't have any kind of a sense of humor.

So I landed in front of what used to be the Good Man's palace. Fuse landed right next to me. Eris was still raising a ruckus.

Fuse looked worriedly at her, his eyebrows quirking. With his brain starting to function, he looked almost normal, despite the network of scars on his face, and the fact that he had patches of hair missing. I wondered if his father had planned on cosmetic surgery after appropriating Fuse's body, and then I wondered how difficult the surgery would be, and then I stopped being an idiot and wondered how to get to Lucius Keeva.

The entrance to the palace was through a massive and rather impressive staircase. At the foot of the staircase were two sentinels. At the top two others.

I stared at them. They wore the sky-blue uniforms that had been newly designed when I'd last been here. But they were also armed with large weapons. I thought that if I knew anything about how bureaucracies and armies worked, just blustering up to the door, particularly in my current, disheveled and rumpled condition, would not get me to Lucius's presence. Or indeed much of an answer.

I flashed a smile at Fuse, "Can you wait here?" I asked.

He narrowed his eyes then shook his head. "No. I know I'm safe with you."

"Ah..." I said, and because I wasn't sure where Fuse's mind was right now and if I was talking to an adult or a six-year-old, I said, "I'm going to lie a lot. Do not act surprised."

His eyebrows rose, but he nodded once, and followed right behind me, all the way to the top of the stairs.

The guards were young and tall, and obviously worked out more than most men bothered to. Clean-shaven, brown-haired, in identical sky-blue uniforms, they could have been twins, only they clearly weren't. Their features were different. And they were both looking at me as though I were something that had crawled out from beneath the rug.

I cleared my throat, "I need to see Lieutenant Colonel Lucius Keeva."

They didn't even change expressions enough to let me know they knew the name. For a moment I wondered if they were some kind of incredibly realistic statues. Then the one on the right said, "About?"

I couldn't tell them anything that would get me to see Lucius but wouldn't get other people curious about me, or Eris, or most of all curious about Kit and about Eden. My father had been on a mission to catch darkship thieves and my father was dead, but it didn't mean that other Good Men wouldn't want to find Eden, particularly if they realized Eden had technology they lacked. As for the other side of the fight, they too needed technology to defeat the Good Men.

So I said what I had planned to say. In any place, at any time, there is a lie that will bring a woman carrying a child to the presence of a man no matter how well guarded he is or how high his station, and no matter how absurd her claim. Or perhaps even more so if her claim is absurd.

Look, I grant you there will be exceptions. Any woman showing up carrying an infant and demanding to see a Good Man would be sent away. If she was lucky she'd be sent off with some money.

Or maybe not. Though the Good Men were biologically the same Mules created and designed to be absolutely sterile back in the end of the twenty-first century, it didn't mean that they didn't wish, sometimes, to pretend to be able to impregnate normal women. Particularly when they were undercover as natural humans.

In the same way, my accusing Lucius Keeva of fathering my daughter was a double impossibility. Or at least an impossibility and a high unlikelihood. Now of course it was only an impossibility if you didn't know I was of the same stock he was. A Good Man-Mule could not impregnate a standard human woman. Me? I was a different matter. And as for the unlikelihood, I happened to know Lucius was in a relationship with my old broomer-lair friend, Nat Remy.

However, I very much doubted two guards as young as these looked were going to attempt to argue the relationship angle, and if they knew that Luce was a Mule, yet they might not put two and two together quickly enough when faced with an accusation. I straightened my spine and I said, "About his daughter."

"His..." the guard on the left said.

I looked at him, then at Eris.

He opened his mouth. He looked like he was about to say something. He closed his mouth. He opened it again. He looked helplessly at his watch mate.

I didn't know how much they even knew about Mules. Mules who had become the Good Men had grown into such scary legends that amid their superhuman brilliance, their cruelty, and their disdain for humans, the "sterile with normal human females" thing might have been lost.

But I swear the message they traded through their look was, *if this is true and Nat Remy finds out, he'll kill us all, so let the big guy deal with it.*

One of them went up the stairs and in, to be replaced seconds later with another guard. And then the guards stood there, staring at us, and Fuse and I stared back at them, until I got tired of hearing Eris cry and knelt down, set her on the step, changed her diaper, then opened my broomer suit strategically so it still covered me, and proceeded to nurse her while Fuse watched with that strangely fascinated expression all males, of any level of mental development, get when breasts and babies are involved.

Since I was sitting on the steps I had my back turned to the front door, and the first I knew of Lucius Keeva's approach was the sound of his boots on the steps. I got up and turned, just before he got to me. He's a huge man, over six feet tall, with long dark-blond hair, and he looked confused and curious in equal measure.

He glanced at Eris—what was visible of her, since her head was hidden inside the chest of my suit, making me look hideously deformed—then at me. "Thena," he said, and extended his hand, before realizing mine were both occupied in holding Eris. He dropped his hand and said, "Thena," again.

He looked at Fuse, frowned, then back at me. "They said, the guard said—" he frowned. "Not unless some experimentation has taken place or I've become amnesiac."

I smiled at him. "I said what I had to say to see you. I need to ask your help."

Now his gaze sharpened, and he nodded once. "I see," he said. "Come with me." He waved to the sentinels that I was all right. I noted that they more than likely couldn't have heard our conversation, and that what they saw was a quick exchange and Lucius inviting me in, and I had to fight not to smirk. By nighttime the rumors would be rife, not that either Lucius or I would care much, I suspected. Unless, of course, Nat heard, wherever he was.

I started up the stairs after Lucius, and Fuse shouted, "Wait."

I turned and realized the sentinels had blocked him, not that I could blame them.

Lucius turned and said, "Er—" Even as I said, "He's with me," and to Lucius, "He's Ajith Mason, or if you prefer, Fuse, a member of my broomer lair. Nat will vouch for him, if you ask him."

"Nat is . . . in some sort of high council meeting, but of course I trust you." He waved for them to let Fuse through, and said, as he led us through the door to a darkened hallway, "I remember him."

Fuse blinked. Then spoke, "I remember too," he said. "A cell? In a prison? And water coming in."

Lucius turned around, "Yes. You were the one who shot the door to my cell, and freed me from Never-Never."

I knew that Lucius had been a prisoner in the infamous underground jail, and in solitary for fifteen years, but I didn't realize that Fuse . . . well, Fuse had been in on the raid.

"Possibly," Fuse said. "You must understand, I've been very ill. I'm just recovering. I have to stay with Athena. She keeps me safe."

Lucius frowned at that, but escorted us into a small room with sofas, and had three kinds of soft drink and little sandwiches brought in. I had finished nursing and probably ate more than good manners dictated. Not that anyone would notice. Lucius looked at Eris, "Your daughter . . . she's very little." He sounded like a man fishing for context.

Which was my opening for telling him everything that had happened to me since Kit's and my return to Eden. When I mentioned the Emperor Julien Beaulieu, he started to open his mouth, then shook his head.

I'd just finished when someone knocked on the door and came in. She was a young, slim woman in an Olympus uniform, and she handed Lucius a slip of paper, which he read. He frowned and took a deep breath. "That's all, Gloria, thank you. You may leave."

Once the door was closed, he turned to me. "Your husband has just turned up in Liberte Seacity with a hostage. They are now . . ." He looked around wildly. "They are elsewhere. Simon requests our help with the situation."

"Simon?" I said.

But Lucius didn't explain. "We have no time to lose."

LOST BOYS

Je Reviens

LET IT BE NOTED I MUCH PREFER TRAVELING IN A COMFORTABLE flyer than on broomback. So did Eris, who fell asleep as soon as I secured her in a seat that had special adaptations for children. Since this was Lucius's flyer, it merited a sidelong glance at him, while I fumbled with the infant-adaptor module, which was sort of a pull-out crib.

He looked amused, and I got the impression he enjoyed puzzling me. After a while, he reached over and set the proper adaptor. "Nat has siblings," he said, in the tone of voice one uses when trying not to laugh. "And often I'm the only family member who can work with them around, since most of my work is writing things and appearing in holocasts. I do a lot of my work at parks and zoos."

He waited till Fuse and I were strapped in, on either side of the pilot seat, then pulled up at least three screens' worth of info before programming a route into the flyer. I said, "Difficult route?"

"No. I just don't like to find myself in the middle of a shooting match. And some of the things used...could bring us down. So I check what is happening on the route. A lot today, apparently."

"I just flew," I said. "On the broom."

"Yes, but Nat says that angels protect you. Or something. Which considering some of the things he survives..."

"It's safe with Athena," Fuse said. "She's always safe. Because she'll kill anyone who tries to hurt those with her."

"I don't normally mean to hurt anyone," I said. Though it wasn't precisely true. I'd tried to hurt people with malice afore-thought several times before. And sometimes even managed it.

Lucius was programming our course, and spoke without turn-ing around, "It's not a bad idea, or a bad thing to hurt people when they're trying to hurt you or those you love. It's something I had to learn." His voice had the sort of slow, thoughtful cadences that betrayed he had put deep thought into the words.

"You said Kit was with Simon?" I said.

"Yes, though perhaps I shouldn't have said it."

"But Simon is dead. I saw it on—"

Lucius pushed the button to input the route, then turned his chair around. "There have been . . . issues. There was a revolution in Liberte," he said.

"I know. I saw the holos."

He shook his head. "It's more complex than the holos show. Simon . . . set the revolution off without meaning to, and the only way it could be brought under control was for someone to take charge who was experienced, someone who understood and could control the armies and the loyalty of those who knew how to run the domain. As you must understand, that person was . . ."

"Simon? But he—?"

"Ah, no. What was killed was one of his replacement clones. Acephalous or nearly so. Created as emergency bodies for . . . for the Good Man."

"The what?" In Eden it was normal for people to grow bodies, or at least body parts, in order to replace their own in case of injury or accident, as well as to forestall aging. Just not conscious bodies or bodies that moved under their own power. "But it could move!"

"Yeah, the Good Man made them that way. Healthier. It can be exercised and develop muscles of its own."

"But that's disgusting. And bioengineering is forbid—"

"And you think that means totalitarian, secretive rulers haven't done it." Lucius gave me a look that enjoined me to be my age. "We know they cloned themselves, plus whatever went into creating you. We don't have much provable knowledge, because we only have one of the doctors who did this. Most of the others ran away, went underground, or are missing. Simon's was a Usaian and tried to mitigate what he did, but we do have a clue as to what went on. Anti-bioengineering laws were and are for the little people."

I opened my mouth and snapped it shut. I'd seen how much my father cared for rules that hampered or mattered to other people. Lucius smiled. It wasn't a good smile. Just a mirthless stretch of the lips. "Precisely," he said. "Anyway, so he had a near anencephalic—without a brain—clone killed, and he... It's complicated, but we'll say he had surgery to change his features and he proclaimed himself—"

"The Emperor Julien Beaulieu," I said. "The rat bastard. I should have recognized the style. Beaulieus as a currency, now. That should have told me it was Simon behind it. Megalomania."

Lucius smiled, a tight smile. "Precisely."

"So, we're going to his palace? Kit is there? With... a hostage?"

Lucius made a face. "It's not that simple."

"Nothing ever is." Honestly, when I die, if I have a grave, and if anyone wants to give me an epitaph beyond *Thank all divinities, she's dead,* I would like *Nothing is ever easy or simple.*

"Well, as you'll probably understand, we can't go to Liberte Seacity and visit the Emperor Julien. You know that. In fact, your husband could not stay there."

"So?"

"There is a place," he said. "An abandoned algae-processing platform, in the middle of the sea. It's far enough from any routes and small enough that we shouldn't be in danger. Sim— Julien had your husband and the... hostage brought over by submarine. They await us there."

"You keep saying the hostage. Who is this hostage?"

"I understand your husband said it's one of the people who tried to capture him. But that you have to see him to believe it."

I didn't know what to even answer. My mind conjured thoughts of tentacle monsters, but I was fairly sure that wasn't it. For one, if Kit had been captured by a tentacle monster, he'd probably have said so. I mean, "I have a hostage and he's a squid" would be an irresistible line for anyone, particularly my husband. But I also didn't understand why he wouldn't have given us a description of any outlandish enough captor. Was this really Kit? Was he being coerced or otherwise under duress?

Luce went back to fiddling with the controls, and scanning a scrolling screen that indicated—as I understood it—the danger spots. He made minor corrections to our course as we went. When he got closer, or at least, I assumed so, he started pressing the link button and saying "Come in, Slasher." It took me a moment to make sense of it, and realize it was Simon's old broomer nickname, *Gutslasher*. Frankly, I'd never seen Simon slash any guts, but he had taken a fancy to the name, and I think gave it to himself, which figured.

No one answered. At first I wondered if there was some answer in the screen Luce was staring at, but he kept pushing the button and repeating his call, and after a while I said, "No answer?"

He shook his head looking upset.

"*Kit?*" I called mentally, and got back a sense that he was nearby, but no answer. That had never happened. Unless, of course, he was unconscious. The idea made me want to punch something.

I unbuckled. Fuse and Eris were asleep. I came to stand behind Luce's chair, where I could look at the other . . . well, not screen. It was actually a hologram of the terrain behind us and a little to the front, materialized in a cube beneath the dash. The tech had still been too new when I'd left Earth two years ago and it was amazing to see it fully functioning in a normal flyer now.

The hologram itself showed nothing but water, except for a structure in the distance.

"The algae-processing platform?" I asked.

Lucius nodded.

It was becoming more clear by the minute, as we approached it. These platforms had been cutting-edge science a hundred years ago. Built more or less by the same process as the seacities, but more cheaply, they were assemblages of dimatough, ceramite and metal, often with terraces of dimatough underneath to create shallow seas where they didn't exist, and ideal conditions for the cultivation of food-purpose algae.

In their heyday they had housed thousands of people who worked, shift on and shift off, at turning the aquatic plants into semblances of other plants and animals, generally speaking more appetizing to humans. I'd had algae-steak once. For a steak, it had tasted an awful lot like a marine plant, and that was about the best I could say for it. However, at one time, after the "improvements" the Good Men had made to agriculture, which had rendered vast portions of the continents uninhabitable, algae had been the food of the world.

And they'd come almost exclusively from these platforms.

This one, as we neared, looked . . . almost mystical. Years ago, when Father had to make a visit near them, I'd seen the ruins of Petra. They're in the Middle Eastern protectorate, and they're these great big, reddish-stone buildings and cliffs, some of the cliffs carved into entrances to . . . I suppose cave dwellings, though that's not what they looked like.

Seen in pictures, they look like just red rocks and red buildings, but looking at them in person, one gets the feeling they're the forgotten remains of something greater than us.

Oddly, the abandoned station looked the same. It was reddish, possibly because it had been made with more metal than most, or maybe because someone had poured dimatough in an interesting color. Its molded forms rose and fell, like cliffs on an island, but all the surfaces looked rounded as if the wind and the sea had been working at it for millennia. And it was vast. I mean vast. Not as vast as a seacity, but I suspected that was because, like many other such installations, most of its space was underwater.

I looked at the buildings that must, at one time, have housed thousands of workers. We were now close enough to see seagulls fly around and to hear their calls.

"How are we going to find Kit or Julien in this?" I asked. I was making an effort. As hard as it was, I meant to remember to call my old friend by his new name. I suspected, among other things, that it was a matter of safety. His, surely, and possibly mine. It had been my experience, growing up as the daughter of a Good Man, perforce close to secrets of state, that letting others know what you knew was rarely safe.

Luce made a sound. It wasn't a word, or a sigh, but a sort of click of the tongue behind the teeth. It had a tone of annoyance as well as of worry. "They were supposed to answer," he said. "I've tried everything including Si—Julien's private com ring."

My gut tightened. "Uh," I said. "Is it possible—I mean, if Kit took a hostage, and someone had captured him before, is it possible that his captors followed him? I mean, is it?"

Lucius waved his hand. "That, or that someone else saw Julien leave and followed him, or ambushed him or otherwise captured him." He made the clicking sound again. "This is not a good place, or a good thing. Julien is too . . . He's always been too careless. And he has enemies. Some of them I even sympathize with."

"Yes," I said. "But his Machiavellic plans have a tendency to turn out all right," I said.

"Only if you assume that what they result in is what he wants. I mean, the man is so sharp he cuts himself, and he often doesn't know how his own plans are supposed to go."

I didn't say anything. It was often very hard to know what Simon had planned, and whether he'd just rolled with the punches and adapted and made the best of a bad thing. In a way he was rather like a cat, by which I don't mean the pilots from Eden, but the real cats from Earth. He could fall and roll and end up on his feet, appearing dignified and giving a good impression of "I meant to do that." Even when I knew things had gone completely out of control.

"The problem is," Lucius said. "I'm not sure what to do now. They arrived by submarine so I'm not sure that we can spot it from the air. And I really don't know where to look. If they're in trouble in there, it could take us days of searching before we find them and help them. It seems we ought to return to Olympus and resign ourselves to wait for a call, if they come out of this all right."

"No," I said. "The birds."

This piece of eloquence merited me a look from Lucius over his shoulder, a look that said as clearly as words, *What?* Only perhaps with more emphasis and implied swearing than any words he could use.

I shook my head and disciplined myself to explain. Sometimes when I have a flash of insight it is really difficult to moderate my impatience and take people through it word by word, till they get it. The fact that I could communicate with Kit with near-instantaneous thought-images that carried their own emotions had done nothing to make me better at explaining things in logical steps. "No. Is it possible to arrange this hologram thing so we see better, without needing to go nearer?"

"You mean for size?" he asked. "Sure." He did something on a touch screen and not only did the image size increase, but the tank they were in increased too, which was startling, as I'd been assuming it was some sort of glass. I had to get me one of these.

"How does this help?" Lucius asked. "I mean, we can overfly the island, but I don't think we can see them. Not if they're in one of the buildings. Or even in the part of the buildings that's underwater. We'd have to get very lucky."

"The seagulls," I said, and before he could turn around and look at me again as though I'd sprouted a second head, I said, "You see, there are a certain number of them in the air at any time, but you can see there are a lot of them also on the buildings, on land, everywhere on the station. My guess is that in the absence of visitors or inhabitants, they've colonized the entire station and are used to having it to themselves."

"Probably, but it's not like we can interrogate seagulls."

Is it my lack of ability at explaining, or are people, even smart people, unusually dull when I try to communicate my ideas? Or do they do it to upset me? So many suicidal people, so little time.

"No," I said, and only added *stupid* mentally. Mostly because I wasn't seventeen anymore. Also because though I don't think he would, the man could break me in two with one arm behind his back. "You know birds, right?" I remembered he was rumored to have spent fourteen years in solitary confinement and realized he might very well not know birds, so I hurried on, as fast as I could, before he could say anything, "You see, they startle easily. If they're used to the station without people and suddenly there are a bunch of men tromping around, possibly fighting, they're going to fly up, alarmed."

Lucius tilted his head sideways, looking at the tank and at the white and black dots of the seagulls on the screen, "I suppose—" he said.

He never told me what he supposed because at that moment, at about ten o'clock on the station's circular plant, a flock of seagulls flew up suddenly, in great numbers, screaming.

"As good as we're going to get," he said.

And I stumbled to my seat with some difficulty, almost falling to my knees, as he made the flyer dive down towards the spot from which the seagulls had flown up.

Come Out, Come Out

I JUST WANT TO SAY THAT I AND LUCIUS WERE BOTH CREATED by bioenhanced madmen. And at that moment, between my stomach plummeting somewhere below my feet and my hands clutching madly at the arms of the seat, I realized that I was very glad the madmen had been bioimproved and had designed bioimprovements into us at well.

Look, I'm married to a man who, besides being as I am, designed to be faster than normal humans, had further been enhanced via a virus introduced while he was gestated, to make him faster, more accurate, with better reflexes than normal humans. Which was all needed and important when flying amid the powertrees, with their dark trunks, their explosive pods. All well and good.

And all of us were faster than natural-born humans and had better hand and eye coordination. Which was also good. But dear sweet gods of the ancients, it was still scary to be in a flyer flown by someone of whose specific capacities I couldn't be sure and who was engaging in what would in other circumstances be suicidal maneuvers.

We flitted downwards, swaying within inches of a corroded reddish building, its windows like blank eyes. All the while, the seagulls disturbed by our passage raised a white and black cloud that obscured the potentially lethal obstacles around us. And all through it, Eris slept. Which meant my daughter had her father's sense of self-preservation.

We swayed the other way just before hitting, then went sideways, the flyer on end, and my inner ear screaming that we were falling. We rushed down a narrow street between buildings, straightened again, and plunged under an arching bridge, before coming to rest on what looked like a plaza. An ancient plaza, the surfaces of the surrounding buildings softened by time, so it looked like they were natural cliffs into which windows and doors had been cut. In the center of the plaza there was a sculpture of some sort, but it had been so corroded by the salt winds that I couldn't tell what it had once been: man, or dragon, dolphin or abstract. Just a jutting form, with what might be arms or perhaps flippers raised to the uncaring sky, trying to uplift people who'd forgotten it.

I felt both dizzy and queasy by the time we landed. Fuse woke up, stretched and said, "Are we there, then?"

I didn't answer mostly because I wasn't sure what the *there* was. I got up as soon as I realized we'd stopped moving, and checked Eris, then started strapping her to me. I felt a need to have her with me in this unknown place, facing who knew what dangers. I needed to feel she was protected.

Lucius got up and clicked his tongue again, this time with a tone of impatience, opened a compartment in the back of Eris's seat and threw something at me. I blinked, before I realized it was a real sling, of the sort one could carry an infant in, that would support her back and not let her slip. Luxury. I put it on and put Eris in it. She didn't wake, but made a sound like a creaky hinge. Then I headed for the door, looking in my pocket for a burner.

Lucius grabbed my arm, "Athena, are you sure you want to go out?"

"What? It's my husband out there. And Simon. We came here to find—"

"Yes, to be sure," he said. "But I don't mean that," he said. "I mean, do you want to take a baby into the middle of a potential firefight? And you can't leave her in here alone."

I most certainly couldn't leave her in there alone, and if he thought I was going to stay there alone, with her, he had another thing coming. I'd read altogether too much history of the wars of mankind to let the men go on and fight while I stayed behind, to be claimed as some sort of prize by the victors. But then I thought of something more immediate, "Firefight? Why—"

Lucius pointed. Now that we were on the ground, windows had opened some layer admitting images into the flyer, and I could look out. We'd parked in a plaza, and there, close enough to the shadow of one of the buildings that it wouldn't be visible from the air, I could see a small vehicle that looked like a miniature of the triangular ship.

I cursed mentally. This wasn't exactly unexpected, but it changed everything.

Okay, so we didn't know whoever had flown that had been armed. Or that they'd get into a firefight with Kit, necessarily. Except that we did, of course, know they had kidnapped my husband in space, and I couldn't imagine anyone kidnapping Kit without at least the threat of firepower. And I couldn't imagine them following Kit, knowing what he could do, without being armed. Because Kit was good enough in a fight to scare even me. In fact, I'd lost several fights to him, before we'd arrived at our present good understanding. So—

So I wanted to go out there and kick some righteous butt. Or more likely some unrighteous one. I had never been the kind who stays behind at home and prays for the fighters. For one, I wasn't a believing woman and wouldn't be sure, exactly, whom to pray to. For another, I had great faith in the power of my fighting, a faith reinforced through all the military schools, reform academies and mental hospitals Daddy Dearest had tried to confine me to in hope of taming me.

Whenever there was fighting to be done, I'd always been there in the thick of things, doing for myself what no one else could: fighting to keep me alive.

And I had vowed to fight to keep Kit and Eris alive too. Kit because he fought for me, and Eris because...because I was responsible for her existence.

And that, of course, was the problem. Before, when I'd leapt into battle with both feet, I had done so risking only my life, and often risking it in order to save it. But now I was responsible for Eris who, for the moment, was wholly dependent on me for food and care. Lucius was right that I couldn't leave her behind in the flyer. No matter how we locked that, someone could get in and hurt her or take her, and that was simply not acceptable. But going into a potential firefight with the men, taking her was also unacceptable. I'd worry about her getting hit as I'd worried in the fight in Circum. But more importantly, concern for her would slow me down and make us both vulnerable. It could lose the fight.

I said a very bad word, and Lucius's eyes widened as though he'd never heard it before. "Fine," I said. "I'll stay. But you shouldn't take Fuse," I said. "If whoever is after Julien is in league with the Good Men, Fuse could be in danger, since his father is looking for a whole-body donor."

But Fuse—I swear—patted me on the arm as he passed and said, "Don't worry. My father doesn't have triangular ships." And then he was out. Lucius hesitated long enough to give me one of his rings. As it landed on my palm, I saw it was a com ring. "I'll call you if we need help," he said. "And if you need to run away."

I thought both of those were fairly useless, since I suspected he'd rather be torn to pieces by wild seagulls than call on a woman with a baby for help, and that I'd rather be torn to pieces by wild seagulls than to run away just because I was told to. But I supposed we were both keeping up appearances. Or appeasing the back of the mind, which was much alarmed by separating before facing the, for lack of a better term, bad guys.

I watched them leave the flyer. I locked it. I felt possessed of a sense of unreality. This had never happened before. I'd never stayed and let anyone else go fight for me.

Kit? I called out in my mind. And I got back a sense of his presence, but no reply, again. So he was here, very near, he wasn't dead, but there was some reason he couldn't answer. The feelings that came with it were of being busy and also somewhat scared. And that was odd. Kit didn't scare easy.

There was also a feeling like he wished I'd hush. I'd never got such from him, except when he was in the middle of a difficult collection, so maybe that was it, maybe he was in the middle of something difficult and couldn't afford to have his concentration disrupted.

I was sorely tempted to call again, to make him say something that might give me a clue. I didn't. The worst part of being a grown-up and responsible is that you have to hold back on the things you really would like to do. Or even feel a need to do.

If Kit felt as though my calling to him would endanger him, I'd have to be very uncaring to actually call out to him again. I suspected that I was in fact very uncaring, but I'd learned to act like real humans. Kit was a real human and the last thing I wanted to do was disillusion him and destroy his love for me.

I watched as Fuse and Lucius—and was Lucius really handing Fuse a burner? Did he have any idea how far that man would go for a good explosion? And that Fuse, damaged and half healed, might not have a full sense of his own mortality let alone other people's?—cautiously approached a large, darkened doorway. They must have heard something coming from there, otherwise why fixate on that particular doorway? I realized since the flyer was landed and sealed, it was impervious to outside noise. It must be, since I couldn't hear the seagulls. But that was no good. I had to know what was happening out there. Even if there weren't a fight imminent, I hated not knowing what was going on. I hated being left behind, at any time, and not knowing what people I cared for were facing.

Now, with my safety and Eris's dependent on what happened out there, I had to know. I just had to. I jumped to the control panel and attempted to turn it on. The damn thing was keyed to a genlock on the dash, its membrane waiting, presumably for Lucius's genetics to turn on.

Normally my way to deal with genlocks was to burn them out. I considered them personally offensive, because they were just a stupid membrane with a circuit behind, and once you burned them you disabled the circuit and could then have your way with whatever mechanism it had protected.

It was offensively stupid to use them as locks because they were so easy to disable. I mean, I could see why people on the street thought they were a good idea, but even my own late, unlamented father had used them, and that was double stupid, as he should have guessed that my genetics were close enough to his in the key components to be able to open them. Of course, the penalties for burning the genlocks were terrible, but they'd never been a consideration for me. While Father was alive, and my status was as daughter of a Good Man, I'd been above the law. And now I was just outside the law, a stranger whose home was in another world altogether, and whose brief sojourns on Earth were as brief as possible.

But I still didn't think it was a good idea to burn out the lock on Lucius's flyer. I suspected he would get a little testy at that, and besides, my dim sense of honor, mostly learned from Kit, told me it was a bad thing to do, since he was helping me. I had to be an adult, yet again.

So, instead of burning out his lock, I opened the panel, and looked at the mechanism, till I figured out which circuit to detach, to do the equivalent of burning the genlock, but in such a way that it could be reconnected in seconds and that the big blond lunk wouldn't feel the need to kill me for it.

I found it and disconnected it, then the alarm that went with it, before it could do more than let out a brief, loud peep. I held my breath, in case that had wakened Eris, but she continued sleeping, and I took a deep breath, pulled up, turned the flyer on, in wait mode, and listened. Listened as hard as I could. Seriously, why would the man leave me with a baby in a dangerous situation without giving me the opportunity to fly his flyer or even to hear in case there was danger outside? And he was biodesigned to be smart. Imagine if he weren't.

I found the button that allowed sounds from outside to penetrate, and jumped. The sound of screaming seagulls was everywhere, as they lifted, again, from the building into which Lucius and Fuse had disappeared. Something must have startled them anew, but they were so loud I could hear nothing else, and now Eris started screaming. I bounced her gently, trying to get her attention, and it seemed to work for a moment.

Outside there were shapes, barely visible among the seagulls. Perhaps human shapes.

In that moment I heard young, strangely accented voices just outside the flyer, "—take their flyer and go."

"It would be stupid," another voice said. "They'll take ours."

"Ours is a damned lifeboat," said a third voice. "I wish them luck of it. You can't maneuver. With theirs, we can go anywhere on Earth. *Anywhere!*"

"That is a point, but where could we go? And what will Father say if we lose our boat?"

"I don't care. This is not working the way we expected. That idiot knew nothing. We must go somewhere where we can find the power brokers and deliver the message. And then we're free. Free, Laz, think about it."

These words were clear, but they must have done something, some movement, some gesture, that set off the seagulls again because all I could hear after that was a mumble, and a fizz and the screams of the disturbed birds.

A fizz. Like a burner. They were burning the genlock on the door.

Damn it! Lucius was going to be upset his flyer was vandalized, but it *wasn't* my fault. Worse, and double damn, these—boys?—were undoubtedly the crew of the triangular ship. And they were outside. And even though it had been said my husband had a hostage, this was clearly more than one person. And they were nobody's hostage.

Which meant that Lucius and Fuse were, what? Dead? Incapacitated? To say nothing of Kit and Simon? My throat closed at the thought of Kit or even Simon hurt in one of those buildings. Not that I wished ill on Lucius and Fuse, and frankly, by virtue of being with me, they were of mine and I'd defend them and avenge them if needed, but Kit and Simon made it personal. If one of them were bleeding to death in that warren of buildings, how would I get in and rescue him? How could I find him, if the coms didn't work? Because I had to find him or them and rescue them. I had to.

I calmed myself down with the reassurance that these people were afraid of being followed, which meant they couldn't have killed all the people on my side and against them. Possibly they hadn't killed anyone, just somehow managed to evade them and get out of the building.

Right. And these voices sounded young. Like really young. One of them still had a relatively high soprano and another's voice wavered between soprano and basso profundo, in the way boys' voices do between the ages of twelve and sixteen or so.

None of which made me feel better about the fact that they were going to be here in seconds.

I was armed. I'm always armed. I'd rather be naked than unarmed. But that wasn't the point. There were three of them. There was one of me. And I had to protect Eris.

Against normal people, this wouldn't be a problem. I was fast enough—a skill not developed, but acquired via genetic engineering, pre-birth—that I could and often did defeat more people than that.

However, here caution applied. I had no idea who these people were or where they came from. They shouldn't be enhanced, of course, but...For all I knew they were the spawn of tentacle monsters. What I did know is that they had been fast enough and strong enough to subdue and kidnap Kit who, on top of being created the way I was and having the same super-speed from his genetic legacy, had been changed by a bioengineered virus in utero, to maximize that speed. If they could capture Kit, no matter if they'd caught him at a disadvantage outside the ship, then they would be able to match my speed. So, a frontal confrontation was out of the question.

That was all right too. Okay, I'd never run up against people—other than other bioengineered clones of Good Men—who could match me for speed, but I'd run up against plenty of them whom I couldn't kill for one reason or another. In my misguided youth, I'd run up against a lot of people I couldn't even hurt without precipitating Daddy Dearest's fury and much worse punishment. So I'd learned psychological subterfuge, finagling, and deception. Which worked against everyone no matter what the level of speed or even intelligence. Most of the time. Practically.

I banished misgivings. Look, whomever my wiles hadn't worked against, they always worked against males. Mostly. Almost. Practically. They hadn't done me much good against Kit, but my darling was a jaded bastard. How many of them could there be in the universe? And could any of them sound as young as those people outside had?

Fast, I made sure of the hidden burners, one at my ankle, one under my hair, and one where it's really none of your business. No, not there. That would impair any fast movement.

Eris had fallen asleep. I engaged my fast speed, because I knew I had seconds only, to disengage the sling, grab her, and stow her in the back, where a net held back an assortment of toys and blankets and stuff that testified as eloquently as his words that Luce did indeed spend a lot of time babysitting young ones. I sort of rolled her in a blanket, so that it protected her from any sharp toy edges, but did not cover her face fully. I was hoping she would pass unnoticed in the middle of the mess, and no one would realize there was a baby back there. I was fully aware that if they grabbed my daughter they'd render me less effective. Not incapacitated, but less effective. Or more effective in a "kill them all" sort of way, but that, too, had its liabilities.

Bless the child, she did not wake up, though she did make a

little aggrieved sigh, which caused me to kiss her forehead, before I returned to the middle of the flyer, the open space between seats, where I did my best to appear surprised as the door burst open.

The surprised look was made much easier by what the intruders looked like.

They walked in, in a group, as though none of them trusted the other to go in first.

They were, as I'd expected, three boys and very young. They were dressed in what looked like those one-piece baby suits made adult size, only they had boots over their feet. This was strange enough, as was the fact that these one-piece suits had been embellished with patches, scribblings and bits of metal sewn on. It was fairly startling that the two who had cut off their sleeves had what appeared to be a welter of scars and blue ink all up their arms.

But none of this—none of it—compared to the strangeness from the neck up. First of all, they all looked startlingly familiar, but I had trouble identifying them, because...Because it looked like a piercing freak had gone insane in an electronic components store. The one in the center, who looked older than the others, had red hair, which he'd carefully shaved so it only grew on half his head. I'm assuming shaved. For all I knew he'd killed the follicles, of course. The half that remained glittered with metal, glass and who knew what the heck else, all of it looking like he'd salvaged it from a computer room. His eyebrows were pierced all along their length with more glittering components inserted. There was something orange and green and metal through his left nostril. There was a blue indecipherable symbol on his forehead. He looked indefinably familiar, but it was hard to focus through all the facial piercings and tattoos.

The one on the left looked really familiar; must be all of twelve and was prettyish in the way boys sometimes are just before or at puberty. What remained of his hair—he seemed to have eliminated random patches of it—was inexpertly dyed blue and straightened, so you could see that his hair was both curly and black. All down one side of his still-babyish face, he had scribblings in blue ink, that disappeared into his collar. His eyes were blue and feral.

The one on the right also looked familiar, but not as much, was maybe fourteen, had a still-round face that would probably turn sharper with age. He had fewer of the blue markings, but his ears were stretched with what appeared to be spools of some sort, his scalp was completely bald and seemed to have electronic components actually growing on it. He had cut off his right sleeve to display a welter of blue ink in designs that included a dragon and made me wonder if these were in fact the sort of primitive tattoos no one used in the twenty-fifth century.

In the middle of the designs was a single word: *Danegerous.* Yes, it was misspelled.

I'm not a prude or an innocent, and there were very few things that people could do with their bodies that shocked me. I grew up between the high class of Earth, the bioengineered Good Men, who treated normal populations as disposable sludge, and in broomer lairs, where frankly most of the population treated themselves as disposable sludge.

But there was something to the way these boys were body-modified that put a chill up my spine and made me realize I was dealing with something completely different.

Throughout the ages, humans had dressed and adorned themselves to look different or to signify membership in some group or family. I was going to assume these boys were adorned according to some tribe or affiliation. I was hoping the tribe was "The Insane Neurotics," because that was how they looked.

Before I could make sure that my air of surprise was just perfect, they'd replied with their own air of surprise. Nose-pierced redhead jumped back. I mind-heard him say *Whoa!*

Danegerous stood rooted to the spot and I heard him mind-proclaim to the world at large *It's a woman.*

And the baby, the little twelve-year-old, was holding two burners out and pointed at me.

The shock that I could hear them mind-talk hit me at the same time that I recognized the youngest one. I recognized his movements, the crazed look in his eyes, I recognized the sort of mind that always, always, reaches for a weapon first; the type of temperament that views anything strange and fascinating as something that should be shot first, so it could be dissected later at leisure.

Staring at me, those baby blue eyes in the tattooed face were my Daddy Dearest's eyes and my eyes too. I didn't know how this was possible, and I was not even going to make any guesses. Just as I wasn't going to make any guesses about their mind-talk. We'd heard that the telepathy bioed into the Mules was limited and bonded. That is, it had to be a bonded pair to allow it to flow. Though really, Kit and I hadn't been when we'd first talked, but an exception doesn't negate the rule.

Unless these three were bonded, of course, which was possible, as there are many kinds of bond. But I didn't want to know why I could hear them, anyway, nor why or how this kid was . . . for lack of a better term, my baby brother. I just knew he was. He'd been made from the same genes that had gone into making me and my late father, Alexander Milton Sinistra. The feral blue eyes were the same that had stared out of the mirror at me for most of my growing-up years. I hadn't even realized they had changed until now.

A cold shot of fear went up my spine, because let's face it, I knew myself, and I'd known Daddy. No one with those genes could be trusted, not even for the simple things that untrustworthy people could be trusted with, like, you know, not doing things that will get them killed.

My face must have turned to stone. He hadn't recognized me, or the relationship between us. Which was good, I supposed. I was measuring the space between us and figuring out how to disarm him. I wondered if the other two were armed too. So far they were not making any effort to reach for guns.

"How do you know he's a woman?" Baby Brother asked, in voice, glaring over his shoulder at the other two while keeping his weapons trained on me.

With anyone else, I'd have risked a lunge at him. I would. But with him, which is to say with myself, it was too risky. It might push him past slightly annoyed into homicidal maniac. I felt a trickle of cold sweat run down my back. From the pile of toys I heard the snuffle, snuffle, snuffle that was often the precursor to a really good Eris cry. Surely not. Surely she wasn't going to start . . . Please, don't start. I didn't want to see what these feral children could do to a baby. I was going to guess they had no protective instincts of any sort.

I took slow, controlled breaths.

The redhead, who was clearly the oldest one, blushed. It was kind of weird to see someone that pierced and tattooed blush, but blush he did. His voice was gruff and low as he said, "Look at her. She—" He made gestures in the front of his chest, even though Baby Brother had gone back to staring at me and wouldn't see him. "She looks like a woman."

"Maybe he's just malformed. How would you know?" Baby Brother was defiant and sneering. "What would you know what a woman looks like, anyway? And how many women can there be? On Earth?"

"Uh," Danegerous said. "Uh. Many. The holos," he said. "From Earth."

"Bah," Baby Brother said. "They could just be differently dressed men. How would you know what they look like naked? That's the only way to tell if there are real differences."

I saw the two older ones trade a look and thought there must be holos that Baby Brother wasn't privy to. But why hadn't they seen women? And why did they seem to think women were rare? Had they been raised in some home for the seriously mentally unstable, kept locked away from all of humanity? Now I thought about it, it made perfect sense, actually.

"Come on," the tallest and oldest one, the redhead, said. "You don't have to see what they look like naked to see they're different. In olden times, they were the people who gave birth. Their whole body is designed for it."

Baby Brother's eyebrows went up. He looked deeply thoughtful, in that way that my soi-disant father had looked before he had someone arrested. He turned to me. "Strip. We'll see if it's true."

Right. And I'd see him in hell.

But I couldn't say that, and I couldn't mouth off. There was that snuffle, snuffle from the toy storage at the back. I had to control my expression. I had to find a way out of this.

I couldn't run at him and pound him into dirt, because the other two might object, and if Baby Brother had the enhanced speed as I did, so might the other two.

And I couldn't intimidate him with words, because I didn't know where he'd come from or what he'd been through. As I said, an asylum wasn't out of the question. Perhaps Father had made him as a back-up body donor. The thing was I didn't know what to hold over him. If someone has already been raised in hell, threatening him with flames is beside the point. Which I'd proven over and over again when well-meaning ladies had threatened me with expulsion from schools where Daddy Dearest had enrolled me.

When sane routes out of trouble are impassible, as my broomer friends had taught me, you take the crazy one.

I let my knees hit the floor, raised both my hands to my head, and bawled in the most sincere way I could manage, "Oh, please, don't hurt me." My noise had the effect of covering any noise Eris might make.

By the corner of my eye, while crying, and cringing, I noted that Redhead and Danegerous had jumped back. Apparently my performance was terrifying.

But Baby Brother also resembled me in not scaring. Or perhaps in scaring angry.

His lip curled up. "He's a coward," he said, and stepped forward, raising his foot. I had to struggle not to smile. The more psychotic they are, the easier they fall. And by genetics alone, poor Baby Brother was laboring under more issues than some long-running journals.

As he raised his foot to kick me, I bent forward, as though to grovel, and said, "Oh, please, I'm just a poor woman." I noted that both Redhead and Danegerous did a little mental shout of *Told you so.* Which was good because it took them off guard too.

I grabbed Baby Brother's foot before his kick landed, and pulled. Up. Hard. With Super Speed.

Look, just because they could move very fast, didn't mean they thought other people could, too. Or perhaps they didn't think women could. Or perhaps they just couldn't think.

As Baby Brother hit the ground with a resounding jar, and before he could roll over and shoot me, which he would have, given half a chance, I had removed his burners. I slipped one into my pocket. Then I lifted the insufferable brat by the tuft of ill-dyed hair, and pointed my burner at his head. My idea was to use him a shield and threaten to shoot him.

But of course, nothing is ever easy or simple. The horrible brat spun around, somehow, ignoring pain. His hair tore at the roots. Leaving me holding a hank of improbably colored hair, he got free. I realized why he was missing tufts of hair. Apparently fighting recklessly was one of his amusements.

He aimed for my crotch with a well-applied kick, and while it still hurt, it didn't hurt me like he expected—I guess he really didn't know any women—which allowed me to bring the burner butt neatly into the side of his head, rendering him unconscious, just as Redhead dove at me.

I shoved Baby Brother out of the way and kicked Redhead

in the crotch just before he hit me. Of all the fighting I learned, both formal and street, for my money, the best training I ever got for combat was the ballet camp I once attended. It allows such precision in high kicks. I jumped out of the way as he rolled on the floor clutching his family jewels. Since I didn't know his resiliency level, I pulled the burner from my hair—look, I didn't know Baby Brother's standards in weapon maintenance. The one I'd taken from him might or might not work—and pointed a burner at him and one at Danegerous, who was backing up, both hands in full sight, his mouth working.

Weirdly, the redhead, on the floor, didn't even look at me. He howled, both mind and voice, staring at his companion, "Thor, don't."

Danegerous gave a little start, and looked mulish, while shaking his head. "If we're going to fail . . . If we fail . . . You know what Father—"

"Fuck Father," the redhead yelled. I felt wordless shock from the other two. "This doesn't mean we'll fail. Just because the guy didn't know anything about Earth, and we let Morgan try his way at making friends and influencing people, it doesn't mean we failed at the mission." He looked at me. "Look, ma'am, I know we started badly, but if you give us a chance, we want nothing nefarious. We're emissaries on a peace mission."

"And I'm Winnie the Pooh," I said.

"No, you're not," Danegerous said with an edge of hysteria to his voice, his hand reaching into his pocket. "We know him. He's much younger than you."

At the same time I yelled, "Freeze."

He didn't, so I leapt across the room, grabbed his hand in mine and pointed the weapon at his head. Only to point it at the redhead who made a jump at us. Finding the burner pointed at his head, he lifted both hands. "Ma'am," he said, the soul of politeness, "you must let me get the stuff from Thor's pockets. He's an explosives fanatic, and he's trying to blow us all up."

"I have to," the so-called Thor yelled. "You know what Father will do to us if we come back defeated."

Which is when his voice, wavering and adolescent though it was, found a place in my head. "Thor . . . Mason?" I asked.

He froze. "Wah?"

"From the genetic line of Ajith Mason?" I asked.

The redhead, who'd been inching closer with all the stealth of a cat, stopped and froze too. He stared at me. And I caught a flash in the eyes that made his features click into place. "And you," I pointed the burner at him, and waved with it. "You're Jarl Ingemar's clone."

I should have known better. Look, perhaps it's genetic. Like Little Brother, I apparently had a way to make friends and influence people.

I'm not going to give you a blow-by-blow account. I don't remember it. I remember Thor Mason squirming, trying to go for his stored bombs, presumably. I mean, what would you expect from Fuse's little brother?

I hit him hard, on the head, and eased him down quickly, just in time to deal with Jarl's—and therefore my husband's—clone who seemed unsure of whether to attack or not and therefore was at a disadvantage when I hit him hard.

I was in the process of tying all of them, individually and securely, when Eris started screaming blue murder, and Kit yelled in my head, *Athena, Athena, answer me.*

We Come in Peace

I TURNED. KIT CAME RUNNING INTO THE DOOR OF THE FLYER. I realized what I had heard was his involuntary reaction to finding the door forced, when I heard running steps behind him, and then Fuse saying, "I told you she'd be all right. She's Athena." I wasn't sure whether to be grateful or scared by such confidence.

My husband's eyes look like cat eyes. It's a side effect of their being bioengineered to pilot the darkships without auxiliary lights, to diminish the chances of being caught in the powertree ring. At first I'd found his expressions unreadable. Utterly opaque and alien. But now I could read them fairly well. It didn't hurt that there was a mind-link, which transmitted in succession worry, confusion, relief, and finally amusement.

It was his cat eyes and his calico hair that had made it hard to identify the redhead as a clone of the same man, but now it was obvious. He looked like a younger, not bioengineered in appearance Kit.

Kit stepped up to where I was tying his clone's hands. I was using for the purpose a pink and purple band with cheerful clown faces that I suspected Luce used to attach a pacifier to a child. It was sturdy, though, and pliable enough. He examined my handiwork when I was done. Then he stepped over to Baby Brother, whom I had bound hand and foot—because I knew

103

where he came from—and then over to Thor, whose pockets Kit started going through methodically.

Fuse looked intently at Thor, in silence, as though trying to evaluate something. I assumed he'd recognized his own clone, but I wasn't going to ask. The new Fuse was disturbing and unpredictable, both in his level of maturity and in his reactions.

Eris continued crying, and I went over to the net, got her, put her in the sling attached to me. Simon and Luce came in.

Well, I surmised the fourth man was Simon. I had reason for it, since he moved like Simon, he was Simon's height, and also, when he looked at me, his features split in an unholy grin that I knew all too well. But he didn't look like Simon. Someone had darkened his skin two shades, his hair had loose curls, much like mine, and his eyes were now a deep, dark green. It was the expression in them that was still Simon's.

There was something challenging in it, at the bottom of it, as though he were daring me to call him by his old name. I pretended great absorption in Eris, as I checked her diaper, which was dry, then said, in an offhand tone, "Emperor Julien Beaulieu, I presume?"

He cackled. Lucius rolled his eyes and stepped towards the control panel. "I disabled the genlock," I told Lucius, virtuously. "I didn't burn it."

"Thank you. I realized my stupidity immediately after leaving," he said, as he pulled the panel and—presumably—set about reconnecting it. "I fully expected you to have burned it in order to hear what was going on outside." He gave a quick smile, as though mocking himself. "And I'd have deserved it."

Fuse was talking to Kit over the contents of Thor's pockets, a series of spheres, weirdly shaped packages, and vials. At one point, Kit turned pale, reached very carefully for a cylindrical object and walked away with it, outside the flyer.

Eris having decided she wanted to nurse, I sat down on a chair and took care of that while Simon, Luce, and Fuse took each of the boys and strapped them into auxiliary seats, which pulled down from the ceiling near the wall. Then they tied them *to* the seats. Halfway through it, the oldest one, Kit's and Jarl's clone, woke. I felt his gaze on me and realized he was frowning intently. I checked there was nothing showing from the nursing that could give him a shock, but there was nothing, except Eris's head disappearing into my suit.

As I looked, his lips moved, at first soundlessly and then, "Who are you? What are you? You look like...Sinistra? Like Morgan. Like you're made from the same genes."

"Athena Hera Sinistra," I said. "Legal daughter of the Good Man Alexander Milton Sinistra. And you?"

He shifted uncomfortably. The rope going up from his ankles to his hands was probably too tight, but having been tied down with too much leeway, myself, and having managed to escape, I was not about to make that mistake. Not with these kids. I had a feeling they'd learned to fight before they learned to walk.

"I'm Laz," he said. Then blushing a little. "At least that's my...my call name. I'm Lazarus Long from Ingemar made from Jarl Ingemar's genes." He turned a wandering look towards Kit. "I think he is too, but...changed. We didn't realize the resemblance when we...when we captured him, because he was suited and...modified."

The name he used tickled something in my deep memory. Something about a series of books I read long ago, in my father's library, now probably reduced to ashes, but for a long time the place where I hid from everyone else in the household. "Lazarus—from a book?"

He smiled, as though surprised. "Yes. From some books by an ancient author. We—None of us had names, just the names of the people we were made from, but that was not us, so we took the names of story heroes."

I remembered the character that name attached to, and I decided that this one bore watching very closely indeed. I could sort of see how a redheaded child with no name could be attracted to the moniker, but I wondered how much he'd modeled himself on his namesake.

"He's Thor?" I said, pointing at Fuse's clone, who had come awake and was staring at Fuse and being stared at in turn.

"Yes. From the god of lightnings," he said, with a small smile, as though realizing the funny idea of an explosives bug naming himself after Thor. Then, with a movement of the head, "And he's Captain Morgan. Of the...Sinistra."

"Yeah. For lack of a better term, my little brother."

Laz nodded. "But you're a woman. How can you be a woman? When Father made us—" He stopped. "I mean, they tried to make women, but they all died or were sterile. So. That leaves us."

I wondered who "Father" was. Some rogue doctor in an unused portion of Circum? It was possible. Only at that moment, Kit came back in. When Fuse turned to look at him, he said, "I threw it away. Far into the sea."

Fuse nodded. "Quite right." Then he turned to Danegerous, aka Thor. "You shouldn't have that in your pocket, kid. It's not stable enough. You were seconds from blowing yourself up. I can't believe you didn't."

Thor looked sullenly at him, and pushed his lower lip out. "I've done it hundreds of times. It's a very effective explosive."

"Well, stop doing it." Fuse sounded like the patient adult. Hair, scars and all, he looked suddenly concerned and... paternal and also very grown up? It was an expression I'd never expected to see on that face. "You could have got killed. And your friends with you."

"It doesn't matter," Thor said. And burst into tears. He bawled with the abandon of a very young child, tears and snot running freely. Between sobs, he got out, "Father is going to kill us all, anyway."

"Hush now," Laz said. He sounded older than his years and very caring. I caught a resemblance to the tones Fuse used, and wondered what role he'd played in the younger boys' lives. Was he the oldest? How many of them were there? And where had they grown up? "No reason to assume that. We can still find... movers and shakers and present the petition."

"What petition?" I said.

Kit made a sound. I can't describe the sound, it being part sigh and part huff, as though he were both grieved at the situation and upset at having to explain.

As I looked at him, he smiled, tight-lipped. "I don't even know how to explain," he said. "Except that I think I can explain better than they do. The proposition itself is a simple one, but I sense undercurrents, and I have questions both about the whole setup of this situation, and the nature of the people who sent them to Earth with this mission."

He frowned, wrinkles forming on his forehead, the sort of worried wrinkles I sometimes evoked, not just because he thought whatever I was doing was wrongheaded, but because he couldn't understand my motivations. When he spoke, he did it slowly, as though he were trying to think through something. "You see,

I heard them talk, and more importantly, I heard them think enough that I can fill you in some, and Laz can probably fill in what I don't know."

"You can hear us think?" That was Laz, his eyes wide.

Kit shrugged and managed an almost-smirk. He turned to me, as he continued, "I wasn't sure they couldn't hear me, either, Athena. That's why I didn't answer you. They ambushed me while I was outside the ship, trying to fix the circuits. I couldn't fight them off without risking drifting off to space. And I didn't want them to find you and the baby, not in the state you were in, tired and defenseless. You wouldn't have been able to fight at all, and I'd have been impaired, defending you because if they captured you, it would all be over. We'd be done. I couldn't risk you, no matter how much I wanted to fight them off. So I went with them quietly, and just hoped you would find my note and come after me."

"I did. That's why I came to Earth, and if you think it was easy toting Eris—"

His eyes widened. "You named her Eris?"

I felt my face get hot. "Well, she was born during a battle. I thought it was appropriate."

"And serve notice to any future young men," Simon said, in that under-voice tone that was supposed to be heard while pretending it didn't want to be heard.

"And we hadn't picked a name," I said. "And Eris is a pretty name."

"I thought we'd agreed on Jane," Kit said.

I didn't dignify that with an answer. Ninety percent of married life is pretending not to hear the remarks to which the only possible response is an almighty argument. Instead, I smiled at him and took a deep breath. "It's good to have you back. And you need a fresher."

"Something awful," he agreed. "I didn't get a chance to bathe in their ship, and then when I took a lifeboat and Danegerou— I mean Thor, over there, there wasn't a fresher."

"So, they took you hostage, and you escaped and took one of them hostage," I said, filling in the blanks. "And you came to Earth." I smirked inwardly that he also called Fuse's clone *Danegerous*. "But who are they? Besides the clones of men three of us were cloned from?"

"Yeah," he said. "Hell of a coincidence that, but perhaps not—" He shrugged. "I gather sooner or later—Look, this is why I chose to come to Earth even after I took Thor hostage, instead of trying to find you in Circum and going back to Eden. First, I was almost sure Eden wouldn't take well to Thor. And second, I thought Earth needed some warning."

"Warning?" I said. Granted, on body decoration alone, this lot looked like slightly more savage Vikings, but I was fairly sure they were just spectacularly feral children. Look, Mules never got prizes for being well adjusted, okay? And whoever had made these kids wasn't even a genetic relation, on account of the fact that the closest genetic relations the boys had were Kit, myself, and Fuse. Nor would he or she have any reason to care for these children. And obviously they hadn't. But feral also meant a lack of discipline. I couldn't understand how these three striplings, aggressive, sure, but not really capable of much complex strategy, could threaten all of Earth—hell, they couldn't even threaten all of Eden—even if my husband weren't able to fully conceptualize a planet the size of Earth and kept thinking of it in terms of his native colony, in a hollowed asteroid.

Kit stared at the boys, then looked at me. "They didn't tell me this, you understand, I just surmised it from hearing their thoughts cross-chatter, that they are sent to Earth with a mission, to find a safe place for..." He paused and took a long breath. "You remember what *Je Reviens* means in Ancient French, right?"

"I'll return?" I said.

"It did."

"What?"

"The *Je Reviens* did return. As far as I can figure out, they are orbiting Earth, somewhere, and they sent down these most unlikely emissaries."

It took me a while to process this. The *Je Reviens* was a—no, *the* only—interstellar ship ever built by inhabitants of Earth. It had been built by the Mules, back when they called themselves the biolords, and when they had more or less reigned over the Earth like absolute despots in a way even the Good Men hadn't managed. They had used it to escape the riots that put an end to their rule.

Correction, that is what I'd learned in my educational programs, but it wasn't... strictly true. I'd found it wasn't strictly true when I'd become a refugee in Kit's native colony and learned their half of the story. Only about half the Mules had left on the *Je Reviens*. It had been intended for all of them, and also for the people I'd learned in my early schooling to call "the servants of the Mules."

This too was a misnomer. Oh, sure some of the people who had been meant to flee with them had been literally the servants of the Mules—or biolords, as they preferred to call themselves— as each one of the hundred and fifty or so of those who'd been improved to be almost a different breed of human, had controlled a vast territory that usually comprised two or three of the old-style land nations as well as some seacities. Government like that, particularly as an oligarchy, needed a vast bureaucracy and, more importantly, a trustworthy bureaucracy.

The biolords employed the best of whatever they required, be it assassins or paper-pushers, and the best, by the late twenty-first century, were always bioimproved before birth, by ambitious or prudent parents. Enhanced for speed or intelligence, for beauty or acting ability or a thousand other characteristics. Or most of them, for those born to ambitious, prudent, and rich parents.

However, when—as I understood it—the Mules had taken panic and decided they were about to be routed, and therefore started building the *Je Reviens*, the primary plan had been to take not only the Mules and their servants, but every conspicuously bio-improved person, away from the revenge, wrath, and destruction that had been labeled "the Turmoils" in my history holograms.

I still didn't know what had caused them to leave in a panic, too, in the barely built *Je Reviens*. I knew some of the people they'd left behind, they'd left behind on purpose: people like my so-called father. Daddy Dearest couldn't be trusted with a ship full of people not as improved as himself and vulnerable to the idea of superiorly bioengineered Mules any more than a wolf could be trusted penned in with a cargo of sheep.

I'd never fully understood if Father's particular kink was sexual—though it was that too—or if his homicidal sadism was a response to deep psychological wounds of another kind. The only thing I was almost sure of was that it was not genetic, since I'd never felt any need to torture or kill my sexual partners.

But I did understand the decision to leave him behind. Others, it wasn't as clear why they'd been abandoned. As I understood,

Jarl had made the decision, and that decision must rest on his knowledge of his own kind, growing up. I had to be satisfied that he hadn't thought them suitable. I suspected some of his decisions might have been rooted quite simply in his likes and dislikes, such as an obvious, deep-seated hatred of the original from which Simon had been made.

The rest of the people, the vast numbers of "servants of the Mules" left behind seemed to have been left through the hurry in which the *Je Reviens* had departed, rather than due to any moral or practical judgment. In other words, there were only so many people they could collect and give warning to, and only so many who'd made it to the *Je Reviens* in Earth orbit, before it left.

And while vast numbers of those left behind had died—burned, beaten, crucified, killed by mobs insane for vengeance and vindication—a number had survived, and reproduced, and many had attained power in the households of the Mules, who'd risen again to power under the guise of Good Men. My friend Nat Remy, and in fact all of my friends who weren't the clones of Good Men, were descended from those highly bioimproved people.

The ones who'd left with the Mules—mostly close retainers and functionaries—had been offloaded in Eden, an asteroid hollowed and made suitable for human habitation for their convenience.

Only fifty or so Mules had left in the *Je Reviens*, and no mere "improved humans." The justification given in Eden was that only the Mules had left because they were the only ones who had a chance of attaining the distant star to which the *Je Reviens* was aimed. And Jarl Ingemar, and Bartolomeu Dias, Mules, both, had stayed behind in Eden to "guide the development of a free society."

I'd never bought either of those, any more than I bought the stories Earth told its schoolchildren. It seems like hiding and whitewashing the past is one of the great vices of mankind, to be undertaken whenever someone feels he can get away with it. Sometimes it's not even for any particular reason, but to make things somehow *tidy*.

But now I looked at these...children. The Mules, by the time they cast away from Eden, had been alone in the *Je Reviens*. No one aboard the interstellar ship had been able to have children: not naturally.

When the Mules were created, back in the twenty-first century, they'd been—as the most extremely bioengineered of all people—all sterile and all male, the last a failsafe for the first. They were so modified, even though most looked perfectly normal, that their creators didn't want them in the human reproduction stream. Originally they had had stops on cloning, too, though that had not managed to survive a hundred years.

And it wasn't out of the question that even creatures who could live hundreds of years—even if the political necessities of Earth had required that they change bodies more often than that—might want progeny. But I had trouble believing that, and besides these three... These three were clones of Mules who had stayed behind on Earth. Why on Earth?

"I don't understand," I said, turning to look at my husband, then back at Morgan, Laz, and Thor. "These aren't clones of the Mules who went. They are—"

"Clones of those left behind, yes," Kit said. "I don't know why. I know how. I'd be surprised if the *Je Reviens* hadn't contained genetic samples of *all* the biolords, as a way to treat them and to grow... spare parts for them, should it become necessary.

"I don't know, though, why the Mules who left chose to clone these people. I understand from the boys' thought-chatter, and some verbal ones, that the ones on board were cloned too, but those... those clones of the people who went are raised more like children, even if in a spectacularly dysfunctional family." He caught my gaze and smiled a little bit, but it was a smile with no joy at all. "Yes," he said. "I do understand that in any circumstances it would be dysfunctional, since the original Mules were raised in crèches, with virtually no real human contact and no understanding of real human family. But that's how these boys were raised. The children whose originals weren't aboard were raised in crèches, mostly by AIs, though I understand sometimes the living Mules intervened, dispensing justice—or sometimes injustice—from above with no warning and no compunction."

"But why?" I said. "And how?"

It was Laz who spoke, eyebrows wrinkled above eyes that were as green as my husband's but not cat-shaped. "They said they had sample genetics of everyone supposed to be on the ship, for medical reasons, and they made us from that because they thought they'd need help... if... if they arrived at a world they could colonize."

I raised my eyebrows. "And they didn't arrive at a habitable world?" The story made no sense. It smelled. It smelled mightily. After all, their intention might have been to go to Alpha Centauri or another such world, but if they'd got there, why were they back here? If it had proven uninhabitable, why not go further?

And if they'd intended to create these children to help with the taming of a wild world, why had they only created them in the last twenty years or so? Laz was maybe all of seventeen; the others were younger. If they'd made clones of all the others left behind, were they of an age? I was willing to bet just from these three's wild adorning that none of them were over forty, certainly none were three hundred years old, because that would be a different dynamic. Then why?

Laz shrugged. "There was . . . Father took control, and he says that there might be some virtue in colonizing a wild planet not fit for humankind, but it is not for them. That they longed for Earth and the beauty of Earth, which gave them birth. That they're as entitled to live here as the rest of humanity is. And so, they sent us, to ask—" He stopped, and said, "Perhaps you're not the right people to ask, but—"

"But I already know it," Kit said. "Yes, and while we might or might not be the right people to ask, at least two of this group have power on Earth, and there are others." He nodded at Simon and Lucius, but he spoke to me, "They were sent to ask for a place on Earth. Any place they can colonize and make their own, create their own independent city-state or kingdom. One of their own, with entry barred to anyone else. They promise to be harmless, if others will not harm them."

"But—" I said, and saw Lucius frown. It made no sense for them to ask for such a thing. After all, who had the right to grant them a place on Earth? On the other hand, in their time, there had been a linked, oligarchic government. Worldwide. Hell, that had been in place until recently. Now with the Earth riven by revolutions . . . well—

"I'd say any place they can take and hold would be their own," Lucius said drily. "Why ask us? And more importantly, why send children to ask us?"

"And why *these* children?" I asked. "Children made from the genes of the people they left behind?"

Simon cackled.

Even if I hadn't known it was him, in the changed appearance of Julien Beaulieu, I'd have known him by that. "Ah, *mes petits*. As usual, you are all too refreshingly innocent." Simon was using heavily French-accented Glaish. It was something he put on when he was acting particularly outrageous. I swear I could hear my husband and Lucius rolling their eyes in unison. "It is obvious they think there is still an oligarchy holding Earth. Likely they approached twenty years ago and scouted Earth, and realized there was one and who was in charge. Then they withdrew and made these children, because what better way to appeal to the Good Men than with their own young clones? Granted that doesn't explain Jarl, but they probably thought he was still revered on Earth."

I snorted. "Which means they had no idea that the Good Men had not only destroyed their own reputations in retrospect, but also in a way cannibalized their own young clones to continue existing undetected."

"Precisely, *ma cheri*. And that's not *in a way*. It is literally what they did, consuming the future to continue the present, to appear to be mortal men, amid mortal men. That's what makes it so funny. That they thought to use immature clones to appeal to men who'd happily kill their own immature clones, so they could have their brains transplanted into the clones' bodies and legally inherit from themselves. It is to laugh. If you have a particularly black sense of humor."

"Enough," Kit said. "That leaves us with the question of what to do with these innocents. Do we let them return with a message that there is no one who can grant them such a thing, and that if they can take and hold any portion of the Earth it is theirs?"

"Father won't believe that!" Laz said. Little Brother was now awake and struggling with his bonds. I kept a sharp eye on him, but all he did was wail, "He'll have us killed, or worse."

I didn't ask what was worse. I'm sure there were many, many worse things that could occur to minds marinated in malice for centuries. Hell, my late unlamented father himself could easily come up with worse.

"He said," Laz said, with an effort at coherency and clarity of speech, "that we were to ask the Good Men, and to have the council of Good Men grant us license to land. They said anyone at all in an official position, even harvesters in Circum would be able to get us in touch with the Good Men, and that once the Good Men knew we existed they would not resist seeing us.

But they said the permission must be official. We can't be led into a trap."

So, paranoia, added to everything else, which also tracked with the Mules I'd known. It was enough to make you wonder if Jarl had been right and if the ones who'd left in the *Je Reviens* were the better half of the Mules. If the better half was this paranoid...

Simon cackled, "I tell you. They scouted! Before they made these children."

Seemed likely, since they knew about the Good Men, and who they were. I didn't bother arguing, but said instead, "Well, if we can't give them assurances ourselves, should we speed them to the Good Men side?"

Two people answered simultaneously. One of them was Fuse, who yelled, "We can't let my father know that Thor exists!" and Lucius, who said, in a tired, tight voice, "I don't need any more blood on my hands, thank you so much."

"But they'll try to get there, since we can't help them," I said. "And I know my own little brother, as I knew the old bastard, and as I know myself. He'll try to escape, and he's quite likely to manage it, if he wants it badly enough."

Lucius frowned. There was a look to his face that resembled nothing so much as the sky before thunder. "You're not the only delegation they sent," he said, rounding on the boys. "Are you? Were you hand-picked?"

There a shake of the head from Lars, a shrug from Morgan. Thor's eyes were fixed on Fuse, as though trying to puzzle something out.

"Who else is—who else did they send?" Lucius said. "Who else did they make? Who are all of you? Is there one of every Good Man who ruled on Earth twenty years ago?" He sounded as if he was in the grip of some great emotion, but I couldn't tell what it was.

"Five other delegations," Laz answered. He was puzzled, probably by this big man being so urgent in that question. "If they all failed, then they'd send others."

"Is there one of you who—who looks like me?" Lucius asked. And suddenly I understood. For reasons hard to explain, Lucius had once had a "little brother." Not really, of course, just a younger clone, but given out as a brother, and raised as such, in his "father's" dysfunctional family. Max had died when his father had needed a new body for his brain. Max had been my friend. I hadn't known Lucius, who was in prison when I had come of age. But I understood from people who'd known them both that Lucius really considered Max his little brother, and had loved him as a sibling. Now here was someone like Max, who might have been sent elsewhere in the world, possibly into a trap, possibly to be killed without Lucius being able to do anything to save him.

Laz frowned at him, but it was Little Brother who spoke. "You're . . . Keeva?" And to Lucius's nod, "It's John," he said. And looking slightly at Laz, "Can't you see it? It's John Carter."

A light, visibly, went on behind Laz's eyes and he said. "Oh. Yes. He was also sent with . . . with Tom. Tom Sawyer and Christopher Robin."

Lucius was all urgency now, "How old are they? Where were they sent?"

"John is my age," Morgan said. "Twelve. Tom Sawyer, fifteen. Christopher Robin is Laz's age or a little older. I don't know where they went. They didn't know where they were going. We were told to just find Good Men."

Lucius said a word he really shouldn't say in front of children, even if the children were feral. He looked like he'd suddenly developed a hell of a headache. He'd pulled his com from his pocket and started pushing buttons before he looked around wildly and said, "Excuse me a moment."

Brands and Fire

HE CAME BACK, LATER, HIS FACE STERN. HE CLOSED THE DOOR, and he started the flyer.

Look, I was never Miss Cautious. I'm not Mrs. Cautious either. Once, when I was twelve, I flew a broom into the façade of a skyscraper to avoid being taken back to a reform school where Father had confined me for—

Never mind. But Lucius Keeva took off from the island too fast, too shallow, almost grazing the tall spires of the former algae-processing station.

I thought something had disturbed him, or that he was so wholly absorbed in some thought that he paid no attention to anything else.

Kit and I barely had time to drop into seats and strap in when it became obvious that he was taking off. Eris set up a low complaining cry since I had no time to put her in the crib, not that I was sure I wanted to put her in it, and away from me, when the boys could conceivably get loose and get hold of her, so she was squished against my chest by the strap.

Simon didn't drop into a seat or strap in. He stood there, his concession to the fast movement being a grab at part of the frame and a spreading apart of his feet. There was a disturbing smile on his lips. And when I say disturbing, I mean disturbing.

It was his "I see something funny" coupled with "I know you just parked your broom on an anthill" smile.

When we leveled off in flight, he made his way towards the pilot's seat, in a controlled stumble from holding on to the back of a seat to holding on to the back of a seat. When he held on to Lucius's seat, he tapped Lucius on the shoulder.

It took Lucius several breaths to respond, and his response was no more than a frown turned towards Simon.

"Eh, *mon ami*," Simon said, his tone still as though he were on the verge of bursting into laughter. "Would you mind telling me where we're going?"

I didn't know Lucius very well. My acquaintance with him was maybe an aggregate two weeks. But I'd known his younger brother, Max, since we were both brats romping around wherever Good Men met to discuss policy and how to keep peace and stability. When Max had done that thing like a half-chew and thrusting his lower jaw forward, it was a good time to clear the decks because he was about to lose his patience.

Needless to say, Simon had known Max as well as I had. But he didn't clear the decks. Instead, he said, "Well?"

Lucius did the jaw thing again, then, abruptly, sighed. A puzzled expression replaced his look of anger. Not so much as though he didn't know what he was doing, more as though he knew he'd forgotten something.

"I can't go to Olympus, can I?" Simon said, in a soft voice.

"Of course you can," Lucius said, again annoyed. "We're not at war with you!"

"Oh, deary me, no, we're not. In fact, we're allies of convenience against the Good Men, but how will it look if I, who have been at pains to establish the personality of a megalomaniac populist, am seen in your company with no pomp, no circumstance, nothing to indicate that I am the great Emperor Beaulieu? In my jumpsuit, and looking everyday and mundane? Worse, if I'm seen in the company of one of the heroes of the Usaian revolution, someone so charismatic everyone knows about him? I'll be judged a puppet." And to Luce's blank expression, "But it is worse than that, *mon ami*. You know it is. Athena's husband would need lenses or disguising glasses, and possibly hair dye, or you're going to find yourself explaining why our side is now bioengineering people into freaks of nature." A look at Kit, and,

"Pardon, but that's what they'll call it. And what's more, Lucius, you can't explain those three little cherubs. And won't they attract attention? *But,* more importantly, we left behind my submarine." He frowned, a little, towards Fuse, "That is, if Christopher here hasn't thrown an explosive device on top of it?"

"I didn't see any submarine," Kit said.

"Which is the main purpose of submarines. To be underwater and invisible from the top. Ah, well, there is a lot of shoreline there. We'll trust Athena's husband threw it into open water. If no chunks of dimatough floated up, chances are we're safe. But there is also the triangular ship, Lucius. We can't leave such things lying about for people to stumble into, because that will lead to all sorts of awkward questions, won't it? We can't afford it, Lucius. You know what Nat would tell you. Hell, you know that you know. You're agitation and propaganda, are you not, my friend?"

Lucius looked upset. I thought he looked mostly upset with himself, but if I were Simon I'd cut back on the heavy cajolery. If cajoling Lucius Keeva when he was in this mood was as safe as cajoling Max in a similar mood, he might find himself looking for his teeth on the floor.

Not that a lot of people didn't feel like doing that to Simon on a regular basis. Even I, occasionally. The fact that he still had perfectly straight teeth either meant people had almost supernatural control, or that he engaged in a lot of dental repair work.

"Where should I go then?" Lucius said, at long last. "Staying on that island is dangerous too, particularly after the explosion, which probably showed on the sonar of anyone watching this area and might have brought patrols out."

"I had to get rid of that bomb," Fuse said. "The explosive was—"

Simon gestured the objection away. "I have control over that area. It is part of Liberte waters. None of which means I want to be there now, when a patrol might very easily come by and it would be...ah...awkward if they found us. But in the long run I can suppress any inconvenient findings and slap a do-not-speak order on any of my units, if needed, by implying that what they stumbled on is secret research from Liberte. All that can be done later, but granted that we had to leave the algae-processing station behind, and that we can't take these people to Olympus or Liberte, do you have a destination in mind?"

Luce shook his head. He faced forward. He was looking at his maps again, and changing our route, at a guess, to avoid passing anywhere we'd be noticed, let alone attacked.

"I have—" Simon stopped and sighed. He turned to Kit, then looked at Simon. "There is that little hideaway of Jarl Ingemar's if Athena's husband wouldn't mind doing the honors of the genlock? I believe all the booby traps have been disabled, and the place itself is not only a resort, but very hard to leave without alarms sounding."

"I gave..." Kit stopped. "Nat the codes to disable the resort."

"Sure," Luce said. "And eventually it will be a spot where those wounded in the war can go to recover. But there has been no time and no resources, and in case you did not notice, Nat is not here. And the inability of people getting out without your say-so..." He looked towards the three teenagers. "Could be useful should these children, or...indeed, any others we gather"—he raised an eyebrow at Luce, but Luce didn't rise to the bait, facing away and keeping his face blank—"prove resourceful. I could give you the coordinates."

Luce gave a look over his shoulder in Kit's direction.

Look, it didn't make any sense, okay? I'm the first to admit that. The place they were talking about had been used as a hideaway and resort by Jarl Ingemar. I believe before that it had been a touristic resort of some kind. It was set in an artificial cave in Northern Europe, with a climate so controlled that it grew plants and fruits from all over the world.

Under Jarl's use it had become a sort of fortress, impenetrable from the outside. And during his absence, with the AIs and cyborgs he'd left in control, two of them imbued with his own personality, those defensive measures had gone completely out of control and turned the place into an obstacle course coupled with cunning traps for the unwary or indeed anyone. On our last visit to Earth, Kit and I had spent a very bad time there.

However, part of the very bad time was that Kit had, at the time, been at risk of being overtaken by Jarl's personality, implanted during a misguided treatment for traumatic brain injury. At any rate, I had destroyed all of the potential traps in the area. There was nothing injurious about the resort itself, other than being old and in some areas ruined.

On the one hand, the place had plenty of abandoned machinery, possibly compounds for making explosives, and was dense and forest-like enough for the children to get lost in it. On the other hand, it was difficult both to break into and to leave, and fairly secret.

They should be asking me, not Kit, if we minded using that place. Only they remembered Kit as being half-possessed by Jarl, and they were probably keeping in mind that Jarl might take offense at the trespass.

Kit sighed. "This is nothing to do with us," he said. "Athena and I, and our daughter, have nothing to do with these children, or with Earth, or with granting the Mules a place on Earth if... if anyone is going to do that. It is only the merest chance that embroiled them with us. I think the best thing to do, for the three of us, would be to go back home, and leave you gentlemen to handle this."

There was a long silence after he spoke. Lucius didn't move or look back. He was looking intently at his controls and remained so, with perhaps a bit of extra rigidity to his pose, as though what had been natural abstraction was now quite unnatural appearance of abstraction.

And Simon stayed stock-still and frowned, not so much as if he were upset, but as if this upset his plans.

Kit had spoken carefully, and politely, but with a sort of cold detachment that was quite unlike him. I wondered if it was because he felt most of all he must take me and Eris out of this situation.

I understood his point. I did. Not just wishing to see us safe, but his reluctance to stay on Earth any longer than necessary.

After all, Kit simply wasn't free to go anywhere he wanted on Earth. Sure, his eyes could be disguised with contact lenses, and then he wouldn't look like the highly specialized enhanced life form he was. But with his calico hair, he was still noticeable. And even if we disguised that, he would stick out as a stranger everywhere. The way he moved, the accent on his Glaish, even his expressions were subtly out of kilter with anyone on Earth. It was the result of growing up in a colony that hadn't been in contact with Earth for centuries, and not something you could easily overcome.

Plus, I knew he still wasn't fond of standing anywhere on Earth where there wasn't a roof over his head. In the hollowed asteroid, in which he'd been born and raised, the sky above was a hologram. He'd confided to me that the only way he could keep from going into an agoraphobic panic outside was to pretend the skies of Earth were the same.

In other words, he was a man out of place. And he wanted to go home. Which I understood. I did. Then why did my stomach contract at his words?

I found I was looking at Little Brother. Captain Morgan, of the Sinistra genetic line, was a pitiful object. Too young to be a man, too old to be a child, and from the look on his face, and the way he looked warily at all of us, too untrusting to ever have been a child like other children.

I'd been created and raised by a man who saw me as his way to a plan: his plan of turning the world into a haven for his kind, one in which normal humans were slowly pushed out, as an inferior species, unable to compete.

Something about that thought sent a finger of cold up my spine and a suspicion crossed my mind that there was something in that I should pay attention to.

But mostly, I was looking at Morgan.

I'm not going to say he was a pretty child, though he could have been one, under different circumstances and different standards of grooming. And I'm not going to say my interaction with him made me think him pleasant or really possessed of any good qualities.

The thing was, where would he have learned good qualities or proper principles, poor sprout? I'd been raised by someone who didn't love me, and didn't really consider me human. But even so, I'd had a foster mother, who had loved me, at least if I remembered my first years of life accurately. She'd disappeared when I was six, but she'd left behind that sense of security and love.

More than that, I'd had the whole wide world.

Yes, of course, my father had mostly made me acquainted with that world by sending me to reform schools and mental hospitals, in an attempt to make me conform to his plans and not question his orders.

But in those, and in my broomer lair, I'd found boon companions, friends, acquaintances. And even then...

Even then, I'd been a sorry mess with no more morals than a cat. I remembered what I'd been like when Kit had rescued me from the powertree ring. Even afterwards, even after he and his family had taken me in, looked after me, and given me their trust and their help, I'd been so disloyal, so unable to have any moral judgment that I'd almost gotten Kit killed.

If Kit had never taken me in, I'd have ended up killed, my own misguided machinations trapping me into what my father wanted me to do. And if I'd somehow survived my father, I'd still be a sad creature, not fully grownup, not responsible for my own actions, let alone others'.

What about this child, who'd grown up in circumstances that made my upbringing look idyllic?

I slipped my hand into Kit's, on the seat, beside him. His hand felt very cold. He looked at me.

Simon said, under his breath, but in a tone that was obviously meant to be overheard, "How . . . typical. Of course, it is none of your business. Though we helped you when—"

Kit opened his mouth, closed it.

Into the silence, I said, "I see both sides," I said. "Yes, Simon has helped us, Kit, as has Lucius. They didn't need to provide us with places to stay, or cover for us, even if once or twice we might have benefited them. But I do understand Kit also," I said, looking a Simon. "This is not his world, nor does he feel comfortable in it. He's afraid of being caught out in something all of us know, but which he doesn't, and which will make it obvious he's a stranger. Considering that my father imprisoned him and tortured him to get the location of Eden and the secrets of darkships, considering that most of the effort of his people is towards hiding the location of his homeworld, you can't blame him. Or rather, you can but you shouldn't."

"Yes, but—" Lucius said. He sighed. His face was taut, the lines on it too sharp, as though he were disciplining his expression by an effort of will. "But Athena, if we are going to keep these children secret—and I'm sure we must—until we figure out what, precisely, is going on, and if we can help them complete their mission without hurting ourselves or them, we have to leave someone with them. You're ideal, not just because Kit can open things that Jarl coded, and will be more at home and more able to arrange things to suit you in Jarl's retreat, but also because you will not be missed on Earth. Simon and I are both relatively prominent. If we are gone too long— As is, taking you to Jarl's retreat and going back would take long enough to be hard to explain. But we can't disappear for days or weeks or even, in extreme cases, months. If we did, it would be noticed and people would come looking for us. Not all of them friendly people."

"You have subordinates," Kit said. "Both of you. You could order someone to look after the boys, or to keep them prisoner."

"We could," Simon said. "But you know who they are, and of whose genes they're made. Do you think many normal people would be able to contain them or to prevent them from going off, perhaps into Good Men hands, carrying information about us?"

I remembered how no school, no mental hospital, no boot camp had been able to keep me. I said, "Kit, they are . . . related to us. Of us. If they belong to anyone—"

He looked at Laz and Morgan and sighed. His mind started, *They are really—*

Perhaps it was the sharpened look in Laz's eyes, meeting Kit's just a moment, that made Kit realize that for the first time, his mind-talk with me was not private. I still didn't understand why their mind-talk wasn't restricted to only bonded relationships, but it obviously wasn't. I didn't know what word Kit had been going to use after really. It could be anything from feral to bizarre. But instead, he sighed, heavily. He looked at me for a moment.

Normally, if our talk had been private, I'd have said more, but all I said was, *Remember what I was like when you found me. Remember my attempt at stealing a ship?*

Even though we were still paying for that piece of hooliganism— literally, since the damage to the ship had been charged to Kit, who was then my legal guardian—and even though in retrospect that betrayal was one of the most despicable things I'd ever done, my husband's lips twitched as if he found the memory of it funny. Honestly, the man had the oddest sense of humor. I was grateful, I supposed, insofar as I amused him.

He sighed, deeply. "All right," he said. "All right. I suppose we owe something to these children, to the extent they share our genetic code. Or not owe, precisely, but as fellow humans, as relations, it is our duty to protect them. We didn't choose them, but we don't choose our relations, do we?"

"I'm not going to let Thor come to harm," Fuse said.

"No. I think they've come to enough harm," Kit said. He frowned. He looked very much like a man deciding to do something he knew would hurt, in more ways than one. "All right.

We'll do it. But we can't stay for months. We are already under some suspicion in Ede—At home. We can't explain months away and get away with it. Or rather, we can, but it will only make us more suspicious and isolated among our fellows. It will only make everyone think we're traitors."

Lucius took a deep breath. I had the impression that he was relieved, more relieved than I expected, as though he had some plans that we could have ruined by refusing to go along with his idea. "So," he said. "Jarl's refuge. If you don't mind?"

Kit shrugged. I said, "It is a place with the possibility for endless mischief."

"Indeed," Simon said. "But which place on Earth isn't? Are you planning to take over a maximum-security prison? I don't think we have anything like Never-Never anymore. Or not under our command. And even that, as we all know, is not impregnable to escapes." He turned and gave Lucius the coordinates for the place Lucius called *Jarl's retreat*.

It took a long time to get there. It was half around the world, and in the middle of the territory of Europe, the place that had got most affected by the "ecological clean-up bacteria" the Good Men had released. If they hadn't lied about it—which they probably had—the intention of creating and releasing those microorganisms had been to clean pollution from the soil. What they had actually done was turn vast portions of continents into deserts. Other parts of the world had recovered, and North America was almost entirely regreened and heavily recolonized. But this part of Europe, where, according to the history we were taught, the infection had originated, remained sandy and deserted, the ground stripped of anything living, so that sand and dust were loose and blew in the air, the remains of cities standing like abandoned sentinels in the wasteland.

Lucius didn't need to refuel his flyer, which surprised me, but maybe it shouldn't have. In an Earth where war—or rather, multiple, small wars everywhere, all part of a larger strife—had become a constant, it probably wasn't safe to run on a small amount of juice, so that you might need to replace the powerpack in a bad area or at a bad time. No, if I were designing for the conditions on Earth right now, I'd have backups to the backup to the backup.

More importantly, Lucius had both fresher facilities and food on board. When those needs had come up, he'd grinned, "Remember, I am often entrusted with the care of the Remy children."

Which probably explained why the food was highly colored, amusing, somewhat bland, and in the case of crackers, shaped like iconic heroes of the Usaians. I found it a little odd to eat a package of smiling George Washingtons, the mythical George that the Usaians believed would come back to establish their republic anew.

We slept too. Not all at once, but by turns. It was decided, without discussion that two of the adults, besides the pilot, needed to be awake at any time. Kit and I took turns amusing Eris, and if I'd thought that Fuse's staring at me while I tended to her had been unnerving, the look on the boys' faces was twice so. They looked as if they'd never seen a baby. Which, now that I thought about it, might be true, at least for their conscious lives, if Morgan was among the youngest batch of clones made.

I confess that by the time we arrived and dipped down to the entrance that would otherwise look like just the rock face of a hill, I was jumpy like a broomer at a peacekeeper convention.

The thing was, I knew these kids. Oh, not them personally, of course. How could I? But I knew the genetic stock they came from, a genetic stock that had been replicated with no outside input. Meaning, I knew the people whose clones these children were, and being clones, they didn't have anyone else's genetics, so sweet reasonableness couldn't have come from anywhere else. These weren't the children of my misguided father, Jarl Ingemar or Meinard Ajith Rex Mason, Fuse's father. No. They were their clones.

Sure, the argument of nature versus nature can go on forever, and sure, Lucius wasn't Max and as far as I knew Max was nothing like their father, Dante. But that didn't mean that the innate tendencies weren't there. Luce and Max, at least, had both been relatively laid back until provoked beyond endurance, and both men of few words.

I'd seen these kids under pressure, and could attest that like their originals, or like myself and Kit, for that matter, they were spitfires, hell on two feet, ready to resolve whatever was scaring them by scaring it right back.

So why were they so passive during the trip? They slept most of the way, save for requests to use the fresher. They didn't even ask for food, though they did ask for water.

I kept expecting one or the other of them to flourish a stolen weapon or a hidden one, and try to take over the ship.

Instead, they sat there sleepy, heavy-eyed. I wondered what was going on. Had the immensity of the Earth scared them?

When Kit had first seen the ocean he'd indulged in a fit of extreme agoraphobia, but we'd been flying above it on a broom, not in an enclosed, totally covered flyer. That surely wouldn't raise their fears.

For that matter, their fears shouldn't be acute when we came out of the flyer in the cavern. Though there was an artificial sky above, it was cycling through night time when we arrived, a beautiful summer sky, studded with lights like stars, which was clearly not the sky outside, which had been the middle of a summer afternoon. Besides, they knew we had gone underground into a cavern.

But if they weren't scared, they were still reacting weirdly. I half-expected the boys to look around in wonder, or to be surprised and maybe even delighted by the heavily wooded space, the river murmuring through the mechanically maintained lawn on the riverside, or the rustling of small animals and birds. But they didn't even look either way, when we let them out of the flyer and escorted them to one of the main buildings, which used to be the resort's main hotel and later Jarl's main residence. Instead, they stumbled along, staring at their feet.

I thought they were walking oddly. Laz tripped on his feet more than once, and Morgan looked like he was dizzy. I thought the long trip was telling on them. It had come on top of a lot of effort and fighting and fear. Surely they'd been afraid of coming to Earth. Because it was a different and scary place, if nothing else. But they'd slept most of the way here. How hadn't that made a difference?

It wasn't until Simon, in his own inimitable style, was giving them a speech—which included such concepts as "no one here will have any way to fly out, and you really can't walk out through miles and miles of desert" and "If you behave, we'll find a way to negotiate your request"—that I could no longer fool myself nothing was wrong.

I couldn't fool myself because Morgan, facing Simon and looking, as the other two, half asleep and barely able to stand on his feet, suddenly threw up.

Lucius was the first to rush up, again giving proof that indeed he'd become used to child care, supporting the young man, feeling his forehead. "What is wrong?" he'd asked. "Something not agreeing with you?"

Morgan had tried to answer and thrown up again. His skin had gone very pale, in contrast with the blue-dyed hair.

Then Thor had lost consciousness, sinking in a heap on the floor, and Laz leaned against the trunk of a tree and said, "My head hurts very badly. Please—"

In the end we took them to one large room, wrestled three beds in and put them to bed.

By *we* I mean the men. I wasn't even allowed near the boys, not that I was making any great effort to get close.

"You and the baby must stay clear of contagion," Simon had said. And Kit had sided with him.

"It's possible the boys are just sick from exposure to Earth viruses," he said. "On the other hand, it is possible they're sick from something they brought with them. Who knows what mutations would appear and survive in the enclosed and circumscribed space of an interstellar ship?" And for a moment, for just a moment, in my husband's face, there was a look of intense curiosity. As though he'd like to collect samples and find out what those viruses were.

He was a pilot, raised to fly darkships to collect powerpods from the powertree ring. He'd never shown any interest in biology till his mind had been cross-pollinated with Jarl's after Kit was shot in the head and the imprint of Jarl's brain used to restore his mind. Supposedly most of this had been reversed, leaving just Kit's brain. But I couldn't figure out how that could be true. There would be no way to fully pull the memories apart. The personality, maybe, could be neutralized and stopped from coalescing. But the memories? It would be like pulling apart two sand piles.

Now and then I caught glimpses of a curiosity or interest or knowledge left behind by Jarl's imprint. Jarl had been a world-bestriding biologist, after all, maybe the greatest of them all. He was credited with creating the powertrees, biological solar collectors which survived in Earth orbit, and also with having created several of the—reviled—physical mutations during the war between the seacities and the land states. He'd created, they said, humans who could breathe underwater. Mind you, no one had ever found any proof of that, but it was one of the things they'd said he'd done, and if true it was not just insane, but a great achievement as well.

I certainly had no curiosity about the viruses either from an interstellar ship or from Earth and no interest at all in anything but keeping my small family safe. Marriage and motherhood had expanded my focus, from wishing to save myself to wishing to keep Kit and Eris safe too. The idea of living on without them was scarcely bearable. Rather death than that.

But I didn't feel the need to expand it more than that. I didn't wish harm to the boys, nor to Luce, nor to Simon. No, revise that, I'd been sincerely grieved when I thought that Simon had died. It would grieve me if the boys died too. And I would do what I could to keep Luce alive if only because Nat was my friend and Nat loved Lucius. But the first essential point was to keep me, Kit, and Eris alive.

Simon and Lucius left us alone with the boys after a couple of hours. Both of them had duties and an already overlong absence to explain. They could not stay with us to babysit the young invaders, even if the young men were very ill. This made it impossible to keep Kit away from the contagion. They tried to keep me away but it didn't work.

You see, when two people need to be helped to a bathroom where they can throw up, and the third is burning up with fever and needs water, it's impossible to keep any of three adults safely away.

Not that it mattered. If this was—as became clear when they started coughing—a type of flu, an airborne disease, then I wasn't safe anyway.

The night became something of a death march, a walking nightmare. I was thrown up on twice. Laz, the oldest of them, was burning with fever, and seemed to obsess about the other two and about someone called Pol. He muttered and struggled, in fear they had been "caught" or were in trouble somehow. It was difficult enough keeping him in bed, but if he got up, he'd blunder around like a sleepwalker, walking into walls and beds, hurting himself and getting in the way.

The other two seemed to throw up more, which challenged us to both keep them hydrated and to keep them clean.

I'd scouted the place and found my way into a storage room where someone had stored shelf upon shelf of the sort of courtesy things one might give guests of a resort: pajamas in various sizes, toothbrushes and other toiletries; slippers; extra blankets. I'd also found sheets, intact in the lower layers, though the top ones were grey with dust.

I have no idea what fabric the sheets and clothing were made of. They felt like the best silk, but they must be synthetic, or they would not have survived three hundred years. I think. Not that I'd ever studied the survival of cloth.

Whatever they were, we went through all of them at a prodigious rate. We'd get the boys more or less cleaned, then wrestle them into clothes, and then they'd throw up again or sweat so hard they looked like they'd been dipped in water.

In the middle of all this, I would nurse Eris, and change her when she cried, though I had to let her cry a while, since I needed to clean myself before touching her. I wanted to try to diminish the chances of contagion, but knew most of what I was doing was, at best, cosmetic.

And just when we thought they'd never come to an end of the spewing, we found that what came after was worse, as they lay on the bed, sweating, eyes bright and unseeing, as their temperature climbed. Even Laz quit his fretting and his moving, which was good, since the beds we'd moved in here were the narrow beds that had probably been allotted to servants. Easier to move, and easier to have three of them in one room, but not big enough for someone of Laz's build. His movement shook the weak ceramite frame, and when he threw the covers from him, he almost overturned the bed.

But I didn't like the looks of the boys. I ransacked the place looking for medicines, but found nothing beyond things for headaches and bandaids. Nothing that helped bring down a fever.

Fuse had got bags, and found a machine that could be coaxed into operating and producing ice. I wondered if it had been meant to produce ice. I was starting to think that Fuse had the same innate mechanical ability I had. What he'd done with the serving bot back in Syracuse, and now, his managing to make something make ice seemed miraculous, not just for him, but for anyone. In the time I'd spent here, most of the servos and robots I'd found were decayed beyond help.

He had filled the bags with ice and packed them around the boys. This seemed to help keep their temperature down, but it added another round to our duties. In my case, a third round:

check on the boys. Change out the bags filled with melted ice, try to force some water down their throats, then see if Eris needed me. We'd put Eris in a room next to the boys' room, and brought two beds together for Kit and myself.

I don't know how long this had been going on. It felt like years, or maybe centuries, but in retrospect, it must have been something short of two days. Maybe three or four, at the most.

And then at some point, I found Kit guiding me to bed. I don't remember dropping to sleep. I woke up with Eris crying. She was soaked, and obviously starved. I wondered if there was any formula around, that Kit could feed her when I slept. Clearly, she didn't get any bad effects from three-hundred-year-old formula.

By the time I was done feeding her, she had fallen asleep. I tucked her away in the box we were using for a crib. And then went in search of formula. Surely, Jarl hadn't had a need to feed babies, but some of his guests might have.

I struck gold in one of the storage rooms, with vacuum-packed, sealed bags of baby formula, but when I came back, carrying it in triumph, Fuse was waiting for me outside my room wringing his hands together and looking distraught.

Why is it our fears always go to those we love the most? In my case, my fears went to Eris. Had Fuse tried to pick her up and dropped her, or something equally disastrous? I couldn't even manage the voice to ask, but he said, "Thena, the boys need a doctor. A real medtech, not us."

Fuse seemed to have aged again overnight till he seemed his real age, except that sometimes he missed words or had trouble pronouncing something or seemed excessively frustrated. I thought he seemed older because he was looking after others. Not that he hadn't always been a nice person, but not usually the adult in charge of sick people. For one, because in the time I'd known him, putting him in charge of sick people would mean he'd build some sort of explosive to blow them up, thereby solving the issue.

Now, though, he behaved like a rational human being. A caring one. He moved from bed to bed, providing water, food, help to the bathroom.

"Why? What happened?" I ask.

Fuse shook his head. "They're not coming out of this. Their fever is too high. I'm afraid they'll be damaged. In the head." He touched his own head, with a finger, as though to indicate the place of danger, or perhaps the disastrous results that could ensue. "Athena, we should com Simon. Simon has doctors. Stands to reason. Emperor."

"You're not supposed to call him Simon," I'd said out of reflex.

Fuse sighted. "No. But Thena, I don't want Thor to die."

"I don't want any of them to die."

Fuse shook his head. "No, he said. But . . . different. Thor is . . . is my brother. Is what I was, before . . . before I got sick. He's the only family I have. Father never was family. I'm— I'll be damned if Thor has to run from someone who wants to steal his body. I'll be damned if he blows himself up before he can learn what is dangerous. I'll be damned if he's going to be hurt anymore. They've . . . they've been very badly treated, Athena. Worse than us. And treated each other very badly. They've been taught very badly. They've been taught they're things. Might still save them, change them, teach them better, but only if they live. Call Simon."

I called Simon. We weren't equipped to deal with this alone. Morgan looked like he'd faded into his pillows, a pale little shade so thin and transparent, you fancied you could see his bones through his flesh. The blue hair and piercings, which had looked almost threatening, now looked just like a child's costume, put on for a party and not discarded when illness struck.

So I dialed the new code Simon had given me. The link rang a long time. I knew it was Simon's personal link, and in the past he'd answered almost instantly. We'd seen him just a few days ago and I couldn't imagine that his duties as emperor were very different from his duties as Good Man. I waited. At long last I gave up and called Olympus. I didn't have Lucius's code, but I had his name, and he was part of a military. I had a vague memory of numbers in Olympus, the area code used for official business. I doubted they'd changed that. Most revolutions alter but don't abolish the previous bureaucracy. I called a lot of codes and considered revising my assumptions before a valid com rang. I asked the rather bewildered person who answered for the codes for the military installation that used to be the Patrician's palace and lucked out. The person who answered me was one of Lucius's secretaries, and had heard of me even if not recently. I'm going to assume at some point in the past he'd heard me too, because he never doubted it was my voice, but instead put me through to Lucius.

Who answered sounding like death warmed over. "Head cold, I think," he told me. "Though Si—Julien seems to have a more severe case of it. He collapsed during one of the morning ceremonies and the doctor has been called. His own particular doctor, Dr. Dufort."

"The boys have a very severe case," I said.

There was a long silence.

"I don't know what to do," I said. "We don't want to lose them."

"The doctor here reassured me it was just a flu virus," Lucius said. There was another silence. "We've been getting very odd, very long-lasting diseases, things that we thought were almost entirely vanished from the world, like flu and colds. The war, and the aggregation of people into tiny spaces, let alone the stress and sometimes insufficient sanitation..."

"And I think the boys caught something their immune system isn't prepared for."

"Likely. Let me call Dr. Dufort," Lucius said.

"To come here? Would that be safe?"

"He's—He's a Usaian. I'll talk to him. Quite safe. He...was the St. Cyr physician."

"That," I said, "is hardly a recommendation." I'd found out, on our flight from the algae station, that an acephalous clone had been killed instead of Simon, and that there were any number of these, as well as people who were effectively Mules or close to it, created.

Lucius hesitated. "No. I suppose not, but he—He's a Usaian. Without him, the revolution in Liberte would have gone very wrong indeed, and Liberte would have been taken back by the Good Men. He's solid."

More than solid, I thought, if his mere presence could prevent Liberte being taken by the Good Men who still controlled most of the world. What had he done? Created armies of Usaians to the cause, out of vats? I didn't ask, though. I suspected all Lucius meant by it was "He is a believer in my faith." I thought that if both Lucius and Simon trusted him, he would perhaps be all right. And if he weren't, we could keep him here with us, after all. I mean, what could he do if we confined him in here with us? And the boys did need medical care.

I went back to the room where we'd put the three boys, to tell Kit that we were going to get a real doctor to come here.

I had Eris strapped to the front of my chest, in a sling, as I did most of the time I was awake. As I approached the room, I heard a scream, and then Laz's voice saying, in a rush, "Me, me, not them. Not them."

It woke Eris, who started crying, so that by the time we entered the room, Laz half-awakened, and turned, away from us, looking as though we had disturbed something intensely private.

"What was that all about?" I asked Kit, who looked more somber and grave than when the *Cathouse* had problems. We were living the room the boys slept in.

"You don't want to know," he said. And, to my enquiring look, "They've been talking in delirium again, but he seems quite out of his mind. You really don't want to know." He looked tired too. None of us were trained doctors or even medtechs.

The First Horseman

"IT IS THE FLU," DR. DUFORT SAID.

I don't know what I expected. A colossus of some sort, a man whose very presence bent reality around him. Or someone whose knowledge of science and medicine was so overpowering that all must recognize it.

Instead, he was a lithe middle-aged man, very calm and completely unperturbed to be sent across the globe to examine three children in a secret facility. If he found it strange, he gave no indication. "I will leave some antivirals. It seems to be a very virulent case."

I had heard of him, before, or at least not precisely of him, but of the private doctors of Good Men. My own late, unlamented father had had some on retainer. I'd been made by one of them.

Somehow I'd never expected one of them to be so unprepossessing and so calm. The ones who had served my father had been somewhat more...showy.

He had taken the three boys' vitals through a med-examiner that looked quite a lot more advanced than when I left Earth. I wondered what had been happening in my absence. Other than, of course, civil war and unrest.

"Do you think they caught it from us? Somehow? Sim—Julien, maybe, if he was incubating something..."

Dufort shook his head, then shrugged. "The emperor was in the best of health. I know, because he insists I see him every other day." At my widening eyes and look of shock, because hypochondria had never been one of Simon's issues, as many has he had, he said, "Ah, no, not about his health. About other matters I supervise for him. I am the one who insists on taking a look at his vitals when we meet. He has taken on much too much, and has a tendency to burn the candle at both ends. He always has."

I almost asked him how he had known what the Emperor Julien always had, since the constructed story I'd skimmed said that he had grown up as a humble man of the people. But I met his eyes, and there was no deception there, and we were perfectly understood. He knew who the emperor was as well as I did. And he knew who all of us were too.

I hadn't ever thought of Simon as someone who burned the candle at both ends, either. Simon, at least to me, had appeared as a bon vivant, who strode through life seeking his own pleasure and his own advantage, and trying to do as little of the unpleasant "work" as humanly possible.

It occurred to me, not for the first time, but the most forcefully it ever had, that I might never had known the real Simon, but a constructed personality designed to be seen and appreciated by such as me.

Maybe there wasn't even a real Simon. Maybe he just had a series of personalities, of acts, that he put on for different people.

Certainly, another thing I'd found out on the trip here lent credence to the idea I'd never known Simon. Kit's "sister"—a female clone of Jarl Ingemar, created and raised in Eden—instead of marrying Simon as we'd all assumed she would, had married one of his subordinates and disappeared somewhere into Olympus's North American territories. Simon had made light of it, shrugged and said they hadn't suited, but I suspected when it had come to the sticking point he just couldn't commit to anyone or anything. Not even for love. Not even for self-preservation.

"They should pull through fine," Dr. Dufort said, as he set a handful of vials on the counter. "I gave them a dose, just give them the next dose in two days, and then another one. They are all healthy specimens, the . . . ah . . . body decorations notwithstanding. Whatever else they are—and from what the emperor told me, they are more or less feral—they are near-perfect physical specimens. Just keep them hydrated and fed. These vials will tip the scales a little in their favor and shorten their healing time. I'm leaving extra vials should any of you get ill. And this," he set down smaller vials. "In case the infant should contract this." The idea of Eris getting that sick made my hair attempt to stand on end.

He gave me and Kit the instructions on administering the medicine, without saying anything about Kit's eyes, the obvious mark of his bioengineering, and without saying anything about knowing who we were.

But when I walked with him to the front of the complex, where he'd left his flyer parked in a vast expanse of robot-maintained lawn, under green trees, beside the murmuring river, he said, in the tone of one who had hesitated a long time, "Patrician Sinistra—"

"Yes?"

He sighed. "Two things, and please forgive me for bringing them up at all. I will only plead that you don't know what has happened on Earth in your absence and that I have reason not to want either of you caught in it, if nothing else because it would embroil my—the emperor, and he's having all he can do to keep Liberte from the main strife because after the revolution, we're not ready to ... We're not ready to fight." He looked at me. "If you'll forgive me, *Madame*"—he pronounced it Mah-dah-m in the French way—"I have here a pouch with lenses which will alter the appearance of your husband's eyes. I would just prefer that if you leave this space, no one knows what you are. That you don't attract attention. Oh, I'd love to examine his eyes and know precisely how they were made, and how—the emperor tells me it was a virus—something was designed to change mere human DNA in that way. Just as I'd love to know how you were made, after a long string of failures and sterile female Mule clones. But I will not speak of it, not unless someone wishes to share the knowledge with me. There isn't even a need of creating female Mules for ah ... biolords to reproduce. It is possible to bridge the gap of reproduction with humans in the laboratory. The idea of making females was, I think, predicated on a perhaps natural desire for the Mules to replace normal human population. A thought that their species was the next step, as it were."

"My father did name me Hera," I said. "Athena Hera Sinistra.

As Nat pointed out, the woman without a mother, and the mother of a race of gods."

Dr. Dufort looked at me, evaluating. "Just so, Madame. Your... ah... father... had his notions. But the thing is, right now, to prevent the other Good Men from hunting you down and trying to figure you out. And from trying to do harm to your husband. So if he would wear the disguising lenses, and you'd try to... ah, not be very obvious."

"Why?" I said. "I mean, sure, they know that I am missing and perhaps think I'm dead. But I grew up on Earth and none of them tried to seize me. Even if they had contracts with Father that said they got to sire a child or something, I never heard of Good Men trusting each other in contracts, and surely—"

Dr. Dufort gave me something I'd rarely seen: an exasperated smile. It was as though he'd tried to combine the appeasement of an obsequious smile with exasperation at my slowness of mind. I wondered, for the first time, what it was like for the scientists and techs who worked for the Good Men. They had to know they were a lot more trained than the men they served, but the men they served had been designed to have greater potential. Did they think that they deserved better treatment at the Good Men's hands? Did they think that the Good Men could have done their job easily, and only didn't for some arcane reason? What did people feel who kept the secrets of unreasonable autocrats who might kill them for any reason or none at all? "Madame, yes, while you were growing up you were a point of curiosity, and perhaps hope for the future, but you must understand that, as you said, the Good Men never trust each other. Ever. This means that they didn't trust your father's assurances, or perhaps his doctors' assurances that you were indeed fertile. Which in the end meant you were a point of curiosity but not covetousness. But now, well... Now you have a daughter."

"Oh," I said. I led him to his flyer, and saw him get in, and saw him take off. Kit had given him the getting out codes.

I came back into the room to find the boys were worse, in the throes of delirium, and that Kit and Fuse were having trouble subduing them.

It was a full week and a half before we saw them improving again. Looking after three teenagers who were delirious, unable to function on their own, left us no time to do anything but fall asleep, exhausted, usually one at a time, while the other two stayed on duty.

Nonetheless, in our times awake together, I noticed that Fuse was coming to himself; becoming more adult... No, more himself by the day. And though he worried about Thor, perhaps most of all, he could now be trusted to look after the other two also, and to come to us if he couldn't handle it. The only time he woke one of us, it was Kit, because Laz was fighting in his delirium and Fuse could not hold him down alone.

At the end of what seemed like an endless succession of days, I woke up and Kit was standing by the bed, "The fever broke," he said. "They're asleep. Fuse is keeping an eye on them."

That was early morning, the first day in the refuge when I was aware of daybreak. I drank coffee outside, looking at the fake sun climb the holographic sky, and listening to the river and the birds, and feeling... relief? No. I didn't want the boys to die, but what had made these days grueling was not the fear they'd die, so much as the sheer amount of work, the grueling effort of looking after three incapacitated juveniles. I savored my moment with my coffee, and then Eris cried to be fed, and I hurried to look after her.

It seemed this was a time for me to look after everyone else, and that I wasn't going to have any time for myself, ever, ever again. Life would be a never end of caring for other people, younger people, people who were dependent on me. I never wanted to be a mother.

And then Kit had woken up and taken Eris from me, and reminded me that the bedrooms upstairs contained a sybaritic bath. I had slept in the immense bathtub, relaxing in more warm water than we could afford in Eden, or during transport in the *Cathouse*.

We had dinner that evening, the three adults together, after we'd given the young men food, and Fuse asked, "They'll live now? They'll live."

"They'll live," I told him. "The doctor said they would." Part of me thought it was very easy for him to say it, when he hadn't had to actually nurse them through the illness.

After dinner, I received a com from Luce. It was a hologram call, and I could see him, sitting at a vast desk, piled high with papers. He looked tired and old. I knew he was ten or fifteen years older than Nat and I and the rest of my broomer lair, but

I'd never thought of him that way. Till now. He looked like he had aged years since I'd seen him a week and a half ago. "I wanted to know how the boys were doing," he asked.

"Oh, they're recovered," I said. "They're fine."

His fingers drummed on his desk. It was odd, because he was staring at me through the holo communicator, but his fingers were drumming on the desk as though they had no connection at all with his mind, as though they were an automatic gesture.

I could sense something troubling him, something deep and unexpressed, but all he said aloud was "They have no other symptoms, now? They are fully recovered and have no other symptoms?"

"No."

"No symptoms as though of a hemorrhagic fever? Blood seepage through skin? Organ failure?"

I was horrified. "Light! No. Why? Do other people have those symptoms?"

He opened his mouth, snapped it shut. "Some. A good number of the people who caught this...flu." He looked more distressed than what he'd said warranted.

I thought I knew the only thing that could make him this tired, so I asked, "Nat?"

He raised his eyebrows at me, as though trying to make me feel I had no right to ask. Then he sighed. "No. Well—He has the flu. But no. It's...It's just a great number of people have those symptoms and a lot are dying, and we can't seem to stop it. And Julien has thrown all sorts of resources at it, but we still can't stop it. We can slow it down by constant blood transfusions, but our supply is not unlimited, and artificially produced blood seems to have deleterious effects, in mass quantities. Julien has tried everything. His wife is very ill."

"Wife?" I asked, surprised. It had never occurred to me that my scapegrace friend had married. Who had he married? His wife couldn't be one of us. Of course neither had my surrogate mother been, or any of the surrogate mothers of my friends, but somehow it seemed wrong. For that matter, Nat wasn't one of us, one of the clones of Good Men. So I didn't think that Luce wanted to hear my ideas on it.

Luce sighed again and shook his head. "Oh, it's just...He picked her from a row of beauty contest winners, and she was supposed to be a show wife, a trophy of the emperor, to show how vastly powerful and attractive he was, but Thena, I think he's come to love her, and you know Julien was never that stable. He's really tried everything. And if she should die this could affect his emotional wellbeing, and in turn put our position in jeopardy." He gave a mirthless laugh. "Not that it matters, since we're losing so many people, I think everything will be destabilized. The whole world." He seemed to bring himself to a halt with an effort and shrugged. "Look, I'm probably depressed because of this flu thing. I'm probably worrying for no reason."

"Is there any reason to think anyone will die?" I asked. "We weren't even really worried for the boys, and, having grown up in an insular environment, they were more likely to lack the resistance to—"

Luce pursed his lips. "Oh, people are dying. A lot of people. I don't know if it's the same flu the boys had, though—" He paused. "I have this feeling it might be. Whatever it is, though, it's going through the troops on both sides, both the Good Men and us and our allies, and there have been..." He frowned. "Something sets in after people recover or when they're recovering from this flu. They...The med techs say they don't make enough platelets in the blood. The upshot is the blood doesn't coagulate as it should. It hits some people differently from others, and some just get bruises and fatigue and jaundice, but we've had people die from sudden strokes, as a bleed let loose in their brains. Watch the boys. We don't know if it's the same thing, but..."

"You're worried. About the boys."

"Not about those three particularly," he said, but was frowning, as if in deep thought. "But yes, about them, too. It's just that... We're losing people we can't afford to lose. And even just the ones who are ill...Never mind, that is my worry, and not part of yours. We're a smaller fighting force, holding out in the face of a much larger enemy, and the truth is they can afford to lose more people than we can before our force becomes nonoperational."

"It's not that I don't care about your battle. A free Earth is preferable to—But I don't know what I can do."

"No, of course not. Your worry is, I suppose, to go home, once those boys are out of danger."

I tried to think of it. Going back to Eden, without resolving this situation...

I hated to admit it. I never wanted to be a mother. I truly never wanted to be a mother, and I hated being responsible for anyone else. But something had happened between giving birth to Eris and finding Little Brother, yes, and Laz too. These boys were probably worse raised than I'd been. I didn't know what they were doing on Earth, but I was sure that those who had sent them didn't care if they lived or died. And I knew if we left them to their own devices, in war-torn Earth, between rival factions, they'd be lucky to remain alive.

From the things they'd muttered while raving out of their minds with fever, I gathered Laz had spent a long time protecting these and others of the boys. I couldn't be less of a parent and protector than a half-grown stripling who could never have been taught any principles.

"I don't know," I said. "I don't think we can leave like this. For one." I hesitated. "It's possible we'd be taking contagion back to ... To the colony. For another, I feel strangely responsible for the boys." There were other reasons. In the upheavals in Eden, the role that Kit and I had played had left us under suspicion of creating dissension and less than popular with most people. I didn't want to go back to Eden just yet. Oh, I'd have to face public opinion at some point, and I did miss Kit's family, but right then, going back, with Eris, was like going back into confinement. Sure we could live again to gather powerpods, but how long could our little family hold out against the world? Did I really want to raise a child in an enclosed ship with just Kit and me? An upbringing even more artificial than mine?

"But it is dangerous for you to remain on Earth," Lucius said.

"I know. Dr. Dufort told me."

"Did he?"

"Yes. He said I could become a prize of contention among Good Men, but it doesn't matter. He gave us lenses, if Kit should need to leave this refuge, and I have survived on Earth a long time. What can I do? What do you want me to do?"

He took a deep breath. "We're going on the assumption that the flu was brought by the children. Dr. Dufort thinks—"

"Yes?"

"Dr. Dufort thinks that there is something different about this flu. Something wrong. He thinks that it's a designer disease, though he can't figure what it was designed to do. But that strange after-effect of your platelets count dropping and dropping worries him. And he thinks it might be the intention in the long run. But whatever it is defies his attempts at figuring out so far."

"And?"

"And getting more of the boys would help. Also establishing some sort of quarantine. At least prevent the spread of this to our side, until we can cure it. If we only knew where the others were. Didn't they talk? Tell you anything?"

I shook my head. "No, I genuinely don't think they know. It was all targets of opportunity, and finding someone who would lead them to the council of Good Men. Look how they latched on to Kit, whom anyone born on Earth would identify as an outsider."

Lucius sighed.

"This is not what you want to hear, I know, I said. Have you tried figuring out—I'm sure you have spying operations—where the disease is propagating from among the Good Men? The centers of those should be where the other boys are."

He made a face. "A lot of our spies are down too. A constant worry that those in the field speak when they're out of their minds. But our cyberspying, and breaking into hospital record centers, is at least so-so. We might be able to get something from that. I'll put some of my kids on it . . . My subordinates. Most of them are so young. Hard to think of them as anything but kids. They're used to doing that sort of analysis for public opinion, though, so they should be able to do it for this. It's a little different but they're adaptable. More adaptable than I. Thank you. I hadn't thought to use them that way, and most of our other leaders are too sick to think straight. I shall do it."

He had worried me enough that I played with the com devices in the compound to get news of the rest of the world. By the next morning, the news were full of this strange disease tearing through the various armies of the world. It was rumored that the Usaian troops were particularly affected, though I wasn't sure how they were getting that news.

The boys started improving almost immediately. Two days later, Eris caught the flu. The boys were recovering without showing signs of the secondary infection.

And on the sixth day, the news was full of stories about how

Yolande St. Cyr, Empress of Liberte, crowned by the emperor's own hands, had died.

And that night, I found that my thinking was becoming fuzzy and confused, and I went to bed. I thought I'd slept through the night, nothing else, but I woke with two men speaking by my bed, and a smell of something burning.

Gambit

"HOW LONG HAS SHE BEEN OUT?" A VOICE THAT WAS FAMILIAR, but not immediately identifiable.

"About a week," Kit said. "She's been semiconscious, mostly sleeping. I think she just got so exhausted. I mean, I don't think the flu is that terrible, just that she was horribly tired and it worsened it."

"You haven't caught it at all?" the other man asked. The smell of burning was briefly more intense. He'd moved near the bed on my right side. The smell was coming from him, I thought.

"I had something like sniffles," Kit said. "But I took the antiviral, and it passed. Fuse had a little worse flu, but just the flu, and it was gone in three days. Same with Eris. I think Athena's is a little more severe because of exhaustion. Her fever never got as high as the boys'."

"Umph," the man said. "I suspect the boys were deliberately infected, with a stronger version, or perhaps a greater load of the virus." Pause. "I am not a biologist. But I think they were given this in such a way that the period of greater contagion would last the most, and also so they would necessitate caretakers, who would in turn be infected."

I had been struggling to open my eyes, and now managed it. My eyes were only partly open, but the sliver of vision admitted

145

was enough for me to identify the person talking to Kit. "Nat," I said, and struggled to sit up.

Nat is whipcord thin, pale blond with seemingly incongruous black eyes. The smell of burning originated from the cigarette in his hand. He'd started smoking obsessively after Max died. I knew he'd slowed down on the smoking when I'd last seen him, and I wondered if the habit was now back full force due to stress.

He looked stressed, not in any way in particular, but in holding himself a little too tautly. There was an almost brittleness to his posture, as though he must keep himself from showing weakness.

Kit rushed to help me sit up, all the while scolding me for even trying to, but I ignored him, till I was sitting against the pillows, my eyes fully open. I felt fine, really, just like I'd had a really long sleep. Thirsty and strangely "gritty" in every joint, but not necessarily ill. "Is Eris?" I asked Kit.

"Perfectly recovered. She's asleep," he said, indicating her little box. "She eats an awful lot."

"Yeah, materials for making more Eris," I said, and turned to Nat. Luce had said he was ill, and there was something odd to his being here, and to his posture. I didn't like odd things, not when a plague was killing people. "You?" I said. "Are you recovered?"

He shrugged. "Not... precisely. I am medicated. I have recovered from the flu, and they've given me meds to try to prevent the onset of the other thing, whatever it is. I feel fine, really."

But I understood what he didn't say. What he didn't say was that he was afraid he was already doomed and that there wasn't anything anyone could do to save him. It was a moment of weakness, and then he shook his head. "It doesn't matter. The idea you gave Luce was a good one," he told me. "We have found several foci of infection, and we think we located... Lucius's younger clone. We have reason to think the boys are the carriers, but we need more carriers, because Dr. Dufort is having trouble isolating the virus from the boys here. Or rather, figuring out how it causes the after-effect illness. And I thought, if we could get a... another of the boys or... or two."

I looked at him. He looked sheepish. No one ever accused me of being tactful. "You want to get the Keeva clone..."

"No," he said. "I mean, yes, but only because if I have to get one of them. Also, he's... that is, he is at La Mancha Seacity.

He's accessible. Or should be. Easy to get at. So . . . I will be going there and trying to rescue him. If I succeed, I'll bring him—and his companions—here."

"Why did you come here first?" I asked. "If you've determined you're going to do this by yourself?"

"Oh," Nat said. He glanced at Kit. "I tried to com you, and couldn't get an answer. I thought you might all have died, or you might all be very ill and need help, so since La Mancha is relatively close to your location, I thought—"

If I remembered clearly, and since geography was never a passion, I might not, La Mancha was in fact several hours away, but granted, closer to central Europe than to Olympus Seacity. "I don't understand," I said.

"He came to make sure we were alive and well," Kit said. "Or at lest the rest of us were well. With you not being awake, and me trying to watch Eris, and Fuse and the boys . . . If the com signaled, I didn't notice or wasn't in the room at the time. He got concerned."

Nat stood up, tall and lean, holding a cigarette between his fingers, and I remembered something my late friend, Max, had once said about him, in exasperation: "World's most unlikely mother hen."

"I think," I said, sitting up fully and only remembering afterwards to check and be relieved that Kit had dressed me in some sort of loose gown, "I'll be all right. Go and get the boys if you can. I feel bad about any of them being in the hands of people who might use them . . . I mean for more than getting a treatment for this illness. I don't think any of them ever had a chance."

Nat's lips went thin. "I'm almost sure they didn't. But we can't save all of them. Not on our resources right now. Besides, I might get away with one raid, but two would be suicide. They'd know to expect me. There would be a trap."

"Isn't it dangerous . . ." Kit hesitated. "Going on this mission all by yourself? Even if it's the first? Surely there will be guards and surely the boys are watched, at least if they made contact."

"They made contact," Nat said. "We—we broke the code for that particular cluster of Good Men some time ago, and we caught references to the boys. They made contact and they're alive, but kept isolated because they're not trusted." Pause, and he lit another cigarette. "There was some talk of using Luce's—John to get concessions from us. So we know where they are, and can guess at the defenses. I wouldn't do this on my own without on-the-ground intelligence. I might be foolhardy, but despite rumors to the contrary, I'm not actually insane."

"Still," I said, worried now. "Shouldn't you take someone? You're a military man. Surely you have underlings who—"

"Whom I'd rather don't know what is happening, Athena. We're in a very delicate situation. Remember—No, you wouldn't know. The reason Simon lost control of the Sans Culottes in Liberte is that we had to publicize what the Good Men really are. The Good Men spent so much time distancing themselves from what they'd been before the Turmoils that they taught everyone to fear and hate the Mules.

"We're all right in Olympus, because so many people are Usaians and Luce is a known Usaian, and...and in a relationship with a normal person. But Thena, if people find out that this plague started with the Mules, in orbit on the *Je Reviens* sending down infected teenagers who are also Mules..." He pulled deeply on his cigarette and released a cloud of smoke into the air. "The Turmoils are nothing to it. Civilization as we know it will be leveled. There won't be two stones together. And Luce and anyone they suspect of being a Mule, or enhanced, which could well include myself and my family, and many others, will be killed. You'll pardon me if I don't think it's worth risking that on the chance that one of the people I pick to help me will recognize similarities and speak."

"I suppose it's why we're here, with the boys," I said. "To keep it as secret as possible."

Nat nodded curtly. "I'm not a master of propaganda, like Luce is. I don't study mass psychological reactions every day, but I'm not stupid either. This situation has the potential to blow sky high."

"And you think the infection came with the boys?" I said.

"We're sure of it. We just don't understand how it's activating the secondary plague, and without it, we can't fight it. But we're sure of it. We're sure this is...well, the revenge of the Mules. What the boys were told was substantially right. They were told the Mules had decided they wanted the Earth for themselves, after all, and that was true. They were told they were necessary for this endeavor, and that was true. What I don't think they told the boys is that they had sent them down as the instruments of the Mules' revenge, the Mules' plan to clear the planet of *homo sapiens sapiens* and make room for them. They want the whole Earth. I presume the boys didn't know, because that was the way to get maximum efficiency in the attack. It's possible, of course—"

"No," Kit said. "They've been delirious enough, they'd have told."

Nat nodded again. "So, you see, I can't take just anyone, because I can't risk their recognizing one or all of the boys and... well... turning," he told me. "I can't ask your husband to go, because he's a stranger on Earth, and because his mutations are obvious. Should he be captured he'd risk his entire world, but worse, should he be captured, I don't suppose you could make it out of here and back home on your own."

"No," I said. "Probably not." It wasn't so much a problem of navigation, but more that if both Kit and I were under suspicion in Eden, I'd be under a hundred times more suspicion if I returned without Kit. But I didn't need to explain this to Nat.

"I can't take Simon because he's very ill." A look at me. "Not physically. He really was in love with his wife, and the shock of her death, combined with the events of the last few months have been too much for it. Simon..." He shrugged.

I had some idea what he might mean. Simon had always seemed to me an unstable concatenation of personalities beneath a brittle shell he'd fashioned for himself. It was quite possible under the stress of several months of hell, he'd split wide, or was in danger of doing so. "Also, frankly," Nat said, "Since the Emperor Julien threw in with the Usaians, he's even more hated than I am on that side."

"Luce," I said.

"No! He's more important than I am to the cause. He's the figurehead that holds us all together. I couldn't do that."

Whether that was true, or whether Nat was trying to protect Luce and not risk him was unknowable. He probably didn't even know it himself.

I cleared my throat. "There's Fuse," I said. "I know what you're going to say, but he's really in much better shape than he ever was, and he would go if you asked him."

Nat shook his head. "No way, Thena. No way. You have no idea how actively his father is hunting him. We've been keeping track of that so we can keep him alive. His father could die at any minute, and knows it, and is trying to capture Fuse with all the desperation of a dying man. I would not risk him. Even though this cluster of Good Men is not the same as Fuse's father belongs to—because their overall alliance is a patching together of small alliances, of course—if they caught Fuse, they'd have a valuable bargaining chip, and they do know it."

I looked at Kit. He nodded almost imperceptibly, and I heard him mentally. *I'd tell you no way,* he said. *But if the situation is as Nat says, we can't go till this is solved. We can't risk carrying the infection to the normal people of Eden. And if they really need more specimens, and he goes and fails, it won't do any good. Nat will just be dead. I don't want to risk you, but I've long ago realized sometimes I can't protect you. If something happens to you, Eris still has a parent. And anyway*—he smiled—*Fuse is right about you. You tend to be all right in the end.*

"I could go with you," I said.

Nat looked horrified, which was a fine thing for a man who had gone on uncountable broomer raids and one attack on Circum Terra with me, and who knew very well I was trustworthy in a fight. "Oh, come," I said. "You know you can trust me. Remember when I—"

"Hell, Thena," he crushed his cigarette on something that he took from his pocket, and which appeared to be a portable ashtray. "I know I can trust you in a fight. More than I trust myself, some ways. There's no one I'd rather have at my back, actually, but Thena, it's not that simple. If the Mules want the Earth, and I'm fairly sure they do, what do you think they want to do with it?"

"Uh...live in it."

"Yes, thank you. Give the woman a star. Seriously, they want to replace *homo sapiens sapiens*. I have no idea what they call themselves, but I'm sure they call themselves something different. I'm sure they think they're different. If they get wind of your existence, you'll become one of the main objectives of whatever they're planning." He put up a hand, to stop me, and I realized I'd opened my mouth to protest that we weren't dealing with those Mules, the ones in orbit, the ones who planned to inherit the Earth, but only with their cousins who'd stayed behind on Earth. "I know, Thena, that we're not going into the *Je Reviens*. But the Good Men are also Mules, and some of them might even have put two and two together. They might know what's being done, and what's in store. I'm not sure how it would stand between the two groups, the Mules who stayed and those who left. From . . . from things we understood and read, the ones left behind were judged unfit to go to the stars, and might have some definite animosity against the ones who went. But in either case, either as a peace offering, or to gain their group an advantage over the other Mules, possessing the *only* female of their kind and one who has proven herself by birthing a daughter, would definitely be a coup. And some of them probably know who they are, and an exam would tell them you have a child. No, Athena, you're too important to risk. Or at least you're too much danger to risk. I'll have to do this alone."

"She isn't the only woman," Kit said. "Zen—"

"Zen married one of Simon's retainers and disappeared into the unexplored and newly forested continental territories in North America. Yes, we've tried getting in touch with her through this, but from the character of her husband, and from her own experiences, I'd guess they're both trying to stay lost. At any rate, she doesn't enter into this equation because only a handful of us know what she is, and none of us talks, even in code, except face to face in places we're sure aren't bugged. As far as the Good Men are concerned, you are the key to their future. And as soon as the Mules hear of you, you'll be the key to populating the Earth. I'll do this alone. I've done crazier things. Trust me. We have the best intelligence."

I trusted they had the best intelligence. I did not trust he could do it alone. Look, Nat was one of the best, an amazing fighter on broomback, and as fast and efficient as any bioengineered person. I suspected he, like many descendants of families who'd served a Good Man for a long time, had in fact been extensively improved. But he was one man. And the Good Men were paranoid and had the ability to indulge their paranoia with guards and systems of surveillance.

In a way it was one man going up against an army. Even if he got to the boys, if they were in as bad a shape as the ones here had been, how did he propose to bring them all out?

Of course, in my heart I was sure he meant to rescue one of those boys, even if the others died. But I don't think he'd admit, even to himself, that any of them were disposable. And there was no way he could carry three of them, if they were very ill.

In some tales, the lone man goes up against the evil army and emerges unscathed, because his heart was pure. I could say many things of Nat, but I'd never say his heart was pure. And at any rate, I was fairly sure no one cared about purity of hearts. If he went alone against an army, he was going to die. And we needed him not to die. And he was so stubborn there was nothing I could do.

I got dressed and Kit and I walked him to the entrance of the refuge, and the flyer he'd left parked there.

"Why a flyer?" I said. "A broom would be less noticeable."

He sighed. "Because I'll need to bring boys back, and considering how they were raised, agoraphobia is a consideration."

"Um. I can't convince you to let me come?" I asked.

"Definitely not," he said. "I cannot in good conscience put you in danger."

Kit was walking around the flyer, as though inspecting it, which got him a weird look from Nat. "I...I hope it's armored in some way?" Kit said.

Nat shrugged. "As much as flyers are these days. Even civilians get shot at."

Kit nodded. Nat shook both our hands, and left to meet his doom.

What a Woman Has to Do

KIT AND I HADN'T MIND-TALKED FOR A LONG TIME. NOT SINCE we'd had the young men around. I had no idea why their telepathy was non-bonded, nor what activated it, but I was so used to my thoughts at Kit being private, I didn't want to forget and think the wrong thing "out loud" inadvertently, around them, because given their upbringing, it might give them really odd ideas. And they might even act on them.

This was odd after years of thinking images and ideas at each other.

But the thing about a happy marriage is that you often don't need to think anything clearly at each other to know what is going on.

I'd known that Kit's attention to Nat's vehicle was unusual, and that his attempt at explaining it was even odder. And I knew Kit actually thought I should have gone with Nat. I didn't have to think very hard to figure out what was going on.

As we walked back, I asked, "You put a locator on the flyer?"

Kit nodded. "On the bottom of the door, where he'd have to suspect something to look. Besides, I attached it there where he wasn't looking, so if he suspected anything it would be in another place." And, because he too doesn't need telepathy to answer a question I'm just formulating. "They were in Jarl's old desk. I had a vague memory." He paused, but I didn't ask anything. I'm not stupid, and I know it was impossible to restore Kit's brain completely, after we'd used an imprint of Jarl's to save him from death. We'd managed to banish Jarl as a coherent personality that could overwhelm Kit's, but it was impossible to eliminate every single memory the imprint had created. Jarl had left behind a goodly knowledge of biology, and possibly other memories. And since this retreat had been Jarl's favorite place over his very long life on Earth, it was impossible Kit didn't know where some things were. But Kit was afraid of making me uncomfortable by speaking of it, and delayed a long time, before saying, "I am worried, of course, about your doing something like this after you were in bed, ill."

"You said it yourself I was mostly tired," I said. "And I do feel fine now, truly."

He gave me a look, shook his head, as though reproaching himself. "I would go instead of you, but—"

"But you're not as conversant with Earth as I am," I said.

He shrugged. "That could be overcome. But the thing is that I'm not sure if Eden—"

"Would let me back in if I came back without you."

"It's not discrimination against you," he said. "Or not particularly. Remember how they treated me after my first wife died while traveling, and when I didn't have a body to bring back."

I remembered. His first wife's family had attempted to collect on the blood feud by killing him. It had almost killed him before we could prove he hadn't done it.

"But also we already stopped on Earth, and if I didn't come back . . . Besides, I might have revealed Eden's secrets and—"

"I know." I said. "That is a very good reason for you not to go. But I feel fine, truly.

I'd made my way to the room, and was locating the various pieces of my broomer costume, even as I spoke. Kit watched, then nodded and disappeared. He came back minutes later holding a broom, which he handed to me. I stared. "This does not look three hundred years old," I said.

He smiled. "No, it's one we left here before, but I have made sure its power pack is charged. Before Nat's visit," he added. "I was afraid one or the other of us would need to leave to get help. If the boys had not gotten better. Speaking of the boys, you'd better leave without their noticing. They're becoming very active, and if they find... they might find a way out, which would be disastrous."

"Yes," I said. "But I'll nurse Eris before going."

Kit didn't actually protest, but had that feeling of repressed protesting that people can give off when they think you're doing something particularly stupid.

"I have to," I explained. "I don't know how long this will take, but if my idea is right, of where La Mancha is—somewhere off the coast of what used to be Spain—it will take at least six hours to get there, rescue or kidnap the young men, and get back. Depending on how wrong I am in my geography, or how much trouble we encounter, we could end up taking twelve hours. My breasts will hurt." Which reminded me. "Why aren't they hurting now?"

Kit pulled a small machine from shelves near our bed, and threw it at me. "It's a breast pump. We used it and supplemented with formula. I don't think you'll be able to save the milk, but if it starts hurting too much—"

I nodded. "But I'll still nurse her before I go." And to Kit's distraught expression, "Truly, it doesn't take as long as all that, and brooms are faster than flyers."

He shut up and let me do what I wanted then. It involved waking Eris, something that even in my short time as a parent, I'd learned was not something to be done lightly. If the little darling was asleep, a condition that made her the most beautiful she could be, and also the most appealing, you let her sleep until she woke. Waking her up meant she woke up complaining and moaning her terrible fate. But she shut up when I put her in the proximity of my breast, and even if she mostly slept while she nursed, this was important. Oh, she could find sustenance practically anywhere else. Okay, anywhere that had baby formula, which both worlds we had access to had. I was also sure if needed Kit would stock the *Cathouse*.

I needed this time with my daughter, to contemplate the miracle she was, so tiny and helpless and yet, already, irrevocably, her own little person. When she was done, I handed her to Kit and kissed him. I refused to consider what would happen to him if he returned, once more, with a dead wife. At least I didn't have any relatives in Eden who might wish to kill him or make him pay blood Geld.

He gave me a mechanism that could be attached to the front of the broom, where I could track it at a glance. It was a tiny screen that displayed the direction Nat had taken and the distance he had covered.

I tightened my hood around my head, slapped the oxygen mask on my face, lay low over the broom, and climbed to an altitude at which I was unlikely to be tracked. Though brooms were illegal almost anywhere on Earth, at least if they weren't being used as a way to escape a flyer in trouble, they were fairly safe to use at certain altitudes. At least they were if you beat the "brains" out of it, so it wouldn't track where you were and tattle on you to the nearest traffic control tower. You see, the brooms were too small to be easily tracked any other way.

It felt good to be flying free, but would you believe that I missed Eris after about fifteen minutes. I missed her snuggled against me. I missed her squirming. I even missed her high-pitched whine when I had to descend fast.

I tried not to think on what it would do to her to grow up without a mother. At least she had a sane and decent father, unlike the man I'd grown up with.

There was something of a pang to realizing I might not have a say in how my daughter's life would unfold, which was strange, since it was a responsibility I'd never wanted and hadn't sought. But then again, who gets to control how their children's lives go? At any minute, we could be taken from her, or her from us. The best I could do was try to protect her. Which was what this exploit was all about.

Emergency

THE GADGET KIT HAD AFFIXED TO THE BROOM DIDN'T EXACTLY show me if Nat's flyer was losing altitude. What it told me was that it had stopped. I'd been keeping a constant distance from him, in case he was using some kind of sweep to monitor traffic near him. Which I'd bet he was, because of who he was, and because of where we were: on a war-torn Earth, in the middle of serious trouble.

Truth be told, Nat had never been the most trusting or easygoing of men, even before all this. Until I'd found out he'd been a member of the forbidden Usaian religion, I'd never fully understand why, but he was the kind of man who watched everything and everyone, everyday, lest an attack should come from where he didn't expect. Or as though he expected the world at large to attack him at any minute. As I said, finding that he was a devotee of the Usaian religion explained some of that, since allegiance to the cult was punishable by death in most of the civilized world. But I suspected now, when his co-religionists had started their longed-for revolution, and were in charge in Olympus and influential in other parts of the world, he'd been even more vigilant, because he fought in an actual military and the state of the world was such that he'd have to keep himself alert.

So I'd kept a good distance away, following him carefully, but not so closely he could find me, even if brooms, in general, could catch up with flyers, and this broom in particular was one of the fastest models.

But suddenly, I started closing in rapidly, without having changed my speed. That could only mean he'd landed, and it meant, incongruously, that I had to speed up. You see, if he'd landed he was probably proceeding on foot—he wasn't so stupid he'd park right next to the place he had to enter—and in a seacity, that meant he could get lost in the crowd. Alas, I didn't have a tracking device on him, only on his flyer. So I must rush.

I lay down over the broom, minimizing air resistance, and I played my fingers, my memory, along the controls. This was a Phoenix 7000, a kind I'd flown often enough in my broomer days. Often enough to have muscle memory of the controls.

I felt the speed more like a kick in the pants, and also, the air rushing around me seemed to be fast enough that the cold seemed to cut through my padded leather suit. It wouldn't actually freeze me, and honestly, I don't even think I could feel it that much. It was part a psychological effect of the greater speed, and partly the sense that it was colder than it had been.

In minutes, the city of La Mancha came into full sight. It was, like the other seacities, built at a time when independently wealthy businessmen had taken to the ocean, just outside territorial waters of land states, to escape the punitive taxes and regulations of those ever-more-grasping governments.

Those businessmen, in La Mancha's case most Spanish-speaking ones, had either been romantic or a little crazy, or in La Mancha's case both, as witnessed by the name.

Like Liberte Seacity, the seacity of La Mancha was built upwards, more than sprawling. It resembled nothing so much as a sort of fantasy island, a mountain in the middle of the sea, climbing up and up, with a narrow path winding along the mountainside. I suspected the real roadways, the real stairways to climb the levels of the house were disguised inside what appeared to be wholly verdant slopes. For one, doubtless, the houses that dotted the verdant slopes all looked too small and self-consciously picturesque to be where the inhabitants lived.

Listen, I'm no expert on urban planning, but I'd never seen a city, not even in Eden, in a wholly artificial, hollowed-out asteroid, where there were no poorer houses, no tumbledown neighborhoods, and no—not a single—place of commerce. Unless La Mancha was now and had always been just a pleasure resort. But seriously, even then, there would be restaurants, and shops, and who knew what else. So, this was a shell, and the real life, as in Eden, took place on the inside. That was fine. There was one residence that I was sure was that of the Good Man in charge of the place, which was visible from the outside, and probably really the place where someone lived: a grey castle, trying hard to look like it was made of granite, but probably really built of dimatough, perched on top of the pretty-pretty mountain.

I eyed it dubiously, because it was quite likely that Nat had gone there. But the thing looked fortified and intimidating enough that I wasn't sure I wanted to go in there.

La Mancha was not in my normal sphere of exploits. I hadn't known anyone there, and if the local Good Man had a son my age, he must keep him so far under his thumb that he didn't join with any of us or do anything outside the family. So I knew nothing about the isle, which made me nervous.

As I approached, I could at least see that Nat hadn't left the flyer up in the castle. Not to say that wasn't his ultimate objective, just that he'd landed elsewhere. Not that—as I approached—the place the flyer was stopped seemed much better than the castle. Picture a dark mouth opening on the side of the artificial mountain-island. No, it's not an exaggeration to picture it as a mouth. It was dark, vaguely round, and it opened on the slope. Okay, unlike a mouth, it had many like it nearby. It must be some sort of garage entrance. Or that is what I told myself as I plunged into it on the broom.

I found the flyer easily. It was almost the only vehicle parked in there.

And my unease increased. Look, I didn't care if La Mancha was built so as to present a pretty picture to the outside; inside there had to be all the necessities of life. The garages like holes on the slope seemed to indicate I was right.

But what kind of seacity had underground garages that were kept dark? And why was it deserted? And why had Nat parked in a deserted underground garage? Unless he had actually managed to spoof the transmission of a local flyer, this flyer would be identified by anyone who saw it, either as being from Olympus, or transmitting no registration whatsoever. And either of them meant it would become the target of very special attention.

I knew my friend intended to do this raid on his own. I didn't know he intended to make it suicidal.

As I landed, I clipped the broom to my back—this model being too large to clip to the belt of someone my height without dragging on the floor—and walked around the flyer—just to make sure it hadn't somehow been forced down, and that Nat wasn't dead inside—I felt the hair prickle at the back of my head, and put my hand in my pocket, holding the burner.

The flyer was empty. So far, so good.

I still didn't feel reassured. I stood very still and listened. I knew that whoever designed Daddy Dearest—whose enhancements I had inherited when I had been made—had given him senses that were more acute and worked better than the normal human issue.

Normally I didn't notice I had any kind of special ability to hear things, though. Not unless I stopped and listened really intently. Which I did now.

There were, I thought, steps, one level above. I couldn't tell if they were Nat's, only that they were from a single cautious person. Which might be anyone. Except there was only one flyer parked here. I headed deeper into the garage. Something that might be a sign activated when power cut out glowed hesitantly in the gloom. It pointed to the right for stairs and to the left for a grav well. There was a chance the grav well would be out due to lack of power. On the other hand, I don't like stairs in these type of places. They are normally little-used and a perfect place to be ambushed. Oh, yeah, they also tend to have blind turns.

The prickling at the back of my neck picked up.

My ears, still attuned to whatever was going on up there, now picked up other steps. There was a sound of voices. I can't tell you why they sounded hostile, but they did. And then I heard a burner zap. If this was Nat out there, he was in serious trouble.

I ran to the grav well. If it was working, it was quicker. I stepped into its field, was pulled up by antigrav, had a moment to give a sigh of relief, before I threw a foot to each side, to stop being sucked further up, and jumped sideways.

Into the middle of a firefight.

The good news is that it was Nat up there. The bad news is

that he was facing armed men. He had apparently cut one of them down and surprised them enough that they hadn't shot him yet. But it was a matter of time. Nat was enhanced, but there were more than ten of them, at a quick glance.

At my appearance about half of them trained their weapons on me.

It is a really bad thing to have many men point burners at you. Why? Because you can't kill them all, or jump out of the way of their burner rays very well, before one of them burns you dead. On the other hand, when you have a buddy show up unexpectedly and they get confused and half of them turn burners to your buddy, you have a chance to prevail. That is, you have a chance to prevail if, before they recover, you shoot those aiming at your friend, while he shoots those aiming at you.

It's not a foolproof strategy, mostly because one of them might be fast enough to kill one of you before the other can nail him. It is just the best strategy in a bad place.

The weak point, in this case, is that I didn't have telepathic communication with Nat, with which I could tell him to shoot the idiots aiming for me while I shot the ones aiming for him. The saving grace is that we had, after all, been members of the same broomer gang for years, and therefore could sort of guess the strategy. It wasn't the first time we'd used it, though that had been in mid-air battles.

I dropped down, just in case they were aiming for my head or heart, and set my burner on cut, which allowed me to do a continuous sweep.

Yes, it's messy, but also takes less time than burning, and there's less chance of the light alerting someone.

I don't remember holding my breath, but I must have, because I let it out when I heard the low-level hum and the screams indicating that Nat was doing the same from the other side.

There were other burner noises. Some of the enemy managed to press their triggers before they fell, and some, undoubtedly, let loose with a ray before I managed to shoot, or even dropped down, judging by the fact that some light beams went over me as I shot. I sort of threw myself sideways in a long, low jump when I shot, which was good too, as some of these people had enough discipline to shoot as the friends next to them were shot down. But normal human reflexes couldn't follow my movement.

I landed on my butt and pulled myself up, to see Nat nail the last of our attackers while he was running away. Yes, it might not have been strictly necessary, except that when we were here on a stealth mission, allowing someone to escape and carry word of us to anyone else seemed like an unnecessary risk.

You'd think the first words out of his mouth when he spoke would be "thank you," right? You'd be completely wrong. The first words out of his mouth, as he stood up—having dropped to one knee to shoot the fugitive, I presumed—were "What the hell?"

"You're welcome," I said.

He glowered at me, "I am grateful, Athena, but what the actual hell are you doing here?"

"Saving your ass."

His pale eyebrows climbed up towards his hair. His dark eyes looked skeptical. "Are you insane? You have a daughter and a husband. Why in hell would you come into this?"

"Because I have a daughter and a husband, whom I'd like to keep at least somewhat safe," I said.

He opened his mouth, but didn't say anything.

I approached the corpses. Note to self, when killing people with the cutting function of the burners, it makes the floor really slippery. Really slippery. And seeing exactly whom you killed can be kind of difficult, as the whole thing is obscured by blood and an excess of guts.

I stood a few feet off, frowning. It was close enough to see what I wanted to see. They weren't wearing armor or uniforms of any kind.

If it weren't for the fact that many of them still had burners clenched in their hands, and that they'd tried to kill Nat, I'd think that we'd just shot a bunch of unremarkable passers-by.

Nat gave me a look, and his voice was curt. "I wouldn't get much closer, Thena, unless you're desperate for weapons. I wouldn't advise getting blood on you. It's a good way to catch the plague."

"I have had the plague. At least the flu portion. I'm going to assume if the Mules sent the kids down to infect the normal humans, I'm immune to the actual lethal portion of it."

Nat made a noise, "Or not. We don't know if they care about the portions of the Mules left on Earth. In fact, judging by the way the Mules left on Earth were treated, we could expect the Mules from the *Je Reviens* to suspect that if they survived they might wish for payback."

"Well, none of us, Fuse, or Kit, or I have suffered any of this platelet-destroying disorder you say people get in the aftermath of the weird flu. Nor have the kids. Has Luce? He said he had a cold when I talked to him."

"No, but we have no proof, Thena, and it does well to be cautious. Unless you're desperate for burners."

I looked again at the burners. Unremarkable and rather cheap models. They might not have had a cutting mode, for that matter. "No, I have enough, I just wanted to make sure they weren't soldiers."

"No. Normal hooligans. They wanted my flyer. Which meant I had to kill them, because they'd seen me come out of it, and some of them might know me, or know someone who'd identify me from description, even if I try to stay out of holos."

"Why would hooligans try to steal a flyer? And is it a good idea to leave this as the only flyer in place?"

He glared at me. "Fascinating discussion. Can we get out of here, and I'll explain. The garage might not be wholly deserted. They were in it. And if there's someone, they might have heard the fight, seen reflected light, or even smelled the blood."

"Right," I said. "Where?"

There mustn't have been anyone else in the garage, because we made it up two more levels of antigrav well, and then down a short tunnel, to a place where the lights suddenly came on.

At the edge of the lighted place, before we even looked around, we looked at each other. "No blood on you," I said.

He nodded. "Nor on you."

Then we looked around. Despite the lights, there wasn't anyone nearby. And the lights weren't exactly lights, but looked like piped-in sunlight from above. It was hard to tell exactly, because above was the hologram of a sky, the same sort of things used by Edenites.

We were in what could be called a narrow pedestrian way. I didn't know if flyers were forbidden within La Mancha or if they had different tunnels. At any rate, taking a flyer into a tunnel into which traffic was channeled was asking for trouble. If you were flying outside, you could go at levels where no one saw you and disable the responder so that you didn't broadcast your location. You were then relatively safe.

But in tunnels they could have cameras and visual inspection of every car, or even ways of counting cars, and one that wasn't broadcasting would only call attention to itself. I mentioned this to Nat and asked about his flyer.

"Yeah, no. We're not going to the flyer tunnels. And don't worry about the flyer. We have spoofed transmissions. I got it from headquarters."

"So your mission is official?"

He shrugged. "Kind of, sort of. My superior knows, and his colleagues have authorized it, but—" He shrugged again. "I haven't told Luce. Or my parents. There would have been . . . objections."

I imagined. "What is the plan?" I asked. "I don't know La Mancha at all. I imagine you have some type of a map? Some sort of intelligence on the place the boys are?"

He nodded. "Yeah." He pointed above. "In the Good Man's keep. Not exactly his residence, though part of it is, but his . . . garrison and prison."

"Oh?" So we were going to the castle, after all. "Charming. I presume you have a map to get there."

He tapped his forehead. "Memorized."

Great. Which meant if I got separated from him I would never find my way. "Uh," I said. "Right. I'll stick with you."

"You should go back," he said. "Wait in the flyer. You shouldn't—"

"Nuh-uh," I said. "That garage will be crawling with busies." Which meant we should find another way out of La Mancha and back to our hideaway, but I wasn't about to tell Nat that. He seemed to be in that state that men sometimes get into when their plans get disrupted and they don't have any replacement to hand. They'll hold on to the original plan buckle and tongue, even if it doesn't make any sense. It's like a child with a security blanket. I'm sure they derive great comfort from it, and if you pull it away too early, they'll fight. "Besides, Kit and I talked, and we decided the best and possibly the only thing I can do is help you figure out the plague before it destroys the world. If I die, Kit can go back to our homeworld, maybe, but it's unlikely he'll go for a long while, because he has to make sure he doesn't take the plague there. But if I do nothing, neither of us can go back until we make sure the plague has subsided. And then there are political issues, which I don't propose to explain. The best solution is if I go with you, we get the boys, and we determine what the plague is and defeat it. And we both survive. So let's do that. That's why Kit bugged your flyer."

He gave me a dubious look. "Your husband seems like a good match for you."

"Thank you. That wasn't a compliment, was it?"

He smiled. "A little. Fine. If I can't talk you into keeping safe, you might as well come." Which was about as good an invitation as I was going to get.

We walked for a long while before we started meeting people, and then it was only a very few people, men and women, looking tired and haggard, some of them seeming to walk at random.

"Why are there so few people?" I asked Nat, when the crowd had thinned. "And why was the garage deserted?"

"The seacity was shut down when the plague became obvious," he said. "A lot of seacities and cities in the territories are doing that. No one comes in, no one goes out till the whole thing resolves itself. I flew in using several kinds of obscuring technology to avoid detection." He shrugged. "One of the advantages of being in the military. I don't know how you flew in, except it's possible no one is looking at brooms going very fast." He almost smiled. "No one is coming in, and vehicles are shot down if they try to go out. That's why those charming critters wanted my flyer. They wanted to escape the seacity. I gather they've had a large number of deaths, and they're spooked. From some words, I suspect they wanted to go to the territories, since the news of death is lower from there."

"Fewer people dying in the land areas?"

"Oh, hell no," Nat said. "At least not those we have contact with. But there are a lot of places out of contact, or not reporting, so it looks that way."

"Oh." I added to my list of worries how we were going to get out of here, if they were shooting out outbound traffic. Seriously, Nat was usually better than this, as I knew from our broomer days. Still had to be to have attained high military rank. So, why didn't he think of those things? No amount of disguising could hide us taking off when no one else was. And if we couldn't get back to our flyer, how would we get out in a non-camouflaged flyer? But I didn't think telling him this right now would make for a clearer head or an easier plan for either of us. Maybe it was that he'd been so ill. Maybe he was really worried. "Wouldn't they have got shut out?"

"They rightly presumed that if I'd got in undetected, they could get out the same way."

Duh. But that would mean to get out we'd have to get back to the garage. I did not like that. At all.

Gambit

"THIS ONE," NAT SAID. WE HAD GOT OFF THE MORE HEAVILY traveled space, not that it was particularly heavily traveled, and into one of the side tunnels, a narrow space, and again completely dark. I suspected this happened because the smaller tunnels, instead of piped-in sunlight, had artificial illumination. And I was going to guess all the artificial power had failed, which was going to be truly interesting. If they didn't have enough people to keep the power going, how would they have the people to guard the boys? And if the boys hadn't just walked out, they probably were too sick to.

I told Nat all this while he knelt and pulled what appeared to be a ventilation panel high up on the side of the tunnel. "Maybe," he said. "I mean, it's quite possible they are still ill. Like the young men you rescued"—they'd probably called it "captured," but I let it pass—"they arrived very ill, and I'll remind you not all the doctors the Good Men can command, a lot of whom have taken the opportunity to defect anyway, are as good as Dr. Dufort. But, besides all that." He paused and visibly struggled with the grate until it popped out. "Besides all that, the flu itself progresses at different rates, and it all depends when they got the medication. We got the impression from our intelligence-gathering that the young men are almost well, if not completely well, but also that they are still very much guarded." He stood by the place where he'd pulled the vent hole cover and looked back at me. "No way I can go in first," he said. "You'd never get in. You can't reach." He sighed. "Well, if the map I memorized is right, there's a join-ing further in that would allow us to exchange places. Now, I'm going to grab you and lift you."

Nat had been my companion in a dozen battles. I appreciated that he understood that attempts to lift me without warning, or even to lay a hand on me without warning, at least if they didn't come from Kit, would result in withdrawing a bloody stump back.

I allowed him to lift me. Look, we were broomers together a long time. The only thing I could think was that none of the non-enhanced men had been strong enough to lift me without visible effort before. I wasn't sure if this was a good side of being at war, or actually a somewhat sad reflection on the effort and work expended on the worldwide conflagration.

As he lifted me up, I grabbed onto the edges of the tunnel that the removal of the vent had uncovered, and found myself in a grey ceramite shaft, quite big enough for me, if not big enough for me to turn around. The big surprise is that there were lights, placed at regular intervals. Well, perhaps not so much of a surprise, as many of the seacities had been built as luxury places, which meant a lot of expenditure—some of it superfluous expenditure—had gone into building them. These must be fed by solar, or some other inexhaustible supply. That they were still working after four hundred years or so was definitely a mark of how well engineered the whole thing had been.

I saw what Nat had called a jointure a few paces off, and crawled to it, turned around, and came back. You see, the strange thing was that I hadn't heard Nat come up, and it was entirely possible something untoward had happened.

In fact, what I found as I came back was that, as I'd feared, there was something not quite right with the way Nat was func-tioning. He wasn't visibly ill, and he wasn't being outrageously stupid. It's just that I'd been on broomer lair fights and raids with him, I'd gone with him on at least one major expedition he'd organized, and if what I understood of his military career was true, he'd climbed pretty high, yet he seemed to be running into weird patches of hesitation and indecision.

In this case, he was standing below the vent entrance, holding the vent cover in his hand, as if he couldn't figure out quite what to do next.

My limited knowledge of platelet-forming issues allowed me to infer it was a blood issue, and if it was a blood issue, was the brain functioning quite as it should? Even with whatever meds he was taking.

"Here," I said, guessing he was having trouble figuring out how to climb up holding the cover. That he had to pull the cover up after himself was a foregone conclusion, but I suspected he hadn't thought it through. I reached down for the cover, then crawled backwards to the junction, watched Nat pull himself up and crawl in. "Thena, the cover. If someone comes by..."

"Yeah," I said, now frankly alarmed, because it was obvious and trust me, please, Nat was not stupid. "Go past me, please. I'll crawl back, put it in place, then turn around again."

Securing the cover proved a little more difficult than I expected, but I secured it well enough that it would hold, unless someone pulled it out or there was an earthquake. In which case, a fallen cover would not occasion any remark.

Nat had gone ahead of me, in the ventilation tunnel, by the time I got to the junction and turned around. This had one advantage: he knew the way and he was leading. On the other hand, I was worried about his reaction time and his mental processes. And I confess it didn't make much sense. What about a blood disease would cause Nat to not function as well as she should? He said he was taking medication.

"Can we talk?" I asked, in a semi-whisper.

He paused a moment, and I stopped to avoid colliding with his retreating shoes. They weren't boots, I noted, which mine were, but a sort of slipper I'd seen worn by climbers before. I wondered if we'd come to a point where I'd need that kind of foot sensitivity and agility. If I did, I might as well go barefoot. "For now," he said.

"You said the young men would still be under guard," I said.

"Yes. The patrician's household is still functioning. If our intelligence is right, he's had to replace a few people and he sent for replacements from the continents, testing them for antibodies to the virus, to make sure they were not infected. So far, we think about forty percent of the population are infected or dead, but the patrician's household continues to function."

"And the young men are in the patrician's household?"

"The most secure place," Nat said.

We crept forward for a while. At least the interior of the vent was smooth, and there was enough space for Nat, much less for my curvier but still smaller self. He turned left, then right then left again, and then we went forward for a long stretch. I half expected him to stop and act confused any minute. It was horrible to know the maps were in his head, and his head wasn't functioning exactly according to spec. But he turned right again, then sort of turned around in a junction and moved his fingers, fast.

It took me a minute to realize he was using broomer language. Up there, on the brooms, flying and coordinating attacks, we couldn't talk. For one, for many of the raids we were wearing oxygen masks, but even when we weren't it would be hard to talk while flying. Over the centuries of illegal brooming, we had developed an entire way of communication using finger movements, usually just one hand because that's what one could spare from the broom. When I realized Nat was talking, I caught it "...Get out at the next vent. It should be the Patrician's fresher and it should be empty at this time."

Uh. I flashed back "Cameras?"

"In the patrician's bathroom? Why would he provide blackmail material?"

It wasn't quite that clear. There's no term for "blackmail" in the broomer sign language, but there was a word for "that which you hold over," and I got it. Right. Made sense. Most patricians were careful enough to not give anything of their private lives away. Oh, sure, a lot of their life was lived in public, and watched by everyone. Many patricians in fact conducted business while bathing and dressing. But Good Men couldn't afford for their less orthodox little hobbies to get out into public knowledge. And most of them had less orthodox little hobbies. Father's had been a doozie.

"What about cameras en route?" I assumed that the boys were not in the Good Man's fresher, though I'd seen weirder things, frankly.

Nat nodded and flashed back, "Have disrupter."

Oh, good then. The damn gadgets cost the Earth, but more than that, were difficult enough to get hold of that almost no one had them. In your normal broomer raid or less-than-legal operation, you shot the camera as soon as spotted and hoped no one would think much of it beyond "it's just a glitch." Disruptors ranged from the ones that were as good as shooting the camera, but only when it would have caught you, to actually recording and playing back the last two seconds of the recording, so that it looked like the place was empty all the time. And they were little gadgets you wore in your pocket. I was hoping that Nat's was the second kind, mostly because it made everything cleaner, but even the first was better than having to get just the right angle to be able to shoot out the camera without being captured.

If they ever became cheap or easily available, it would be impossible for surveillance cameras to do any good, which I suspected was why they were restricted. And it showed the advantages of having a friend in high position in the military.

I followed Nat till he got a vent cover off. I didn't see how he did it, but he must have a special trick, because just punching it out would cause it to fall on the floor.

Instead, he caught it and put it back, then climbed out, then helped me out, which was a little difficult since I had to come out face first.

The fresher was . . . amazing.

Even Daddy Dearest hadn't thought of gold plating the toilet, but hey, to each his own. Mostly everything that could shine, shone, from the mirrors to the gold-plated appliances. And really, who put mirrors on the floor and the ceiling? Unless they staged far more interesting things in their fresher than I could even think of.

Nat must have been thinking the same, because a corner of his lips went up, in a case of not-happy amusement, and his eyebrows arched.

He touched his finger to lips, which was frankly not needed. Was he afraid I'd shriek with laughter?

And then he led out of the room, and I followed.

I had burners in both hands, but we met no one, as we came out into what I presume was the Good Man's bedroom, because most mansions have more walls, and the furniture didn't center on a giant bed, as it did here.

Nat opened a door and headed confidently in. I followed and blinked. I tapped him on the shoulder, "The Good Man's closet, really?" I flashed at him, fingers moving fast.

He sighed. It was almost inaudible, but an unmistakable sigh. "This wall," pointing. "Leads to the boys' fresher. It avoids dealing with guards outside."

"It's a wall," I pointed out, hoping it would be obvious that walls were not in general the most permeable of things. It's not like we could just walk through it. I mean, normally Nat would know this, but...

He nodded. Then he pulled a burner from his pocket. This was in addition to the burner he was carrying in the other hand. This burner was different, very small, and...

And he put it in cutting mode and started cutting the ceramite window. I blinked, and realized this was not really a burner as such, but another of those specialized tools one had only heard about.

He caught the ceramite as it fell. And that's when all hell broke lose.

Trippingly into Hell

THERE WAS A SCREAM. I SAW NAT DROP THE CERAMITE FRAG-ment, kind of tossing it to the side, in the Good Man's closet, and dive through the opening into what I presumed was the young men's fresher. I followed, burners drawn.

Okay, there is a problem with going traipsing about in the innards of a house without following the normal ways of getting between rooms. The main one is that people don't expect you. When the room you're breaking into is a fresher, there is also a very strong danger that you'll catch someone in an unwary and vulnerable position.

In this case, we caught a young man I didn't recognize—not even by scanning back to all my memories of various Good Men's functions—in the middle of dressing. Or undressing. I wasn't sure which, since his shirt was off.

He was maybe fifteen, at that age when boys are all height and haven't started filling in with muscle nor, frankly, with much of anything else, all their energy going towards growing. His hair was brown and short, his eyes were some kind of dark green. An unremarkable young man. Unlike our lot, he wasn't tattooed all over, and for a moment, I thought we had the wrong person.

Nat was pointing a burner at him and appeared to be counting mentally.

The boy had stopped, shirt in hand, and was staring at Nat, and at the burner, alternately. My friend wasn't, at the best of times, the calmest person in the world. I'd once since him berserk in the middle of a fight and— Never mind. It hadn't been pretty. But right then, he was intent and pale, and looked like he just needed an excuse to shoot.

I realized the young man had screamed, as one would when one's fresher was broken into. And Nat had told him to shut up and pointed a burner at his head. I assumed he was now trying to listen for anyone who might have heard the boy scream. I listened too, and said, "There are people in that room. But no one running in. Either no one heard him—"

"Or they paid no attention," Nat said, relaxing a little. He looked at the young man, "Tom Sawyer?"

There was imperceptible nod of the head. "Yeah, but—"

"Don't scream. Don't act alarmed. We need you to come with us."

The young man blinked. As one would if a perfect stranger broke into one's fresher and demanded one accompany him. I wondered if this was Nat's brain not working properly, or if the military had broken his ability to understand people wouldn't naturally follow his orders. Was this really his plan? Hadn't he brought knock-out juice or something?

"We need you to come with us, you and our friends," I said, softly. "So we can keep you safe."

"Safe?" he said.

"You brought plague to Earth," I said. "Sooner or later people will turn on you."

My presence seemed to confuse the young man. He stared at me for a minute. "You're a woman," he said.

"Yeah, I said. In the flesh."

"I always thought—" He shook his head. "I thought it was a legend."

Nat made a sound. I wasn't sure what the sound was, but I remembered how Little Brother had reacted and his demands that I undress. I wasn't about to get caught up in the same sort of thing, not counting the fact that while Nat might have no personal interest in women, he still had ingrained chivalric training, and this could get really ugly, really fast. I remembered the curiosity I'd heard in the boys' thoughts, and a way to bypass all this occurred to me. Should have occurred to me earlier, except I really was not used to being heard by anyone but Kit. I mind-spoke, *I'm Athena Hera Sinistra, the daughter of patrician Sinistra. I don't have time to explain it to you, but I promise you that you're in more danger here than you'll be where we'll take you.*

Among other things, and I did my best not to let those thoughts out, because here he might get Nat to flip on him, and because in Jarl's hideout he would have a hard time hurting himself and others.

For a moment I thought it was only the other set of boys who could hear mind-talk, then I saw his eyes go really wide. *You can mind-talk. Sinistra. Like Captain Morgan.*

Not like Captain Morgan, I said before I thought about it. *That boy is a mess.*

I regretted it as soon as I said it, but weirdly, I could feel the boy calm down. *Yes,* he said. *He's Urrahn.* And then, *but I can't see what good it will do to go with you. We're in negotiations with the Good Man. He will—*

He's stringing you along. Most of his people are dying of a plague that seems to have been started by the virus you carried. He's keeping you here so he can analyze and use you to cure the others.

He said he'd give us land . . .

He doesn't have the power to give you anything. Earth is at war. The council of Good Men has no power to grant you safe landing space. And besides, you're not stupid. This last was a plunge into the unknown, but I couldn't think that someone who had been enhanced for intelligence, as these boys had been, or at least their originals, wouldn't have figured out that being infected with an odd virus as they landed wasn't a coincidence, and that it must mean something. *You know they infected you with this because they wanted to use you as biological weapons against Earth, not because they wanted space.*

Father— he said. It wasn't so much a rational argument, or an argument of any kind, more like an almost-prayer said under pressure. And then, rapidly, *you mean Morgan and his lot were sick too?*

Very, I said. *We barely pulled them through. And the people—the normal people, not of us—who caught this have another disease after, a . . . an inability to form platelets, that is, things that make the blood coagulate. People have died and are dying of this.*

He looked concerned. I had given him a corroborating point to what he knew was happening. *Here too,* he said. And then seemed to be in deep thought.

"What is going on?" Nat asked. "Were you mind-talking?"

"You know of mind-talk?"

He shrugged. "Family bioed to serve Good Man, remember. We can sort of . . . Luce and I. I kind of recognize the look. But not—"

"Anyone else? Yeah, they mind-talk everyone."

I was trying to figure out what *Urrahn* was, but this was not the time or the place. For whatever reason, Nat had not planned to have the boys actually controlled or brought back. I realized, surprised, that he'd never really expected to get this far. So it was just whether they believed me. The fact that I could mind-talk them might tip the scales, but I felt our argument was weak.

Hey, what is going on? A different mind-voice echoed, and a very young man, just on the threshold of puberty, said, putting his head in the door. He looked enough like Max when I'd first met him that it was disorienting. Nat made a really weird sound.

Tom Sawyer turned around. *Come here,* he said. Then he pitched his mental voice differently. I can't really explain it. It was the sort of thing like when you raise your real voice so it will reach farther. It was possible to do mentally, but it's almost impossible to explain. I'd done it when I was unavailingly calling Kit. *Christopher Robin? Can you come here?*

I kept the ideas from anywhere they could listen, but thought that at least they'd all be in the same place, and we could herd them at burner point. Maybe. I told Nat he'd called Christopher Robin. Nat was looking jumpy. I'll be honest, Nat when jumpy was only slightly more scary than Nat when not jumpy, but Nat when not jumpy lived on the edge of a berserker fit. So I didn't want him jumpy. I looked at Tom Sawyer. "Can we talk voice? My friend can't hear us."

He nodded, and when Max's little brother joined us, and then a young man who looked almost full grown, he said, "Tell them what you told me."

I told them what we were almost sure had been the real reason for sending them.

"And who are you?" asked the young man referred to as Christopher Robin, who had long brown hair, and facial hair.

"Athena Hera—"

"No, I mean, who are you? You told us the whole Earth is at war. Which side of the war are you on? What is going on?"

"Let me explain," Nat said. He put his burner away, probably because he looked faintly ridiculous holding it when we were talking to the boys as equals. And he proceeded to tell them the truth. Both what we thought the plague was and what we thought it would do—i.e., depopulate most of the world—and why he wanted them to come with us. "I don't know if you're in physical danger here," he told them frankly. "It's possible you're not. But on the other hand, as people die, things might get violent, and La Mancha was very seriously affected." I thought it was stupid to tell them this, but Christopher Robin and Tom Sawyer looked thoughtful. Then they both turned to John Carter, whom I was having trouble not thinking of as "Little Max."

"Well?" Tom asked.

"It feels right," he said. "It feels like he's telling the truth."

"Feels?" I said.

"John can feel when people are telling the truth. His... mind-talk is stronger than the rest of ours; that's why he heard you and me talk."

There was a long silence. Then Christopher Robin said, "Excuse us a minute."

He pulled the others, not out of the room, but to an opposite corner. I caught *If what they think is true, the Earth—* And then *Voice. She can hear us.*

Followed by whispers. I took the opportunity to turn to Nat. "That was your plan? Is that all the plan you had? If I couldn't have mind-talked him, it would have ended badly."

He looked at me. His face was impassive but his eyes looked scared. "I had a plan. I just hit the point at which I should execute it, and I couldn't remember it. It was like hitting a wall. I need a dose of meds. I didn't bring them with me. I meant to."

I felt a cold finger down my spine. Oh, this was not good.

The boys came back. "We will go with you."

"If it were done," said Christopher Robin, "it were better it were done quickly."

"I don't think Macbeth is precisely the best augur at this point," I said.

You know Shakespeare, John said, delighted. *None of the adults here do.*

Some of us do. Come on, I said.

We started to retreat through the Good Man's closet and into his room. Which is when his door flung open and three goons with burners came running in.

There was the sound of others behind them, of more and more of them massing in. They sounded distinctive because the protective forces of Good Men mostly wore dimatough. Dimatough suits, dimatough boots, dimatough—

Dimatough resists burner fire, even on cutting. You can hit the men, sure, but you have to hit in the space between neck and suit, where the helmet was not actually joined to the armor. It was a difficult hit, but could be done if absolutely needed. Just not done fast enough to catch all of them.

Mentally I screamed at the boys, *run, run, run, run,* and with my voice, I yelled at Nat, "Take them back."

Nat hesitated, then turned around, a snarl caught on his lips. "Like hell I'll go and leave you to die."

"No, no, no." I physically shoved him. "Go, I'm right behind you. I'll be right behind you."

I was in my field of experience here. Nat, being the child of Good Men's servitors, probably never had to fight actual guards of the Good Men.

There was a reason that the residence guards, the palace sentinels, wore dimatough. There was a reason that operatives, field forces, and the Good Men's legendary and horrible Scrubbers didn't.

The dimatough armor has two weak points. It's not very good for mobility. And you will trip if there is anything at all on the floor. In which case, all these men coming towards us were more of a liability to each other than a threat to us. I stepped back, facing backwards. What I really wanted was a nice bottle of ball bearings. Why was there never one around when needed?

I kept my eye on the goons. More and more kept coming through the door, backing us up towards the Good Man's bathroom. They weren't firing. They couldn't fire. I realized they were afraid to hit the young men. I wasn't absolutely sure why they wanted the young men alive, but I suspected something like bargaining with the Mules. Surely it wasn't because they'd developed any affection for the young ones. I'd been raised by one of them, and I knew what the Mules here had been doing to their own younger clones for generations. Even supposing that the ones who'd left were marginally saner—at least Jarl believed so—during their rule as biolords they'd all proven they were branches of the same rotten tree.

Still, it handicapped them. If I could sow confusion, we could escape.

I said a silent prayer to gods I didn't believe in and turned to make broomer signs at Nat. They were complex, since the situation wasn't often encountered on the air and on brooms, but I told him, *Cut through the wall, don't try to get in vents.*

Cutting through the wall would get us to a more exposed position, and it might be difficult for Nat to make his way, but now that I knew where we'd been, I had a good enough sense of direction to guide us. And it was hard to trap us and cut us out with burners.

Nat didn't argue, which was also a surprise, as my friend had never taken orders easily. While he was cutting the wall, one of the few walls without appliances, and I was hoping it led to a hallway, I looked around for something, anything, to make the goons fall.

I found it in the cleaning area of the fresher, in the form of a pump. I didn't know if it pumped soap or shampoo or shaving cream, nor did I care. Those things built into the wall, though, held about a month's supply. I hoped it would be full up, as I aimed it at the marble floor just as the goons came running in.

Nat had made such quick work of the wall, he was shoving the boys through somewhere, even as the first goons hit the slick pavement and went flying, their feet going out from under them.

I repeated a mental encouragement to the boys of *run, run, run.* Then I dove after them, spraying more of the foamy stuff on the floor as I went.

We were in a utility closet, briefly, then Nat cut into a side corridor, and we ran past a woman who looked ill, and whose face was one large bruise. I wondered if she'd been beaten. But only briefly, because Nat cut into another wall.

"What?" I said.

"We can't take expected routes. They'll send people to block us."

"Do you have a clear sense of where we're going?"

He gave me a feral grin over his shoulder. "If I go wrong, correct me."

We progressed in the direction we'd come from, cutting through rooms, though I stopped Nat opening one wall because I could hear voices on the other side. In a seemingly erratic pattern, we now followed hallways, now broke into rooms. Two of the rooms had corpses in the beds, the visible parts of their skin looking bruised. I wondered if some battle had taken place.

We made it to the garage and took the grav well down. I was as shocked as anyone else that we weren't ambushed there. It meant they hadn't located our flyer. Which meant this area must be horribly depopulated for no one to have noticed the killings or the smell.

The boys shied at the corpses. We steered them clear of the pool of blood and less pleasant fluids, and towards the flyer.

As we got in, Nat punched some sort of preworked program on the controls.

"Thena," he said, looking exhausted. "Take over. If something unexpected happens, maneuver it. I can't—I can't—"

By the time we took off, he was unconscious, and by the time we got him into the shelter, he had a welter of bruises on his face and hands.

Care and Comfort

A QUICK CALL TO LUCE GOT ME A LONG STRING OF SWEARING. Not directed at me. "He should have prepared syringes in the flyer, Thena. Find them and give him two. It should hold him while I bring the doctor out. I told him—"

He'd turned the screen off without finishing the sentence, and disconnected the call after that, with some mumbling about finding whoever had let Nat go out.

I went back to Nat's flyer and looked. Kit joined me, and we found the syringes. We gave him two, but there was no reaction. "It's platelets, I presume. Probably cultured from his blood. It will delay symptoms, but it won't be enough, clearly."

"There were bruised people dead in La Mancha."

"That's this plague," Kit said. "I've been listening to the 'casts."

"He was acting confused."

"Probably having microstrokes. Be fair, his bruises are also small. He'll be all right for a while, but I hope the blood from the new young men pinpoints something, because there are millions in this position, if what the news says is true. Hundreds of millions. And most people don't even have the ability to culture platelets. And once the dysfunction is in, it's not just that you start bleeding at all times, and bruising with nothing, it's kind of like hemophilia. The wrong injury at the wrong time will kill

181

you. That's how Simon's wife died. He's very—Simon is worse than usual."

Um...I didn't even know what that meant, but I had not much time to think about it, because at that moment, Fuse came in. "It's Morgan," he said. "He ran off. He said he wouldn't stay here with them."

"Them?"

"The new arrivals. He said he'd get out of here if it killed him."

Kit looked at him. My curse rivaled Lucius's verbal brilliance. Yeah, I understood, this one was on me, because when it came to understanding Little Brother's mind, I was the local expert. "You see what the other boys did," I said. "I'll go find the idiot."

"No, no," Fuse said. He was twisting his hands together in panic. "He took Eris. Eris was asleep and he took her."

I grabbed Kit by the shoulder. "Stay," I said. "Find out what the other boys know. I get a feeling from everything that Laz knows Morgan pretty well, so see if you can get his help. I will find the insufferable brat and our daughter. Panic won't help. Besides, he's the one that should be panicking, because when I find him he's going to die screaming."

My first impulse was to get out of the building we were in and find my way to the single entrance to the refuge. There, I could wait for Morgan and catch him. There was only one entrance. I had a vague idea Kit had told me that Jarl had once gotten out by other means, but if I remembered clearly, that involved immersion in the river, and I didn't think even Morgan was crazy enough to take that route with an infant who wouldn't know how to hold her breath.

But I couldn't be sure. The problem, of course, is that Morgan probably had no idea at all how babies worked. He was one of the youngest of this group, unless I missed my guess, and that meant he might never have even seen babies.

I tried to tamp down images of his failing to support her neck, of her being already dead. They did no good. And while they might be true, they might not. He'd seen us hold the baby for all these days, and one thing these kids were, having been designed to be, was smart enough to realize we supported her neck. Of course, smart was tempered by crazy and dysfunctional, but really, worrying about it did nothing.

I hoped he wasn't about to try the river. His being my younger male clone, I kind of knew how his mind worked.

If it were me, what I'd do is hide someplace and wait until the other flyers came in. He probably understood we meant to have other flyers come in, if he hadn't actually overheard my conversation with Lucius. And I'd not swear he hadn't, at any level. After all, listening in and in general taking advantage of that sort of information was the one thing that had kept me alive in boarding schools, mental hospitals, and military academies.

So, he would hide, and probably do it well. Jarl's retreat had been a resort before he bought it. It had countless rooms, most of them in disrepair, inhabited only by memories and cobwebs.

Some had furniture, and some had machines, or parts of machines and parts of broken furniture. From what remained it looked like Jarl had used maybe ten of the rooms, and those had been outfitted with all the luxury possible at the end of the twenty-second century. The others had simply been closed.

By the time he had acquired this place, Jarl Ingemar was the leader of the biolords who governed all of the world, which is to say, he was in many ways the ruling monarch over all of Earth. Which meant that he didn't need to run the resort at a profit and he hadn't. He'd used it as his getaway, his hideout, possibly a place where this man, built in a test tube, raised in crèches, by total strangers, could pretend he was just a normal person. A normal person with a lot of room between himself and the rest of the world who knew what and who he was.

I knew that he had had his best friends: Alexander Sinistra, who would age into my Daddy Dearest, and Bartolomeu Dias, whom I'd known as Doc Bartolomeu, and who'd help bring Kit up, and I knew from certain letters we'd found that he'd sometimes entertained female company, but other than that the resort had been mostly empty, as it was now, and I suspected even in Jarl's time, a lot of it had been allowed to decay.

No matter how much I felt like screaming and taking off in search of the little bastard who'd taken my daughter and was doing who knew what to her, I was going to have no luck at all going through this place room by room. And that's if he hadn't gone outside. Outside, there were acres and acres of once-pseudo wilderness that had been going wild for the last few hundreds of years.

I'm not the calmest of women, and when something like this happens, when someone I love is threatened, my instinct is to run headlong at the problem, find the person causing it, and end him.

But finding him was going to be more than just running around and looking under every leaf. Eris would be marriageable age before I looked in all the nooks and crannies of this odd and mostly abandoned place.

The alternative...

I knew that Jarl Ingemar had been insane. Impossible not to be insane when you were raised by strangers who treated you as both scary and special. Impossible not to emerge scared. And then after that he'd survived being treated as a machine, taking power, orchestrating several wars, always with the danger of other biolords attacking him and taking everything he had, and even killing him. He wasn't sane. He was just marginally more functional than the others. But he was still paranoid. Which meant he would have bugs all over the place, and a control room where he could view everything.

When we'd been here last, we'd found that Jarl had left behind a cyborg made from a replica of his brain. The cyborg had Jarl's uploaded memories up to the time that Jarl had built it, and it had run the entire place. I was going to guess all the controls and leads for the resort came from that room. I was also going to guess that most of them still functioned. The last time we'd been here, that cyborg, who had conceived a misguided passion for me, had spent a considerable amount of time tracking us around and sending robots after me. And robots... could be useful, I realized.

Among the qualities engineered into Daddy Dearest, which were, therefore, by default, engineered into me, was an unerring sense when dealing with machinery. I could look at a machine, have a vague description of how it worked, and figure it out in no time. Okay, a little longer when the machinery was from Eden, where the tech had taken a completely different path after their colonization. But on Earth? On Earth I knew what most machinery components were supposed to do, and it was easy enough for me to figure out how to make machines work.

I ran to the room, then paused outside the door. I'm almost sure paranoia itself was not bioengineered into the Good Men, and yet, I too suffered from it. Some writer or other had once said that paranoia was a perfectly well-adjusted reaction to growing up in hell.

So I stopped outside the room and really listened, because

if Little Brother had run into this room, of all rooms, to hide, I wanted to be ready. But there was no sound of breathing. No sound of anything. In the room there was the broken, once liquid-filled container that had held the brain. I'd shot the brain. It had, believe it or not, been an act of mercy. The poor thing was so desperately lonely and insane, there alone for hundreds of years.

Now the shards of the container were still on the floor, and if I looked really closely I might see something that resembled desiccated brain fragments, but it took a lot to be spooked. It had been over a year, after all. Instead I marked all the receptors that were on the column in which the brain container had rested.

I would need screens to which to attach them. I could not, unlike a brain connected to a computer, simply receive the inputs without the use of sight.

I found most of what I needed in the adjoining room. Jarl must have used it as a store room for components he needed when he was building the cyborg and attaching it to his surveillance system.

It took me a couple of hours to attach the inputs from—well, all the inputs coming to the room into hologram projectors. I wasn't sure I could get sound also, but I could do without sound if I could see everywhere from here.

Just as I attached the last holo projector and turned them on, I heard a voice say, "Thena!"

I jumped and turned. Fuse was staring at me from the doorway. "Thena," he said again. "Have you found her?"

"No, I'm just connecting the stuff to the . . . to the cameras and stuff, so I can look."

He nodded. "Is she going to be all right?" He sounded more adult than he'd ever sounded, but he looked like a scared and lost child. I didn't know what to say. To the Fuse of old, I'd have said "Yeah, she'll be fine," because there was no point distressing poor Fuse with the complications of real life. And to a full adult, Kit, say, I'd have admitted I hoped so, and if she wasn't, Little Brother was going to regret the day he'd been decanted.

But before I could decide, Fuse added, "Anything I can do? Any way I can help?" And it was so adult that as I turned on the various projectors around the room and looked at the various projected views of the resort, I said, "What about the other boys? Is anyone watching them?"

"Kit. He's trying to get them to say what happened." Pause. "I know what happened."

"What?" I asked.

"The first group, Thor . . . they're the misfits. For . . . for whatever reason they're the ones the people who raised them treated really badly. They . . . worse than our fathers treated us, Thena. Laz mostly, though also the others, talked while they had fevers. It's not something that— They were treated really badly. When it was just us, and we were treated badly by our fathers, at least there were no other kids, no other people like us, who could treat us badly. But there are a hundred of them, Thena. A hundred, and maybe more. The ones who are the clones of the people aboard are treated like children, and everyone else has to curry favor. I think some of them were killed for annoying the Mules. And if they wanted anything at all, particularly any human attention, they had to ask the Mules for it, to beg, to make themselves seem like they deserved it.

"It wasn't easy for those who didn't have clones aboard. I don't remember things very clearly, but Kit and I talked, and Kit says the ones who stayed behind were left behind because there was something wrong with them, and I think part of that carried over when the Mules had their clones made.

"Perhaps it started that way. They thought these kids were dangerous, and perhaps bad, perhaps not to be trusted. But they hated Jarl. I'm not even sure why. Kit can't explain, and neither can the boys. So they hated Lazarus. Because he's one of the oldest, he started gathering around him all of those others they hated particularly. The other boys call them Urrahn. I'm not sure what it means. I think it's an invented language. Kit thinks it means something like damned. They were the first ones to be punished, the first ones to get in trouble."

I'd been scanning now one location, now another, a dozen locations a minute, and suddenly, near the gate, I caught a movement. Not on the ground, but in the leaves of a tree. It took some squinting to catch a hint of blue hair, a tattooed arm. My heart about stopped while I focused the hologram and tried to see clearer. Did he even have Eris, or had he killed her on purpose or by accident and dropped her somewhere, hoping we'd never find her? Then the arm shifted and I caught a sling and my daughter's round head protruding from it. I took a deep breath. "So they were afraid of the other kids?" I asked.

"Morgan was," Fuse said. "I think because he's the littlest. And these other boys have been used to lording it over them."

"Are they behaving like that? Hostile?"

"Mostly they're ignoring them, I think." Fuse caught my movement as I sharpened the picture so I could see more clearly. "You found them?" he asked.

I nodded. "Yes."

"Let's go get them," Fuse said.

I shook my head. "Not like that. He's my . . . younger clone, like Thor with him. In a way that means I know what he's likely to do. Does that make sense?"

He nodded.

"Well, if you startled me, when I was young, if I had a little one, I might have thrown her down so that I could run more easily."

It took a moment but then Fuse nodded. "I will go get her for you."

I shook my head. "I think this one I have to do on my own, Fuse. You go help Kit keep an eye on the other boys and Nat. How is Nat?" I couldn't believe it had taken me that long to think of my friend's welfare. I really was completely concentrated on my daughter.

"He's . . . conscious. He says he doesn't feel so good."

"Then help Kit keep an eye on him, or at least look after the boys, before another of them gets the idea that they can hide near the entrance and run away when someone in a flyer comes in, okay?"

Emotions I wasn't sure I understood warred in Fuse's features. After a while he said, "Yeah. I'll do that."

If it were with anyone else, I wouldn't trust it. If it were at any other time, I wouldn't trust it even from Fuse. But the thing was that I didn't have time to keep an eye on Fuse, to make sure he was doing what he said, or any of that. Right then I needed to go save my daughter.

I almost took the burners out of my pockets. Almost. I know I am a hothead, and I knew I couldn't afford to shoot, under any circumstances, certainly not when I might hurt my daughter. And truth be told, I also didn't want to hurt Morgan. He was a little bastard, in more ways than one, and probably would invent new ways to be a little bastard, but he was still young enough and probably malleable enough to have a choice to be destructive or productive. I'd made that choice when I was older than he. And I suspected Daddy Dearest had never got that choice.

So I didn't want to kill Little Brother. Or rather, I wanted to, but I couldn't. Not and live with myself.

I took the burners anyway. The thing is, they're such versatile tools. You can use them for all sorts of things, not just for shooting at bad guys. You can cut trees with them and . . . and other stuff. Like bad guys.

I grabbed some cables for the supply room. Before, when I'd climbed the trees here, I'd been without any sort of equipment. This time I intended to be prepared. As I rolled the cable, I realized I also needed gloves. In a couple of my escapades, while young, I'd cut my hands on cables thicker than these.

I dropped by my bedroom on the way out and collected my broomer gloves. Laz was waiting at the door as I came out, "Morgan doesn't mean anything bad," he said, and as I looked up he must have caught something in my eyes, because he added, "Don't kill him."

I might have muttered something. It might have been that killing was too good for the brat.

As I headed for the door, Laz pinched my sleeve. "No, listen. He is little. He was picked on. They said his original was a murdering lunatic and he would be too. They said—"

"Who said?"

"Father. The other gangs. Everyone."

I continued to walk towards the door. My daughter was in danger, and I was not about to wait to discuss the hardships experienced by her kidnapper. Just no. It very much and for sure wasn't happening.

"They did that in the twentieth century," I snarled. "And part of the twenty-first. They gave excuses to murderers. Hardship in childhood and all that. And then they wondered why their cities were abattoirs. No." I was about to shake him off at the door, when I caught something in his expression, something . . . "You're mind-talking him!"

Laz stopped, frozen, pale, shaking, as if I'd hit him or cut through him. He didn't say no. His mouth opened a little.

Damn. I hadn't counted on that.

"Did you tell him I know where he is?"

Laz shook his head. His voice trembled as he spoke, "I don't know where he is. I—I've been trying to convince him to come back."

"And he won't?"

A head shake.

But the problem here is that I couldn't trust Laz. Look, it wasn't taking into account their childhoods, but it sort of was. Their entire childhoods they'd only had each other. That was all they'd had, and all they could rely on. Which meant that groups, particularly what appeared to be a group of misfits consisting at least of Laz and Morgan and Thor, and possibly others, had bonded strongly. I wasn't stupid. Humans are tribal. He might wish nothing ill to befall me or my daughter, or my family, but he also would happily sacrifice us to save his "tribe" and those he considered of his own group. I'd heard much that suggested that from him, in his delirium. Which meant, hell and damnation, that I needed a portable holo projector to take with me so I could track the maniac should he try to leave.

Fortunately I'd seen a small one, which I attached to my arm with tape. And synchronizing it with the main ones was a matter of moments.

I could now see Baby Brother, sitting stock-still on the branch of the tree, holding my daughter. At least she was squirming, and I could see a chubby arm pumping. I suspected she was hungry and probably dirty.

"Ma'am," Laz said. "I promise you he didn't mean anything more than to protect himself. They told us we'd blown it, and we'd . . . we'd caused the mission to fail, and he's afraid of Father, and he—"

"Tell him," I snarled. "That if she's hurt, in any way, he doesn't have to worry about Father, because I will tear his arms and legs off and feed them to him, do you understand?"

In my vision, the little arm was moving, and Little Brother shifted restlessly. And I was out the door.

When we'd been here last, long ago, the path had been strewn with traps, and the only way for me to get from the entrance of the refuge to the entrance of the building was to take the path among the trees. At the top. Fortunately, the resort's once-gardens had grown wild enough to permit that.

I ran down the path, leaving Laz standing at the entrance.

When far enough from him, I clambered up a tree, and then moved by shimmying and jumping and sometimes crawling from branch to branch. I did it in such a way that I made the least noise possible. One had to assume Baby Brother, too, was enhanced.

I followed my sense of direction, deviating only when there wasn't a tree convenient. But I followed it around in a semi-circle. You see, Baby Brother was turned and probably watching intently in the direction of the path that came from the resort. Staying alert.

I came at him from behind from the other side of the tree. As I got closer, I caught a whiff of Eris, and thought at least I couldn't say he hadn't been punished. Closer still. He was holding Eris on a sling while he had a burner in his other hand. I calculated the chances that he would drop Eris if I grabbed the burner, then I decided that the sling would hold her well enough. Just in case, though, I snaked an arm around that way, while my other hand grabbed his burner and took it away.

He screamed and tried to claw at me.

I flung his burner down and got my daughter.

He came at me. There was no way I could kick him down without kicking him too far down. All the way down to the ground. Instead, I pulled him to me, confining him with my free arm. He was screaming, his scream caught and amplified by Eris, and I realized both of them were the full-throated, openmouthed screaming of infants, of grief given expression with no restraint and no compunction.

The way my arm was around him, he couldn't claw me, but he was trying to kick me. "Stop it," I said. "If you cause me to drop Eris, I will kill you."

"You're going to kill me anyway," he screamed.

"No, but I might," I realized that the noise had attracted my husband, and that through the noise, I hadn't heard him run out or clamber up the tree. He'd come up on the other side of Morgan, and his face was set in an expression of rage such as I'd never seen on it before. He pulled Morgan away from me, but he asked, "Is she all right?" as if Morgan were of no consequence.

"She's dirty, and probably hungry," I said. And then, "Don't kill him. In many ways he's little more than an infant, incapable of paying attention to anything but his own needs. No one has paid attention to them before, you know? He's a moral idiot."

"Moral idiot is right," Kit said. "And I bet you he'll only get worse."

"I didn't," I said, and saw something change in Kit's eyes. He was still murderously angry, but I didn't think he was going to wring Morgan's neck before we could all get to the ground. He got the sling, and I put it on, with Eris snuggled to me, which allowed me to climb down using both hands, and then I was on the ground, holding my smelly, screaming daughter, and I realized I was shaking.

Kit came down, holding Morgan immobilized. "Give me a cable," he said.

I hesitated and looked closely at Kit, because in that mood he might very well have decided the best thing to do with Morgan was to hang him high.

Except now the other boys had got here, three of them, the weirdly tattooed and the completely unmarred, all staring, fascinated, as if they'd never seen anything like this.

They elbowed each other, and stared, and Thor looked anguished, and Laz said, "Please," which told me they also expected Kit to summarily execute Morgan. But I'd caught his eye, and knew that's not what he meant.

He tied the cable around Morgan, in a not-terribly-strong position—he was never very good at tying people—but enough to hold him. Morgan collapsed to the ground, his knees folding under him, crying, "You can kill me," he said. "But I was only trying to take the baby to Father. I thought if he had a woman, a girl of our kind, he'd give me safety and protect me and give me honor." He paused a moment. "And ice cream."

It was pathetic. I'd done some horrible things in my time. But never for ice cream.

"No one is going to kill you," Kit said. "At least not yet and not like this. But we are going to have"—he paused—"a talk."

It was at that moment that the flyer arrived, carrying Dr. Dufort, another doctor I didn't know, a very worried Luce, and a pale, shaky-looking Simon.

I didn't stand in their way. Morgan had started to cry. I found myself curiously filled with mixed emotions about him. Make no mistake, the part of me that had been worried about Eris wanted to beat him till he stopped protesting. But the other part was worried. What kind of childhood had he had that led him to commit kidnapping for safety and ice cream? I noted the expression of the other boys, too: Tom, John, and Christopher looking vaguely puzzled and somewhat sickened. Laz looking guilty. Thor...I dove towards him and got the round play-doh-like circle out of his hand. "No booms," I said, in the tone I'd use for Fuse in the old days. Just on cue, Fuse showed up, took the lump from me and sighed. "There are things you can't solve by blowing everyone up, Thor. Come with me. They want to take your blood again."

Without seeming to, Fuse herded all the boys towards Dr. Dufort and they went into the building.

I was left with Eris and Morgan, who had his arms tied, but not his legs. He was still sobbing, full, openmouthed, snot-emitting sobs. Eris had joined in the fun. She had an excuse, being dirty and probably hungry. He had an excuse too, likely, being feral and completely devoid of moral sentiment.

And I had to deal with both problems. Fun. Conquering the desire to throw myself on the floor and start to howl—which might work to startle Morgan into silence, but probably wouldn't do anything for Eris's problems—I put my arm on Morgan's shoulder, and said, "Get up." I said it gently, as if I were talking to Eris. For a moment it looked like he understood it about as much as Eris did. Then he stopped bawling, his mouth still wide open, and turned tear-filled blue eyes to me, as though checking my mood and reaction.

I remembered this and felt a pang. I used to do that. And I remembered when. It was when someone had seen me actually be weak. I'd look at them to see if they would take advantage of it. Part of me wanted to console him and reassure him, but I was really careful not to let him guess those feelings. The problem with Morgan is that he truly was feral. I was sure he'd shown me his true vulnerability, but that was only a part of it. The most unpredictable animals in nature are the tiny ones, when they think they're about to be eaten. There is a reason people talk about a cornered rat, not cornered elephant or cornered lion. Morgan really was pathetic and lost. He really had been pushed around and treated with contempt and cruelty all his life. But what people and judicial systems in the ancient age failed to understand is that suffering doesn't make you noble or good. And being treated as a thing doesn't make you kind and nice and full of all that's good. What it makes you is a cornered rat, a trapped animal, amoral, not caring about anything but surviving.

I had no illusions about Little Brother. But I also knew it was possible to change. There was probably some caveat like "while you're young enough" before habits of despicable behavior set in. I cautioned myself as I thought this, that "young enough" was probably variable. I didn't know if Father had been redeemable by the age I'd met Kit. Some things I read, and some memories of Jarl's that Kit had acquired, had told me he might not have been. I'd been young enough, though, and I'd cared enough.

Sure, I'd fallen in love with Kit. But I thought that only happened after I started feeling I was letting him down. In the end, what had reached me was Kit's basic decency, his family's basic decency, and my understanding that my bad actions would hurt him.

I'm not claiming I'm as moral or as capable of discerning right from wrong as my husband. I'm not sure I'll ever be. But his example made me capable of faking it, of acting morally even if I couldn't sense right and wrong. I could think through it. And I'd learned not to hurt others who hadn't hurt me and that sometimes merely being human imposed obligations on you. Like caring for Eris. And perhaps, just perhaps, caring for Little Brother, who, after all, had never had anyone else's care.

I kept my face implacable, but I said, neutrally, "Come on now. *No* more drama."

He looked speculatively at me some more. "Are you going to punish me?"

I tilted my head. "I'm going to make you take a shower. And eat. And then I'm going to let Kit talk to you."

He tried to run. I grabbed him by the back of the ties around him. They were too loose to actually leave him alone and tied up. He'd have wriggled out of them. It was amazing how Kit didn't learn, sometimes. Granted, telling your husband he needs tutorials in tying up people might be a little embarrassing.

However, my pulling Morgan didn't give him a chance to wriggle out of his bonds. He stumbled after me, until we got to the building, where I met Laz coming out from somewhere inside, holding a piece of fabric to his finger. I said "Laz?" And he shook his head. "Just blood drawing," he said. "Your husband has asked

Dr. Dufort to draw twice as much, so that we could... So that he could run comparisons. He's also taking Mr. Remy's blood."

I was fairly sure that Nat had a military title, not Mr. Remy. But I didn't say anything, because I suspected no one had told the boys. After the coup Morgan had tried to pull with Eris, I wasn't sure I'd trust them with the idea Nat was important, either. Not while he was ill and semi-helpless.

I can't say I was absolutely sure of Laz's moral compass, but I was sure, from what I'd heard when he couldn't possibly have been controlling his thoughts and actions, that he would do anything to protect the younger clones, particularly whoever counted as Urrahn. So, I shoved Morgan at him. "Get him washed and fed. I'm going to take care of my daughter. Oh, and don't let him go anywhere. He'll get hurt bad if he tries. Next time I might not be able to prevent Kit from killing him."

Laz's eyes grew really big, but he nodded and put his hand on Morgan's shoulder, neatly foiling Morgan's attempt at evasion in a way that indicated he was wise to Little Brother's tricks.

I walked to my room, passing a small room where Simon appeared to be on a call on his portable link. At least I hoped so; otherwise my friend had picked up the disturbing habit of screaming at his own finger. Which would be a real bummer when he was trying to be the high and mighty Emperor Julien.

As I passed he was yelling, "No, come here. I'll give you the coordinates. Kit—No, wait, your DNA might let you in, but if not, Kit will. Yes, we have medicine, we—"

I was somewhat curious as to whom he was inviting here, but not so curious that I would forego changing my very stinky daughter, or feeding her. Her screams had acquired the ragged quality of a baby who has become hoarse from crying, and besides the fact that I really didn't want to listen to them, there was also the fact I didn't like seeing her suffering.

Call it instinct. Call it insanity. Call it maternal love. I did not want to see Eris suffer any more than I wanted to see Kit suffer. She was small and helpless and mine to take care of.

I ended up bathing her too, in the little fresher that had once been a hotel room fresher, and which Kit and I had been sharing. This meant, in practicality, stripping and getting in with her, since there was no baby appliance in the place. I used water, because there was lots of it, and it came out beautifully warm.

In Eden, where water was the most expensive of commodities, and where the currency was based on the unit of water used by a household per day, I had to be careful of water. And on the *Cathouse*, where our water was drastically limited, I had to be a miser about it. I would enjoy it here. Even if it was the only enjoyable thing.

Eris stopped crying under the water, and looked faintly puzzled when I rubbed her all over with gel soap. We emerged from the experience clean and nice smelling, and for a change, I was able to get a diaper on her before she started peeing. Possibly because she was bordering on dehydrated. At least unless Kit had fed her just before she was kidnapped.

I threw a shift on, one of those we'd found in storage here. It was a very soft material similar to towels. That and its generic simplicity and white color made me suspect it had been designed to cover up women undergoing some sort of beauty treatment, or relaxing experience that involved bathing. That was fine. It was very comfortable, even if I had to shift it around my shoulders and wear a size too big to be able to nurse Eris.

Simon came in while I was nursing Eris.

Babies are like cats. If you disturb them while enjoying their food, they won't growl or give another warning, like cats do. Instead, they follow you suspiciously, with their eyes, as if afraid you're there to steal their sustenance.

She could have saved her suspicions. If anyone had told me, even the last I'd seen him, that Simon St. Cyr could walk into a room where one of my tits was visible, and not stare at it, I'd have thought the person was crazy.

But Simon didn't do more than glance at me, before setting about walking up and down the side of the room, between bed and fresher. He straightened a print of Sea York on the wall. He picked up my boots from the floor and set them, neatly, side by side, in front of the fresher door. He picked up the coverlet on Eris's improvised bassinet, folded it in squares, and set it at the foot of the bed.

"I really loved her, you know?" he said.

I said, "I'm sorry. I was told. I never got to see her."

He pushed on one the rings that glimmered on his hand. A holo came up. It was a beautiful redhead, with pale, even skin and a sweet, gentle gaze. Simon made a sound that was neither sniffle nor sigh but could be confused with both. "Yolande started out as just, you know, a trophy wife. But she was so kind, Athena. And so nice."

I didn't say anything. From a sometime lover of mine, having fallen in love with someone for their sweetness seemed odd. Then again, I had fallen in love with Kit for his unswerving rectitude, his honor, and I didn't think Simon could even spell rectitude. As for honor . . . well, none of us had got any instruction in such things. We all did the best we could.

"I'm very sorry," I said. "I'd hoped you were happy."

"I was," he said. And again there was that sniffle-sigh. "I don't know if I'll ever be again, but I think Yolande would want me to save people . . . normal people. People like us. She believed in me, you know. She believed in my devotion to the people of Liberte. Oh, she must have had some inkling that I wasn't what I seemed to be. Impossible to live with me and not guess. But she still believed in me. In who I really am. In my essential goodness."

Did Simon have essential goodness? And who was I to question that?

He sighed again, then stopped pacing, looking at me. "I thought I loved Zen, you know?"

"I know," I said. I'd seen what I thought were the beginnings of a relationship between Simon and Kit's clone-sister before we'd left Earth. At the time I'd suspected that was why Zenobia Sienna wanted to stay on Earth. Now— Well, things hadn't gone as expected and I wasn't so sure why.

"I didn't, you know. I just thought I did because she was so pretty, and everyone who saw us together was jealous of me."

Did Simon care if other people envied him? The things you don't know about your friends.

"But she fell in love with my . . . friend Alexis Brisbois, who is by far the better man. I was actually happy at their wedding." He swung around suddenly. "Alexis is ill. Zen called me to say she was flying him to Liberte for treatment, but I asked her to bring him here."

I opened my mouth to ask if this was a good idea. Unlike Kit, Zen has no modifications, and there was no reason she couldn't take her husband to a normal hospital, in a normal city or seacity. Before I could form words, Simon lifted his hand to stop me. "No, he said. She can't be seen anywhere near Liberte.

Too many people knew of her involvement with me—with the Good Man Simon Saint Cyr. And Alexis, well, he was my chief of security. Of the secret police, you understand. Yes, there were some modifications done to his looks. Not many, because he already— Ah, it doesn't matter. There were modifications done to his looks, but not enough, and he's probably—by DNA—on a lot of wanted lists, both in Liberte and other places."

I didn't ask him why on a lot of wanted lists. I didn't need to have it spelled out for me that chief of secret police, even for Simon's regime, which might not have been as bad as the normal Good Man, could spell a lot of deaths and worse on his conscience.

"So they will come here," Simon said. It wasn't a question, and it got my hackles up, though I suppose it shouldn't have.

"While you were gone," Simon said. "Your husband found a laboratory, outfitted by Jarl, and most of it is still state of the art, and some only Kit probably knows how to use."

Found or remembered? It didn't bear asking Kit. He was convinced I'd leave him if I found any particle of Jarl in him. It was a stupid belief, but one he'd hold on to, no matter what I told him.

"Kit says that her blood will be useful to analyze, too. She's just recovering from the cold, so at a useful phase. And Alexis is—" He was folding and refolding Eris's blanket. I switched Eris to my other breast and she resumed suckling, greedily.

Simon sighed. "I've called Alexis my brother most of my life. There is a reason for this."

I raised my eyebrows. If he was Simon's clone, it would explain why he'd had his appearance altered before.

"Oh, he's not genetically, *ma petite*. But he was made by Dr. Dufort, as I was. We all considered ourselves brothers, and him, our father. And Alexis protected me, as an older brother would." He sounded momentarily wishful. "And corrected me and forced me to behave when needed, too." I thought he missed external breaks, since he had so few internal ones. "But he is designed, you see. Engineered. Not a...a biolord, a Mule. Not one of us. Perhaps a Mule in the ancient sense of being genetically created, but still not really, since he sired a daughter. Do you understand?"

I shook my head. At his best, Simon was annoyingly eloquent. At his worst, he was incomprehensible, like a human simulator machine stuck on "ebullient babble."

"Your husband, *ma petite*, Monsieur, ah, Sinistra," he betrayed the little hesitation before remembering that in Kit's culture men took their wives' names. "He thinks that it would help to have someone artificially constructed who is not designed to our specifications and whose original wasn't around since the time of the Mules. He found it curious that Alexis caught the platelet problem after his virus."

I remembered with a pang that I hadn't asked about Nat. I felt like I was trying to coordinate three lives at once. I was a bad friend. "How is Nat?"

Simon looked shocked at my question. The supreme and natural egotist, he thought that of course everyone else was secondary to his own story. Maybe that too was the result of being raised feral or close to it. "Fine, fine." He frowned. "Or maybe not so fine." He looked like he was trying to remember some far away, unimportant detail. "Lucius said something about cryogenics."

"What?"

"To slow the disease," Simon said. "Should we not find a cure soon."

I glared at him.

He turned his hands palm out. "Kit says it will work. Do not fixate me with the death-ray eyes. Lucius says it might be the best solution."

Men. They're the most romantic and emotional creatures in the world. Until they aren't. I had the impression the three of them—or possibly four, since Nat was also quite likely to have joined in—discussing freezing Nat, with the complete detachment of . . . of robots. Are we sure men and women are one species? An ancient author I used to read, almost certainly the one who wrote the character Lazarus Long, asked that question. He thought they might very well be symbionts. I thought he had been trying to make a joke, but I wondered.

"I just wanted you to know. Kit said to prepare one of the rooms down the hallway. I don't think they will be any more trouble. Unless, of course, we have to freeze Alexis," he said, as though it were the most natural thing in the world, then pivoted on his heel and left.

Eris had fallen asleep, and as soon as I put my tit away, Laz appeared in the doorway. It was as though he had been waiting till I was decent. And perhaps he had. I laid Eris in her bassinet and said, "Yes."

He dragged Morgan in.

Little Brother was still a pitiful object, but he was a clean pitiful object, with his blue hair looking shiny and combed, and with fresh clothes on. What they'd put on him was obviously a workman's outfit. It had the advantage of hiding all his tattoos.

As I looked at them, interposing myself between them and the bassinet, Laz said, "It's all right. I told him what he did wrong."

I looked at Baby Brother. I think he was trying to look contrite. His face was inclined, so all I saw was the blue hair. I waited. He looked up. The blue eyes were mutinous. "Sure," I said. "And did he understand?"

"Yes," Laz said. "I took him to your husband first, but he's very busy in the lab and he said to bring him to you."

"Oh, did he?" It didn't surprise me at all. Kit was always the same whether what he was pursuing was a new route to the powertrees or an unknown virus with strange effects. "Fine. You may go. You may leave me with Morgan."

Laz hesitated. He backed away two steps. I waved him out the door. He turned and walked to the door, then turned again, and stared at me. I shook my hand at him, the fingers loose, like someone frightening chickens. "Shoo, go."

He went, but I got the impression he was afraid of leaving me alone with Morgan, or maybe with Morgan and Eris. I understood it, too. I'd have been afraid of leaving me alone and unsupervised with anyone who didn't know him. What Laz failed to comprehend was that Morgan and I were built on the same substrate, had the same general nature. Even our upbringings weren't that much different. All right. I'd benefited from having a mother, at least for the first six years of my life. But unless I was much mistaken in Laz, he'd supplied that kind of nurturing to the young ones, to the best of his ability.

"Sit," I told Baby Brother.

He sat on the edge of the bed. His movements were the wary actions of an animal, stepping sideways, sidling, always keeping an eye on me, as though I might at any minute pounce and do something unimaginably horrible to him. Which was true in a way. I was going to make him think about his actions, something I suspected he hated as much as I did.

"Did you understand why you did wrong?"

The eyes evaluated me, while the head did a slow up and down.

"Really? What was it?"

"Laz says kidnapping people is wrong. He says babies are people. He says if you kidnapped them in the old days, someone would put you in prison for a long time. And he says now, and with us having no one to defend us on Earth, or even to look for us, and Father not caring what happens to us if we don't get him a place to colonize for our people, he says, Laz says, that you'll just kill us. He says you and your husband both are quite capable of killing people. He says that Thor's—Fuse, you call him, he says he's told him you've killed people before."

This was all said in a big rush, and I looked up at the ceiling for a moment, wondering why Fuse had chosen to give the impression we were mass murderers. Perhaps it was his intention to scare Morgan out of doing something stupid. Or perhaps he simply said what crossed his mind. It was hard these days to know which Fuse was running the body: the addled, severe trauma victim, or the recovering responsible adult.

"But that's not why it's wrong. It's just why it might get you killed," I said. And made a mental note that Laz himself might be unclear on the idea of "this is wrong" and "this will hurt you." The latter form was usually the one very young children understood, and I thought emotionally all of the boys were very young. Learning anything past that, on the emotional level, required the example of adults, and they hadn't had that. They hadn't even had the example of normal, functioning humans as most humans had been throughout history. "It's wrong because when people do something good for you, they don't deserve to be paid with bad. Because people don't live in isolation. Even in . . . where you grew up, you needed friends and—"

He frowned, looking at me. "Laz protected me and Thor and Clark."

"So, would it have been all right for you to betray Laz?"

He looked at me. I had the impression he was mulling something deep and dark, not sure what answer he should give me. I heard shuffling outside the door and had the sudden impression that all other five young men from the *Je Reviens* were all listening. I didn't know why, but I waited for Morgan's answer.

He sighed. "I don't know. I don't know if I could survive without Laz. But if it were me or him . . ."

"Yeah, but see," I said, floundering wildly. I wasn't sure how to explain it. After all, my incentive for realizing that it wasn't all just me, and all about saving myself with no regard for whom I might hurt or how, was that I had cared for Kit's family. But no, that wasn't true. At first my incentive for changing couldn't have been loving Kit, because I hadn't even particularly liked him. It was just that... I looked through my mind, in retrospect, trying to figure out why I'd changed. I decided part of it was all the six months that Kit had spent arguing with me and convincing me there was more to life than simply Athena getting her way.

But I wasn't Kit. While I'd grown up in a better environment than these young men—it would have been really hard to grow up in a worse one—and had been around normal or at least decent human beings, my main influence and instructor was my father, a Mule like those who had raised the boys, but one who had been left behind because he couldn't be trusted in an enclosed space with normal, non-enhanced beings. But Kit had been raised by a normal family, and he'd been instructed in how things worked and what you had to do to live like a decent human being. I'd never had that. I'd acquired it through being around Kit. And I didn't know if I could explain it to Morgan or the other boys. And I had to, because Nat might be dying, and apparently so was Zen's husband, whoever that might be, and Kit was doing really important work in the lab and— And we couldn't afford for these feral and amoral children to do something heinous like what Morgan had done this morning.

How had I ended up stuck with the care of the children? Yes, I knew it was the traditional thing for women, but why me? I wasn't a traditional woman. I wasn't cut out to be a mother. Luce had said how much time he spent watching children. Of course, those were small children. It was quite different to look after teenagers, or to make almost-men understand right and wrong. If the things I'd heard from all the stories and all the sensies were true, the only way to talk morals into not-quite men was with something heavy and hard applied repeatedly to the skull.

On the other hand, after I'd lost Eris today, I wasn't about to let her out of my sight. And Kit was doing things in the lab that I couldn't do, and no matter how much Luce might or might not know how to look after juvenile humans, he was with Nat. Nat's condition had worried me, and I couldn't tell myself he wasn't going to die of this. And if it were Kit dying, I wouldn't want to leave him. Even if I talked brave talk about putting him in deep freeze until a cure could be found.

So, curse it all, it was all up to me, talking some moral sense into these particular feral juveniles.

We couldn't afford for another of them to injure us. And I didn't want them to injure themselves either. Their innocence wasn't the absence of evil, but they were still innocent. They had no idea what the Earth was nor what could happen to them. And some things could happen to them, some even deserved, that were worse than even what they'd grown up with.

I took a deep breath. "You see, the thing is exactly that. Laz protects you and you owe him loyalty. If you don't respond to his protection with loyalty, not only will he not be able to protect you, but no one will want to, because they can't trust you. This is why it's wrong to betray those who are good to you, do you understand?"

He blinked at me, looking exactly like I imagined I did while working difficult math problems in my head. "Right," he said, as if he'd understood part of the problem. "But what about the baby? It's not like she can do much, or like you have much invested in her. You could always make another."

I suddenly realized two things: that this boy, possibly that all the boys from the *Je Reviens*, had grown up being measured by that metric. "What do I have invested in this child?" reduced them to the level of objects. Possibly objects that improved with time, but still objects.

And that he'd thought he was doing something entirely forgivable, a minor transgression. She wasn't worth that much to me, I could always make another, and the Mules in the ship would pay good money to be able to study her, if not grow her. She was the key to their being able to have women and genetic descendants and populating the Earth they were in the process of conquering. In fact, she probably would be worth more to them as a dissection object, and as tissues to keep frozen and be studied, than as a living human being, much less a child to be loved and taken care of.

For a moment the back of my throat closed with a bolus of horror and anger so great that I couldn't express it. If I moved, if I gave it a chance, I was going to strangle this feral non-human. And then the others like him.

I sensed the other boys outside the door listening.

The thing was, it wasn't their fault they were feral. And yeah, some of them might not be redeemable, but a lot of them would be. They were young enough. I'd read things from back in the twentieth century and then again during the war between the landstates and the seacities, of children raised as mercenaries, taught to do all sorts of horrible and despicable things. Even they—most of them—had been redeemed and taught to live like normal people.

I sucked in air through my nose, let it out through my mouth. Here's the thing. They'd never be like Kit or like other people I periodically met, who'd had real families, with real love. Those people seemed to know what right and wrong were instinctively. But like me, they could pretend. They could try. They could do their best. And most of them would pass. And sometimes, when the decision was murky, they might be better than the normal people. Why? Because people who hadn't ever had to think about what was right and wrong, what was good and what was evil, could be tricked with things like the idea of greater good, which could lead to all sorts of evil. While it was admirable to sacrifice yourself for your friends, it was the purest evil to sacrifice one of your friends for the rest of your friends, or even for the whole world. The balance hung on a knife-edge that other people often failed to see. At least Morgan had grown with the idea of sacrificing whomever and whatever to survive. He could be taught, mentally, what was wrong and why. I hoped. Oh, hell, Kit had promised to give them the talk. Why was I having to do it?

I realized Morgan's gaze was on my face, his eyes very wide. And there was something to the way he sat, the foot farthest from me slightly extended, as if he intended to land on it and run to safety out the door. My face must be very threatening indeed.

"No," I told him, and took a deep breath. "Babies are not disposable. It's not a matter of making another one. My daughter is not just an object I could discard and start again."

"Why not?" despite his obvious fear, he sounded somewhat impatient. He sounded like I was making no sense. At the back of his somewhat variable teen voice was the complaint of the toddler, "WHY?"

I took a deep breath, "You know what I told you, before? That if you kill those who are good to you and protect you, there is no one else who'll step up to protect you?"

He nodded, once, curtly.

"Right. I figure that's how humans started to band up. I don't know if you know this, because I don't know if you had to study anything besides fiction—"

"We had things we needed to read," he cut in. "History and culture and languages and *stuff*. About what happened on Earth before even Father was made. As if it mattered."

"Only a little," I said. "Most of that stuff is how you find out where you came from, and what other humans have done before you, and what has been tried and failed." I saw him opening his mouth, and barreled on, very fast. "Humans in nature are not isolated creatures. We are related to the great apes of Earth, and they're all social creatures. They move in bands, not alone. If you find a lonely one, he's usually dangerous. An outcast. And he's short-lived because everything else can kill him.

"Look, I think at first it started because if you look after other people, they'll look after you. You're not so strong, so infallible, that you'll never need help. You can fall, break a leg, get sick. You can be weak, and then you'll need someone to look after you. So back when our ancestors were still animals, we banded together."

"But my ancestors were never animals. I was made in a lab."

I put my hand out. He almost ran. He started to move, but I put my hand, palm up, on his leg. "So was I. Look at my hand. Five digits. Goes back to the first life on Earth. Look at the opposable thumb human ancestors acquired probably through random mutation." Yes, I knew the theories of a creator perhaps acting through evolution, or perhaps putting his own thumb on the scale, but I'd be damned if I was going to get in those waters. I'd never been taught to be religious, and I understood that idea even less than all the rest. "We were made in labs, from human genes. We're made a little better, a little faster, a little smarter. Not enough to make any difference. We are still humans. And many humans on Earth are close to what we are, because their ancestors were enhanced, and it's inheritable. You're human. Your impulses, your thoughts are human.

"Like other humans you want to have a group, because that instinctively feels safer. And it is. And that means you have to respect those who take care of you, and you have to be loyal in return. But here's the other part, you have to look after those who are weaker than you. You have to. Partly because all babies are much weaker. And babies are the only hope of the human societies."

"What? Why?"

"Because we get old. Yes, I know, we personally get old slower than most normally born people. And if you use cloned body parts and other devices you can live a very long time." I'd be damned if I explained to him about the Good Men who'd stayed behind using their own clones, raised like their children, as whole-body donors to keep themselves alive. "But you will get old. You will get weak. You will get vulnerable. And the only thing that will keep you alive then is if those people who were once weak and whom you looked after now look after you. Babies are the ultimate in that. They start out very weak. But they grow. In twenty years Eris will be a full-grown woman and able to help me and her brother, and to protect us. As for replacing her? Not done. In the whole of humanity, even with cloning, there have never been two humans exactly alike, even those born of the same egg and the same sperm. You grow differently, even before you are born. And this too is instinctive: In a human society, the more variety you have, the better. As she is." I gave a look at Eris in her bassinet, sleeping on her belly, with an arm extended high above her head. "She's already unique. And she might have some ability that will save the world, or at least some people. You can't know. You can't know till she grows up, but it's worth a bet. It's why from the oldest antiquity, people protected children and mourned for them when they died. Because they are chances. Chances that they'll be the ones who survive and help others.

"I think that's why adults have an attachment to children, a need to protect them. We know at gut level that they might save us some day, one way or another."

He was shaking his head violently side to side. I swear there was a repressed sob from outside the door. I couldn't understand—

"They never wanted us to look after them, did they?" Morgan asked. And now his voice was a complete wail. "The ones who are just like them, maybe, their own clones, but not us. And they didn't make us because they needed our help colonizing a new planet. No. They didn't do that. I know. They didn't care about us, if we were really young. The machines looked after us, and sometimes the older boys. But if an older boy killed a little, it just got him shouted at. They could make another. They only got mad if it was a half-grown boy, one who could take care of himself. Then they punished you for wasting resources." He yelled the last word, and I gave an instinctive glance at the bassinet, where my unfathomable daughter ignored the scream and slept on. "I didn't know— I don't know why they made us. It wasn't as their children, or in hope we'd save them in the future. Why was it?"

The other boys came in the door. Five of them. Two outrageously tattooed, though in the work garments most of that was hidden, three looking far more like normal teenagers, but with a tension about them, an expectancy one didn't see in many normal teenagers or, for that matter, many normal human beings. Their faces, at that moment, looked older than themselves. Set, serious. No, not so much old as timeless. Faces carved in granite surmounting the frail, whip-thin bodies of still-growing boys.

"It wasn't to send us down to plead for land, either," Laz said. His voice was hoarse, as if, were he just a little younger, he'd be wailing and crying like Morgan. "Because I've been looking around. I know we look like freaks of nature. Most of the people like us do," he did a head gesture towards the other three. "These guys are the freaks of nature among us and I never understood why they didn't tattoo or pierce. Well, that much. But we did to distinguish the tribes. And to look, to look intimidating. But if we'd been raised to serve as ambassadors to ask for a place on Earth, we'd have been told not to. We'd have been taken care of so we looked handsome, or at least well taken care of. We'd have been taught what to do when we got to Earth, or even whom to interact with."

"We never needed to look that scary." It was Christopher Robin. I looked at the three of them and realized that all were of relatively sturdy body build, compared to the other three. "We learned to defend ourselves in other ways than by looking like freaks." He looked at the other two standing with him, then at Morgan, and his lip curled up. "But he's right," he said, with a head gesture to us. "He could have been one of us anyway." His voice sounded both justifying, as if he had to explain why a freak like that could be right, and vaguely baffled. "He just chose to stay with the Urrahn and play guardian to them. I guess he wanted to be their king." Even as Laz opened his mouth, he pushed on, "But he's right. Even to us, no one ever told whom to approach or what to do. It was 'go to anyone and talk to them. They'll take you to someone who can give us land.' That is stupid. They've monitored transmissions. They know who has power to give land and who doesn't. They should have sent their most convincing people, and they should have sent them to a specific person. And if they didn't want to risk their most convincing people, why waste resources by sending so many of us, or by making so many of them they didn't care about? Send the most convincing ones, perhaps with a letter to those people they still knew, who still survived. Why didn't they do that?"

The silence hung for a moment. I was trying to think whether I should tell them what I'd started to suspect. The problem of ferals, even ferals raised by AIs, who have read the literature of mankind, was that they reacted unpredictably. They could bolt or attack me or whatever. I remembered the way they'd acted when I'd first come across them. There was no predicting them, because there were no rules to them. They'd been given none.

"And then we all got sick, really sick," Laz said in a tone of thinking and worry. "And now there's a plague, sweeping the Earth."

"We think that's why you were sent," I said, ready to jump and protect Eris, and beat them to death with their own heads if that's what it took. I didn't want to wantonly kill them, but if they threatened my daughter, they'd die.

They looked blankly at me. "We think you were infected with a virus before you left the *Je Reviens*," I said. "And that the virus had a payload that would carry another illness or something, which seems to kill normal people. So far it doesn't seem to kill those of us who are of the same genetic heritage as you or the masters of the *Je Reviens*, but it kills normal people. It must do something. They said it interferes with the mechanism that makes it possible for your blood to coagulate. But they don't know how or why we're spared. So they're studying it, Kit and Dr. Dufort."

Laz took a deep breath. "What happens if they don't find a solution?"

I shook my head. "I don't know," I said. "People will die. A lot of people."

He shook his head and took another deep breath, and despite it his voice was tiny. "No, not a lot of people, all the people. All those who aren't made or descended from the same stock we are. All...all the people of the Earth but maybe a hundred or less. That's why we were made. That's why so many of us. Oh, not their own clones, no. Those they treat like you treat her." He gestured with his chin to the bassinette. "Those are their children, really, whom they expect to grow and protect them when they're ill, and help them take over the empty Earth. Maybe help them find a way to reproduce naturally. But we? The rest of us? The damned? Those made after the people who were left behind on Earth because they were too dangerous to take aboard? We were made for one reason only: to come to Earth and infect it and cause everyone to die.

"They wouldn't risk themselves that way, and they thought because we're still children or at least juveniles, most people would look after us when we got really ill, and that would allow us to infect even more people, in a shorter time.

"We were created as weapons."

From out the Wilderness

I STARTED OPENING MY MOUTH TO ANSWER, THOUGH I COULDN'T deny any of his deductions, when there was a noise from outside, running feet, talk.

There are things I've learned, through my growing up in various institutions that Daddy Dearest thought could tame me, through my time in Eden, through my past adventures on Earth, and one of them is that no matter what fascinating events you're involved in, if there's that kind of sudden disruption, you'd better get on your feet and figure out what is going on, because otherwise it could kill you.

I jumped to the bassinet. The sling was folded next to it. I put it on and slipped Eris into it. She continued sleeping. I'd guess being kidnapped, or more likely crying herself hoarse, had been an exhausting experience. The young men were moving out the door, and I followed.

The hallway outside, between this room and the set of rooms where the young men and Fuse were staying, and where they'd put Nat, the hallway that ended in the laboratory where Kit and Dr. Dufort were working, was full of people.

My first impression was that an entire crowd had arrived.

It wasn't that, of course. The only people there were the ones who had been there before, except for two. But everyone who

209

could walk was in the hallway: Fuse, Luce and Simon—and Luce
took up more space than anyone should—and Kit and Dr. Dufort
and the six young men. The new arrivals were Zen and a large,
ugly man she was lowering onto one of those antigrav platforms
they use for transports in hospitals.

Zen looked haggard and scared, something I'd never thought
I'd see in the most carefully put together woman in existence. Like
Kit and Laz, she was a clone of Jarl Ingemar. Like me, the people
who built her had managed to shift her gender. And while my
husband was a handsome man, and Laz might be almost pretty,
were it not for the tattoos and disfigurations, I suspected—not to
say I was sure—some more genetic manipulation had gone into
Zenobia Sienna. Enough to make her look like a replica of the
central model in Botticelli's Birth of Venus. Add to that the sort
of poise and control that you don't often find in anyone, male or
female, and we'd heartily disliked each other at first sight. No,
change that. I'd heartily disliked her. I didn't know if for Zen
Sienna I'd ever rated as much as a mild annoyance. If I had to
guess, she only noticed me when absolutely necessary, and the
rest of the time didn't think of me at all.

Which was why both her obvious tiredness and fear, and the
solicitude with which she bent over this man, whispering something
to him, looking weirdly tender, made me stop cold. You know how
I said my husband was a handsome man. The same could be said
for most men I'd grown up with, most of them either the children
of Mules or of those servants selected and improved to serve those
Mules, even if they called themselves Good Men. Most of them
were at least handsome, even those like Simon whose designers had
striven to make them unremarkable. At least none of them was ugly.

The man that Zen was so solicitous about—had Simon said
it was her husband?—was frankly ugly. Brutal, rough features,
bluntly arranged and scarred at that, layered scars, as if he'd
made his living as a professional fighter for a long time. Well, if
he'd been Simon's chief of security, he would have, wouldn't he?
Granted, the bruises on his face, the same kind of spiderwebby,
spreading bruises Nat had, didn't help his looks. But the brutal
face, topped by unremarkable and badly cut brown hair, was a
face only a mother could love. He wore a white shirt, and rough
pants, the sort of clothing people often wore out in the territories, and his body looked as roughly hewn as his face, even if

I suppose attractive enough, in that it was muscular and large. There were spiderweb-like bruises on his exposed hands too. His feet were crammed into what looked like homemade moccasins.

And yet, Zen was looking at him like he was all her hope and delight, and this made me blink and stay very still, and gave Dr. Dufort a chance to take over and start steering the transport platform towards one of the empty rooms, the one next to where Nat was, which I presumed must have been arranged in advance while I was talking to the boys.

When Dr. Dufort came into view, the man on the platform looked up and said, "*Mon Pere,*" so low that it was almost inaudible.

It was the old French words for "father." More precisely "My father." If the small, dapper Dr. Dufort had sired that ill-begotten giant, some serious mutations were at play. But the doctor answered only by touching him gently on the shoulder and saying something back in French, very fast, something my scant knowledge of the patois of Liberte Seacity couldn't follow. I spoke the French of the French territories, of course, having had it forcibly taught to me at a very young age, but it was not the same. The seacities had first been founded as business consortiums, and many varieties of French, plus quite a bit of Glaish, had gone into making the everyday tongue of Liberte.

Zen said, "We didn't even know what was happening. We've been staying in the cabin. But when we went to town to sell—we must have caught it. I got sick first, and it was a bad cold, but Alexis—"

"Yes, yes," Dr. Dufort said. "We've got stuff that will slow down the progression. If you're lucky and don't get a bleed in your lungs or your brain, we can slow it down quite a lot and get a cure."

"And if you're not lucky?" Zen asked, her voice cutting. "What then? I'm not willing to risk this to luck."

"That," Dr. Dufort said, in a tone I thought older men must often take to Zen when she attempted to get masterful, "That might not be your choice, Madame."

Zen looked like she was going to say something else, but the man named Alexis said, "Zen." It was the one word, and barely audible. He looked and sounded like he was at the end of his strength, frankly. But the one word was enough. She said, in the tone of a petulant child, "I won't let them let you die."

Alexis sighed. "Let people help you, Zen. And help me. That's why we're here. They can't guarantee the outcome."

She put her hands on her hips. "Well, why not?" she asked, sounding much like me when I was on the verge of utterly losing it. "Why not?" She looked up at and down the hallway at Kit, who looked also exhausted and vaguely helpless in a way I couldn't define. "Kit, you have his memories. You have Jarl's memories. He was a biological genius. Why in hell can't you fix this?"

Kit blinked, "We know a great deal about it, but there are puzzles too. We need blood samples from both of you." He hesitated a minute. "Is it true you are..." he seemed to struggle for words, "pregnant?"

A wild red color climbed up from Zen's neck to suffuse her face. She pressed her lips together, then nodded.

"Your husband's?" my darling asked, with that complete lack of understanding of how things might sound to others that had made me almost kill him several times when we'd first met.

I saw Zen's mouth open, and instinctively interposed myself as an interpreter. "He means as opposed to lab-built."

Her mouth snapped shut. She did one of those things all women learn to do to hide when they are embarrassed, lifting a strand of hair off her face and pretending to pin it behind her head, with the rest of her hair. Pretending because from where I was, it was fairly obvious she couldn't find the hair clip with her blind, searching fingers and was merely playing for time. "Yes. Unplanned. We didn't know it could happen. We assumed it couldn't."

Which just goes to show you I wasn't the only idiot around. Though she had perhaps more justification, because unless something underhanded had gone on, the man she'd married wasn't one of us, and our original clones had been made specifically not to be cross-fertile with normal humans. Or really fertile with anyone.

Kit nodded. "Good. That will help." I wondered if he'd descended to a primitive state and meant to sacrifice children to avoid the plague, then decided that no, that wasn't Kit. On the other hand, it might very well be Jarl. I know, he was considered the best of the Mules, an idealist, a man of high ideals. But I'd met him—granted, in a rather insane condition—or what remained of him when his brain imprint had been superimposed on Kit's, and he had sometimes taken over Kit's body and his actions. I hadn't been overly fond of him. Like the other Mules, he'd displayed near-pathological arrogance, combined with a total lack of understanding of other humans. The mind of a century-old genius, but the emotional maturity of a twelve-year-old who thought he could gain the attentions of the woman who caught his eye with silly displays, many of them of cruelty and boasting.

I didn't know how much of Jarl remained in Kit. I knew that those remnants of personality that had come with the brain imprint, and that hadn't reverted when we'd managed to treat Kit, weren't enough to control my husband's actions. But were they enough to influence him?

On the other hand, Zen didn't look alarmed. She accompanied Dr. Dufort and Kit into the room, and moments later the men left with vials of blood in a carrier.

Five of the boys were huddled in the far corner of the hallway, talking. I wondered about what, and rather prayed—yeah, it's possible to pray when you're not too sure who or what you're praying to—than knew that my talk to them had done more good than harm.

A quick look told me the one who was missing was Max's clone. What was his name? Oh. John Carter.

Just because the thing with Morgan had taught me never to trust one of them again, because at least some of them were bioengineered to be good with mechanics, because I was and others must be, and because we now had a lot more of the flyers to steal, I went looking.

My powerful intellect allowed me to realize the voices coming from the room where Nat was might include the boy's. Hell, no, it did, because neither Nat nor Luce sounded that young.

I looked in at the door. The boy was standing at the foot of the bed, shifting his weight from one foot to the other the way people do when not absolutely sure of themselves.

Nat was sitting up, on a pile of pillows, and Luce was standing by, protectively holding his hand. For a moment I had a pang of panic. There was no way you could look at those two and not know they were a bonded couple, and primitive societies in general had had a poor opinion of such associations. Only—

Only John's discomfort seemed to be of another kind. He was saying, in the stilted tones of a child who is not sure how to address adults, "I know they treat their own clones better, so I think there must be some of that there. What Ath— the Sinistra woman says is protecting the young so they'll protect you. So I thought, since I am your clone—"

Luce let out breath, in a long exhalation. John shifted the weight of his feet. From the look of his shoulders, he was holding his hands together in front of his body, like a petitioner waiting a verdict.

Nat looked up at Luce, and something passed between them, some silent understanding. I'd swear they weren't mind-talking. At any rate, from what Nat had told me, they couldn't, or not really. Feelings, impressions, the occasional word. But they knew each other very well, and I realized they were consulting each other on the advisability of this. They also were probably not precisely in the frame of mind to make big decisions. Nat looked better than he had, and some of the bruising looked paler, or perhaps like the blood was being reabsorbed, but he was very pale, and looked wan, like he was on the verge of passing out. And Luce looked like he hadn't slept for days.

But Nat smiled at John, a smile that would probably have been impressive, had he been well, but was still quite warm. "We're in the middle of a war," he said. "We don't even have real quarters together, Luce and I, though I stay with him when I have leave. But if we can wrap this up, soon, we—"

"We plan to get a farm, in the territories," Luce said. "You'd be welcome to live with us. We figured we'd have a few children and a few dogs, and we could use another pair of arms." He hesitated, as if he meant something warmer but didn't know how to say it, then said, "You are my brother, I think, in a way. I had a little brother before. A . . . a clone, but I thought he was my brother. You are a lot like him. Which I think makes sense, right?"

"What happened to him?" John said.

"He died." Nat's face closed on the word, as though he'd lost some sort of strength.

"Oh."

"But we'll try to protect you," Luce said. "You're family. We'll do our best to keep you safe. That's what family does."

None of them had noticed me. I realized, on second thought, that two males as a bonded couple were the only kind of bonded couple this young man had ever seen. They hadn't seen a woman.

I walked away, past the boys huddled in some sort of conference. Whispers came from it, mostly names I didn't know.

Zen and Alexis weren't talking in their room. She was sitting on the bed, next to him. I wanted to ask about her being pregnant. I wanted to ask why this undistinguished-looking man, and I wanted to know what bound them. I couldn't. Zen and I had never been friends like that, and at any rate, she might not be able to tell me. I wouldn't be able to tell why I'd fallen in love with Kit. Why Kit?

I left them alone, and peeked into the lab. Dr. Dufort and Kit weren't talking in a foreign language but they might as well have been. It was all scientific jargon. And I didn't like the look on Kit's face. He looked worried, sure, but his features had also fallen in the expression that reminded me of the terrible time when Jarl had been fighting for control of Kit's body.

I tried to tell myself this was just because he was using Jarl's knowledge base.

In either case, I had a feeling I wasn't going to like this.

Hunting in the Dark

WE DIDN'T KEEP WATCH ON THE BOYS IN THE NEXT FEW DAYS.
Part of it was that we couldn't. Well, I suppose I could have
strapped Eris on and followed them around, but the idea seemed
counterproductive. We either trusted them or we didn't. After
the talk I'd had with them, if we didn't trust them, it would be
easier to kill them.

I explained to them, further, on the morning after, that we
were keeping them here not for our protection, but for theirs.
Whether they'd believed me, I couldn't tell. But we had to trust
them. Had to. The alternative was to keep them under lock and
key or do away with them.

I wasn't sure, precisely, that the best thing wouldn't be to kill
them painlessly. I wasn't sure they were redeemable or that they
would ever be self-sufficient, capable human beings. But when I
mentioned this to Kit, quietly, in our room, he thought I was
joking, which I suppose I was. The old Athena might have been
able to kill young men who'd not done her irreparable harm, but
the new one could not. And maybe that fact alone was reason
to have hope for the boys.

Even should their very inventive minds allow, the worst they
could do was leave the refuge and talk to the outside world.
Telling the outside world where we were was not a big problem.

217

Jarl's refuge had been hardened against unwanted entrance by a paranoid and very competent man. One or two people might get inside, but never enough to cause any big problems or be any great danger to us. So I didn't mind their getting out and giving away where we were. Or even their getting out and telling the world that the *Je Reviens* was in orbit and what they were doing. And surely other people would put two and two together.

The young men proved less trouble than I thought. At first they stayed close to the entrance of the hotel part of the resort, then they branched out. Four of them did, at least. Thor tended to follow Fuse around, which meant he spent a lot of time in the lab, fetching and carrying and doing whatever was needed, including fetching and carrying for Zen and her husband. So did John, who also spent time bothering the heck out of Luce with questions. Or reading. One of them had found him a gem reader, and I'd trip on a tall, gangly twelve-year-old, folded up in corners, the gem reader clutched to him and his eyes glued to it. At least he wasn't trouble.

Nat, hooked up to medicine to keep him from internal bleeds or hemorrhaging to death, had demanded and got—probably from their flyer—a link with holo capabilities.

I asked Luce what he was doing, in bed, seemingly working. Luce shrugged. "Intelligence. And trying to find out what is happening to his friends and underlings."

"How is the war going?"

Luce shrugged. "We are retrenching. That's what you call it when you retreat to relatively defensible places, so you don't get your few, pathetically few, healthy troops killed." His face was impassive but I had the idea that if he allowed it, he'd have cried with as much noise and fury as Morgan had done the day before.

"But aren't the other side suffering as many casualties? Weren't they infected too?"

His face worked. It looked like he was attempting to chew through something with his mouth closed. "We're most of us in seacities, and that's where we got infected. They have more of the still habitable parts of Europe, more sparsely populated. Oh, we have the territories, and as far as we can tell, all the people in the territories are still healthy. But if we bring them together, and to the seacities—" He was quiet a long while. "We have people like Nat, not quite as ill yet, whose illness is kept away with infusions of platelets created from their own blood. It won't work forever. You end up hooked to the medicine, all the time, or you die. Which is where Nat is. Nat is trying to coordinate those still well enough to fight. Trying to get them to strike, in small coordinated strikes. Trying to get them to keep the wolf at bay, but the wolf is gaining ground. He's monitoring, too, what happened to the other boys."

"And what happened? Why has no one else figured that the *Je Reviens* is in orbit? Unless they have?"

"Nat has access to channels I don't have. Ask him."

And I did later that day. "No, see," he said, "there were ten groups sent down, maybe twelve. The boys are only sure of five, but I've been tracking...we have decoders and stuff, okay. There are at least nine triangular ships found, so ten groups of boys must have landed, because Simon had the one that our set came in destroyed. But the thing is where they landed."

"You mean like they landed in the sea?"

He shook his head. "No, they all had some control. They all landed in populated areas. All of them. But most weren't traced. Only their ships."

"They died?"

He shrugged. "We only have two confirmed instances in which the boys were killed—their corpses found."

"Relatives of anyone we know?"

"Impossible to tell. Some seem to have landed in a really bad part of Shangri-la. Really bad. They were found dead and their corpses noted in police reports. No one else seems to know where they came from, but I'm going to assume they're from the *Je Reviens* both because the corpses were not just tattooed, but tattooed in a style not used in that area, and pierced with ornamental electronic components and because there is a focus of the disease radiating from the slum where they landed.

"In old Paris they were destroyed by a mob that connected them with the disease.

"But the rest, except for the three we recovered, and who apparently never managed to convey they came from the *Je Reviens* because the bureaucracy in La Mancha is so byzantine that no one ever heard their full story, are lost. Disappeared. They never reached anyone important, and no one even knows they should look for them. The ships were found, and the ships concern the military on both sides, but the boys themselves were swallowed up by the world."

"Swallowed up how?" I asked.

"Thena, be your age. Think of the size of the world. We grew up in a limited set, probably smaller than the smallest villages. It might have spanned the world, geographically, but not...not in the number of people. And none of us, certainly none of the children of Good Men, would be allowed to travel and mix with the masses. But you visited Spain in childhood, didn't you? And China later?" I nodded. "Well, think of the big ancient cities. The Good Men of those regions can't even get an accurate census. Most of those cities are built on the ruins of their own previous incarnations. Those boys dropped in and got...swallowed. Disappeared. There's places everywhere, and they either went to ground, convinced they couldn't find any rulers and wouldn't get anywhere with their petition, and that they'd be killed if they went back, or they were...co-opted. In my good moments I hope most of them found nice families, with mothers and fathers desperate to adopt a child in need. Doubtless some did. Not all are horror stories, and a lot of people are very decent. I know if they landed in the newly colonized North American territories, and at least one set did, they're probably learning to operate farming robots, how to milk cows, and how to fish and hunt. But the people around them are also deathly ill and need help.

"The ones who landed in Rio and Old Seville, in Milan and Moscow? If they're lucky they're not acting as drug mules or being sold as underage prostitutes." He shrugged. "We can't look after them, and most of them are better equipped to look after themselves than the average human. Part of the reason we needed to recover John and Tom and Christopher is because they were with a Good Man, and sooner or later they'd get where they'd come from, and what was happening."

"And this would be bad why? How are we to thwart this alone, Nat? Kit and Dr. Dufort—"

"And labs around the world are coming up dry on examining this virus, yes. But listen, the problem is this: The Good Men might ally with the *Je Reviens*. They might like the idea. They might make it more efficient somehow, or join their troops to the great killing. There are horror stories in the Good Men archives, Thena, things I wouldn't share with anyone, not on purpose, though my father made Luce read them. Plagues that killed entire populations. We think that's what this one is, but what if the Good Men here on Earth thought this was a great idea and released a better and quicker plague? If we had no time to fight back? We needed those boys. We needed a bigger sample, too. Though the clincher might be Zen. I don't speak doctor, and what I'm getting is filtered through Simon, anyway, but I understand Zen and her pregnancy are the key to all of this."

That night I asked Kit, "What did he mean? Why is Zen the key?"

He was undressing, and I didn't like the expression on his face, not because it was tired, or because it was stern, but because it wasn't quite him. He turned around, "What?"

"Nat says that Zen is the key to your figuring out what is going on, and how to treat it. Or at least that her pregnancy is."

"Oh. That." He chewed on his lip. "I think it's more . . ." He sighed. "I think it's more that she didn't expect to get pregnant. She shouldn't have got pregnant. It would never have happened, unless her husband was modified in the exact same manner we were."

"You're saying unless her husband was a Mule?" I said.

Kit sighed. "Unless her husband were a Mule, built well after our originals were. I wasn't sure about it, and even Dr. Dufort, who made him, wasn't sure of it."

"Doctor—"

"Oh, yes, turns out unbeknownst to you—at least I presume unbeknownst to you—people on Earth continued to be bioimproved. In the case of Zen's husband and, apparently, quite a few others, they were made in Liberte Seacity by Dr. Dufort. I don't think he's like us, or not really, and certainly he has no stops on his reproductive genetics, because he had a daughter by a woman with similar genetics.

"Here's the thing, though, Dr. Dufort wasn't following the plans for us, and he confesses he doesn't know if Alexis and others like him will be as long-lived, but he did all the same things: maximize for intelligence, speed, enhanced physical strength and sensory abilities. The fact he impregnated Zen, who is not averse to the idea, but who thought having children would require laboratory work, means that he's close enough to us for that to work. It doesn't work with normal humans. I could explain to you why, but it will take too long."

"So they essentially recreated the Mules and let them loose in the world with no reproductive stops," I said. "And there are females, too?"

"We don't know how many of them are that modified, certainly Alexis's daughter, though," Kit said, "But— That is not the point. The point is that Alexis still caught the disease."

"And so you're afraid the baby won't survive?"

"The baby is fine, at least while he's sharing Zen's blood. She didn't catch the plague after the virus. No, Athena, think, our kind catches only the cold. We could say it's because we're naturally more resistant to disease, but that's not it. If that were it, then Alexis Brisbois would also be more naturally resistant to disease, but he caught it. And yet he's close enough to us to be able to impregnate Zen with no reproductive assistance of any kind."

I blinked. "So you don't know why we're resistant and the normal humans, even enhanced ones like Nat or basically the same as us, like Alexis, aren't."

"Oh, we know. Or at least we have a good inkling."

"And that is? Does it mean we can fix it?"

"Well . . . no."

"Explain."

"The . . . biolords, before the Good Men, the biolords released viruses into the population, sometimes."

"Nat says the Good Men did it too," I said. "I don't know why."

"I suspect mostly to shut down rebellious areas. It's why we—why the Good Men of Jarl's time did it."

"How do you shut down a rebellious area?" I asked. "With a bug? There was this disease they did in some territory I don't remember when, but early on, before the Mules were made, where they put in the disease to stop something, I don't remember what, mice? No, there was a domesticated population too, or maybe— Oh, yeah, rabbits. There was someplace rabbits were out of control, and they gave them something they called mixie, and it killed all of them, but also all the domesticated ones in other seacities and continents and stuff. I know that people say the Good Men released deadly stuff, but mostly it was stuff that really got you very ill. It spread, but it didn't matter because at the time when it happened it got people to stop fighting and you could restore order. And it eventually burned itself out of the population."

"That's one way to put it," Kit said. He pulled his arms back, as if the muscles on his back hurt, but standing there, in his underwear, he was still one of the most beautiful men I'd ever seen, golden and muscular. The first time I'd seen him almost naked—not an intimate occasion—was also the first time I'd realized his essential humanity. Before that I'd been distracted by his gengineered eyes, his calico hair. But his body was all human, all male, and good to look at.

He turned around and must have caught something in my eyes because he smiled. But he didn't start anything. Both of us had some idea we were supposed to wait after birth, though neither of us knew how long, and neither of us wanted to ask. I supposed a couple of months would be enough. And not easy.

Kit sat on the bed, his smile vanishing. "No, the biolords, when they called themselves that, created two-stroke plagues."

"Two-stroke? Like engines?"

He shook his head. "No, look, viruses are an ideal way to spread a virus. And it might be something like a cold, that burns itself up and leaves no memory it even happened. A couple of days of the sniffles, say. And then later you release another. And it hooks into what the first virus left behind."

"What did the first virus leave behind?"

"Markers. Markers that say hook here, or cut here, or change here. Think of them as bookmarks left on a book that tell you 'This part is important. Read this later.'"

"You can kill people that way?"

He reclined and pulled the blanket over his legs. "Easily. In fact, we're convinced this is a two-stroke plague, one of the worst ones. But you can do others. You can kill people very quickly with them too. Say the second virus makes you start producing metabolic poisons. You'd be dead in a couple of days. Or have the second virus make you stop producing serotonin or the other things that keep you on an even keel."

What there had been in his face that wasn't quite his, that expression, that distance that I identified as Jarl was gone. Now there was just Kit, a tired, very sad Kit.

"But how does that save it from having a worldwide effect? From killing everyone in the world?"

"In this case I think they want to kill everyone in the world," he said. "Maybe. It's the length of death that doesn't make sense."

"Length of death?"

"Depending on how lucky or unlucky you are," he said. "Sure a platelet deficiency can kill you very quickly, if you were on blood thinners, or if you get unlucky enough that you have a tiny hemorrhage at the wrong time. But most of the time they'll not kill most of the people for months. Simon's wife got unlucky and got a brain hemorrhage. Nat was having too many of them, and one was bound to kill him, which is why he's here and watched. I'm not sure anything is wrong with Alexis, beyond a tendency to get visible tiny hemorrhages—a skin too transparent, for instance.

"They're both in the early stage of the disease, just reacting to it a little too hard. As are the people who have died so far. The majority of the people aren't that ill yet. They've caught it, and they're bruising easily, and sometimes tiny hemorrhages in the brain will cause them to become confused, which has upped the number of accidents of all kinds, but really, the big dying is not happening yet. It will happen in . . ." he said and looked like he was doing calculations in his head. "Well, platelets have a median cycle of about ten days, the boys arrived roughly two weeks ago . . . don't make me count. It's been sleepwalking hell. Let's call it two weeks. The platelets replace maybe in tri-phasic cycles, don't make me look it up either, that's not what I've been looking at, which means two-thirds of platelets are active at any given time, and are your regular count. So if you're simply not creating new ones, it will take a month to the full dying off. We have two weeks. The people who have already died . . . well, unlucky with bleeding in the wrong place, or perhaps some genetic reason their platelets replace in greater numbers or faster. But the average human who has this, and by now the whole world has, will die in two weeks."

"So we must find a solution in two weeks?"

"Yes, but here's the point: why wait? The biolords did this before and they killed everyone they wanted to kill in a week or less."

"How did they keep it to only the people they want to kill?"

"Easy enough," he said, and I was pleased to know his mouth was pinched and his eyes looked as if he were looking into unimaginable horror. "Easy enough. You can infect scientists, or daycare workers, or whomever you want by concentrating them all in the same place and giving them the first virus. Not as easy if it's all the people in your domain, or all the people in a certain city, but not impossible either, Athena. In the twentieth century people got paranoid about vaccines, and third-world countries had theories about payloads on vaccines that could turn their men homosexual or their women sterile. It was crazy, but it was as though they were having visions of the future, when genetic engineering really allowed to do things like that—or close enough—and hide the payload in vaccines. With the biolords, or later the Good Men, controlling all forms of information, it wasn't hard to insert the idea of a plague threatening a particular area, and you're going to vaccinate them against it. And then you give them water, with a payload that you can use to kill them later. They don't get sick, or only get slightly sick, a head cold, and you can warn the symptoms are the result of the killed virus. And they think they escaped. When in fact they cooperated in their own murder."

"But how do you get people who are rioting or rebelling to show up for a vaccine?"

"You don't. You lay these things in place years or sometimes decades in advance. And you leave it in place."

I blinked. "But then . . . if this virus is that, we were . . . prepared decades ago."

He smiled, but it was a flash of a smile with no joy whatsoever. There was irony and maybe an edge of ruthlessness, but also disgust. If the disgust hadn't been there, I would not have been able to go on living with him. "No," he said. "No. Centuries, Athena, this was laid in place before the Mules left the Earth."

"But how?"

"Heredity. Whatever was deposited in our—definitely not ours. I'm going to conjecture something about the Mules then on Earth made them immune to the original virus. No, I don't know how, but they'd been given so many vaccinations and strange things in childhood, it's not impossible—in the genes of normal humans, or people of Earth, something was gengineered in such a way as to be inherited. The proof of it are Zen and her husband. He's close enough to us to be cross-fertile, but she caught the virus as a mild cold, he caught it as a mild cold with a killing payload of blood disease. Do you see it?"

"I see it," I said. "And I wish I didn't. How much of it . . . how much of this is your memories, Kit? The memories from Jarl? Are those accurate?"

He shook his head. "Almost none. I remember mostly the technical things of biology, which is why I can help Dr. Dufort. But we have Jarl's writings between here and Eden, and in Eden most of this is known. Part of our distrust of authority, of constituted government, is the fear of things like this. When people are in charge of you, it's hard for them not to believe they own you, and once they believe they own you they think they have the right of your life and death, and of making you do anything they want.

"The people of Earth were dissatisfied with their all-too-human rulers, and they thought if only they could create perfect rulers, life would be perfect. But I don't think it's possible to have perfect rulers without having them be wholly inhuman. Which the Mules weren't. But even inhuman perfect rulers, I think, would end up thinking of people as things, as units. The Mules came close."

"To lay in the murder of millions—I presume different viruses for different areas so it could be controlled?—centuries in advance," I said. "So you're murdering not-yet-born people. You'd need to be a conscienceless monster."

"No, merely a human who doesn't consider himself part of the human race, and who considers himself simultaneously better and worse than normal humans."

My hand was on the bed, between us, as we sat up, half reclined on the pillows. The rest of the compound was very quiet. Even exerting my sensory ability to the utmost, I could not hear the boys move, or anything, really. It was as though Kit and I were alone, in the dark of night. Just us and our baby girl, alone, in the night. It must feel this way for every family. Just us, just our little unit. I wished it were possible to seal us from the rest of the world, from the evil and the darkness out there. But the darkness was in us. Even in families there's oppression and violence.

Kit put his hand over mine. He'd been speaking in a low voice, probably, like me, conscious that there were things it was better for our feral guests not to hear. "I know you worry that I will turn into Jarl, or not that, but that he has so much power over me, he's slowly changing me into him, but I couldn't, Thena, even if I tried to. Short of my entire brain getting remodeled so I don't exist and he does, it couldn't happen. I was raised by a real family. I knew love. He never did, not after his toddler years. Like these children here, it is possible to imagine turning into something that resembles a normal human, being able to function in society.

"And he functioned magnificently. But he wasn't right inside. Ever. He only kept from atrocities like what we've been talking about because he knew his companions did them and he knew enough of human history to know they were wrong. Not because they were morally wrong, mind. His idea of morality was shaky, his whole life. But because he knew that such atrocities begat other atrocities. He had a biologist's respect for life. Not for individuals as sentient beings, but for individuals as different configurations of genes, which might never happen again, never in the whole of an organism's history, and which were precious because variety is strength when it comes to genes." He shook his head. "But he wasn't like me, not inside. I don't know if he could ever love. I know his incarnation, as memory patterns uploaded to a cyborg in this lair, had a crush on you, but that's not the same as love. I haven't read his love letters, or his diaries in various places in here, but—" He stopped abruptly, not a hesitation, not as though he'd been speaking and suddenly didn't know what to say, but as though he'd been speaking and had been interrupted by some sort of internal censor.

"But what?" I asked. "What is wrong?"

"Don't be afraid, but I dream as Jarl sometimes. What I mean is I have dreams in which I am him, and I know they feed off real memories. They've been coming a lot these last few days, because I'm working on things that were his, on his life's work. Almost every night. And it's a dark and bleak thing, being Jarl Ingemar. I couldn't be him. Not even if I lost you and Eris, and my family and everything I know and love, I couldn't be him, because he didn't lose those things. He never had them. Those who created the original Mules went as far as they could to make them into things, into creatures that didn't understand human feelings. And they almost succeeded."

I don't know when we fell asleep, our hands entwined on the bed covers, but I woke with Kit's hand jerking, twitching, and something that would have been a scream if he hadn't cut it off midway, tearing out of him.

I woke up fully to see his eyes wide, his open in horror, his head shaking.

"Dream?" I said, because we'd just been talking about it. I remembered his restless sleep the last few days and realized they too had been nightmares.

He nodded, but said in a whisper, "Oh, light, oh, hell. Wait."

He got up, and went into the fresher next to our bedroom, one of the reasons we'd picked this room, and came back with a glass of water. He drank maybe half of it. His eyes shimmered in the half-dark, something like tears sparkling in the light of the nightlight I kept on to see when I needed to feed or change Eris.

"Want to talk about it?" I asked.

He started to shake his head, then nodded. When he spoke his voice came out hoarse, as if he'd been screaming a long time, instead of being almost silent. "I know when this virus was implanted. At least if what I dreamed was true, and they tend to be."

I snaked my hand into his free hand, while he took another sip of water. "You know how we always thought Jarl took all the functional ones in the *Je Reviens*, or at least that's what we got from the clues we had? From Jarl's memories, from—

"I think Jarl did his best to forget it. He rushed the removal, not because the riots were about to erupt. I don't know if he caused the riots to erupt, honestly. Maybe he thought it would kill the rest of them on Earth. But he arranged to get out of Earth all the Mules with biological knowledge. He found... he found that there was a conspiracy to unseat him as the leader." He swallowed hard. "And that this involved releasing the first stroke of the virus into Earth, with the second ready, so it would be released at the right moment and kill everyone on Earth."

"And he removed them?"

"He couldn't bring himself to kill them, both because they were his kind, and because of that biologist's decent respect for life. But he took all of them who knew and knew how to create the second virus, including himself, out of Earth. He got them and all their biologically savvy servants who might have known of it, with warnings about impending riots, Turmoils, which did happen, but I'm not sure if they were really starting, or if it was Jarl being Jarl. He then arranged to be dropped off in Eden with the humans, because he didn't like or trust the people he was in with. He was dropped off with his only friend, who held the key to a threat that would retaliate against the Mules should they release the virus on Earth."

"What was the threat?" I asked.

"I don't know," he said. "But I suspect the *Je Reviens* never went anywhere. That story of going out, changing their mind, deciding they missed the Earth? Lies. They stayed somewhere where they could monitor Eden."

"And seven months ago, Dr. Bartolomeu died."

"And they could act."

Whom Shall We Send

WE ENDED UP MEETING AT THE BIG TABLE, IN WHAT HAD ONCE, probably, been the dining room, at least when Jarl used this as a private residence. Before, who knows? It might very well have been a meeting room for the staff of the resort.

Whatever cloth touches or other perishable materials Jarl had added to it had been scrubbed away. Kit explained, "I set robots to clear it and clean it a few days ago."

What remained was almost antiseptic in its cleanliness and its simplicity. There was a vast white dimatough table, which might have been meant to pass for carved quartz and might have, if the chairs weren't made of the same material, molded whole, probably in a single pour, big fluid shapes with integrated arms. It was as though a chair-animal had grown and then moved on, leaving its discarded shape to be used by humans. Very artsy, very simple, and very, very antique dimatough use. I'd seen similar chairs in museums. I slid into the one next to Kit, and people came in and started taking seats, even those of us who were ill, who moved perhaps more carefully than usual, but who were still there, nonetheless. Nat dragged his link with him, I don't know if in hopes that he had to take notes, or ready to look up something.

Even the boys came in. We'd sent an announcement of the meeting via mind-talk, and they'd come back from the grounds, but must have come some time ago, because they were clean, dressed. The tattoos remained, but Little Brother, sorry, Morgan had cut his hair very short, so that it just showed as short black curls, not an outrageously dyed mop. They had removed the components-as-jewelry from their many piercings. They looked more like the other three boys, and less like outcasts. I would have to talk to them and soon about light regen treatment to remove tattoos, particularly Thor's, who sat next to Fuse. They looked, I thought, like father and son. Yes, Fuse too would need skin regen to look perfectly normal, but he'd cut and combed his hair, or someone had done it for him, in a way that you didn't see the patches missing where the scars crisscrossed his scalp. And I'd be damned if I knew where he'd found the narrow-waisted white shirt with ruffles at the collar and wrists, which was what was being worn in the best society, or the form-fitting, silky-looking pants. Perhaps he'd borrowed them from Luce. One didn't associate someone of Luce's size, let alone his history, with sartorial splendor, but he was usually very well dressed, and he and Nat, after all, had come here on purpose. They might very well have brought clothes. My second shock was realizing that Fuse and Luce were much of the same size. I was so used to thinking of my old friend as a child, with a child's reactions and emotions, he'd always looked smaller to me.

Now, serious and well dressed, he was every inch the patrician, even to the way his hand rested on the table, not fully open, but relaxed, waiting to hear what Kit and Dr. Dufort had to say.

I betted not very many impeccable patricians knew what to do with various explosives, though. And I'd bet that Fuse still knew it.

John was sitting next to Luce, looking like one of those dioramas in which they show the person at various ages. I wasn't sure if I was offended or gratified that Morgan wasn't sitting next to me or Laz next to Kit, but across the table from us. At any rate, I was almost sure that Morgan not sitting next to me was a good thing. Across the table made it easier to keep an eye on him. I put a hand behind Eris, where I could feel her little heart beat. I wouldn't trust her alone anywhere that Morgan could reach.

Simon was sipping something and looked like he was half asleep. I hoped what he was sipping wasn't alcohol, but he was a grown-up emperor, and I wasn't his mother, or his sister, or his wife. At any rate, the story in all the news was that the Emperor Beaulieu was in seclusion, mourning his wife.

First, Dr. Dufort got up and explained a two-phase bioweapon. Well, that's what he called them. I thought it was more understandable and far less stupor-inducing when Kit described them, but then, unless they are speaking a language I understand myself, most experts put me to sleep. I once used a teaching sensi on building cleaning-bios to sleep at a time of great stress.

Then Kit got up and explained it in a more down-to-Earth way, starting with how he'd acquired some of Jarl's memories; how they helped with the biological stuff, giving a retrospective of what he'd learned in his homeworld about what the biolords had done, how they had used targeted viruses.

Then Nat had spoken of the use of disease by the Good Men—still used—of what it meant. How a lot of it was targeted and two-phase like what we were facing, but most of it had been a blunt-force weapon, either designed to incapacitate people for a time period that allowed governmental forces to restore order, or to cause just enough mortality to ease the way past some crisis. But not something delicately targeted.

Then Dr. Dufort talked again. He had assembled people, gengineered them according to the way he'd learned from his father and his father's father. He'd created people at the behest of the Good Man he served. As a Usaian he didn't approve of the form of government, but it was better if he did it than if other people did it. As a Usaian he didn't approve of creating people to serve as essentially slaves, but there was a sort of arms race going on between Good Men, each one striving to have the fastest, best, strongest, smartest servants. He'd basically created equals of the Good Men. It had been his revenge, his joke. He'd also raised them, through surrogates and servants, and kept in touch with them. His wife and he had had trouble having children, and he considered these people he'd created his sons and daughters. He'd in fact created his legal child the same way, using his and his wife's genes.

Alexis Brisbois was one of his first creations, his eldest surviving son, in a way, but he didn't have the immunity that clones of Mules seemed to have to the plague, so the first phase of this plague, the thing that created the place for the second virus to attach to and deliver its payload, must be something that had been introduced long ago, and something to which the Mules were somehow immune by virtue of a very specific gencode.

He'd tested the clones of Good Men present, and he could tell what this was.

At this point, he moved to a wall and pulled down something. It seemed to be a paper, until he started touching it in various spots, and it lit up. It was undoubtedly a screen of some sort. I wondered if it had been there since Jarl's day, if he had used this for his presentations to his guests.

I regret to inform you that I got absolutely nothing from his presentation. He said a word a lot, which I thought was *locks*, but which turned out to be *lox*, and I understood it was some sort of genetic mechanism, but there my so-called powerful intellect deserted me. I'd long ago learned that even in mechanics, before I trained I had known the lingo. I might know how things fit, after seeing a machine work once, but I completely lacked the deep knowledge of the principles behind it. And for bioengineering I lacked even the instinct.

Looking around the table, I thought the boys were about to go comatose. At least Morgan was engaged in picking intently at a scab on the back of his hand, while at his right, Laz was sitting, relaxed and long on his seat, reclining as much as his seat would allow, his legs probably most of the way under the table to where Kit was sitting. His eyes followed Dr. Dufort's movement on the screen, the letters and symbols he drew, and I realized, startled, that he understood it, or seemed to.

John had got a gem reader, and had the device in front of him, obviously reading whatever Luce and Nat had given him. Nat had told me it was mostly the history of the last three hundred years which they were trying to bring him up to speed on.

Fuse and Thor were whispering together. Their hands weren't moving, so I hoped they weren't comparing the bombs in their pockets. Of course, they might be talking of the bombs in their pockets.

Two more of the boys were following the presentation. They didn't have Laz's easy, laid-back way of seeing what was being said, as if it were an old subject, but were clearly making an effort at understanding all of it, which meant they knew more of it than I did: Tom and Christopher Robin.

When the doctor finished talking, Laz was the first one to

speak. "Have you tried regen? The machines, I mean, to fix this? They can fix missing limbs, shouldn't they be able to fix a missing sequence of gencode?"

Dr. Dufort nodded, seeming not in the least surprised with what amounted to a feral boy having followed his presentation and having a pertinent question. I've noticed that experts seem to think their knowledge should come naturally to everyone, and are only ever surprised when one fails to speak their subject at expert level. He opened his hands, as if to show helplessness. "We tried, but it didn't work. You need almost a rewiring of the regen tanks, a whole level of technology we don't have."

Laz opened his mouth, closed it and frowned.

Kit said, "We don't know what to do. We know there must be a solution to the problem, because the only reason we can think of for them to have used this slow-acting effect is that they mean to save some of the people."

Laz sat up straight. Christopher Robin made a rude noise. "Of course they do. Catch them farming the Earth even with robots. They plan to have serfs." Laz threw him an odd look, which I wasn't sure I could interpret.

"Couldn't you use a virus?" Tom asked. "A virus the way they used, but with the missing DNA?"

"It's harder to do than to remove it," Kit said. "But yes, it's possible. The problem is that the viral infection would have to run its course, and many if not most people, by the time we have it ready to go, would be too frail to live through it. And yet, the Mules— Ah, the people in the *Je Reviens* must have a solution. I would assume they intend to come down to Earth when we're reduced to a small number and can't really fight, and—that means most people will be very ill. They must have a means of fixing this."

Laz stood up. It seemed to me he stood up without meaning to, and then he sat down again, heavily, as if his legs had given out. "I," he said, so loudly and in such an odd voice that the whole room quieted, even Fuse and his—for lack of a better term—brother. We all stared at him. "I think I know," he said. "That is, I've been working on a project for them the last...the last two years. Making...making regen machine chips, designed to change how they function. They chose me because I'm the one who has...who has repaired the chips. I like machines, though they made me study bio also. I—I think they mean to retrofit all the machines on board and on Earth, maybe, and . . . and save the people they want to save. If . . . If that makes sense."

The next few minutes were complete pandemonium. Everyone was up and everyone was shouting. Okay, not everyone. Nat remained sitting—which worried me a little—but Luce was up and shouting for it, and the gist of the shouting was that he really wanted to know where these chips were right this minute, and he must have them, and he must—

"Gentlemen," It was Simon, speaking in full voice of command, and bringing complete silence to the meeting, such as I'd never heard before. "Gentlemen, nothing can be gained from yelling at the top of your voices. Lazarus Long Ingemar, tell us what you know."

"I know they've been making program chips for regen machines for three years. We—I mean they have thousands of them. I don't know what they are, because no one told me, but we never needed to make all of those before."

This is when some crazy maniac stood up and announced, loudly, that she was going to go to the *Je Reviens* and bring back the chips, or at least one of them that could be replicated and used on the machines of Earth, to save the population.

I realized it was me after a second or two, due to some subtle clues: I was standing up. Kit was looking at me as though I'd lost my mind. And so was Zen, who was the only other woman present.

Simon looked tired. "Thena, sit down."

I looked at him. And continued being a lunatic. "I don't think so," I said. "I think—"

Luce, in a tired voice said, "Thena, sit down. Of course you're not going to the *Je Reviens* to retrieve these chips."

Laz stood up. He was shaking all over, and it reflected in his stammering, "I-I-I will g-go with her."

Little Brother looked at him sideways and stood up. "And I also," he said, throwing his head back.

Slowly, Zen stood up, ignoring Alexis's attempts and grabbing for her arm. Then John stood up, and Christopher Robin.

Dr. Dufort opened his mouth, let it snap shut. Fuse stood up, and Thor. "We will go too," he said.

"In what crazy world," Simon asked, in a tone of withering

hectoring, "are we allowing a mother, a pregnant woman, and a gaggle of undergrown boys to go on a dangerous mission?"

"I'm not an undergrown boy," Fuse said, very calm. Simon looked at him, and I could see what Simon wanted to say, the words burning their way into his tongue. At any other time, he'd have said them. I might have said them too, only a month or so ago. But Fuse was different. I still wasn't sure I'd trust my life in his hands, but I'd trust him to watch my back. I wasn't a hundred percent sure, mind, that his enthusiasm for big booms wouldn't overpower his enthusiasm for staying alive and keeping me alive, but it was at least possible.

As for the others . . . "I can see a risk," I said, slowly, "in taking back the young men who were raised in the *Je Reviens*. Any who volunteer must understand there is a high risk they'll be captured."

"So you're saying we're at risk of living as we have all our lives?" Laz asked. "I don't think there will be a problem."

Morgan frowned. He looked far less outrageous and more adult with his new hairstyle. "Maybe, Laz. I don't think Father will take well to being told we failed. Do you?"

Laz shrugged. "How can he get much worse? Killing us? That will be a form of release, don't you think?"

John sighed, "I want to go. I'm willing to go." He turned to Simon. "Understand, I know what life is like in the *Je Reviens*. Part of the way they tempted us to this mission was telling us if we succeeded, we got to go to Earth, to live free, or at least to live free in comparison to everything we've always known. Now we've found this is a lie. We were just the bait, the decoys, to come to Earth and depopulate the Earth and allow it to become a much larger version of our life in the *Je Reviens*." He shrugged. "That means our only hope for freedom, our only hope for a future in which the same people don't torture us over and over again is to save the Earth from . . . the elders of the *Je Reviens*. And because we never fully understand how other people, normal people like you," he said as he looked around the room with touching naiveté, "behave, or why, unless from books, we have to, in a way, pay our way in. We did you grievous wrong without knowing we were doing it, but truth be told, none of us are so stupid we could not have figured it out, if we'd thought for a few minutes. Which means we are responsible for the harm we've done you.

"I don't want to go back to the *Je Reviens*. I don't want to risk staying there. I have found family here," he said, with a glance at Lucius and a hint of a smile. "And even a promise of a life in which I get to decide what I do and who I am. But I can't do any of that, and feel like I deserve it, if I don't earn it. This is my way of setting myself free from the way I was raised; setting myself free from being an object, a means to an end. I've come to the place stories happen, and I want to be the hero of mine."

There was a long silence. I recognized the personality there. His speech, as young as he was, reflected the verbal facility I'd known in my friend Max and in their older clone, Lucius, as did the stubborn decision to take the guilt for some things they couldn't help.

Simon said, "So we're sending children and women. Is this smart or rational?"

I'd had just about enough. Look, I love Simon, love him like a brother, or a best friend. The time we were lovers was a piece of insanity on both our parts. We were too much alike to have a stable relationship. Except that Simon *wasn't* like me in one thing: I knew what I wanted and pursued it openly. I wasn't one for subterfuge or pretending. To anyone, least of all myself.

Simon...I wasn't even sure he knew what he thought at any time, much less that he ever stated an opinion without wishing for a reaction. And the reaction wasn't always obvious.

I wasn't sure what he wanted now, but I was sure what I wasn't willing to give him, and I was sure there was only one thing we could do. Or at least one best thing we could do. "What are you saying, Simon? Do you wish to go, Emperor Beaulieu? Is your idea that you can sacrifice yourself, fulfill whatever drama is playing out in your head? What about your seacity? I thought you'd only taken leadership because you had to, because there was no one else equally qualified, no one else who knew the layers of government there? I thought it was a sacrifice, and you'd rather shed it. Is that what you're trying to do? Shed it without recrimination? Is that what you want, and your seacity be damned?"

He turned bright red. I wasn't really hoping to score a hit, but I saw in his deep blush, in the way he shrugged, in his incoherent defense of, "I didn't mean that I— That is, I'm not sure that I'm the best person to go—" that I'd scored a hit. What hit I'd scored I didn't know. It was entirely possible at some level he'd wanted to commit suicide by adventure, to escape his current grief and manage to live on in legend as the savior of his people. Or something. There was a strong streak of the romantic in Simon.

But there were more streaks in Simon, or perhaps more accurately, more layers. Simon was and would always be a person of layers. The same way nothing was ever simple or easy in life, nothing was ever simple or easy with Simon. Simon was... complex. It was entirely possible that at the same time an impulse pulled him into suicide-by-Mule, another impulse, warring with it, just required he act reluctant to let us go so he didn't feel guilty for our inevitable demise.

And both of those, and a dozen other contradictory impulses could be absolutely true for Simon, at the exact same time. But whatever it was, I'd managed to stop him. Or at least undercut some of his insufferable certainty for a moment.

"As for the rest of you," I said. "Luce can't go. If he's lost to the Usaian revolution, so I am assured, he'll be a deeper loss than Nat, who is enough of a loss, if we can't find a way to save him. Luce is the public face of the revolution and some of them think he's the George, come again to free his people." I think Luce mumbled *that's crazy talk*, but I didn't know. Or care. In popular movements, what people think or believe is often far more important than what the actual objective truth might be. "Kit can't go. Like Laz, he is the clone of Jarl Ingemar. That means he's hated and despised for reasons we might not even fully understand." At least if Kit's dream was true. "Add to that that Kit is capable of remembering a good portion of Jarl's biological knowledge, some of which the...ah...elders in the *Je Reviens* might not have reproduced yet, and what you have is the chance not just of sending Kit into a living hell, but of making the Mules even more powerful."

"But sending Zen is the same," Simon said, his voice lower, and possibly a fraction more whiny, but objecting nonetheless. "I mean, she is a clone of Jarl Ingemar, and by being a woman will give them clues on how to create women."

"I'm not sure their creating women is the worst possible thing," I said, and looked around at a series of faces turned to me in shock. "Listen, part of the problem of the Mules—the original Mules—is thinking they didn't have a future. Every human longs for immortality, but none so much as the ones who think no piece of themselves will live after." I waved my hands wildly, since I was making this up as I went, and was not sure at all that it was true. "Lots of history and literature testify to that. If they have women, and particularly if they realize the normal humans are themselves changed by the gengineering that went on in the twenty-first and twenty-second centuries, maybe they'll just become another bunch of annoying people. Strange and possibly genocidal, sure, but no more so than many groups of humans throughout history."

I thought Nat laughed, but I wasn't willing to look at him. I remembered his telling me in the past that my mind worked in funny and frankly strange ways, but of course he should talk. "The point is, in the series of dangers we could worry about, the Mules figuring out they could make women and have babies is really, really, no, really low on my scale. I think worrying about them not killing everyone not them is far more important. Or not creating a neo-feudal state with them at the top and everyone else unwilling serfs is much worse. So, it doesn't worry me that we take Zen. As for her being the female clone of Jarl Ingemar." I shrugged. "Has everyone else failed to notice she's far prettier than Kit or Laz? They're not likely to figure that out on a short acquaintance. Her getting captured is something we don't want. Any of us getting captured, really. And if it happens, it's the end of the world, more or less. I think we should agree right now, those who want to go, that we're not willing to leave behind anyone who gets captured. That this mission is win or die for all of us."

Everyone nodded, even Morgan and John, who were, frankly, babies, and not capable of making the decision.

Tom Sawyer cleared his throat. "What if I don't go?" he asked. "I'm not a coward, but with everyone volunteering to go, it seems to me like you're crazy. I wouldn't be dragged back by force."

I shrugged. "No one will drag you back by force. You're able to decide." He was, we'd found, the clone of a Good Man, Robert Edwards, who had perished early on in the battles for control among the Good Men. Having met Tom, I realized why his original might not have survived. There was very little room in the insane-eat-insane world of the Good Men for a sensible person with a modicum of rationality. He'd probably failed to be sufficiently paranoid.

"I'm not sure so many people should go," I said. "I presume the ships take only three people since that's what was sent per ship."

"What ships?" Kit asked. He didn't sound like he objected, but more like he was half amused and half horrified.

"The ones they came in. The triangle ships. The lifesavers of the *Je Reviens.*"

Morgan put his hand up, as though he were in an assembly room and asking to talk. "Those are pure bugger to steer," he said, his profanity passing unnoticed to himself, I think. Meaning he was just speaking as he was used to, not trying for best behavior. Which was interesting. Was Little Brother starting to feel at home with us? "They are lifeboats, really, only supposed to take people and supplies from the *Je Reviens* to a planet. Flying them back will be..." He thought about it a moment, as though seeking for a descriptive-enough word. "Interesting."

I nodded. "Yes, sure. I get that point. But the thing is, Morgan, that we must use those ships."

"Why?" It was Lars. "You have much better, and if you think you don't want to give them the technology—"

"Oh, hell no," I said. "I don't care if we give them the technology. I'd be very surprised if they don't have ships like ours, or something way better. No, no. The thing is, they'll know the ships approaching, right? Or worse, they won't know the ships approaching, and that will put them on guard. While if it's these ships, they will assume some of you are just coming back to report."

"But there's nothing for us to report," Morgan protested. "And Laz, we should have known it. We should have seen it, from the fact that they sent us in ships that are almost impossible to pilot back."

Laz blushed and nodded. If he blushed because he had guessed and said nothing—possible, I suppose, though I'd not understand why, except for a chance of running away—or if he blushed because he hadn't guessed and that made him an idiot, is anyone's guess.

"They don't know you know there's nothing to report," I said. And to his blank look, "Imagine that you hadn't been told or realized what caused the plague or that it was intentional to infect you and send you down. You might as well be reporting that you hadn't managed it."

"We'd have to be crazy," said Thor. "That would be death."

I refused to comment on their mental health. Instead I said, "Sure, but think about it this way: You could also be reporting with something you think is a game-changer. Like when Morgan tried to steal Eris. He thought he could get special treatment by doing this."

Christopher Robin rubbed his hand on his face, and there was a grating sound, which made me realize, startled, that he was old enough to have beard growth even if held in control by some product like our men used. "She is right, you know. Though it might require us to lie. One of us per ship might need to lie outright to their faces and then evade whoever they send to corner us."

Laz sat down, "More than one ship," he said. "There must be more than one ship."

"Of course," Nat said, making notes. "It's important to have more than one ship, so that at least one can get through and make it to the lab."

"I think I'll need to draw the layout of the *Je Reviens*," Laz said pensively. "And get everyone who is going to memorize it, so that if all of us who were raised in it die, the others can still get to the lab and find what they need."

There was a long silence, then Nat said, "Of course. So you need at least two ships, though three might be better, and both need to dock to the *Je Reviens* simultaneously."

"Of course," Laz said. "And here's the thing: The ships will need to be retrofitted, so they have enough power charge to get there and back. Some improvements in steering wouldn't go amiss. Right now they'll really be very hard to maneuver, much less all to a simultaneous docking. But retrofitting three ships in a day or two, which I think is the most we can take, given the disease and its progress, will be very difficult."

"Which is not to say impossible," Kit said. "We have two expert mechanics, and others who can lend a hand."

"Why isn't anyone listening to my objections?" Simon asked, and he really sounded aggrieved. I thought my old friend had got way too used to being obeyed and to his opinion being law.

"Because there is no other option," Luce said. "Yes, what we are doing sucks and has lots of dangers, but there isn't an option for perfect and with no danger. If there were, I'd be the first to suggest it. So, unless we have one, kindly shut up."

Simon did, which might be the first time.

If I Lose Thee

EVERYONE HAD SOMETHING TO DO. THE FIRST THING TO DO WAS track the ships in friendly hands, or those that, while not in friendly hands, could be recovered.

That job, by default, fell to Lucius, who got in touch with various underlings. That he not only seemed to have an endless supply of these but that they seemed to be in most unlikely places, including deep in the strongholds of the Good Men, should not have been a surprise to me, but it was.

I had no idea what "head of propaganda" of Olympus Seacity meant, much less that it apparently entailed an entire army of . . . operatives? Spies? Embedded subversive elements? I must have let a comment like that escape near Nat, because he looked at me quizzically, as though trying to figure out what he could tell me. Or perhaps, who knew, trying to figure out exactly how stupid I was.

Yes, I am aware that all of us had been bioed to have greater intelligence than normal humans, but I'd long ago come to the conclusion that unless both normal and non-normal humans, both the naturally born and the genetically engineered, had been raised in the exact same situation and had close to the same personality, raw intelligence might count for nothing.

Take these feral boys, who would have been infinitely better

241

off being raised by wolves. I shuddered to think of what had happened to the ones who had been dropped in parts of the Earth where they'd had no one to help them or protect them. Naturally smarter they might be, but that was like your knowledge and understanding of poker—a game I despised, and had resisted Kit's attempts to teach me—you might be the best poker player around, but the hand you were given couldn't be changed. You could play a bad hand very well, but you weren't going to overcome someone with a good hand, even if he wasn't quite as good a player.

Nat had been given a very good hand. Like Kit had. Oh, sure, there were things you could say against both of their families. No family was perfect, from what I understood, and I shuddered to imagine what Eris would think of ours when she was old enough to judge. But both Kit and Nat had had parents who loved them and valued them, and tried to instill in them an understanding of people and the world.

I'd never had that. I'd had a woman who thought she was my mother, and who'd done the best she could for me until she disappeared when I was six. She'd probably joined the ranks of Father's victims. I refused to believe she had escaped without taking me. Possible, of course. I was too young when she left to really know her. But it didn't seem likely.

But other than that, it had been Father and me. Father determined that I shouldn't sully his name or make a public spectacle of myself, for reasons that would only become clear years later, and I determined not just to live my life any way I wanted to but to disappoint him at every turn, just to show him.

This had left me curiously unprepared for any relationship that didn't involve locking wills on a regular basis.

And being raised as the Good Man's daughter, a Patrician of Earth, had made me different, too. I didn't understand very well how people established networks or relationships of equals. Sure, there had been my broomer lair, and that had helped socialize me. But none of my broomer mates had precisely average upbringings, either. My relationship with Kit's family was a sort of baby-step towards that; my relationship with Zen was best described as armed detente, and my understanding of how other people worked was limited.

All this to say that if Nat thought I was subnormal, he might be somewhat justified. But it didn't prevent me starting to bristle and looking for a response that would sting him back, when he shook his head. "I'm sorry. I forget people don't really understand how our religion works. Lucius is not our head of intelligence. He's not commanding spies. We have other people for that. What he's done is get in touch with a network of Usaian families, where each of them will do what he asks, to further the cause."

"There are Usaian families in the domains of the Good Men?" I asked, genuinely surprised.

Nat's pale eyebrows climbed, high above his dark eyes. "How not? We're everywhere, Thena. And that is why we are feared and why we were first proscribed."

I nodded, pretending I understood all of this and turned my head to my job in the preparations, instead.

The planning had, probably not strangely, fallen to Simon. Simon had many layers, and many were distinctly unsavory, but the one thing he'd learned to do and become good at was planning and strategy. He'd had to when his father had become incapacitated when Simon was still young. In a world where the "son and heir" only became Good Man after his putative father had used him as a whole-body donor for a brain transplant, Simon was an oddity and an abnormality.

The normal thing when someone inherited who wasn't, actually, the same man who had inherited since the beginning, is that all the Good Men united to take the intruder down.

The fact that this had not happened was in part due to strategy and planning on Simon's side. I still didn't fully understand how, and I might never. He had adroitly managed the expectations that his father would wake up from his long-term vegetative state, with whatever he had on the other Good Men intact, against the gain other Good Men could get from attacking Simon and taking over Liberte and its territories.

He was aided, both in that initial gambit—as I learned—and in the current planning, by Alexis, who apparently had been more than a thug and his guard's captain.

I'd find them sitting at a table, trading gestures and the occasional word, sharing an understanding only people who knew each other very well could have.

It turned out that their calling each other "brother" was more than a rhetorical flourish.

As for me, I was relegated to mechanics and to working with Zen. I didn't mind mechanics. I had an instinctive understanding of them, something programmed into the way my brain worked, and I'd augmented it with the knowledge of two very disparate civilizations.

Working with Zen was something else. I even understood there was a lot to Zen that was similar to my beloved husband: the quick temper and the deep reserve. But they were not even close to the same person, and unfairly or not, Zen got my back up by being too beautiful, too effortlessly put together, too... right. I'd always felt like I was a scapegrace, crosswise to the world, and she seemed to be my antithesis.

We had comparable mechanical knowledge. And both of us were bioengineered for an ability with mechanics, her by the same means Kit had been bioed to be a pilot of darkships: a virus introduced into the biowomb that gestated her. And both of us had worked as mechanics of darkships.

I'd even worked with her before, both in repairing the ship that had got us to Earth before, in the trip from which she'd refused to return, and in retrofitting a *Je Reviens*-era ship to take those of us who'd returned to Eden.

But none of that—none of it, really—could make up for the fact we seemed to rub each other wrong at every possible opportunity.

We were working on the first ship, one that Nat and Lucius had recovered in the middle of the night, from some stronghold near La Mancha. Turned out the reason the city was so affected was that this had been an early arrival, probably two weeks before the triangular ship we'd intercepted. Why the boys hadn't told us that initially we didn't know, except there was a lot of "just assuming" on both sides.

But it made sense the mortality would be greater if they were reaching the month mark. Apparently there had been another ship that had been sent early. The people infected by that early mission might be impossible to recover. The others... We'd have to hurry.

Which was the problem, as we were being asked to do, more or less, the impossible. The ships were slick pieces of machinery, but Little Brother had been right about them. They weren't designed for a trip out and back. They weren't designed for easy maneuvering.

As they were, it was possible—barely possible—that the boys could have flown it back to the *Je Reviens* to report. As such, it would have been difficult for the Mules to say that it couldn't happen, that it wouldn't happen and that anyone who tried to come back must have modified the ships. Good. But that was the only piece of good news.

After a very frustrating afternoon sticking hands and heads where no one was meant to, in the entrails of the ship, I sat down on the floor to nurse Eris. Kit was changing her and monitoring when she needed to be fed, while he worked at a seemingly crazy task: trying to recreate the chip that would go into a regen machine, to reproduce the one the Mules had created. He had explained it this way: "If you fail, if we manage to do it on our own, it will take longer and there will be only a remnant of people alive, but there will be a remnant of people, Thena, people left alive who don't owe their lives to the Mules and who can still fight back."

It seemed like a forlorn hope to me. But hope, no matter how forlorn, is the only thing humans can't live without. They can curtail food and drink, and even ration air, and go on living. But if you remove hope from humans, they die. That's all there is to us. As a species, we subsist on hope, even foolish hope.

So I left him to his work with Dr. Dufort and whoever else could help, and to watching Eris. He'd built her a secondary bassinette from a box in the lab, and he brought her to me when she wanted to eat.

As it happened, Zen and I had just about given up on working any more just then. We'd surveyed the situation thoroughly and both of us understood to a nicety how impossible our task was, which was why we'd spent the last hour or so sniping at each other with snark and curtness.

Now I washed my hands, took Eris from Kit, and sat against the wall of the place where we'd parked the triangular ship.

It was a garage. The boys had discovered, in their exploration of the place, that one of the artificial cliffs that seemed to rise above the artificial little valley opened. It opened, to be precise, to Laz's thumb, which made perfect sense, since his genetics would be close enough to those of Jarl Ingemar to open a genlock. Which meant we must all be very grateful he wasn't inclined to leave or lead the other boys out.

Inside the "cliff" was a whole other cave, almost as big as the artificial valley and the residential resort next to it. It could park thousands of fliers. More importantly, though, it had a whole shop attached to it, with service robots and other amenities. Once upon a time, I supposed a guest might arrive with a flyer that was giving him trouble, and find complete repair and other services here. Which was good, as it meant we had all the tools we needed. Mechanics had progressed since the twenty-second century, but not in the matter of tools. It was all still computers, and machines that read computers for the diagnostics, and various tools to manipulate the chips and components.

This cave also concealed an entrance above us, cunningly disguised in the lip of a real cliff, which had made it easier to fly the triangular ship in here.

We had been working on it in the shop, a surprisingly antiseptic space, made of poured silver-grey dimatough and lighted with piped-in sunlight from somewhere above. I didn't know where that hadn't been covered by the shifting sands of the man-made desert above.

I waited for Eris to latch on and closed my eyes. Win or lose, I was going to be away from her for probably two days. Simon had said something about a drug that inhibited milk production for a week, without drying the milk permanently, and that meant I didn't need to worry about taking a pump with me, or spending time pumping in the middle of a potential firefight.

Eris could be fed by formula. Simon had got some that wasn't even three hundred years old, though she didn't seem to react badly to the old one.

But I was going to miss this. There was a connection, a tenderness in doing this. Don't laugh. I know that, with giving birth, it is one of the functions of females, something you don't even need to be human to do. So is sex. And yet, nursing your child is as far above merely feeding her, as human sex is above the reproductive mechanism of non-human primates. Yeah, they use it for bonding and other social needs. But we can elevate it to a near-sacrament of love, by imbuing it with meaning, in our clever monkey minds.

In the same way the time I spent nursing Eris, even if it always happened at the worst possible times, which I'd learned was a function of any interaction with a child, was a time for bonding.

It was instinctive, but more than instinctive. She accommodated her body to mine, and presumably derived comfort from being held. And I looked at her face, petted her hair, and day dreamed of grown-up Eris, a combination of myself and Kit, and raised in love, more than either of us, and capable of doing whatever she wanted.

It was like holding a piece of the future, for just a moment, a link to everything she would do and be, and beyond, a link to everything her children would do and be, world without end. It was a little like feeding eternity.

I liked to think that we had many such moments, stretching a year or so, and then other moments, watching her grow, and trying to stay out Kit's way while he imbued her with sound moral principles and the skills of living with others.

But I didn't know. It was possible this raid would go incredibly wrong, and all that was left to her was to live with Kit on Earth, while they either fought a retrenching battle against ruling Mules or organized for future resistance, as forlorn and stubborn as the Usaians.

"First." Zen came back from washing her hands, stood in front of me and ticked points on her fingers. "First, there's not enough space in that forsaken shiplike thing to put in a larger power unit. Second, the steering is such I'm amazed they did anything as sophisticated as kidnap your husband. They could have done better falling from orbit in an airtight barrel. What *is* this thing? One of the ships from ancient navigators? Third, can we please, for the love of Nature and Nature's God, just take another ship and load it with radar-evading and scan blinds, and everything we can to keep it opaque. At least we stand a chance of getting there in one piece and not being met by a reception committee."

I looked up at her. There was really no visible sign of pregnancy unless you counted a little basketball-sized swelling in her midriff. I'd gained weight all over, which had caused Kit not to figure out what was going on for quite a while. It made sense, I thought, that Zen, who didn't look quite real, should also not have a quite-real pregnant look.

"Zen, I think we're going to get a reception committee anyway," I said, seriously. "There is no possible way we're going to make it so opaque to detection that they won't actually feel something opening into their hull. You must know that's impossible."

She put her hands on either side of her waist and looked mulish. A few months ago, this would have exasperated me. I was talking sense, and she didn't understand. But she looked so much like Eris, when Eris was making a face in displeasure, that I laughed aloud. Which made her look startled. She tried very hard, I think, to get a look of displeasure on her face, but couldn't quite get it.

"You don't understand," she said, and there was a small smile on the corners of her mouth. I'd never seen her smile against her will, and I revised my opinion of her marriage. Alexis must be doing something right. She sighed, as if at her own tantrum. "The thing is, I don't want to do it this way," she said. "I want there to be a safe, easy way for us to go up against these evil, ancient people and their trained armies of minions."

I shrugged minimally, so as not to disturb my daughter's feeding. "Nothing is ever easy or simple. I've got used to it."

"Oh. Yeah. I guess. I still fight against it now and then." There was a pause. "Is it terribly painful and difficult, this birth thing?" And then in a rush, "Understand, I never expected to do this the natural way. It just isn't done in Eden, unless you're a crazy religious person, and I might have been less than all there, but I never was that religious."

I opened my mouth, then closed it. "Let's say that the old holos don't lie about how painful it is. They do lie about the beauty of birth. It hurts like hell, and it's nasty and bloody and smelly."

"Oh, joy," she said.

"But you get a baby," I said. "I mean, I think all the pain and stuff is so we attach to the baby. You know, we value that for which we've suffered. But part of it feels right too. I mean, you're bringing a new life into the world. It's a privilege and a...an honor? Not quite what I mean, but more like a miracle. Someone should pay for it in some way."

"Are you ever doing it naturally? Or are you using a biowomb?"

"Oh, hell," I said. "Biowomb all the way." And we both laughed, even though it probably wasn't that funny.

When the giggle fit had passed, she said, "So, we need to increase the power capacity, get some sort of veiling, because otherwise, like Eden, they'll be able to scan and tell how many people and what mass are aboard, and we're going to need better steering. We can't negotiate those."

"But you said it's impossible," Kit said, from the doorway, and I realized he must have come back for Eris and heard us discussing.

"There are degrees of impossible," I said, and gave him a goofy grin. "Now take this child away," I said, handing him Eris, who had fallen asleep at the breast and who made only a small sound of protest as I handed her over. "I am going to perform miracles."

He laughed and started to turn away, then turned back, pulled me to him with his free arm and kissed me hard. "Thena, I don't like this. I don't like the chance of losing you. Please—"

I don't know what he wanted me to tell him. That I wouldn't go? That there was no danger? That nothing bad would happen?

I told him the most comforting lie I could think of, "I'll come back," I said. "I promise." It might not be a lie, after all. I was certainly going to do my best to come back.

We went back to work, and Little Brother came to lend a hand. He was intuitively good with machinery, and after all, it was the machinery he'd grown up with.

I noted, with quite a bit of alarm, that he wasn't behaving as I'd expect.

Look, Little Brother, the old bastard, and I were made of a piece. Our genes were the same. No one, not even the people who played with genes, were sure how to control them fully. I understood that in the making of the original Mules there had been far more discards than finished products. There were things they'd found went together that they didn't want to go together, like, say, high connectivity in the brain often correlated with depression. But then there were other things, like if you raised children a certain way, you could overcome some of their genetic tendencies, to the point no one who didn't know the genetic makeup knew what they were.

The original designers hadn't been trying for reproducible results. What I mean is that when they'd made the original Mules, they hadn't cared if the clones of the original creations had the same traits. They had instead done their best to put stops and traps in the genetic code to make it as impossible as they could that these creatures could ever clone themselves. And then, if I understood how they had been raised, they had set about breaking their spirits.

All the original Mules were supposed to be docile and obedient, and ready to lay down their lives for their masters, those who had created them and the people they had been created to serve.

Maybe it had actually worked with some of them. I knew that

all the high-end Mules, the ones created to be the functionaries of the super-state, had made it to power as biolords. I suspected the docile ones had disappeared early on, in internal fighting. Or perhaps, I thought with some alarm, a lot of them had simply walked away and aged and maybe died as common people.

But I knew none of the ones who had made it to biolords, much less the ones who'd stayed on Earth after the Turmoils, and become the ruling "Good Men" under new identities, and new regimes, had been docile, or even very capable of taking orders.

And I knew the bastard who'd called himself my father. I knew the bastard who'd raised me. And I knew myself. I had grown up determined not to do what I was told, unless it was absolutely necessary. I preferred being a free agent even if it hurt me.

So seeing Morgan fetch and carry and do as he was told made my hair prickle at the back of my neck. What was he planning? What did he intend to do?

I didn't have time to play stupid games with a rebellious teen-ager who would have been better off being raised by wolves…or by Daddy Dearest. Earth was in dire danger and Eden…Eden might already be lost.

He caught me looking at him after Zen had set him a difficult piece of assembly work, and raised his eyebrows at me. "What?" he said.

I sighed. "I'm wondering what you're planning."

He gave me a startled look and almost dropped the tweezer-tool he was using to assemble the components used for steering. "I? Why?"

"Because you're my clone and the clone of the person who raised me, and none of us would willingly take orders."

His rather dark eyebrows, thicker than mine, as Daddy Dearest's had been, descended over his eyes. "I have reasons," he said.

I waited.

"I don't like taking orders, and I'll tell you if you order me to do something stupid." He threw the words out like hammers, like blows. "But I don't want the Earth to be empty, because then when they land, it will be easy to find us, to control us, to make us do what they want to.

"I want to run away. I want to go with you and do this, and bring back the chips, and save people on Earth, and then I want to—to—"

"To?"

"Disappear. We've spent time outside, but Laz says this is only a little fake forest, like the one in the bio area of the *Je Reviens*, and that there are miles and miles and miles like that in the rest of the world. Miles and miles. And Zen's husband, the man, Alexis, he says they live out in the middle of nowhere. They can go days and days without seeing anyone." Something like a dreamy look didn't completely dispel the anger in Little Brother's face, but made him look somewhat more human. "I want to go out there. I want to be alone for a while. Maybe not forever. For a while. I want to find out who I am, what I am, what I want to do. I want to hear myself think."

"You've never been alone?" I said, startled, which was stupid. After all, he'd grown up in very odd circumstances. I'm not going to say I was prone to solitude, myself, and the idea of going out in the middle of nowhere by myself would only occur to me as some form of punishment. But he wasn't me. Yeah, sure, similar, if not exactly the same genes. Things like the eyebrows were often expressed or not depending on sex hormones. And that was fine. But there was the way he was raised.

I had had my hours of solitude, my hideout in the abandoned library of my father's mansion. If he hadn't ever had anything like that—

He shrugged. "Not really. Sure, there are places in the *Je Reviens* where we can be alone, but not places where you're not under surveillance. There are eyes and ears everywhere. The whole ship is wired for sound and vision."

I felt my throat constrict, and mind you, not just because I felt sorry for the boys growing up that way, without even a moment of privacy. "No part is free of surveillance?"

"No. Not a single bit."

"Oh, hell."

Later when I found Zen, I told her, "It's worse than we thought," and explained.

She pressed her lips together and looked like I'd punched her. "So," she said. "Not much point putting shields on the ship. They'll see us the moment we go in, they'll see us every step of the way."

"Yeah," I said. "We're going to fight our way in the moment we step into the *Je Reviens*."

"Lovely. It's us against what? A hundred of them?"

"Let's hope there are so many they choke the hallways with their dead and we can scamper through."

She grinned. "We should be so lucky, Athena, if we talk of this in general."

"They'll never allow us to go. I got that. In fact, I was going to talk to the boys and ask them not to mention it to the men. The thing is, I got the impression they think this is perfectly normal."

"That's probably why they didn't try to escape the area out there," Zen said. "They think it's completely wired like the ship."

"It is. That's why I found Morgan. He just doesn't know we don't look at them the whole time. The way I found him would fulfill the idea we are tracking them all the time." Which also, somewhat, more perhaps than the reward he expected, explained Morgan's docility. I too had been good at behaving while watched.

"I'm still not sure I trust him further than I can throw him," I told Zen. "I want him and Laz in my ship. I want him under my observation, and Laz seems to be the only person he respects, perhaps loves, the equivalent of a parent for normal people."

She nodded. "Yeah, but that's not our greatest problem, Athena. We must find a way to talk to the boys about not telling the men anything. They'll never let us go. Simon is not too fond of the idea, already. It's the Gallic thing."

"That and I think the 'father of his people' thing."

As she started opening her mouth to respond, I cut in, "No, I don't think he's gone around impregnating all his female subjects, Zen. I just think that he needs to play whatever role he's given. He's always been like that. When he's being something, he's that thing absolutely. And I think he's being the Emperor Beaulieu, which means he's the father of his people, and by extension, the father of everyone he's with. He's, you know, feeling responsible for us."

We'd returned to work. There was no way this machine was going to be elegant or beautiful. The engineering we were doing was simple, brutal, and sometimes weird, like distributing the sources of power all over the ship, so each of them took a partial battery. We couldn't have a whole powerpod anywhere without it protruding to the outside.

The steering was probably the most satisfactory modification job, but it had to be done in tiny miniature details, in cautious moves.

I was half under the steering console, staring up, by the light of my head lamp, at a bunch of confused circuits, wishing they were self-repairing and color-coded like the ones on Eden, when Morgan said, "Athena?"

I had a moment of panic. He wasn't supposed to be here. He was supposed to be in the improvised workshop, doing things we'd set him to do. I was trapped, with my head under the console. I didn't like him out there, able to do anything.

My entire body felt like a target, exposed. He could stab me, or cut me in half, or do anything. I couldn't retaliate. I couldn't—

It took all my discipline—and I never had much—not to pop out, not to jump out of there and immobilize him. It would be stupid if he was planning to attack me. With wild animals, I remembered, it is important not to show fear.

I'd always wondered if that was true. All the books said it, and okay, they'd been right about giving birth, except for the wonder thing, but I wondered how much a hungry lion or tiger really cared if you showed no fear. But Little Brother was not a lion or a tiger. He might be a feral creature, but the creature was human. And at least half raised as a human. I mean, he wasn't a wolf-child.

"Yeah?" I said.

"I lied," he said. His voice came in a hoarse whisper.

I didn't move, mostly because my body had activated the *oh, shit* circuits, the ones that pretty much assume you're going to die and there's no point doing anything. "About what?" I asked, shocked that my voice came out casual, almost disinterested. My hands, inside the console, raised above my eyes, were shaking so much I was afraid they were going to rattle against the sides of the console.

"About the privacy thing."

Breathe, Athena, breathe, damn it, I told myself. "Oh? You had privacy?" I splayed my hands on the inside of the console, against the walls, to stop them shaking.

"No, and yeah," he said.

Slowly, very slowly, I pulled my hands down, pulled my head out from under the console.

Robin was sitting cross-legged on the floor, a few steps from me, his mouth set, his face worried. He wasn't holding a burner or a knife. In fact, his hands were joined in his lap. He looked at me, as though he was afraid I was mad at him. His whole aspect was of a child who was about to tell on friends. "Look," he said. "We've never told anyone who wasn't . . . who wasn't one of us. But Laz . . . he created something that disrupted the eyes and ears." And perhaps interpreting my look of interest as disapproval, he said, "He had to, Thena. Sometimes we had to defend ourselves. Laz took under his protection everyone the elders hated, everyone Father wasn't interested in having survive. We had to defend ourselves. Sometimes that meant setting traps. It meant making sure that the others couldn't come to our territory. Only if you beat some of them, or hurt them, and Father saw it, he was going to kill us. Do you . . . do you understand?"

I understood. They'd been raised in continuous tribal warfare overseen by crazy gods. They weren't the only humans to be raised that way. There was a flavor to their upbringing of Greek mythology, which I suspected was itself derived from the primitive structure of hominid bands.

People in the twentieth and twenty-first centuries—if their books were any indication—had created this fantasy version of what early primitives had been like. No, thinking about it, humans always had. The Christians believed in that Eden for which Kit's world of origin had been named. But everything I'd read from scientists, and from the early history of mankind, indicated that early humans had been, like late humans, prone to excesses and to seeking power over other humans and to abusing that power when they had it. There were no noble savages. And there had never been.

I processed the horror that must have been these children's upbringing, and I didn't want to think more about them, I didn't want to go any deeper. I just wanted to free them of it; I just wanted to make sure they and we survived to have a better future than their past.

I realized Morgan was looking at me as though he expected me to chastise him. Instead I felt a great relief, as I realized he said they could block the eyes and ears. "They never caught on?" I asked.

"No, what it does is take the last two seconds of surveillance and repeat them in a loop as long as you need. You don't have things like that?"

"We have things exactly like that," I said. "For our surveillance mechanisms. But our technology and yours aren't precisely congruent."

"You mean yours wouldn't work on ours?"

"Probably not."

"But you have some?"

I wondered suddenly if he meant to use it to escape. But then I thought, what if he did? Yeah, we wouldn't have him with us, but we didn't need all of them with us. And hell, if he escaped to Earth here, we'd either save the people on Earth and he could get lost here, or he'd—be caught by the people who'd raised him again.

"Sure. Why?"

"Because I think it would be easier to modify yours. I know the frequencies and stuff. For ours, I mean. Laz taught me to do it."

"Right," I said. "Then I want you to make them for each of us to carry, always activated, to make sure none of us are seen. I mean they might catch on—probably will catch on—but at least—"

"They won't be sure where we are," Morgan said. "I'm glad you understand."

I understood. I also understood the risk Zen and I were taking. Maybe not Fuse. I had a feeling he and Thor had bonded. And it hadn't even been because of the quasi-parental concern that Fuse showed for Thor. No, it had been because Fuse could blow things up better than Thor. But whatever it had been, there had been a bond formed. I doubted Thor would do anything to hurt Fuse.

The others—

Maybe not Laz. He seemed to have the sort of personality that needed to protect others. From what I'd seen of both Jarl and my husband, that might be genetic. Most of the issues both Jarl and Kit had, most of the mistakes they'd made, were the result of perhaps trying to protect others too well. So Laz was likely to prove trustworthy. If anything he might risk himself to protect us.

But Morgan and John and Christopher? I thought John wanted to come to Earth and live with Luce on that farm Luce kept talking about. And Christopher Robin seemed like a kind and protective young man, a sort of younger version of Laz.

Still they had been raised in tribes, and with their hands against everyone else. Morgan, I wouldn't trust very far. I understood his desire to disappear, to run away on an Earth not controlled by the Mules. But would that win out, if he found himself in danger? Or would the sheer desire for life of an abused and feral creature take over?

I didn't know, and I didn't want to test it.

Two days later, we boarded the triangle-ships on our way to the *Je Reviens*. The one I shared with Morgan and Laz was called *Satisfaction*, after Captain Henry Morgan's flagship, and Little Brother claimed the right to pilot it, with me as a backup.

Fuse, Thor, and Christopher Robin were flying the *Mjolnir*.

Zen, John, and a last-minute joiner, Tom Sawyer, flew the *Barsoom*.

It was a crazy last-ditch effort, but it was the only one we had.

SAVING THE EARTH

Bearding the Lion

THE *JE REVIENS* WAS NOT AS CLOSE TO EARTH AS CIRCUM TERRA. It took us three days to reach it.

This mean we all piloted by turns while the others rested.

We observed radio silence while on the way, because we couldn't be sure we'd not be intercepted, and I kept mind-talk silence, because you couldn't be sure what the boys would pick up. At any rate, keeping up a talk with Kit would not have done any good. What I wanted to tell him, I'd already told him, in voice and mind and every way possible. And he'd already known it anyway. By some strange, inexplicable alchemy, he and I were one. The idea of dying didn't scare me, except for dying without him. It wasn't right. I didn't know if there was anything after death, but I had a feeling as though I'd be setting off on a journey with only half of me.

Of course, I also felt scared at the idea of leaving Eris to grow up as I had without a mother. But at least Kit, and whomever he might choose, should he not be able to raise her, would be people who loved her as something more than a whole-body-transplant donor.

But after a few hours, I missed the feel of Eris, warm and heavy in my arms. The milk-suppressor worked with no problems. I didn't have a physical need to nurse, but the emotional need remained. I said a prayer to divinities I wasn't sure I believed in as we flew into what was almost certainly battle.

We'd coordinated how we'd approach and to which port each ship would go.

Laz had drawn the outside of the *Je Reviens* and then diagrammed the inside. If we took the immediate halls? Avenues? In front of the ports in which we landed, we'd meet where the three pathways crossed.

I had been thinking of them as hallways, or at most as the roads in Eden. Until we came within sight of the *Je Reviens*.

This was a good way away, because it shone in the night like a beacon.

I'd been imagining it as a very large version of the *Cathouse*, or maybe as a ring like the original Circum Terra.

It was . . . vast. We couldn't see all of it as we approached, but it looked like nothing so much as a seacity in space. A vast seacity. There were at least three layers. I didn't know what it was made of, or not precisely. I'd never studied it, you see. Probably dimatough, because whole seacities had been sculpted of dimatough at around the time it was being built. Only it didn't look like dimatough, certainly not the poured black dimatough that constituted the beaches of places like Olympus and my native Syracuse Seacity.

Instead, it was black, yes, but dull, unreflective. The light from it came from what seemed to be lights affixed every few meters along its carapace, illuminating the intricate structure.

On my own, I didn't even recognize the ports, much less what port we should aim for. I was suffering the disorientation of the field mouse in the city. It was too vast, too confusing for me to understand.

I flew towards it, my mouth slightly open. There was enough space there, I realized, that if the Mules had taken all their "servants" with them to space, there would have been no need to colonize a planet for many generations. It probably could accommodate close to the population of Eden.

I felt a hand on my wrist. A small hand. "Let me," Morgan said. He'd been asleep when I'd last noticed, both he and Laz, curled up on opposite sides of the triangular ship, wrapped in some sort of reflective blanket.

I blinked at him, and he eased me aside, gently, and took

the controls, his hands confident and practiced. "They made us learn," he said. "They made us learn to pilot in and out, many times. I don't think they intended for us to come back," he said, "but they probably realized we'd notice that, if they didn't teach it. I can do this in my sleep. At any rate, when we approached first Eden, then Earth, we had to fly patrol around the ship."

"How could you not have privacy in that?" I asked, my mouth dry. Had we been led on? Were we walking into a trap? Worse than we'd imagined? Had the Mules created a million clones? Were we about to—

"We didn't have the use of all of it," Laz said, behind us. He stood, the blanket around his shoulders, almost like a cape. "We had very tight confines and a few restricted paths we could use to get to our work aboard. And at any rate, any place we were in was always full of eyes and ears. Electronic spy devices."

He stood beside me and pointed at a section. "We lived there, there, and there." The areas he identified were maybe the size of my father's palace. Spacious, but not massive.

"But then, you don't know the layout of the rest of the ship."

His smile was almost a grimace. He looked like he'd slept restlessly and had nightmares. "I know the whole ship," he said. "I got blueprints. Among the things they gave us was access to electronic materials, mostly reading materials. But you know, it's not hard to hack the rest of it. Oh, there were parts I couldn't get in. There were parts not even Morgan could get in. Parts that were walled off, passworded off, closed to us. Most of them were private to the elders, or to their . . . to the heirs."

"You mean the actual clones of the Mules aboard?"

He nodded curtly. "Yes. They called them the heirs. We had to behave to them like peasants to nobility."

"Not that we often saw them," Little Brother said. "They are— They had the run of the areas we can't get into. They were probably looked after by robots, as we were when we were very little, but they had fathers who supervised it all. We just had robots. And then the older kids, but most of them just liked to torture the younger or weaker ones. Not Laz, of course. I don't think most of us would have survived without Laz."

I turned to see Laz with his face averted, seemingly very interested in the wall beside us.

"He fought for us. He kept the others at bay. He kept us safe.

We—twenty or so us—ended up under his tutelage. Without him we'd all be dead."

"Are the others still in the *Je Reviens*?" I asked.

"If they weren't sent out," Laz said, his voice flat. "I wasn't given a choice about leaving, and I imagine they weren't either. At least they let me have Thor. I'm glad he found his brother. He worried me."

I didn't say anything. They all worried me. He was what? Sixteen or seventeen. Did he feel responsible for all the other misfits aboard? Did he feel responsible for keeping them alive?

I knew from his talk while he was delirious that he'd sometimes failed. And that those deaths still haunted him.

At least in my misguided youth, I hadn't been required to be responsible for anyone's life. I didn't know if that made me more or less human.

There was a crackle from the com panel and both boys gave out with "shhhh" even though I could tell the sound pickup was closed out.

A threatening voice echoed through the ship, "Unit Two Hundred, why are you returning?"

Little Brother hit the com button. He looked very pale. Not the sort of pale anyone should be able to go naturally. More like someone had opened a faucet at his heels and let out all his blood, leaving behind a bleached shell. He licked his lips, increasing the impression of dryness, and spoke in a rustle, "This is Sinistra. We seized this ship. We have a hostage."

I tensed. I was wearing my broomer suit, because it doubled as armor, and I had weapons in places these two misguided children wouldn't even think of. Sure, they were armed too, had to be, but there was something to be said for age and experience when fighting youths, even if those youths had grown up in hell.

"We have . . . a child," Morgan said, apparently reverting to what would have been his script if he had actually managed to kidnap Eris. "A child born of my . . . my female clone and a male clone of . . . Ingemar."

There was a long pause. The voice that came back was different, more human, more eager, but also strangely scarier. The first voice had been booming and threatening, as though it meant to get something from us, something that was forbidden or illicit. The tone reminded me of an addict reaching for the thing that would kill him, but kill him in bliss. "A child of those two? You mean Athena Sinistra and Christopher Ingemar?"

A shiver went down my spine, as though my name and Kit's pronounced by this creature were a sort of incantation that dirtied us and our names.

"Yes, yes," Morgan said. He sounded . . . different. I recognized the strangely unctuous and vaguely threatening voice he'd first used to me. For the first time it occurred to me to wonder whether he really had been unable to identify a woman. Laz said he was a computer expert, and if so, surely he'd watched sensies from Earth before the Turmoils. Also considering whose this ship was, some of them would almost certainly be rather . . . ah, instructive in the difference between men and women and the common interest of those differences. "We have their child. She's less than a month old, but she should be able to give you clues on how to create females of your own kind, so you can dominate Earth and displace the old humans."

I thought no one would buy that. Particularly not with the strange, slavering, weird voice Morgan was using. It was blatantly false. I'd known the little creep for less than a month and I already knew that voice wasn't right. No adult would be stupid enough to buy the sound of it, let alone the words.

There was a silence, and I thought the next sound we'd hear was *boom*, as the ship exploded around us, after which our life expectancy would be measured in seconds, even if we weren't personally hit.

Laz had told me they'd installed burner-cannons all along the outside of the *Je Reviens* with the intent of taking out any defenses that Circum Terra might possess, and which might still be active. Of course, Circum Terra had no defenses, except the personal weapons of the people aboard. But that wasn't the point. Even if they had been listening to our communications—and clearly they had since they knew both Kit's and my birth names and who we were—they didn't understand it was possible to have an outpost of Earth that wasn't defended against space attack. They also probably didn't understand that no one expected them to come back.

I confess that in retrospect, I too didn't understand why we hadn't expected it. Seemed like a stupid thing to write off members of a group that continued to cause problems on Earth no matter how thoroughly put-down. How could we have sent them to space with their own ship, the capacity to create biological and force weapons, and we hadn't guarded against them? Maybe we deserved to go extinct.

The voice came back with "You've done well. Dock in port fifty-five."

"I—I—I—am already aimed for port twenty-two, and I don't know if I can—"

"Oh, very well," said the rather bored voice. "You'll be met."

I wanted to ask Morgan if he'd just set us up to be arrested, but both of them kept touching their finger to their lips, demanding silence, even though the com was turned off. I wanted to tell them they were insane, but then I thought perhaps they knew something I didn't. Zen and I had changed many things about this ship, but the com system was not one of them. For all I knew these could be overridden from the mother ship, and the boys knew it.

I saw their hands move and realized they were talking, but the gestures were not broomer language, and I could not do it. Instead, I gestured to the pockets I knew hid the burners, and mouthed the words "Are you ready?" They both nodded. They looked tense.

I mouthed "Are we going to port twenty-two?"

Little Brother shook his head, and I had to be content with that.

He piloted us, tensely, in jerky movements. I'd seen him pilot elegantly, with gentle movements, before, but now it was as though he couldn't move except by overcoming some internal fear.

I felt a jar that almost rocked me off my feet, and thought we'd hit the *Je Reviens*, but Laz pushed a lever, and the door whooshed open.

There was a current of warm and smelly air. I can't put it any other way. The first time I'd entered a long-distance ship, as it happened, my beloved's darkship, the *Cathouse*, I'd almost been knocked out with a smell like all the dirty socks in the world had ganged up to ambush me.

And while my husband wasn't the best when it came to vibroing his clothes on time—in fact, I'd never been able to break him of the habit of leaving a trail of clothes from wherever he started undressing to the bed or the fresher—it wasn't because his housekeeping was terrible.

It was that over time, with humans confined inside a ship, the smell of human seeped into the ship itself, fused with the metal, became part of the space. There was no air scrubber so powerful, no cleaning bots so thorough, that the ship would ever not smell again.

Fortunately, after some time you stopped smelling it. It just became the *Cathouse*. I could smell new scents added to it, like if something leaked, or if we cooked, but not the pervasive, everlasting smell I knew was there.

The smell was in the *Je Reviens* too, but not as overpowering, because the ship was so much bigger. There was also a smell of vegetation, as though the ship contained forests. But there was another smell. I'd smelled it, even if not often. Mostly I'd smelled it because the broomer lair was truly appalling at cooking and housekeeping: It was rotten meat. Worse, it was a lot of rotten meat, nearby. It smelled like something very large was dead nearby. I didn't like it. And I liked the look the boys gave each other even less.

We left the ship in a wedge. We hadn't planned it. I couldn't trust them at my back, and perhaps they felt the same way. So Laz took point, and Morgan and I each took one side, facing out.

The place we exited into was a very broad room. It took me a moment to reorganize my thoughts into realizing it was not a room but a passageway of some sort. Not a hallway. In Eden we'd have flown flyers in it.

We walked out, and the place was deserted. There was no vegetation on the side of the road, but there were packing crates of some sort.

Laz said, "They'll be on us any moment."

I said, "Shouldn't we have flyers or something to make it there?"

"No," Morgan said, in a tone like it was the most stupid thing he'd ever heard. "No. Not that. We can't hide in a flyer. If they send flyers against us, it will be easier to run among the debris."

"Debris?" I asked.

"This is why we picked these docks. There are debris and stuff that never got unloaded when they left people out in Eden. I don't think it was an orderly separation," Laz said. "But debris allows you to run among them and hide. We have entire tunnels," he said.

I was going to ask him what he meant, but instead I asked, "How far is the lab?"

"Not far," Laz answered.

And that's when the flyers came down the tunnel. I saw them flash, but I never saw or even knew if they had weapons.

Instead, before they could even get close, Laz grabbed me and pulled me.

I thought we were going behind the boxes. I had my burner out. I was trying to get a fix on the nearest flyer, even though I realized it was probably too big to be brought down by a mere burner.

But the boys push-pulled me at a half run, yes, behind the boxes, but into the boxes.

I can't describe it, partly because it was all done at a run, but amid the boxes piled high, there was a space for us to run.

It seemed to me that this was stupid. The materials we were running among looked far too flammable. And as we ran, I wondered why the boys thought this was safe.

I heard weapons and stopped, but Laz said, "Never mind. You're safe here. We spent years building a shell of ceramite over it. Even if the boxes burn we're safe till we get to the place we cross paths with the others."

But before we got to the crossing, the tunnel had got unbearably hot, and the smell of something dead had become almost unbearable. It felt really scary running towards the horrible smell, in the half-dark, since I couldn't tell where the light was coming from.

Morgan, who was running ahead, burner in hand, in the half-dark, tripped on something.

He stepped back, looked down, and something not quite a scream escaped him.

Laz knelt, looked down, and felt at something.

"What happened?" I said. "Who is it?"

"One of the littles," Laz said. "He's been dead a while."

The Home Team

WE SPENT VERY LITTLE TIME ON THE DEAD KID. I COULD BARELY see him, but from Laz referring to him as "one of the littles" and from his size, he looked to be under ten to me. He was dressed in the same sort of outfit the three young men had worn when I'd first met them.

Laz tried to take off his coat, presumably to cover the dead child, and when I stopped him, he made a sound of frustration, ran to a box and dragged something over, which he laid over the child. I don't know why he bothered. I mean, it did the child no material good.

It was Morgan who pulled and pushed at Laz to get him to hurry on.

We ran on as the surface of the tunnel grew heated above us. There were steps behind us, too, now, running. Which made sense. No matter how much we defeated the cameras, the port had probably reported a ship coming in, and then the flyers would have seen three people duck into the tunnel. Whether they'd had enough distance vision to see that one was female didn't matter. They knew the three people in the tunnel were unauthorized. When setting fire to the piles of trash on the side of the pathway hadn't got us to come out hands up, people would be sent after us. I knew that sound, the sound of boots on dimatough.

"Who the hell will they send after us?" I asked, turning around to look in the back, seeing a group of maybe six people running. They wore shiny armor. Dimatough makes the best armor that humans have ever invented. Its drawback is that it doesn't articulate well. Which is why most dimatough armor was made of tiny scales, layered. And it was near impregnable.

Its advantages were that there were only two ways to get to the occupant. One was to use your burner on high heat and kill them by cooking. Another was to aim carefully, on cutting mode, and slice the head off where the helmet joined the body armor.

There were no ways to disarm people in dimatough armor.

I wouldn't have cared. Not a few years ago, I wouldn't have. I don't know how many people I killed in my mad career, getting out of hospitals, military academies, and mental hospitals to which Daddy Dearest confined me in attempts to tame me, or at least to try to keep me quiet till I served my purpose.

I'd done what I had to do, struck how I had to strike, hit whom I had to hit. And I didn't even remember it afterwards. But Kit was different, and he'd spent years telling me that everyone I had to deal with was someone's brother or sister, some mother's child. This made killing them with no thought very difficult. Kit, who had the devil's own temper, used this mantra to control himself. He'd also made me see that people sent against me weren't necessarily villains. Most of them, truth be told, were earning Daddy Dearest's salt, or in the case of most of them, narcs.

And in this case, unless the people coming up against us were the actual Mules, I thought they'd be coerced in some way. Either by force or with bribes, either by propaganda, or simply by virtue of growing up in a virtual prison camp, and in what amounted to a cult, only worse.

I didn't think the Mules would risk themselves in this.

"Some of us," Laz said. He sounded hoarse, his voice tiny. "Some of us were trained to kill, to defend the elders. Some of us—"

"Shit," I said. "You mean enslaved babies with no real choice."

They were now close enough, I could see the burners in their hands, which meant any minute now— I dropped and rolled. Laz dropped and rolled in the other direction, and came up taking a perfect knee and firing. The boy was good. A head rolled, a man in dimatough armor fell. He fell just so others tripped on him.

"Don't know about choice," Laz said, as he beheaded another. "I know they were trained from birth to be killing machines. They were trained on us, and taught not to flinch at taking life. Either fire on them or run, damn it."

And I shot, beheading one. And then Little Brother, behind me, took another one.

Suddenly they were all dead, and I was running. I'd killed three probably very young men, who never had any choice about what they would be, and there was something heavy and cold in the pit of my stomach, something like regret or remorse. Only not really regret or remorse. I thought of how Laz and Morgan had fired on them, and I thought that they would know best, that they, if anyone, would be more likely to have mercy on these people, raised as they were in a similar environment.

Okay, these weren't precisely some mother's child, except for some very distant mother who might have provided the gestation environment for the original Mules. And those would be at best surrogate mothers. But they could have been the brothers—at least the spiritual brothers—of those who'd grown up with them.

Yeah, they'd probably not made a choice to become killers. They had probably been chosen from infancy to be the enforcers. I could tell, even at the distance we'd seen them, they were all over six feet, and unless the armor greatly exaggerated their proportions, built like brick shithouses. But whether they'd chosen to or not, I knew what a concentrated program of brainwashing and programming could do to a mind.

Sure people could be deprogrammed. People could be brought back. Maybe. Sometimes. It was possible that in circumstances completely different from the ones we faced, circumstances in which we could have made a raid and kidnapped these kids, and put them through a thorough deprogramming course, using the best techniques of our mental rehabilitators, they might have come out of it more or less normal. Maybe. None of those rehabilitators had managed to make me stop rebelling, and heaven knew they tried, and that I hadn't been put through a program to encourage rebellion, or at least not on purpose.

It was all academic, anyway, we didn't have those resources, we didn't have that kind of time.

I ran after Laz, and tried to think of these men who might— who would, because certainly somewhere, somehow, the death of

those sent against us had already registered—come against us as
nothing more than enemy assets, like so many robots, sent to
kill us. "How many of them are there?"

"What?" Laz asked, his voice strained. He was running full-
on, like a sprinter, and Morgan was keeping up with him despite
considerably shorter legs.

"How many guards might they send against us?"

"Probably about a hundred?"

"Probably?"

"There were a hundred and fifty made, but some washed out
and some died. Probably about a hundred."

"Washed out?"

"I...I was made for that. Most of the older ones were. Most
of them were made from three lines only. The...the ones most
conducive. Some of us didn't work out."

I processed this as I ran. Joy, oh joy. Not only was I likely
to have to fight my way through a hundred or so indoctrinated
murder-machines, but there was a good likelihood a third of
those murder machines were the identical twins of my husband
and Laz.

"They don't look like the sort of people who would allow you
to just drop out of the program."

"Nah, those of us who could ran away. We were about five
years old. We grew up in the tunnels. These tunnels. On scraps
dropped from the colonization of Eden. By that time there were
other kids, and when we went into the crèche they didn't care
anymore. The elders. I guess they liked that we could keep discipline and do a better job than raising robots."

I tried to picture that, to figure out how these kids had grown
up, but I actually couldn't. The mind wouldn't bend that way.
There are things that anyone raised in semi-normal circumstances,
even circumstances like mine, can't conceive. And I took the
fact that Laz had run away to avoid being turned into a killing
specialist, and yet was willing to kill those coming after us, to
mean that I should just kill them and shut up.

It was a good thing I came to that conclusion, because just as
I thought it, there were sounds from in front, running towards us.
I took only a moment to realize it couldn't be our fellows from
Earth, whom we were supposed to meet. Because the sound of
feet indicated military boots and the weight of dimatough armor.

And yet, we couldn't fire straight on. Because I didn't know how close we were to the place the pathways crossed, or whether stray burner fire would not burn one of our own.

So I jumped to the side of the tunnel and aimed part sideways, as I took a cutting ray through two necks in succession.

Little Brother, taking his place against the crumbling wall of boxes, behind me, did the same, while Laz had taken a position against the ceramite wall and did the same.

They fired at us, of course, while we were trying to cut off their heads, and they threw themselves around and tried to evade our rays.

I don't remember it. I don't remember being in danger. I was aware of burning rays going by twice, so close that I felt their heat on my face, and smelled the singeing of my own hair.

I saw a cutting ray go so close to Laz that his sleeve was sliced.

But I don't remember being afraid or thinking there was any doubt of the outcome. More that we'd kill them, and go on, and could we find our friends—and were our friends still alive—before we had to deal with another batch of attackers.

When the last of the dimatough-armored men fell, we ran. We ran among them, leaping over corpses obstructing the way, and not even pausing when Morgan tripped on a head that rolled in his path. Instead, Laz and I grabbed him, one from either side, and lifted him, and ran with him half-suspended until he regained his balance.

We came out of the tunnel of rubbish. It was as abrupt as emerging from a cave into sunlight and nearly as blinding. We'd been in semi-dark. I still didn't know how the improvised tunnel was lit, though I suspected it was some system the boys had jury-rigged. But the pathway was as much larger than the tunnel as a street is than the hallway in a house, and it was bright, lit with either artificial or piped-in sunlight.

Bright enough to blind us, which was good, because we stopped.

It was just a few seconds, but it might have saved our lives.

Because before I could blink, I was aware of a dimatough-clad guy falling at my feet, his blood pouring out of his severed neck to soak my boots.

And Zen's voice said, "About damn time."

She stood, flanked by Tom and John, both holding weapons, and wouldn't you know it, that not one of her hairs looked out of place? It was the sort of thing warranted to drive every other woman to hate her, but there it was. She looked like the perfect goddess of battle, makeup and a couple tiny splatters of blood applied just for effect. Not that she was wearing makeup. This was just how she looked. And the blood was probably real.

Tom and John at least had the grace to look as breathless as I felt, and John had taken a shallow cut to the face, on the left side, which he was letting bleed as if it didn't matter.

"We were chased," Tom said, taking big gulps of air, as though he had gotten winded and had no time to recover. And these were waiting for us here.

"No sign of Fuse?" I asked, turning towards the left, where another path met ours, the path I presumed Fuse would have taken. I wondered if Fuse and Thor, even with Christopher Robin's help, would have been cunning enough to fool the Mules to allow landing. I wondered what they'd met on arrival.

I was starting to feel greatly despondent about my friend's chances, and thinking we should never have allowed someone who was still mentally impaired to make the decision to come with us, when an explosion made the floor under our feet shake, and debris came flying out of the tunnel, as well as three people.

Don't ask me how. It shouldn't be possible, considering the young men were well nigh his size, but I swear even in the confusion of the moment I had a clear picture, and now have a clear memory, of Fuse, with Christopher Robin and Thor, each under one arm, jumping just ahead of flying debris.

We all hit the deck, by instinct more than thought. I felt... something patter on my back, and refused to guess of what kind the debris would be, and whether organic or not.

When they stopped and I got up, everyone was getting up. The answer to the debris was "yes." There was obvious blood spray and bits of flesh. But there were also a lot of pieces of what looked like machinery.

"Oh, hell," Laz said. "Not the cyborgs."

Why can't anything ever be easy or simple? Why did it have to be cyborgs?

Run!

"WE NEED TO GET OFF THE OPEN PATHWAYS," LAZ SAID.

"How are we going to do that?" Christopher Robin asked belligerently.

"I know ways. I needed them when we had to hide from you guys." It was thrown back slyly, but I got an impression of tribal warfare.

And Laz headed back into the path that Fuse's group had come running out of.

We slipped and slid on blood and circuits until we came to a portion where the wall looked damaged by the explosion, but you could tell there was a grate there. It was bent outward by the explosion. Laz said, "Bonus," and pried at it, then said, "Inside."

We all went in, one after the other, till he came last and pulled the grate back into place. As I watched him doing it, I thought it wouldn't fool a child, except for the fact that the entire pathway was so much damaged by the explosion, it might take time to notice. Of course, they'd also realize their bugs were useless, since they would have been transmitting a spotless corridor, then shown it blown up and then . . . well, probably continued showing it blown up as it didn't show us. Never mind.

There are two ways that you can make your way through a building, a ship, or anything that has functional arrangements

273

for living. One is through the air ducts, as Nat and I had done in La Mancha. This was the other way. To be specific, this was the sewers.

I'm not squeamish. Sometimes, even we had to make it through the sewers, when our broomer lair was avoiding attention by peacekeepers. My boots and my suit were waterproof. It was the smell.

Perhaps it was that something had changed since I'd given birth. I've been told that pregnant women get all sorts of hormonally induced changes. Or maybe it was instinctive: the need to keep surroundings clean for my baby.

In any case, the smell stung my nose and throat and made me gag.

The sewer itself was large. Probably double the width of the hallway in my father's mansion, and those were spacious for household hallways. It was tall, probably double my height. And it had only enough water to reach just above the top of my boots. Well, not water. The staining on the walls, though, indicated that at some point or other it had run much higher.

Visions of someone turning sewage on full force and washing us down...somewhere...were not good. I'd once been submerged in medical waste to escape a hospital to which I'd been confined. It wasn't an experience I remembered fondly, nor did I want to repeat it with variations.

But the best way to avoid it was to move fast.

We followed Laz at a trot, which meant that we had to inhale more of the stink that burned my throat.

None of us spoke, and there were no thoughts exchanged. I assumed our pocket disruptors were still preventing any bug from locating us, and I presumed they extended far enough to disable bugs in rooms and hallways beyond the sewers.

What I didn't assume is that those rooms were empty. None of us did. I noted that while running full tilt, we were all trying to land on tiptoe to diminish the splashing, and I didn't think it was just for reasons of hygiene—though it was that also—but to keep the noise to a minimum.

After a while, we heard voices above or to the side of us, and once, a sound like an explosion. We didn't stop. It couldn't have anything to do with us, or if it did, the best way to deal with it and avoid any repercussions was not to stop.

We seemed to be going downwards, the sewer curving in a gentle slope, and the water at our feet growing exponentially. I was trying not to have the dreads about it going over where boots met pants, because it was almost impossible for it not to seep in at that point, when Laz stopped abruptly.

In front of us was a deep pit into which the sewage flowed, and a noise of machinery came from it. Some sort of pump, I thought. And if he gestured for us to jump in, it would be the biggest mistake of his short and misguided life, because I would end it.

But instead, he turned to the wall, slightly above his head, where there was a fan.

The fan pointed inward, towards the sewer, and through it came a vaguely floral or at least vegetable scent.

Laz's hands flashed in quick movements, and Thor and Morgan moved to help him as he started unwinding the finger-bolts holding the fan in place. Morgan couldn't do much but stand in place, ready to ease the fan down. He simply wasn't tall enough. However, as what they were trying to do became obvious, Fuse joined in, his fingers working fast at the bolts above Laz's head, and I had a momentary shock at how tall Fuse was, again. It's weird when you've been used to thinking of someone as the logical equivalent of a six-year-old to realize he's tall enough and competent enough to tower over most people and to get things without explanation.

They moved as if they'd practiced this, and I thought the young men probably had done it before, but Fuse managed to fit in. When the bolts were loosened, Fuse, Thor, and Laz eased the fan onto the floor. Through the opening came a definite vegetable smell. It was like the smell of a garden or a forest.

As the taller men started to methodically boost us up, starting with Morgan, who was the shortest, and then myself, I realized why.

My head protruded from a square opening at floor level, and the whole thing fell in perspective. I realized that the machinery at the end of the pit was probably ventilation. Oh, probably pumps and incinerators, too, or whatever. I suspect solids were incinerated, liquids were filtered, and quite likely gases were burned. But the point was to create a negative draw on the bad smell, so it didn't seep back into the tunnel.

And because you might need to do maintenance in the sewers now and then, and also because you really didn't want droplets of sewage drawn into the air, you'd have to replenish the air. It was best to do it with outside air from places where you really didn't want the smell of sewage. Like this garden.

This garden was gorgeous.

Morgan had knocked a filter-cover from the wall in crawling through, and was lying on a carpet of soft grass. That soft grass thing was not poetry. It really was soft grass, with thin and abundant blades, much like the biocarpets of Eden, only quite obviously less artificial.

As I crawled after, I smelled it, and it was like heady perfume. Oh, I'm fairly sure it smelled like lawns everywhere, okay? But it smelled wonderful after the truly horrible sewage stink. There were little yellow flowers growing in it here, and I wanted to remove my gloves and feel them. I wanted to remove all my clothes and roll in the grass, which made me wonder if either the sewage or the grass had hallucinogenic properties. I've never been one of nature's nudists. I have no body modesty, mind, always thinking of my body as something not only very handy to carry me around, but also something I could use to bribe or coerce others.

But most of the time I found the idea of being naked in the outdoors, or the equivalent of the outdoors, disquieting. I wasn't even fond of my father's gardens while fully clothed. The outdoors is full of things that bite, sting, or crawl into inconvenient places. And that's not counting all the plants whose sole justification for existence is the ability to inject toxins or tear into unsuspecting human skin. Yeah, I know, my nannies also insisted this was silly, and that the plants weren't specifically out to get me. None of them managed to convince me, though. I knew better. If they weren't out to get me, Father wouldn't have planted them in his garden.

But this place was so beautiful after the horrible things we'd seen and done since entering the *Je Reviens* that I had trouble controlling myself not to get naked and roll around. In the end, what helped me control myself was the stern admonition that Little Brother didn't need his prurient, and in this case perverse, curiosity satisfied, and neither did the other boys who had never seen an unclothed female in real life, and who had—in fact—only seen Zen and me in real life.

I crawled away from the entrance as John emerged from the opening, and lay down beside Morgan, chuckling.

"What's so funny?" he whispered.

"I was thinking you boys will have a very weird idea of the proportion of males and females in the human race," I whispered back.

John gave me a weird look, and Morgan said, "Yes?"

"It's really about fifty-fifty. Our group is different because we have the blood of—we're made after people like the elders, and women are hard to create from that stock."

Tom emerged from the sewer, followed by Christopher Robin, and then Thor.

I sat up. John was sitting nearby with a weird expression on his face. He caught my eye and grinned, and whispered, in a tone of breathless wonder, "Fifty-fifty? Oh, I'm going to enjoy Earth."

"None of us is going to enjoy Earth," Laz said, as he emerged from the sewer opening, "unless we get moving, and fast. Because an Earth in which the Elders rule is really not that much different than what we've been living with." He was whispering, but his voice was really determined. Those of us who'd sat stood up, and Morgan bounced to his feet.

"That's better," Laz said. "We're now deep in Elder territory. I only found this place because of the maps, but I've used it a few times, and I know how to cross it to get us to the lab."

"What is this place?" Morgan asked, sounding awed.

"I think it's a park of sorts. They rarely come here. But it's no reason to get foolish. And some of the heirs do come here. Play here, in fact. So be alert."

He led us. It was a different progression than in tunnels or semi-open pathways where the best you could do was stay close to the walls.

Here, our progress was mostly made—it seemed—through tall grasses, amid bushes, or under the canopy of tall trees. I knew that our disruptors disabled bugs, so we must be doing this to avoid the eyes of casual observers.

The place really was beautiful. Like the open area of Jarl's resort, it seemed to mix vegetation, trees, and flowers from all over the world, and not to be overly cultivated. Just allowed to grow in pleasant disarray. Which was good, because it meant some of the grasses were at shoulder height for Laz, and completely covered the rest of us, in an experience not unlike being submerged.

Weirdly, we crossed a sort of flowing rivulet of water. Sort of flowing, because it was very shallow and had stuff growing right on the riverbed, tall plants with plumes. I think it was really some sort of planned irrigation. But the water looked and smelled clear and came right over the top of my boots, cleaning away the mess from the sewer. I wasn't the only one who stooped and cleaned my gloves, either. In fact, every one of the others did it.

We moved cautiously and kept our eyes open. Or at least I did. Which is why I spotted the turtle-like thing at my feet, and took great care to walk around it, because it was mechanical, which meant it would holler if disrupted. I hoped it didn't have any bugs that our disruptor didn't neutralize, but whether it did or not, shooting it would be a sure way to get the busies on us.

A word for those of you embarking on a life of clandestine movement: While it's best of all to avoid police and machinery that reports to the police, if you can't do that, at least try not to disrupt the operations of either human or mechanical peacekeepers.

Humans are fallible. Human peacekeepers, or the humans who reviewed data from the robots, might miss your presence if you simply passed by as fast as you could. But no peacekeeping organization in the world, or in any world, or even aboard a ship, will ignore something that takes out one of its own, human or mechanical. If you shoot a peacekeeper or a peacekeeping robot, you just made your chances of escape that much slimmer.

I had just finished going around the mechanical turtle and looked up when I saw fast movement through the plants around us. Lots of fast movement. I lifted my burner and pointed. And stopped.

They were children. The oldest was probably Morgan's age, and the others were younger than that. I didn't count them. Just had the impression of a small crowd, probably around twenty or so of them. They were all male, but there the homogeneity stopped, as they were all sizes and descriptions.

I couldn't just shoot them. I mean, it's one thing to shoot adults one considers irredeemable, or at least irredeemable without considerable and at the moment impossible work. But children? I couldn't have shot children to save my life. Possibly literally. And it was a viable strategy, I realized.

Before the guards had come at us, I'd thought we were dealing with one-Mule-one-clone or something close to that, but now I realized it was no such thing. The Mules created people as they needed them, and in different varieties. I suspected there had been thirty or fifty clones of Jarl Ingemar, and wasn't even sure that Laz was the only one who'd dropped out of the attractive "become a killer" program. For all I knew there were dozens of them lurking around somewhere. In the same way, I could see at least one kid in the crowd that looked a lot like Little Brother, and one that bore a resemblance to Fuse. If the Mules had made hundreds of these little children, and realized we were hesitant to shoot them, they could simply bury us in children.

I waited as first Little Brother then Thor obviously saw the children. They also didn't go for the burners, but Morgan sighed, and I thought he saw it as I did. The children would run us down and we'd be—

"Laz!" a little voice piped up.

Laz, up ahead of me, stopped, and fell into a squat to be at the child's level. I could see him fully—and not as glimpses of his broomer suit, through the tall grass—for the first time since we'd started moving. He smiled at the child, a dark boy with unruly dark curls. He took his finger to his lips, though, and spoke back in a whisper, "Well done, Etienne," he said. "But don't speak so loudly, all right? It could get them to hear us all, or there could be an heir somewhere around and he could notice us, and that would get us killed."

The child's face fell. "You didn't come back for good? You're not going to take us to Earth?"

Laz's face fell. He looked at us. He seemed to be doing calculations in his head. He said to Fuse, "They have so little mass."

This is when I intervened. "We overengineered," I said. "I think we could."

Laz let out breath, as though he'd been holding it a long time, and I realized that he'd been worried about this. I also realized several other things, such as the fact that he'd obviously been planning this from the beginning. He wanted to come with us, because he wanted to take back his . . . protégés? Morgan had said that he was the protector of those weaker than him, so I couldn't exactly claim this was unexpected.

He smiled at me and said, "Thanks." Then he turned to the children. "Listen, we have to do something dangerous, and there is absolutely no point in endangering you with us, so you stay here and keep the others safe, all right? I'll come back and get you, and take you to Earth with me on the way back."

A couple of the children hugged him, a few hugging his knees as he stood up. He looked like a weight had been lifted from his shoulders as he led us diagonally across the vast, cultivated space and then paused, still within the protection of the grasses, but within sight of the outer door. "Now," he whispered, "once we're through this door, we're in public corridors, and some of these corridors, we're even allowed to use. I suggest we put the people who grew up here on the outside and the ones from Earth, particularly the women, in the center. Look, it is possible that anyone we encounter—most of the elders here are scientists—will not realize we're not the ones supposed to be here. There is a good chance they won't even notice us. Unless they notice Fuse is much too old to be here, and that two of you are women. So just keep your heads down and try to pass. If anyone looks like giving the alarm, though, we must kill them. Is that clear? We can't afford for the alarm to be sounded. The Elders and the heirs still have a lot of guards, human, cybernetic and robotic. If they spot us, there is no way we get out of here alive: any of us. And then all of Earth will die and the elders will get what they wanted. Is that clear?"

It was crystalline.

Hell Breaks Loose

WE MADE IT WITHOUT SEEING ANYONE A GOOD LONG WHILE down what was more of a hallway than a path, like the one we'd encountered back where we'd first boarded the ship.

If I'd been dropped in this portion of the ship without warning, I'd have viewed it as a building, some sort of commercial structure, laboratories or warehouses, or something like that, with proportional hallways and doors opening on either side.

Since the boys couldn't technically surround us, we walked with Fuse and Zen and me close to the wall, hoods pulled over our heads and goggles on, as though we were about to take to the air on broomback. We won't even mention how badly I wanted to take to the air on broomback. Because I did. In fact, I thought, even in these corridors, it would have been much easier to take to the air and fly over the heads of those seeking us, or, even better, those not seeking us.

The problem was that, as Laz had noted, it would be much easier to pick us out up there. So we moved at human step speed, at ground level, with the more conspicuous ones of us next to the wall, even if the wall was punctuated by doors. The boys were on the outside, forming a sort of shield, and clearly moving with what they thought was nonchalance. Perhaps it was nonchalance here. In the same way that Morgan's performance aboard the

Satisfaction had seemed horribly unconvincing and contrived to me, but had clearly fooled the Mules, perhaps the boys, having been raised in a place where danger was always around the corner, had no idea what fully relaxed body language was. In fact, I'd never seen any of them act completely unselfconscious, save for when Morgan had broken out bawling.

I noted all the boys had their hands near the pockets that contained burners. I hoped they wouldn't have to use them.

You always get what you don't want.

In this case, what we got was a relatively young man coming out of one of the doors, pausing, staring at us, and his eyes going huge. Before he could scream, three of the boys had shot him through the heart, burning a hole through his white tunic and his body. He looked surprised, but only for a second, and then he looked dead and was on the floor bleeding.

Which should have been the end of the incident, as far as we were concerned. After all, he'd collapsed before he could scream, right? And unless someone else saw it, we should be out in the clear until someone found the young man and gave the alarm.

Except that things never happen in a logical way. As the young man fell, he was dead. He had to be dead, and he had to know it too. Where his heart used to be, there was a hole, instantly cauterized by the fire of three simultaneous burners. I wouldn't have moved that fast to kill, not now. I'd probably have jumped him and beaned him on the head with the butt of a burner. But of course the boys had grown up here, and anyone who had grown up here was as likely to be fast—as fast—as the boys with us were. And maybe they couldn't be overcome that easily.

But what the boys had done, killing the poor unsuspecting man really fast, should have ended it. He didn't have any heart. He was dead. Except, as he fell, his hand went to a necklace around his neck and grabbed at the pendant there.

"Oh, shit," Laz said.

And then alarms sounded. Really loud alarms.

It was like every possible alarm had gone off, like something had activated every possible state of emergency aboard the *Je Reviens*.

The light in the hallways throbbed, turning from sunlight into a sort of flickering red and yellow, and klaxons sounded very loudly, while a voice with a strange accent admonished that there were intruders aboard, and they should be captured right away.

Doors opened. From down the hallway there was a sound of running boots.

"Shit," Laz said. His shoulders sagged. "We're dead."

It could be true. He could be right. But if I'd given up every time all seemed surely lost, I'd never have survived childhood.

"Damn it, no," I screamed. "At least we go down swinging. Where is the lab, Laz? Lead us."

He looked at me with a blank expression, as if I were speaking a strange language. Perhaps I'd talked too fast. Everything around me seemed to have slowed down. But I thought he was just in shock. I slapped him hard. "Take us to the lab, damn it," I yelled.

He took a breath in, deep, like a drowning man. And then he started running. We ran after him, though I noted that Fuse and Thor threw something over their shoulders as they ran.

Explosions came, and the force caught up with us and lent a little extra speed to our running, but we didn't even slow down, not even when we were slipping on dimatough and flesh debris.

Laz slammed his hand into a panel on a door to our right, and it opened, and we ran through it.

Inside was a vast laboratory, crammed with work tables, some of them littered with circuits or crowded with microscopes. But there were vats along the wall with what looked like tissues growing in different colored liquids. And there were, on a far corner, not one but two regen machines.

Regen machines are unmistakable, since they look kind of like the square, blocky medieval tombs you find in ancient monasteries throughout Europe, except that they're made of glossy ceramite. These were both grey and looked new, unlike the outer surface of the *Je Reviens*.

Laz had run into the lab in a sort of panic, and the rest of us had followed the same way, but Fuse and Thor had taken positions by the door, looking out, and before any of us could do much more than stand in the lab, breathing heavily, they threw something out of the door. Flesh and bits of unidentified components came raining in tiny pieces through the door, accompanied with a flash and a smell of burning.

"Thena," Fuse said confidentially. "I don't have enough bangs to hold them off forever. Get to finding whatever the hell we came to get."

I found the word bang incongruous in his speech. Sure, when he wasn't functioning, Fuse had called bombs *booms* or *bangs*, and it seemed to make sense with the rest of his vocabulary. Then it occurred to me that what he and Thor were holding in their hands, ready to throw, looked about like glass marbles, and that for all I knew "bangs" were the slang for those things.

Conscious that my mind wasn't working normally, that I might be in shock, or just really scared, I turned to Laz. "Laz, find them."

He ran.

He started ransacking tables, throwing things on the floor, looking through shelves, as though he were a burglar looking for hidden silver. He was muttering to himself as he did it. I had the impression that whatever he was looking for had been moved, and a cold shiver ran up my spine. Great, just great. We'd come all this way, and we were probably going to die here, and we hadn't even got a chance. If I'd known, I'd have stayed on Earth, while Kit tried to recreate the chip. We might at least have survived.

From above me came a sound like digging, and I looked up. The ceiling was panels of ceramite, inset in a frame. Probably to allow people to get up there and change wiring or illumination. Made sense. Pour the ceiling in ceramite, and you won't be able to get to anything.

But now the ceramite was cracking and flaking. And suddenly, through the panels emerged a head. It was a robot head, and it looked exactly like a giant beetle with sparkling jewel eyes and a dimatough carapace. Why did it have to be robot bugs? I'd fought them once before, in Jarl's resort. Actually that made perfect sense, now that I thought about it. After all, the Mules, the original set, had all been raised in the same way, and it made sense they had the same hang-ups and some of the same things they considered interesting or cool. None of which made this better.

I jumped away as the thing dropped on the floor and started slithering towards me. Look, I can take mice. I can take snakes. But some of these bugs could do strange things, from shocks to, potentially, mind control, and I'd be damned. I'd just be damned. I screamed and hit it with a blast of the burner on the highest hit setting. It stopped moving, but there were others behind it. I hit another one, and another one, and now the boys joined me, all but Laz, who was on top of a ladder, madly ransacking a stack of semitransparent boxes.

Zen was saying something over and over—it sounded like "ew"—and burning them away, while she stood on top of a table.

"Young man, get down from that worktable," an irascible—and unknown—voice said. "How many times do I have to tell you a laboratory is not a bar and that—"

We all turned to look. The man had come in through a door that looked like access to a closet. He reminded me of Dr. Bartolomeu, the one Mule I'd known who had eschewed cosmetic rejuvenation. He was tall, and his face looked like his wrinkles had decided to acquire wrinkles. His hair was long, very white, and wispy, and his eyes were dark and sharp in their nest of wrinkles.

As we all turned, he took a step back. His face went pale, and he said, "Young lady," mechanically, staring at Zen, and then in a tone of great and complete confusion, "Young . . . lady?"

Morgan let out a feral yell and fell on the man. I noted the man wore a necklace like the young man killed in the hallway had worn. Morgan tore it off his neck, which was probably stupid, because alarm had already been sounded. Then he put his burner to the man's head, and said something.

I didn't understand the something. For one, a bug touched the tip of my boot, and I fell back, screamed, and burned it as Morgan was talking. For another, Fuse decided this was a superlative time to throw another bang down the hallway, or maybe we really had that much of a threat headed our way.

I heard the answer loud and clear, though. "Well, why didn't you say so, instead of making this unseemly display? I always said that whole thing was a stupid idea anyway. Earth would be interesting for experiments, but I'm going to guess more trouble than it's worth. Ingemar!"

This was obviously directed at Laz, who said, with an edge of panic to his voice, "Sir?"

"Components cabinet. No, not that one, the one to the left," as Laz scrambled down the leader and went to a big piece of furniture next to the shelves.

I lost track of what they were doing at that point, because

Zen had apparently run out of power in the burner she'd been using, and had gone into a very feminine freak-out. I knew for a fact that she had other burners. But instead of reaching for one to burn the bugs, she had got hold of a "dead" bug—I hoped she'd waited long enough for it to cool and didn't now have third-degree burns in her hands, even through the gloves—had jumped down from the table and was using the dead bug to beat the live bugs in something that approached frenzy.

Dimatough is almost impossible to break. Almost. If you're going to have a chance at it, your only choice is to hit dimatough with dimatough. But more importantly, she was hitting the things hard enough that it was destroying whatever the mechanism was inside. There was no way machines could be made of solid, poured dimatough, after all.

Between Zen and the young men, they were taking care of incoming bugs, and I looked back to see Laz receive a shoe-box-sized clear box containing a bunch of components from the elderly... Mule, I presumed.

I could only hear their conversation intercut with the noise of Zen beating the holy hell out of the bugs, but it went something like this:

"...with us?" Laz asked.

"Daft... Young... Told you, no use for Earth."

"...Quite safe?"

A wheezing laugh. "Safe enough... I've lived with these psychopaths my entire life."

I was strategizing. I too had lived with these psychopaths my whole life, or rather, with psychopaths like them. I knew how Daddy Dearest's mind had worked, as well as the minds of all his closest friends and enemies, which were often the same people.

Fuse and Thor threw a bang. The fine rain of, this time, mostly components came blowing in, and the old man, whoever he was, screamed, "Close the door, damn it. This is a lab, not a barn. You're getting contamination everywhere. Mason! I'm talking to you."

It was like magic, and both Fuse and Thor jumped to it, closing the door. Which made absolutely no sense, as they wouldn't be able to clear the next wave of whatever was sent after us. And we'd locked ourselves in the lab, which meant we were sitting ducks. On the other hand...

On the other hand, only one wall of the lab was dimatough. If you grew up with the stuff, as well as ceramite, you could more or less tell one from the other on sight, though don't ask me exactly what made them different, because I couldn't describe it, just identify it.

The other three were ceramite, as was the floor, and obviously the ceiling.

Unless I was being more idiotic than usual, I thought, looking at the ceiling and the seemingly unending bugs raining down, the sort of escape Nat and I had taken in La Mancha should be doable, particularly if we made it random enough while approaching the ships. And the ships were overengineered. All we needed was to get to one of them, or, well, any of the other triangular lifeboats still berthed at port in the *Je Reviens*. If the sketch of the interior of the ship Laz had made was right, there were hundreds of them. We didn't actually need to take the ones we came in, if those happened to be too strongly guarded. It might be better to take random ones, in fact, because that would allow us to make sure that not only weren't they too well guarded, but that none of the psychotic bastards had put a bomb aboard that would go off as soon as we hit space. One of those would be trivially easy to rig, for instance, by attaching it to the artificial gravity mechanism.

Mind you, I could sweep for a lot of these, certainly for a locator mechanism. But I could not sweep all possible locations for a bomb. So. It would be better to go for one of the unused lifeboats. Or two or three of them, if possible.

And it would be better to go through the walls.

The world gyrated in my head, the diagram of the ship superimposing itself on my location, and I knew exactly where I was going. I cut through the wall, quickly even for me, and shoved the piece of wall down, then walked over it into another lab. I was vaguely aware that the old man behind me had said something about barns, but I ignored him. Instead, I looked back towards our group and yelled, "All of you. Run."

They ran. I waited for them all to go past. I had a vague idea we should kill the old man. Not sure why, but my gut feeling was that we should leave no witnesses. However, when I looked back, he was busily beating one bug with another, and I thought that no, I couldn't do it. I liked him. Not all Mules were bad, not matter how many of them had been swept into reprehensible or outright evil things. They too had been raised without the slightest sense of right or wrong. And it didn't really matter what Jarl thought of them either, or which ones he'd thought were dangerous. The truth was that Jarl had been a very smart human being, but not a god, no matter how much people tried to revere him as such. I'd met a version of him, in a way, and knew him to be as fallible as the rest of us and imbued with the same ability to take a hearty dislike to a good person or to love a bad one. In fact, one of Jarl's best friends had been Daddy Dearest, who not even Jarl could pretend was a decent human being.

When I ran through the wall, I found Laz applying the burner to a wall. It wasn't quite in the right direction, but it was close enough, and I let him.

The next one I chose, and I rearranged the direction.

Halfway the way we meant to go, Laz grabbed my arm. "Thena, the children. We must go get the children."

I might have sworn at him. "We can't," I told him. "We'll be lucky enough if we can get out of here alive. You told them to hide. They should be safe where you told them to hide. We'll come back for them."

"Thena," he said. And it might have been a protest, or it might be because at that moment another of the walls came down in a man-sized hole and men in armor stepped through, burners blazing. If I was right, and I always was in matters of direction, my sense of direction being one of the things bioengineered into me, that was in the direction of the little park and where the children were. But that was a passing thought, as I concentrated on beheading as many of them as possible, and Laz got the rest, and then we ran after the others. Little Brother had the general idea and had cut the next one, so we headed in the direction of the ships we'd brought in. As the others ran through the hole, I grabbed him by the shoulder, "No, Morgan, we can't go back to those ships."

"So?"

"They'll be booby-trapped, even if they're not guarded. We need to go to other lifeboats. Random ones."

He didn't say anything, but the time after next, when he got to cut through the wall, he took us in the direction I thought was right.

Once or twice, Laz tried to cut in the direction of the park, but either Morgan or I redirected him. I wish I could say he looked worried or reluctant. I've thought and thought about it, and to the best of my recollection, he looked panicked. But we all looked panicked. There was something that—I swear—looked like a mechanical octopus, which woke in one of the rooms we crossed. The rest of us killed it while Morgan cut a hole, and then we ran through that, and through the next.

We emerged, without preamble and with a feeling of suddenness, into a vast space. There were ten of the triangular ships parked side by side, and behind them were the sort of membranes that enclosed airlocks. Which meant that was a way to get to space. Of course, whether the other side opened automatically or not was something else, but I'd trust the boys to know that.

I pushed Zen, Fuse, and Thor to the nearest of the triangular ships, saying, "Go, go, go, go."

The others were still running in as those three entered the ship. And then Thor came back and poured three marbles into my free hand. "Remember to throw them far enough they don't kill you," he said, and he ran back into the ship.

I started to grab at Tom, to push him with Christopher Robin and John to the next ship, leaving me and Laz and Morgan to our own. I pushed out of my mind fears we'd be shot out of space. We'd just have to perform evasive maneuvers, that was all. If we couldn't do it, who could?

I had shoved Tom and Christopher Robin towards a ship, and was grabbing for John, as Morgan came into the bay, followed by Laz. I was going to assume from their expressions that Laz had been trying to get back to the kids again. I even understood, I did. Impossible not to. Laz had been responsible for the children, probably from birth. I could imagine what he felt like. In fact, I didn't much need to imagine, because I knew exactly what he'd done and what he'd endured to keep the younger ones safe.

They'd no more than stepped into the bay, when a voice came from everywhere at once. It was the same frightening voice we'd first heard in the *Satisfaction*. Now it seemed three times at loud and it came from every direction imaginable. It shouted one word: "Ingemar!"

All the boys froze. John's lips formed the word "father." But he did not say it aloud. Morgan had gone white again and was shaking.

Laz, frozen as if in the act of running, one foot ahead of the other, looked up, giving a curious impression of being blind, or as though he were looking past the ceiling at something very distant. "Father?"

He clutched the transparent box to his chest, in the position of someone guarding a treasure.

"We have your . . . children," the voice said.

Laz trembled. "Father?"

And suddenly there was a hologram, projected between us and Laz, a hologram so vivid that their technology must be better than ours.

If it weren't for the fact that in addition to showing a group of young boys and a group of heavy dimatough-armored guards, it also showed trees and a shrub caught in the middle of the human actors, I'd have thought that these people had somehow been teleported in front of us.

A keening sound came out of Laz's throat, and I think he tried to reach for the children, because suddenly he and one of the armor-plated guards occupied the same space, his pale face visible through the helmet of the guard.

"Laz," Morgan shouted. "Come on. To the ship."

"Ingemar!" the voice said again, and Laz stepped back and to the side, so we could see him clutching the box, and looking up, eagerly, desperately.

"We will be there in moments. Just wait, give us the box, and we will release your children and let you all go away. All you have to do is leave us the box."

Laz froze. I could see his mind work; I could almost hear him. Or perhaps I could hear him, in fact. None of the boys was very good at controlling their telepathy or directing it.

If I give them the chips, all of Earth dies. But if I don't, my charges die. Those I swore to protect. If I can just take them. If I can get them away. Maybe Kit will have found the way to rebuild the chip.

Christopher Robin tackled him. It was a flying tackle, through the hologram, bringing Laz down with a thud and reaching for the box, but Laz was holding onto the box and shoved Christopher Robin away. "No, no," he was saying, and repeating like a mantra, "Women and children first, women and children first."

Little Brother made a sound like escaping steam and jumped on Laz. He gave the impression of climbing the taller boy, biting, punching and scratching, screaming, "You daft bugger. Think how many women and children will die on Earth. It's just a book, Laz, not holy writ, give me the box." He might have added a bunch of adjectives to "box."

There was the sound of boots approaching, taking the same path we'd taken.

Laz flung Morgan away. The children in the hologram screamed as the armed guards started toward the center.

Laz started to run towards the approaching armored guards.

A laser beam took him in the chest, barely sparing the box. I screamed, "To the nearest boat, go!" At this point, I didn't think we could get to the box, I just wanted to get the children out of here and back to Earth in one piece.

My mind wasn't very clear. Something ancient and dark had taken over. Laz had yelled that thing about women and children first, and I suspected he hadn't been thinking clearly at all and did not know what he was saying. But I knew. The duty of every able-bodied adult was to look after juveniles, to make sure juveniles were safe. Else, we counted for nothing as a species, and we didn't exactly have a future either.

Tom and Christopher Robin had taken a knee and were methodically cutting down guards before they could shoot. I noted in one case they cut a row of burner-holding hands for a more direct approach.

Little Brother and John had jumped to Laz's corpse. Little Brother had the box under one arm, but both the boys were dragging Laz in my direction. In the direction of the ship.

I ran to them, grabbed the box, pulled at Little Brother, and shoved him towards the ship, "Go, go, go."

He was crying, but so silently that I hadn't realized it. The face he turned to me was washed in tears, his mouth open in a silent scream. The voice he managed was a watery croak. "We can't leave his body here. We can't. You don't know what they do."

Where do people get these atavistic impulses? Laz was beyond reach of any cruelty they inflicted on his corpse. But throughout history, soldiers had died to rescue their friends' bodies from the hands of their enemies, and people had faced death to dispose properly of their relatives' remains.

John was trying to lift Laz, and I shoved the box at him instead. "Go, run, damn it, run, all six of you to the ship. *Go.* I'll bring Laz."

I put him over my shoulder, heavy, almost impossible to lift.

It shouldn't have been possible to run, either, but John and Tom couldn't hold off the enemy forever, and I needed to make it to the ship, to make sure these boys were safe. To make sure the Earth was safe. To make sure Eris and Eden were safe too. Damn it, I had to.

Something like mad strength overtook me. I think I more slid than ran, but managed to make it to the door of the ship, and Morgan and Christopher Robin lifted Jarl's body into the ship, even as Tom and John ran in.

We closed the door, and the ship took off. I was so breathless, I didn't even have time to worry the outer part of the airlock wouldn't open.

Before I could draw two breaths we were out in space, tilting and flipping madly. I was aware that Morgan was at the controls, and also that he was making a sound, a strange, wordless keening, like a wounded animal. I was also aware of flashes, as burner rays from giant-sized burners flew by us.

But none caught us. And the strange artificial gravity of the triangular ships kept us all in place, if not upright, while the ship twisted and turned.

When we were far enough away that we could straighten out and fly more calmly, I realized two things.

The first one was that Laz was laid down on the floor, in such a natural position that for a moment I thought he must be alive and we'd misunderstood what happened. But his chest was burned, and it was impossible for anyone to live when their heart was carbonized. His expression was that of a puzzled, wounded child.

I wanted to scream for the whole stupid thing. I should have hit him on the head and dragged him into the ship. For just a moment, I wanted to make the same formless lamentation Morgan was still making as he piloted.

But then Morgan spoke in a hoarse voice. "Thena, we're being followed. I'm going to go very fast. I don't know how fast we can go, but I'm going to go as fast as we can. The mind-link tells me that Zen and the others are ahead of us and speeding up."

"Followed?" I said. "Followed how?"

"They're coming after us. From my feel of it, some of the heirs. They can't let us have the regen chips when we can still save most of Earth."

I looked down at Laz's corpse and up and around at the boys. "They can't have them," I said.

And then I mind-called to Kit and told him what was happening, more in images than in words.

I got back a strange, wordless reassurance. Why wasn't he speaking?

END AND BEGINNING

Home Is the Hero

WE WERE HALFWAY TO EARTH IN WHAT MUST BE THE STRANGEST chase known to man when I heard my husband's voice, clear as a bell in my head, *Athena! Please pilot to these coordinates, and tell the children to get the same message to Zen if they can.*

The heirs pursuing us will overhear, Morgan protested, hesitantly, revealing that he'd heard Kit's message to me. All I got back was a wordless feel that this was fine. I wondered if Morgan could get the feeling, but his confused look made me suspect not. I said, "Tell Zen anyway. I have a feeling there's a plan."

I heard him broadcast the message and the coordinates. I did not hear a reply. I was not attuned to Zen's transmission, and unlike the boys, she seemed unable to broadcast to all and sundry. Morgan said, "She says fine."

The strange thing about this was to be able to sleep and rest while being chased. We'd found towels in the minimal fresher in the lifeboat. It was only a little strange, since the fresher did have hand-washing facilities and drinking water, out of different dispensers, and both, I suspected, endlessly and instantly recycled. The towels were small, so we used three of them to cover Laz. We moved him up against one side of the ship, the same position he'd occupied in the *Satisfaction* on the way back. The boys and I, whoever wasn't piloting, slept on the other side. At a moment when both Morgan and I were sitting at the back, trying to sleep, while Tom snored gently next to us, I asked Morgan, "What do you want us to do with Laz? What is your idea of disposing of his body?"

He looked puzzled. "I don't know. In the ship everyone got recycled into growing the vegetation."

"What were you afraid they'd do to him if we'd left him behind?" I asked.

Morgan looked at me, and for a moment I thought he'd have no answer. Then his eyes filled and his lips trembled. "They used people they had killed," he said. "People they didn't like, to build their . . . the cyborg things. I was afraid. His brain was still intact. If they'd got him quickly . . ."

And suddenly he was in my arms. It was in no way a hug between two adults, but the frenzied clutching of a child to an adult, in search of reassurance and maybe protection. His shorn head nestled on my shoulder, and he started trembling. I felt tears on my shoulder, even though the suit was impermeable and thick enough that I couldn't feel heat. I knew he was crying, and I felt as though I could sense both wetness and heat against my shoulder.

I raised a hand hesitantly, and cupped the back of his newly-shorn head. I was not very good at being a mother. I never expected to be one. The only experience I had of it now was my experience with Eris. One didn't need to be a genius to know that mothering an infant girl and an awkward boy on the edge of puberty were not the same thing. But it was all I could do and all I could offer him. We were both sitting. I held his head against my shoulder and rocked gently back and forth, whispering, "It's all right, it's all right. It's going to be all right."

I was fairly sure I was lying. We were being pursued by who knew how many ships. And even if the boys felt the heirs aboard, I was fairly sure the pampered clones of the elder Mules would not be the ones engaging in battle. I was sure, as sure as I was of anything, that if they were coming for us, coming to retrieve the chips before we could insert them in regen machines and start healing the population of Earth, they would be surrounded by some of those trained killers, those irredeemable, armored guards, raised only for the purpose of enforcing discipline. And I wasn't sure we could take them. I'd slept when I could, but I felt tired, exhausted with a bone-deep exhaustion. I didn't want to admit it to myself, but I'd grown fond of Laz, perhaps because he had willingly taken the role of looking after the young, which seemed so strange and painful to me.

It had been his weakness, yes. What had lead to his death in the end. But it was also what made him fully human, no matter how feral he had been raised. He cared. He cared about others to whom he, objectively, owed nothing except that sort of noblesse oblige that the strong owe the weak. And he'd never been taught noblesse oblige.

"I should have shot his leg off and dragged him into the ship before it came to that," Morgan mumbled against my shoulder. "I should have hit him with the butt of my burner, and dragged him unconscious. Then he'd still be alive."

"None of us were thinking clearly," I said. "I have been blaming myself for precisely that. I should have knocked him unconscious and dragged him. But he wasn't thinking clearly either, and he'd have defended himself from us. There is a good chance it would have ended the same way."

Morgan pulled away from me and looked up at me. His face was tear-streaked, his eyes woebegone, and his lips shook a little. "He was the only protector we had. We, those who weren't valued, you know? He was the only protector we had, the only person who cared if we lived or died. When I was really scared or really sad and thought it would be easier if I died, the only reason I didn't was because he would be upset. He wanted to leave us with the littles, thought we would be safer. He thought we would be able to help them survive, and also he was afraid we'd get killed on Earth, Thor and I, but Father called us by name. So he took the littles to the park and left them, because they could get food and water, even after rations ran out, and because it's one of the few places in the ship where it's easy to hide."

"What about the one near the entrance we took," I said. "Laz said he was one of the littles, by which I presume he was one of your ... tribe. So why was he dead? Did he come looking for Laz?"

Morgan shook his head. "No. Well. He might. I don't know, because we couldn't stop and talk, not even mind-talk, but the littles said they had all been ill. When Laz went to take them to the park, it was after we'd all been given what we were told were immunization shots for our trip to Earth. I think we gave the littles the disease, and they didn't have anyone to look after them. Nally might have come to look and see if we'd arrived, but was overcome. You know how severe it was even in us."

I imagined Laz had reconstructed that story too, and probably had felt guilty enough over it to confuse him further at the end. In the end, he could neither betray the people of Earth nor those children who had reason to count on his protection and whom he already felt he had failed.

"I'll never be all right again," Morgan said, in a desolate voice. "There isn't anyone left alive who cares if I live or die."

"Sure there is," I said, more positively than I felt. "You are my little brother, or as close to it as makes no difference. Kit and I care if you live or die, and we will look after you." When I mentally added *and may God have mercy on our souls*, I made very sure I wasn't broadcasting.

He gave me a carefully scrutinizing look, like I'd just promised him something as unlikely as his very own dragon or a kingdom, then nodded. "I'll try not to make you want to kill me." He wiped his nose on his sleeve, a largely ceremonial gesture, as his face had dried. "Laz said he wanted to kill me three times a day."

"Just be kind to those weaker than you, and don't kidnap my children," I said. "And you'll be all right."

Eventually he fell asleep, and eventually I fell asleep too.

I woke up to John saying loudly, "Whooo."

In the moments it took me to pry my eyes open, we flitted to one side, then the other and then went on our side. In the peculiar antigrav of this unit, the gravity stayed with the "floor" even when it was on its side, which made my stomach climb somewhere near my throat, but at least didn't tumble us in a heap atop of each other.

Tom was standing behind the pilot chair, holding on to it. From his movement, I realized he was doing "behind the seat piloting," but John seemed to be doing fine with it. Or at least we were still in one piece, though I had absolutely no idea what was causing evasive maneuvers. Had the pursuing ships caught up enough to be so close they could fire on us? But if so, why weren't we returning fire? I knew we could from the battle over the *Cathouse.*

I got up and walked over, which was easier said than done while on our side, with my brain screaming the gravity was all wrong, and my stomach chiming in that I needed to throw up now. I managed to make it behind the pilot's chair, and a few things became quite obvious.

I must have been really exhausted, because I had apparently slept through the usual storm of warnings and alarms on the approach to Earth. We were landing, apparently on a desert. On that desert was something... It looked like a battery of burner-cannons, of the sort I had heard were mounted on the *Je Reviens*, of the sort some seacities used to defend from assault. It looked like what I'd imagined they would look like, since I'd never seen any.

They were firing, the tracks going in the air to either side of us. I figured that was why John was taking us on our side. I wondered who they were and why we were still landing despite being attacked, and what Kit could have been thinking of to tell me to land there if he knew I'd be attacked.

Then something got hit behind us, fragments thudded against our carapace, and the force pushed us down, harder, faster, right in front of the battery of cannons, and under the beams of their power.

John barely straightened us out, and we landed, scraping hard and long against the sand and stopping just short of the cannons.

As my brain caught up with our movement, I saw behind the cannons a calico mop that could only be my husband's. So, those were the good guys. Who were the bad ones? Or rather, where were the bad ones and how many of them were there?

Another rain of debris atop our ship, and I heard Kit say, *You might want to bail out of the ship, Thena, I don't think it can burn, but you're getting hit with some pretty big burning pieces. We'll provide cover as long as we can and try to stop raining debris on you as you come out. Now would be a good time. Now, now, now.*

As he spoke, Zen, Fuse, and Thor passed our ship running. I knew both Fuse's and Thor's penchant to just throw incendiaries behind them, so I thought the best part of valor was to be behind the cannons with them. I opened the door, then realized Robin must still be asleep and went to wake him, to see him trying to drag Laz's body out of the ship.

"Leave him," Tom said. "John and I will carry him."

I heard the tribal barriers fall with a thud. I suspected neither of the two higher-status boys would have done this, ever, under any circumstances in the past.

As I started running, I realized Christopher Robin had grabbed Little Brother and was dragging him along, faster than Morgan could run on his own.

We all hit behind the cannons' emplacement at the same time, diving to the sand, and first one, then another ship exploded in the sky, and debris rained down. Manning the cannons were some very young men.

When there was only one ship left, it was allowed to land. For a moment I thought it wouldn't, but I also suspected even the heirs and their guards were afraid to go back and tell the big-voiced, scary creature they called Father that they had failed. It was that and only that, that must have kept them on track as they fired gamely on our position. This was when the young men manning the cannons performed a neat trick I would have not thought possible. Using their giant burners as I would have used a pocket burner, they turned it on cutting and neatly excised the barrels of the ship's guns, leaving it unable to concentrate or project a burner beam.

After that they fell to the desert sand like a leaf and sat there quite a long time.

This was when Luce arrived and started negotiating. The fact that the ship was de facto helpless and could be burned out of the sky meant they had nothing they could do. Sure, they could come out burners blazing, but that would only end with them dead.

The box with the chips was taken by a very young man; though, being paranoid, I took one of them out and kept it in my pocket, just in case the young man turned out to be a traitor and was not following Nat's orders and taking it to doctors.

Nat was in charge of the very young men, though he wasn't there, being too ill to take part in a battle. There was only so much that artificial infusions with platelets could do when your body couldn't produce them.

After a long while, it appeared that the men in the triangle ship surrendered and were taken prisoner. By that time, I wasn't there, and I didn't get to see it. In fact, I never saw them, though later on I had access to the results of their interrogation.

Turned out there were no guards, at least not in that ship. Only heirs. We don't know why, except that Kit believed the guards who remained were all left behind to guard the elder Mules, in case we did manage to survive and take the fight to them. They had sent their untrained, pampered younger clones to Earth to deal with enemies they must have realized were formidable and wouldn't let them take the chips without a fight.

They had sent the young men to die in great numbers, on the off chance one of them would get the chips back before we could use them.

Kit said it was the arrogance and uncaring callousness of that move that had finally broken the young men and got them talking. Not that Kit was doing that. That part of the work was done by Nat's people, or people who had more experience of war than we did.

Kit and I returned to Jarl's refuge, where regen machines were retrofitted to take care of Nat and Alexis.

A medtech came to the refuge to operate the machines and to learn the settings for others. She was a young and heroic woman. Suffering from the illness herself, she was one of the few volunteers willing to wait for the healing, and set up a station to heal those who could be airlifted from behind the lines of the Good Men side.

The argument had apparently raged from the Olympus legislature to the various ersatz legislatures in the newly resettled territories to the august halls of the Emperor Beaulieu. The argument—on whether it was just and moral to let the people die who had the misfortune of being behind the lines of the Good Men territories, simply because their rulers were evil—was obviously answered with no. But the idea of taking the chips behind their lines and enabling the Good Men to heal their whole army was obviously foolish.

With the army of the free, as they called themselves, getting priority on the healing, a field hospital of sorts was created in the part of Jarl's refuge that used to be a hotel.

Before it was open to anyone who came to turn it into a hospital, we had buried Laz in a difficult-to-reach place, above a gorge, under an apple tree, and had put on his tomb a marker that read LAZARUS LONG INGEMAR, HE SAVED WOMEN AND CHILDREN FIRST.

Morgan had cried again at the burial, but he looked easier and softer now, perhaps not fully tamed—I didn't know if it was in our genes to be fully tamed—but a gentler and more civilized young man, even in a few days.

He'd lost his protector, but he gained a family, and he spent all the time he could helping Kit. I wasn't absolutely sure I should trust him to babysit Eris, but I did sometimes, on principle, because I thought it was important to show him good behavior would be rewarded. He had not kidnapped Eris again, and he even changed diapers, even if he made very odd sounds of disgust while doing it.

Cindy George, a cheerful, brown-haired young woman with very little nonsense about her, set about making sure rooms were clear and operational enough to host regen machines, all the while keeping track of Nat's and Alexis's recoveries.

People were being flown in, in great airlifts, part by the military and part by volunteers who braved fire and death to go behind the lines and lift up the very sick of the common people on the enemy side to treat them.

Some of them would of course be loyal to the Good Men. That was something else. Lucius was elbow-deep in setting up a careful interrogation and evaluation process that would allow him to separate the sheep from the goats, and also in figuring out what to do with the goats. He kept muttering about sending them all to Australia, but I think that was a metaphor.

Cindy George bustled about, teaching a small army of helpers as they were flown in. No one made a comment about Kit's hair or eyes, and it was all just as well, as we'd decided that Eden could no longer be kept secret from Earth, or at least not from the side of Earth that was more or less free.

Yes, I know, the leaders of my adopted world were going to hate like poison that they could no longer manage their cherished secrecy and that they'd be vulnerable to Earth.

But they had no choice. Unless the heirs had lied to us, and lied completely, Eden was not free now, and would not be free again unless they got help from Earth.

They had been infected with the virus shortly after we'd left. But the Mules of the *Je Reviens* had moved in early there, waiting only for them to be weakened and not for most of the population to be dead.

There were two reasons for this, the first being that these people were a personal project, since many of them were descended from families created and molded to act as Mule servants. That they dared leave servitude and that Jarl had aided and abetted them was bad enough. That they were still useful was a reason to save them and show them they needed their masters. The other part was probably that, being smaller, Eden was much easier to control.

The young men who'd come to Earth were not part of those who had planned or executed the invasion of Eden. They knew only that it had happened, that it had been successful, and that right now there were five elders and twenty heirs in charge of the little hollowed asteroid.

They didn't know how hard Eden had fought, nor who had died.

After the news was given to Kit, he was very quiet that night, sitting on the side of the bed while I nursed Eris.

"They'll be all right," I told him, feeling like I was getting better at telling lies. "Your family will be all right. They're survivors."

He gave me a half chuckle. "You really see my sisters knuckling under the rule of the Mules, in order to stay alive."

"They might have," I said. "To fight another day."

He inclined his head, but I could tell he didn't believe me. "We'll have to go, anyway," he said. "To free them. They're my people, even if the crazier of them will see an approaching force from Earth as an invading force, not liberators."

"We'll manage somehow," I said. "But if we're going to be an invading force, we need a force, which means we'll need to wait the week or two until enough fighting men are healed to go with us."

"We'll take volunteers only," Kit said. "It's not an expedition with a high chance of success."

"When is anything we're involved in?"

Defiance

I WON THE BATTLE OVER GOING WITH KIT TO FREE EDEN. THIS meant that Morgan lost his battle against going with us. He also lost his battle about being old enough to be left in charge of Eris. Not that we were taking Eris with us. There were limits to our insanity. Instead, we were leaving her on Earth for what I heartily hoped would only be a few months, a year at most.

It broke my heart to think that when I came back she would be walking and possibly talking, and we would miss all of that. On the other hand, she would not, as she grew up, remember a time without us.

Kit is more sanguine about leaving her behind, possibly because he doesn't have the experience of motherhood, or more likely because people of Eden are more detached about their children, gestating them in biowombs, and more often than not having them raised by a couple out of an entire clan. It had worked for Kit, and I did not mean to cast aspersions on the way he'd been raised. I certainly could not contrast my upbringing as being better. But it was not what I wanted for my daughter, and I hoped I survived to come back and reclaim her.

After much debate, we decided that no matter how excellent a babysitter Lucius was, he really was going to be elbow-deep in vetting refugees for a while, and we didn't wish her to have to compete with Nat's younger siblings for his scant time, no matter how much he assured us he'd make her a priority.

Simon offered, and promised to hire the best nannies. Only when that failed did he recommend us to Dr. Dufort. The doctor and his lady were newly alone. Their son had recently gotten married. More importantly, they were vouched for by Zen and Alexis in the most important way. Zen and Alexis were leaving their newborn son with them, while they joined us in the liberation of Eden.

So it is us, Zen and I, Alexis and Kit, and a thousand hand-picked volunteers of Nat's choosing. We are to free Eden from the autarchs who have taken it over.

We're not quite sure what we will face. Surely the Mules and their heirs are too few to completely control the fiercely independent citizens of Eden? At least unless they've deployed some new technology we don't know about. It is either that or armies of the young men created and trained as killers and enforcers.

In either case, it is likely to be the sort of battle where both sides fight against the liberators, since I didn't see Kit's compatriots ever trusting Earth.

It doesn't matter. As I told Morgan, whom I also left in the charge of Dr. Dufort, there are certain things you have to do if you want to consider yourself a human being. Looking after those who can't help themselves is one of them. Since I couldn't see Eden voluntarily surrendering to Good Men rule, they obviously couldn't help themselves. And the other thing, I'd told him, in which his upbringing was utterly normal, was that humans looked after their tribe.

Eden was Kit's tribe.

Five months after our arrival on Earth, I kissed my daughter and left her in the arms of Madame Dufort. I also kissed Morgan's forehead. He'd hit a growth spurt and was almost my height. He and the others had also gotten rid of the strange piercings and tattoos, on the idea they might want some when they were sure of what was appropriate on Earth. For now, blank skin made it easier for them to fit in.

"Do try not to blow up anything until we come back," Kit told Morgan very seriously.

"I'm not the one who blows up things," Morgan protested. "That is Thor."

"Well, yes, but I won't say that to Thor, because it would be pointless."

Fuse, also newly regened, so that he and Thor looked like what they were, identical twins separated by close to thirty years, was waiting to shake our hands as we went in. He'd declined to go with us, because he said it was his duty to fight and conquer the seacity his so-called father controlled. "If I went with you," he told us, by way of farewell, "it would be a little like running away, taking myself and Thor out of where my father can get us. He's desperate because he's dying. But I'm tired of living in fear. We're going to conquer my birthright and claim it for free men. By the time you come back, I should be able to host you. I was willing to tolerate the danger for myself, but not for Thor."

It seemed a very strange idea, but the idea of Fuse ever recovering had seemed strange too. And besides, he was being a parent. That is something I've learned about being a parent. You don't abdicate your responsibility towards the young. Even if you didn't ask for them, create them, or decide to have them.

Adults of a species look after its young. And by that I don't mean the sort of detached "looking after" the Mules had done with their young clones. Adults protect, guide, and, yes, correct the young of the species. Without that, the species won't survive. I'm not quite sure where the lines of morality are, but I am human—even if a slightly modified one—and I want humans to survive and thrive. I imagine any sentient species would feel the same way.

I never wanted to be a mother. I didn't seek it; had no interest in it. If you'd asked me, I'd say I was the least qualified person to mother anyone or anything.

But my daughter, and Morgan, and the young men with Morgan, needed a mother when there was no one else available. I might not be the best there was, but I was the one who could do it.

Now I am in a hastily adapted troop transport. It's overcrowded, jury-rigged, and prone to break-downs, and Zen and I have our hands full both keeping the thing running and looking after a lot of young men and women, over and above military discipline.

I have no idea of precisely what challenge the liberation of Eden will present. But one thing I know. We're going to go there, and we're going to liberate it. And I'm going to come back.

Because my daughter needs me, and I intend to be a mother to her.